CHUCO TOWN
TALE OF THE SERIAL KILLER

JESUS MORALES

AuthorHouse™
1663 Liberty Drive
Bloomington, IN 47403
www.authorhouse.com
Phone: 1-800-839-8640

© 2010 Jesus Morales. All rights reserved.

No part of this book may be reproduced, stored in a retrieval system, or transmitted by any means without the written permission of the author.

First published by AuthorHouse 10/11/2010

ISBN: 978-1-4520-8634-7 (sc)
ISBN: 978-1-4520-8635-4 (e)

Printed in the United States of America

Certain stock imagery © Thinkstock.

Because of the dynamic nature of the Internet, any Web addresses or links contained in this book may have changed since publication and may no longer be valid. The views expressed in this work are solely those of the author and do not necessarily reflect the views of the publisher, and the publisher hereby disclaims any responsibility for them.

DEDICATION

I dedicate this book to God.
Thank you for this incredible gift.

CHAPTER ONE

THE END OF PABLO DE LA VEGA

It was a terrible thunderstorm and I was standing on the rooftop of some building and I was looking straight at my father's Condo in Washington D.C. There was a lot of rain, with a lot of thunder and lightning and the wind was blowing pretty hard. I had my eyes on my father and he is going to pay for his actions. My father was alone in his Condo while my mother and my sister, Tania went out shopping. And my father was getting out of the shower and went straight into his office to do some paper work. I noticed that the top window was wide open and I ran towards it and jumped inside the Condo. I was walking in the hallway and the door to his office was open. I went inside and was standing behind him while my father was serving himself a drink. The lights where I was standing were going off.

"Don't move, Agent de la Vega!" I exclaimed.

My father started laughing and turn around and said, "The Dark Cowboy what a pleasant surprise! And what seams to be the occasion?"

"Sit down, Agent Pablo de la Vega!" I exclaimed and I walked a couple of more steps and the lights were going off but my father still had some lights where he was standing.

Once again my father started laughing, "So, Dark Cowboy, you have finally decided to kill me. After I pardon your crimes and you became a hero to the city of El Paso, Texas and hero to the world. I told my family and the whole world that you are best Serial Killer of all time and I was going to shake your hand in front of them and also I planned to give you an award. But somehow you still have a vendetta against me. You popped out of a Christmas box and nearly killed us in our living room. What else do you want from me, Dark Cowboy? You're a hero and do you want the key to the city."

I started laughing and said, "I'm not interested in having the key to the city, Agent Pablo de la Vega. Well I am The Dark Cowboy and I'm a hideous looking creature that was thirsty for blood. And I came out at night and killed a lot of people and left them in a pool of their own blood. And I remember Oklahoma having a problems with a lot of tornadoes. There was a rumor that a tornado came into the state of Oklahoma and destroyed a secret Mental Institution and killed so many innocent people." I laughed and my eyes still glow red.

My father responded, "You did trick me! You said that I had a week to save the people from the Mental Institution and when we got there. They were a week dead and the building was destroyed. And I still have the tape that you made for me and we were this close to put you behind bars. But I didn't believe in those ghost stories they were saying about you. Everyone was saying that you were the Devil in person and killed so many people along the way. And we did have a hard time dealing with you but sooner or later we would arrest you .Because I am the great Pablo de la Vega, the greatest FBI Agent that has ever lived!"

I started clapping for him and I was laughing too, "Bravo! Bravo, Agent Pablo de la Vega but you always failed to arrest me and I'm standing in front of you right now. And it's because I was better than the great Agent Pablo de la Vega and I outsmarted everyone in the city. As the matter of fact we are better than you. While the Police Officers were looking me, something else was happening in the city and you never saw it coming."

"You did fool us but I did pardon you for the crimes that you committed and we found out that they worked for the mob. And you still want me dead because you found out about my beautiful history. And do you know why I chose to go after you? I was in Europe when they told me that a lot of bad things were happening in El Paso, Texas. They were talking about a psychotic killer that was dressed as a Dark Cowboy and rode a black horse and killed a lot of people and the Police Officers couldn't catch you and they couldn't find you. I thought my wife would catch you by the end of the week. And they told me that they have failed to protect the people of El Paso, Texas. And I accepted this operation to come after you but you were better than me and the rest of us. So, you took out the top dogs in the business and I want to say congratulations."

"And you put those false crimes that I didn't committed and you were just scared and where is your honor. Well you don't have honor and all you care about was medals, money and messing with people's life." I said.

"I do have honor, I love medals, money and it's fun messing with people's lives. It's so fun and you also joined the club and I wish you were a de la Vega." My father laughed and continued, "And we thought our kids everything we know. My beautiful daughter, Tania Marie de la Vega is going to become a District Attorney and my son well I don't see a future in Mauricio de la Vega, the second. He ruin his life and he should have listen to me right from the start and I knew he would be a great FBI Agent than I was and I was hoping that he will take you down but he chicken out!" He yelled.

I walked in front of my father and the lights went out but he still had lights where he was standing. "That doesn't make you a failure, Pablo de la Vega and I know you are a wise person. My father once told me, "You have the opportunity of becoming somebody important in your life. You need to leave a legacy for your kids. Don't you want to be a legend in your own right and make the family proud?"

He looked at me and asked, "Where did you get that from?

I went up to him and the lights went off and all he could see my eyes glowing red and I said, "From you!" And I grabbed him and made him sit down on his chair and I sat in front of his desk.

"Who are you?" He asked.

All the lights came back and I said, "Your son, Mauricio de la Vega."

My father was in shocked. "Mauricio! I cannot believe that it was you that was doing those crimes."

"Believe it, Dad. Like I told you before and I will say it again. You never saw it coming!" I exclaimed and laughed and my eyes continue to glow red.

"Why, Mauricio? We gave you all the love in the world so you can turn the corner and can kill so many innocent people. That's how much you appreciated what your mother and I did for you!" He yelled.

I responded, "I appreciate what you guys did for me. But it was you dad, you wanted me to become a legend well I did became one. Now I'm going to be a bigger legend once I get rid of you and just imagine in the History books, the great Pablo de la Vega gets killed by the great legendary Mauricio de la Vega also known as The Dark Cowboy and people are going to talk about me and not you. Because you are going to be dead and I will live forever. But after all it was my sweet dear old mommy, the great Beatrice de la Vega that gave me permission to kill more people and you see I obey my mom and you as well. You guys are going to take credit for my legacy. You guys should be proud because you guys were honest Police Officers and I took the corrupted out of the way. You see I can do a good deed to the city of El Paso, Texas. I can give you an example. I killed the top dogs in the city, so my mom can get promoted and along with Perla. You see my mom did earn the promotion and it wasn't handed to her." I smiled and laughed.

"So, now you travel so far and you plan to take out the biggest dog of the Federal Bureau Investigation so you can make yourself legendary but I don't believe that you are going to kill me!" He yelled.

"It doesn't matter if you don't believe me!" I yelled and grabbed his throat. "I want to know everything about Eliza Caballero. And I've asked around and they all tell me that she saw Doctor Juanita Van Der AA, and Eliza was doing drugs, Vito Mancini is her birth father, and you two were together at one time because Primo saw you guys together and you sent those men to come after us. Now tell me everything!"

"You really want to know?" He asked.

"Yes!" I yelled and continued grabbing his throat.

"Yes, Eliza Caballero is the daughter of Vito Mancini and her mom wanted her to stay away from Vito because she was worried that she might also join the mob. So, she lied to him and to her."

"Everyone has told me that same story. And they lied to Eliza and told her that her father went to the Army."

"Eliza was disturbed when she saw you at the Franklin Mountains and killed her friends right before her eyes. That's why she saw Doctor Juanita Van Der AA and to be honest with you, Son. Eliza wasn't on drugs. I gave her the pills that Chris was making in the laboratory."

"Are you sure?" I asked.

He responded, "Yes, I'm sure. And while you guys were going out. I approached her and her mom and I told Eliza to stop seen her father because he was dangerous and we wanted what was best for her. But Eliza didn't listen to us and she wanted to stay with her dad and with you but we knew that Vito Mancini might come after you and kill you. And he would have order you to leave his daughter alone and he was going to sent his men after you and kill you."

"What are you trying to say?" I asked.

"I wanted to protect you from Eliza because she didn't want listen to me or her mother. But being the great FBI Agent that I am, I wanted to protect Eliza from her father and you as well. So, that's where Primo saw us together and I gave her my idea and I saw him looking at us and Eliza didn't like my idea. So, I don't think Primo heard what we talked about but I paid him to keep his mouth shut. And Chris told me that he was making some pills and he was explaining them to me. So, around midnight, I went into his office and took three boxes of those pills. This was a way for Vito to stay away from Eliza and from you. I explained everything to her mom and her brother about what we wanted to do. They said yes. And once again we told Eliza to stop seen her father, and in the summer of 2000 she went to the Hospital for a drug overdose and then she told me that her father was worried for her and we did a lot of things for him to stay away for Eliza. And that's why I hired a couple of gangsters, and they agreed to help out and they sold Eliza those pills because she wasn't in her right state of mind at that time. But it was working and I'm sorry, Mauricio that's why I sent those men to break into Eliza's house. I paid them a lot of money to make it look like a robbery and extra if they wanted to have sex with her but I did warn Eliza to stay away from her father or else. Well she did found out what or else was. And they did break into the house and they were punching her and slapping her and rapping her and I was pissed off when they knocked you out. So, when she was in the Hospital the Nurse gave her half of the pill that Chris made in the lab and everyday she kept taking those pills and we made it look that she died in the Hospital. But we planted one of the patients that was already dying and we made her look like Eliza. So, when everyone who got near the casket they would know that it was her and we knew that Vito saw her too. The plan worked fine." He said and tried to smile.

I looked at him and yelled at him, "The plan worked fine! Have you had any idea what I went through and what we went through! I cannot believe you would this to Eliza and to me!"

"I know you and everyone is going to be upset with the decision we made. But we wanted Eliza to stay away from Vito Mancini. And I had no choice,

Mauricio and remember I am an FBI Agent, and I did everything I could to protect a civilian from her father and I did my job! And I saw your reaction and I'm sorry Mauricio for everything that happened!" He yelled.

"Where is she?" I asked.

"I cannot tell you that because it's confidential." He responded.

"Where is she!"

"Do whatever you want with me." He said.

I looked at him and said, "I'm going to kill you! I have every reason to kill you! I know if I kill you, Tania is going after me and your men will also come after me. And If I keep you alive, you probably want to have an alliance with Vito and come after me with an Army. I can just see it now, a Civil War between father and son, the two de la Vegas going at it, the long awaited rivalry." I yelled and grabbed him by his shirt.

"Now, I know who you are, Son. I cannot arrest you because you are my son. You're mother will have a stroke if she finds out that you killed those people." He said and wanted to hug me. "I love you my son! But I'll tell you where she is!"

"Where!" I yelled and punched him in the face.

"Eliza is locked away in another secret Mental Institution and it's located in New York City." My father said and he looked at me, "I love you my son."

"Well I don't love you and I don't have any respect what you did! I know mom will have a stroke but she is going to have a heart attack if she finds out what you did to Eliza. I know you don't want to arrest me and come after me, or else I can change your mind right now!" I yelled and punched him in the face and he fell on the ground and I grabbed him by his hair and made him sit down. "Have I changed your mind, Daddy? Do you want me to continue? You are going to find out what or else really is!" I yelled at him and punched him in the face and I threw him on the ground and he was trying to get up. "Remember how everyone told you about the horrible Demon that killed so many people in El Paso and in Oklahoma. Well you better start believing in those spooky tales because I am a the monster that everyone described to you!" I yelled and transformed into the hideous creature and he looked at me and he was scared. I brought my dart gun and shot him in the back. "You know dad, you are paralyzed but you will be back on your feet in an hour. Now you listen to me, I killed your friends and sent them to Hell and we took the money from their accounts. And if you are looking for revenge, I will be waiting for you and you know where to find me." I said and grabbed him and I decided to kicked him in the face and his ribs. Once again I shot him in the arm with the dart gun. "Have I changed your mind now? Well in two hours you are going to be on your feet once again. But I want you to think about our little conversation between father and son. You can live a pathetic life and seen me becoming legendary in your very own eyes and you will be a miserable husband to my mom or else you can come after me with an Army and try to kill The Dark Cowboy. And I will be waiting for you or else you will be waiting for me again. Well goodnight and I want you to think about it." I was about to leave but I had too much hatred towards him so I turn around and he was looking at me. I took out my guns and pointed at them and said, "But I know you are going to hurt Luz and my friends and I'm going to protect them from the likes of you. May God have mercy on your soul." I pulled the trigger and shot him so many times.

"No! Pablo!" My mother yelled.

"What did you do to my father!" Tania yelled and she came running and hugged my father.

I walked up to my mother and said, "I'm sorry but he had it coming! But we're going to send you his evidence. My sympathy!" I ran towards the window and broke it and landed on the side of the building.

"You son of a bitch! You're going to pay for your actions!" Tania yelled.

I was walking in the dark alley and I was upset because I killed my own flesh of blood. And I felt that I did the right thing. Sometimes I begin to wonder what happen to our lives.

CHAPTER TWO

THE EARLY YEARS

My mother was born in Mexico City in the year 1954, she brought joy to the family because she was the only daughter in the family and she has five older brothers. My grandparents named her, Beatrice Marie Guzman. The Guzman family was an old school family, the men in the family were raised to be hard workers, to be gentleman with the ladies, to bring food to the table, and take care of the wife and the kids. The women in the family were taught to act like ladies, to look good at all times, and to have good proper manners. They also did the chores around the house and to raise the kids while their husbands were working the eight hour shift. The women in the Guzman family had no ambition of becoming someone that important, other than becoming wives, mothers, and grandmothers, and all they did, is wait to meet their future husbands at Church or if there was a knock on the door and it was a stranger that wanted to marry their daughters. But my mother had a different dream from the rest of the girls in the family. One of my mother's dream's was becoming someone important in life and she wanted a future for herself but her parents didn't approve of her dreams. My mother's second dream was that she wanted to come to America and go to college in the states. But she knew that she needed to learn to speak English if she wanted to live in the United States. So, my mother decided to remain in Mexico City until in the year 1972, where my mother turned eighteen years old. Her parents wanted her to stay home with them. They wanted her to help around the house and she had to sit and wait until she met her future husband at Church or she had wait for the knock on the door. My mother's third dream, was becoming a Police Officer in Mexico City. And without her family's support or permission, my mother decided to joined the Police Academy and it was hard work and dedication but she managed to survive the whole training and she became an honest to God Police Officer. When she finished her training at the Police Academy, they gave her a warm welcome at the Police Station. So, my mother started working right of away and she made the wise choice and moved out of the house and got an apartment for herself. Well my mother until that time was five feet tall, long brown hair, brown eyes, light skin, and she weighs in ninety pounds. She was the smallest and the prettiest Police Officer in Mexico City but her looks were not going to make her into a legend, it was the hard work and the dedication that was going to make her a legend.

My father was born in Madrid, Spain in the year 1954 but my father and his family were raise in Mexico City. And the de la Vega's were raised to be somebody important in life. My father was destined to be somebody important in his life but there was something important about the de la Vega family's history, that made them very successful and very proud of their heritage. My grandparents became close friends and we now know why my mother wanted to have a career because she was friends with my father when they were kids and she loved the de la Vega history as well. Both families were sharing each other's culture. But the de la Vega family had a different tradition than the other families from all over the world. Men and women in the family were taught to be the best and they were encouraged to follow in their ancestor's footsteps and make them proud. And the new generation of the de la Vega's were anxious and scared because how they were going to surpass their family's success in the past. At one time the de la Vega's were the most powerful family in the country of Spain and the people couldn't help it but to admire the whole family's success. Then there was a lot of rumors going around in the country of Spain and it was in the late 1700's. There was a plague that entered the country of Spain and half of the people were affected by the disease and they were dying and half them were the de la Vega's that got infected. Everyone were devastated that every de la Vega died from the plague. Well except for Pedro de la Vega, the last of the de la Vega's, that somehow didn't get infected. And he made the wise decision to come to America and restart his life all over again. He went on his long seven month journey and he finally arrived in America and he settled down in Boston, Massachusetts. And once a month Pedro wrote to his friends in Spain and they told him that the plague was gone and the crises was finally over. And they also told him that he can come back to Spain whenever he was ready. And around the 1850's, the new de la Vega family went back to Spain and they tried rebuild the whole country all over the again and once again the de la Vega's became more successful than ever before. So, my grandparents decided to move to Mexico City with their ten children. Five boys and five girls and my grandfather would encouraged his kids to make the family proud. As they were getting older, they went their own separate ways to find their own success. But my father remained in Mexico City with his parents and also in the year 1972, my father turned eighteen years old and he also joined my mother at the Police Academy and he would find his success as a Police Officer in Mexico City. My father around that time was six feet tall and two inches, short blonde hair, blue eyes, white skin, and weighs in two hundred and twenty pounds. Those pounds were of muscle and my father looked like a wrestler and he could have been the future champion of the world.

For the past six years my mother was a blue collar worker and she already made a name for herself as a Police Officer. My mother had a great reputation of being a Super Cop. Well she was the smallest Police Officer and she was able to arrest more than thirty-four criminals in the next six years and she was just twenty-four years old and she loved tackling criminals to the ground. And all thirty-four criminals had broken ribs, broken arms and legs. My mother may be small but she was the toughest Police Officer and they were comparing my mother to the athletes of Rugby. That's how tough my mother was in her young stages of her life. And my mother killed twenty criminals.

My father was also a blue collar worker and right of away he made a name for himself. But my father had a bigger and better reputation than my mother. And all of his life my father has been motivated of been the best and making de la Vega's proud. My father took his job very seriously and on the other hand my mother didn't care about being someone that famous and all she cared about was taking criminals off the streets and lived her life in peace. Yes, my mother did took her job very seriously and all she cared is taking criminals off the street but she didn't want any medals and she didn't want to be guest speaker at schools. My mother didn't want the spotlight but my father enjoyed the spotlight. The more he took criminals off the streets, the more he appeared on the television, and he also killed twenty criminals. So, their colleagues were impressed with their individual progress and they made the wise decision by putting them together as partners and together my parents took criminals off the streets and they were a great combination.

Then it was in the year 1981 where my parents and every Police Officer in Mexico City decided to work with the American FBI, they had their toughest assignment to date. Because there was a new mobster in the city of Mexico, his name is Vito Mancini. Vito Mancini is a high power Italian Drug Lord and had his drug businesses from all over the United States. The mob business in Mexico was about to go out of business because of the lack work from the other mobsters. The drug business wasn't going anywhere until Vito Mancini decided to come to Mexico City and killed the ten top Mob leaders and he was now the new leader of the Mexican Mob. Vito became so powerful that he even bought half of the city and half of the people were corrupted. And you didn't know who was bought by the Mob. It was a risky assignment so they sent everyone to arrest Vito Mancini and his followers. The Police Officers and the FBI arrived in an abandon warehouse and from there it was a gun fight, it was the fight to the death. Because half of the Police Officers and half of the FBI Agents turn around and started shooting at the honest Police Officers and FBI Agents. But the weird part is that my parents were the honest Police Officers and along with ten Police Officers and three FBI Agents that were already dead. It was an ambush and my parents were running out of the bullets when the cavalry arrived just in time. The citizens of Mexico City decided to joined forces with my parents and together they tried to take out the mob from Mexico. They had baseball bats, knives and you name it they had everything. One by one the Mob was going down and the Alliance of Good was also going down. My parents were left standing and they were pursuing Vito Mancini on foot. Vito went running to the rooftop of the building and a helicopter chopper was waiting for him and my parents were chasing him and my father tackled Vito to the ground. And Vito grabbed a pipe and whacked my father in the stomach and head. My mother took out her gun but she ran out of bullets so she decided to tackle him down too, and that was her specialty. They were wrestling on the floor and Vito threw my mother to the wall until Vito took out his gun and he pulled the trigger and six bullets were going to my mother's direction until my father pushed her out of the away and he was shot, and he fell to the ground. My mother had the chance to arrest Vito but she stayed with my father and Vito Mancini got away in the helicopter chopper.

It resulted that four bullets hit the windows from the other buildings and the two bullets hit my father, one in his shoulder and the other one in the chest. My father actually saved my mother's life, and the Ambulance arrived in time to take my father away to the Hospital. My mother visited my father in the Hospital and they were talking for hours and hours. My mother showed my father her appreciation that they kissed for two minutes and I guess that was their start of their real relationship. My father spent two months in the Hospital and everyday my mother came to visit him and they talked and kissed and they were falling in love with each other. My father was able to recover from his wounds and my parents were still working together and on their day off they usually went out to the movies and they went out dancing until wee hours of the morning. And months went by my father proposed to my mother around Christmas Eve and they got married in the spring of the year 1982. My parents turned twenty-eight years old and they were mature enough to get married and they had their families blessing as well. And it was around September where my mother made a shocking discovery that she was two weeks pregnant. She went to the Doctor and it was confirmed that she is pregnant. My mother remained on the Police Force and she only worked around the desk and all she did was paper work. But my father was a young twenty-eight old year old hot shot Police Officer that continued to bring more criminals to justice and he became more respected in the Police Force and now criminals were terrified of him. Since my father couldn't surpass my mother's reputation of being a Super Cop while she was active. So, in my mother's nine month absence my father did a great job to surpass her and increased the de la Vega family's legacy. My father had a eight month reign of arresting so many drug dealers and drunk drivers and they promoted him to Lieutenant.

Then in the middle of May, my mother wanted to spend her birthday with her brother in Redwood City, California. My parents asked for their vacations and they told them to come back when they were ready. So, her family was there and they celebrated her birthday and a couple of days day later, they took my mother to Kaiser Hospital because she was having contractions. They had her in Kaiser Hospital for two days for further observation until her water broke. She was in a twenty-four hour pain and at twelve fifty-six in the morning I was born. My mother had me in her arms and she was happy that I was healthy boy. Everyone saw me and they were holding me so tight and they were so happy. Well I was excited to be born in Redwood City, California, and it was a couple of hours from San Francisco, California and right on the Pacific Ocean. Well I'm half Spanish from my father's side of the family and I'm half Mexican from my mother's side of the family. Well my mother and I were in Kaiser Hospital for a couple of days until she recovered and they took us to her brother's home. Then in July we went back to Mexico City and my mother showed her colleagues her new baby boy. Well my parents named me Mauricio de la Vega the second. My father gave me that name in honor of the original Mauricio de la Vega but the weird part is that there wasn't enough information on the original Mauricio de la Vega. Well some say that he was just a poet, writer or a soldier but those are the speculations. And I felt honored and I feel so special that my father name me after somebody that didn't do squad for the family. So, they told my parents if they were ready to come back to work. They said yes, and even though my mother hasn't done anything in the last nine months, well she was worried that she might be a little bit rusty from her pregnancy. But she was able to train once again and she was clear to work and she couldn't be anymore happier. My grandparents decided to take care of me while my parents went out to fight crime. My father continued to put his life on the line day in and day out and my mother once dedicated her life to her Police work and taking criminals right out of the streets. Well now it became a regular eight hour job for her because I was her top priority now and my grandparents could tell that my mother was still not ready to go back to work. Then my parents were way behind on their payments because they were buying me food, clothes, and toys. And besides their paycheck wasn't enough to get by for a whole week. They may be Super Cops but they weren't going to get a raise because Police Officers don't get paid that much. And they came to the decision that they should move to Redwood City, California. My mother asked her brother to lend her money and he did loan the money so they can come here and start a new life in America. My father already knew how to speak English, and he also knows how to speak French. My mother improved in her English because my father was teaching her. So, my parents asked for their transferred.

So, my mother called the Redwood City Police Department and they were glad to have them on board. And for the last two weeks my father continued to fight crime while my mother was packing up her things and put them into the moving truck. And at the end of the week we finally moved to Redwood City, California. My mother's sister-in-law took care of me most of the time. My parents went into the Police Station and they gave them a warm welcome. My parents started working for the Redwood City Police Department. Well my father was turning out to be the best Police Officer there is. But my mother had other things in mind, and she only work for eight hours and went home to be with me and took care of me. And later on my mother had another surprise. It was her birthday where she discovered that she was pregnant once again. My parents were happy that they were going to have another baby along the way. My mother told me that she was going to have another baby and I was excited as well. Once again my mother worked around the office and she was doing paper work while my father was on the streets making himself into a legend and making the family proud of his success. And there was this one time that the Redwood City Police Department were working with the FBI. They were helping them with another drug sting operation. The FBI told the Redwood City Police Department that they were after, Vito Mancini. My father couldn't be anymore happier and he couldn't wait to arrest Vito Mancini and it was Round Two. But the drug sting operation went wrong again and Vito was trying to escape once again and he killed three FBI Agents and ten Police Officers along the way and my father shot Vito Mancini in the foot, and he went up to him and arrested him. And as always four members of the Federal Bureau Investigation were sponsored by Vito Mancini and they knocked my father out and helped Vito Mancini escaped once again. The rest of the FBI Agents and along with the Police Offices showed up to see Vito Mancini getting away in a helicopter. They saw my father knocked out and they took him to the Hospital. My father woke up in the Hospital and he had a concussion and they told him that Vito Mancini escaped and he was upset and started cursing Vito Mancini all the way to Hell. Well my father remained in the Hospital for three days and he got out and went back on the streets to find Vito Mancini the crime lord and hoped to arrest him someday. Nine months later my mother went back to Kaiser Hospital, and again she was in pain for thirty-six hours and then at six o'clock in the morning, my parents were blessed with another baby and it was a baby girl. My mother named her, "Tania Marie Guzman de la Vega." She was happy that Tania was a healthy pretty little girl. My father and I arrived at Kaiser Hospital and he was holding her and he was about to cry. My father showed me my little sister and I was excited and loved my sister right from the start and I never left her sight. My mother and Tania stayed in Kaiser Hospital for a couple of days and they finally went home. My sister and I shared a room together and I always took care of my baby sister, "my little munchkin" that's how I call her and she even gave me a smile and it felt like she liked the name that I gave her. The four of us lived a happy life in Redwood City, California and things were going to change for the worse. Because it was the year 1989 where my parents left us with her sister-in-law while they go out and fight crime.

My sister and I were playing in the living room until everything started shaking, I looked around and everything was falling to the ground. My aunt came running to the living room and told us to go under the table because what we were experiencing was an earthquake. And thirty minutes later it was over, we went walking to the living room and we went outside and everything fell on the ground. People were on the streets and they were crying and they were getting hysterical. We heard the sirens of the Ambulance, Fire Fighters, and the Police Officers from all over the city. My sister was crying and my aunt tried to make her happy. My uncle finally came to the house and he asked me if I was alright and I told him yes. By nine o'clock in the night, we kept hearing the Ambulance and the Fire Fighters and my aunt turn on the television. We saw the disaster from all over the city, and all the bridges collapse and a lot of people died on that day. My sister and I were scarred on that horrible day and probably for the rest of our lives and we were traumatized by the whole experience. Then at midnight my parents finally came home and they went to hug us and we cried in their arms and they told us that everything is going to be okay. From there everyone had to be precaution because we didn't know when the earthquake was going to strike next and we were really worried. By the year 1990 my parents saw how I was acting and my sister was crying most of the time. So, on that night my parents decided for our own good to move somewhere where there was no earthquakes and for us to be safe. My uncle told my mother that their family were now living in Ciudad Juarez, Chihuahua and they said that El Paso, Texas is a nice city to live. My parents asked for their transfer and they started packing everything and they put their boxes and the suitcases into the moving van. My mother gave the key to the landlord and we left and we said goodbye to Redwood City, California. My uncle was driving the moving van while my parents were following him. And we arrived in a restaurant in Phoenix, Arizona. My uncle told us that he has a friend that lives in El Paso, Texas and we can leave the moving van at his friend's house and we can go see our family in Juarez. Well we finally arrived in El Paso, Texas and we followed my uncle and we stopped by at his friend's house and we all got to know each other very well. So, his friend let us have the moving van in his parking lot while we go and see the city. And we went to downtown El Paso and we started walking around downtown and it looked to be a nice city and nice people too. My uncle drove us to the Eastside of the city and we fell in love with the Eastside of El Paso and it was a nice place to live. As always my uncle helped us get a house and he paid for everything. My parents left Tania and I with our family in Juarez while they went to pick up the moving van and they started putting everything inside the house. By the end of the week they went back to Juarez to pick us up and we went home. My father opened the front door to our new house and I started running all over the house and I liked how my parents decorated the new house. Then I went outside and I noticed that it's a nice neighborhood to live in.

Later on in the afternoon my father and I went to get some Pizza and we came back home and we started celebrating together like on big happy family. And on that evening our new neighbors came to our house and we got to know them very well and they welcomed us to the neighborhood and to El Paso, Texas. Well the neighbors were proud to have two Super Cops living next door and they even asked my parents for their autographs and they were taking pictures. And later on in the week my parents left us with the neighbors while they went to the Police Station. They presented themselves and everyone heard about their reputation in Mexico City, and in Redwood City, California and they were happy to have them on the Police Force. My parents were once again Police Officers and everyone were honored to have two Super Cops on the Police Department.

By the year 1990 my parents turned thirty-six years old and they were still taking criminals off the streets and they haven's lost a step. So, three weeks later we were in the living room watching a movie and there was a knock on the front door. My father opened the door and it was an FBI Agent. My father invited him into the living room and they sat on the couch. "What's this about?" My father asked.

The FBI Agent responded. "My name is Agent Williams and I'm in charged of the Federal Bureau Investigation down in Washington D.C. I hear that you two are Super Cops and you bring criminals to justice and you also killed a lot of criminals. And for a long time I've been hearing about your reputation. And I know when you were in Mexico City, you helped the FBI with a drug sting operation."

"Yes, I was shot two times and Vito Mancini got away in a helicopter." My father said.

"And I understand that in Redwood City, California, you once again helped the FBI into capturing Vito Mancini but unfortunately he bought half of the FBI Agents and he did escaped in a helicopter."

"Yes, I had two chances to arrest Vito Mancini but he got away and I've been waiting to get my hands on him. When I got out of the Hospital I decided to ask around and no one knows where he is." My father said.

The FBI Agent looked at them and said, "Pablo and Beatrice, you guys have a great reputation of being two Super Cops and you have arrested so many criminals. And I came here to offer you two a chance to work for the Federal Bureau Investigation."

My parents were in shock and said, "Wow, I've been dreaming of becoming an FBI Agent." My father smiled.

"I've read your profile and you two are the best there is." He said.

My father smiled and looked at my mother and said, "What do you say, Beatrice? Let's take this opportunity and we can be more successful in our lives."

My mother looked at them and looked at us and smiled. "It was also my dream of becoming an FBI Agent but that was when I was single and now I'm married and have two kids and I need to look out for my children and I just want what's best for them. If you want to take it Pablo, there is your chance of becoming an FBI Agent because you are the best there is." She smiled and looked at the FBI Agent. "I don't need anyone to remind me about how many people I've killed. You have no idea what I went through. Those criminals I killed had families and I should've arrested them."

"I understand!" The FBI smiled.

My father looked at us and said. "Well I'll take it. And I want to risk my life for my wife and kids and for this country. I want to arrest the most dangerous criminals there are in the world and of course I want to arrest Vito Mancini. And when can I start?"

"Well you can leave tomorrow morning so you can spend this night with your family." The FBI Agent said and smiled.

And just like that my father accepted his new position as an FBI Agent and we went to hug him and we are proud of him. And my mother also had the opportunity to become an FBI Agent just like my father but she chose to stay in El Paso and she felt that we wanted a better life for her kids. So, my mother was turning out like the women in her family that took care of the kids, clean the house, and making dinner but she also remained as a Police Officer and continued to work for eight hours. So, the next day my father told us that he loves us a lot and we saw him leave in a black van and we knew that he was going to do great things if we works hard and he can achieve anything he wants too and of course making the de la Vega's proud. My mother was responsible for us and she was both mommy and daddy. And I waited for the new school year to begin but my mother told me that they were going to held me back in the first grade so why go this year. The three of us lived happy together and I showed my baby sister how to walk and how to talk and we had fun with each other. My sister and I we were getting to know each other and loving each other as well. I would do anything to make Tania happy so she won't be sad.

CHAPTER THREE

MY GREAT DEPRESSION

A year later my mother took me to register at my new school. When we got there I was reading the name of my new school and it's called Myrtle Cooper Elementary School. And we went into the front office and my mother was talking to the Secretary and to the Principal and Vice Principal. I looked around and I felt that I was going to like this school and it was a lot bigger than the one in Redwood City, California. And finally they asked me if I was bilingual and I didn't know what to say and I just smiled to everyone. My mother said yes and they told me that I was going to start school on Monday morning. And we went home and I asked my mother what bilingual was. My mother looked at me and smiled and she told me that I know two languages, English and Spanish and that's what bilingual really is. And on that day my mother took me to the store to buy school supplies and she bought me a lot of school supplies. On the weekend my sister and I were always alone because my mother was out at night fighting crime. Well the weekend was the busiest for her because there were a lot of drunk drivers and people that were trying to rob the convenience stores. Well the neighbor always took care of us and my mother usually came home around midnight and she picked us up and went back home. The three of us stayed together in her bedroom and she wanted to know how our day went and she told us what she did. My mother told us that she arrested ten criminals in one night and she tackled one of them to the ground. That was her signature move. "I still have it! Now bad for a thirty-six year old, Mommy!" She smiled and hugged us. And Tania and I knew that she was working very hard and we are proud of her but my parents told us is not about the medals and the awards, is about working hard and you can achieve anything if you set your mind to it.

So on Monday morning I started attending Myrtle Cooper Elementary School. I was so shy that I didn't want to talk to anyone. As soon I walked into the classroom, all I did was smile to everybody and they also smiled at me. During the time I was there my classmates kept asking me how come I didn't talk and I usually shrugged my shoulders and smiled. I guess I was still traumatized from the earthquake but at the same time I was so nervous of being in a new city and that was the problem right from the start. While I was sitting there and out of nowhere this girl came into the classroom and she was so pretty than the rest of the girls in class. I was in love with her right of way and she looked at me and smiled and very slowly she approached me.

"Hi, my name is Eliza Caballero! And what's your name?" She asked and I was smiling and I wanted to tell her but I was too shy to talk to her.

"He doesn't talk he only smiles and nods his head." One of the kids said and smiled.

So, I decided to write my name on a piece of paper and she read it and I think she noticed that I was drooling all over her but we shook hands and she was my new best friend in El Paso, Texas. "How about we sit together because I know we're going to get along pretty well." Eliza smiled and I nodded and smiled. Eliza sat down and she started talking to me. Eliza is very talkative and is always smiling to everyone and she is not judgmental like the rest of them. She has all kinds of friends and she got along with everybody. Eliza has long black hair, and brown eyes, and she was wearing a white blouse and a long skirt and she is so beautiful. So, I was listening to what she had to say and all the kids in class were staring at us and they were saying that we are going to get married and they were just teasing us. But Eliza didn't mind the torture from our classmates so it was okay. She told everyone in class that I was her new boyfriend and she also told them that we are going to have a lot of kids somewhere in the near future. Well I looked around and there was at least twenty-seven students. And the bell rang and our first grade Teacher came into the classroom and she gave us a huge smile.

Our first grade Teacher introduce herself to the whole class and said, "My name is Martha Falcon and welcome to my classroom." She smiled and open her folder and took out the attendance sheet. And she said, "I'm going to call out your names and I want you all to say "Here." She smiled and said, "Deyna Alberts."

"Here!" She smiled.

"Joanna Bennett."

"Here!" She also smiled

"Christina Bobs!"

"Here" She smiled.

Mrs. Falcon looked at Christina and asked, "Is your father in the Federal Bureau Investigation and is your mother a Police Officer?'

"Yes! They are my heroes!" She smiled.

"Congratulations!" The Teacher smiled and read the next one. "Eliza Caballero!"

"Here!" She smiled.

"Jennifer Callaway."

"Here!" She smiled.

She looked at her and asked, "Is your dad in the Federal Bureau Investigation?"

"Yes! He's one of the best." She smiled.

"Mauricio de la Vega!" And been the moron that I am, I raised my hand and smiled.

Mrs. Falcon smiled and looked at me, "I heard that your parents are Super Cops and I've been hearing about their reputation for so many years."

I smiled and laughed and she said, "Armando Guerrero!"

"I'm here!" He said and smiled.

"Jessica Hernandez!"

"Here!" She smiled.

Mrs. Falcon looked at her and smiled, "I heard that your dad is in the Army and your mother is a Police Officer."

"Yes!" She smiled.

"Lorraine Hondo."

"Here!" She smiled.

Mrs. Falcon smiled and looked at her, "Wow, your dad works for the Border Patrol and your mother is in the Navy."

"Yes!" She smiled.

"Erin Killins!"

"Here!" She smiled.

Mrs. Falcon looked at her and smiled. "We have another one class. Erin's father also works for the Federal Bureau Investigation and her mother is also a Police Officer."

"Yes!" She smiled.

"Jason Loams!"

"Here!"

"Primo Mancini!"

"Yo!" He smiled.

Somehow Mrs. Falcon looked frightened when she look at us and looked directly at Primo Mancini. "Don't tell me your dad is?"

We looked at him and he responded, "My father is Vito Mancini, the greatest crime lord that has ever lived and my mother is a Detective as well." He smiled and has an Italian Accent.

"Moving on class. Lucinda Nagles."

"Here!"

"Cassandra Powell."

"Here!" She smiled.

Mrs. Falcon looked at her and said, "Your parents are Police Officers."

"Yes!" She smiled.

"Karina Reyes!"

"Here!" She smiled.

Mrs. Falcon looked at her and said, "Your dad is in the Central Intelligence Agency and your mom is a Police Officer.

"Yes!" She smiled.

Mrs. Falcon went through her list and there were more surprises on the first day of school. "Sonia Rodriguez." It turns out that her father is also in the Central Intelligence Agency and her mother is a Police Officer. "Roxanne Sanderson." Her father works for the Sheriff Department and her mother is a college Professor at the University of Texas at El Paso.

There you have it ladies and gentlemen, eleven students and our parents are Police Officers, FBI Agents, CIA Agents, Sheriffs, and crime lords. The weird thing is that our parents have known each other since they were little kids but with one common goal. They have been after Vito Mancini for a lot of years. Well all of us just looked at each other and we smiled. At the same time we didn't know what the Hell was going on and maybe it was just coincidence that all of us were in the same class together. So, Eliza sat next to me during class and during lunchtime. Eliza and I sat down with our new friends. Eliza was talking to everyone and she was asking us about our parents and she told us that we should be proud of them but we smiled at her. Then the bell rang and it was time to go home, Eliza and I stayed together in class and the Pac Ten also stayed in class. We were talking to each other well I just listening to them talk until our mothers came to pick us up. We introduced our parents and they were excited to see each other again and they were happy to know that they are now Police Officers, FBI Agents, and CIA Agents and not to mention crime lords. We said goodbye to each other and went home. My mother started making us dinner and she said, "It's great to know that you have something in common with your friends. I was glad to see Perla again, she has been my childhood friend since Mexico City and she came to live here and gave birth to Primo. And I know you and Primo are going to be good friends and even though his father is a crime lord and your father has been anxious to arrest him. But Primo may be different from his father. He can come over whenever he wants to." My mother smiled and served us dinner.

"Mom, I met this girl."

"Really! What's her name?" She asked.

"Her name is Eliza Caballero. She sat next to me during class and lunch."

"You made another new friend. I'm so excited." She smiled.

"But I chicken out and I didn't talk to her. I was too shy to talk to everyone in class." I said and smiled.

"Not again, Mauricio. Honey, I want you to make me a promise that you are going to talk. I don't want you to be in the same situation like when we were living in Redwood City." She smiled and hugged me so tight. I looked at her and smiled and we were eating dinner. And the babysitter came to take care of us and my mother kissed us and went out to fight crime all night long.

So, my first year at Elementary was one of the best memories in my life. That year I received five straight honor-rolls and as the matter of fact, Eliza, the Pac Ten, and I received five honor rolls. We got so excited that we were about to cry. And I could tell Eliza was happy for me and our classmates were congratulating me and they also hugging me as well. Then in the afternoon

Primo's mother took us home and I showed my mother and my baby sister the honor rolls, and they also got excited, they hugged me and we went out to celebrate at *Peter Piper Pizza*. We celebrated all night long.

Then there were a lot of bad things that were happening in the city in the last three weeks. It was Saturday morning where my sister and I were watching cartoons, when all of the sudden the news interrupted the program. The anchor man was talking about that on Friday night, three girls were brutality raped and tortured and that's a total of ten girls that are getting raped and tortured in the last month. The anchor man also told us to be careful on the streets because there's a serial rapist that's on the loose in El Paso, Texas and the Police have yet to arrest him. So, right now they are looking for the serial rapist at this very moment. The news finished and the cartoons were back on and I was hoping that my mother and her team are able to capture that pervert by the end of the week. So, it was Friday night where my mother invited Primo and her mother, Perla Mancini Fuentes to eat at *Peter Piper Pizza*. The five of us were sitting down and we were eating.

My mother looked at me and said, "Mauricio, I know you are happy because you have five honor rolls. It doesn't matter how you start the school year, what matters is how you finish the school year. Is not about the awards or the medals. Is about working hard and achieving your goal to graduate from high school and going to college. Are you willing to work hard to reach college and have a big future ahead of you?"

I looked at her and smiled, "Yes, I'm ready for anything." My mother smiled and we finish eating and went home. And since it was the weekend Primo stayed over at my house and we were in my room.

Primo looked at me and said, "Well I finally heard your voice, Mauricio de la Vega. And I want to know is why don't you talk at school?"

"Well I'm shy and I get nervous around people!" I responded.

"Okay, I'm not going to tell anyone at school that I heard you talk. I'm not going to tell Eliza anything. And it will be our little secret." Primo smiled and grabbed a pen and paper and wrote down something on a piece of paper.

"What are you writing?" I asked.

"A list." He responded.

"A list of what?"

"Remember on the first day of school when our teacher, Mrs. Falcon was taking row. And it turns out that eleven students have something in common."

Primo smiled and said, "Your parents and their parents and my mom are Law Enforcement. And they all want to arrest my dad so badly."

I looked at him with a serious face. "You are right, Primo! My dad had the chance to arrest your father and if it wasn't for his friends that helped him escape twice."

Primo looked at me and smiled, "My father pays people to help him escape and that's how it's going to be. You need friends to help you do the things that you wouldn't do alone. And remember friends help friends to succeed in life."

"I'll think about it and when I do need help in spelling. I'll make sure to call you and everyone else." I smiled.

"Take a look at the list." He smiled and gave me the list.

I was looking at the list he made. "Nine girls and two guys. Are you saying that we are going to need their help?"

"Yes and what's your opinion!" He smiled.

"I like it and now let's play video games." I smiled and we started playing video games. And during that year I got to play with my friends and we played a lot of games in the playground and at Marty Robbins Park. But I had more fun playing with Eliza the most. Our mother's became close friends and we went to each other's house but as always I didn't talk and Eliza was the one that was doing all the talking and me I was just listening to her and I loved watching her smile and I love her laughter as well. And there were many times when Eliza was talking to me and I usually smiled and nodded my head and I wrote what I wanted to say to her on a piece of paper and she read it and smiled and that's how we communicated with each other. I wanted to talk to her and I wanted to know where she was from but I was way too shy to talk to her.

Most of the time Eliza and I usually hang out and played hide and go seek at Marty Robbins Park and knowing the rules of hide and seek. I had to count in my mind because I didn't want Eliza to hear me talk. What if I count and she was in back of me and was waiting to hear me talk. Also we played school and my all time favorite, Eliza and I played husband and wife and pretended to have a baby together. It was exciting to be in a new school and to hang out with Eliza and everybody else. And school was out and everybody went to their summer vacation. My mother took us to Washington D.C. to visit my father and he was happy to see us. My father took us everywhere and we even met the President of the United States. The President invited us to the White House and he was going to have a boring dinner with all the leaders of the world. But he actually order Pizza for us kids and we actually ate the Pizza in their rooms. My summer was great in the White House and I was playing with the President's kids. And we kept in touch right after that great summer and we became pen pals.

Then summer was over and I was excited to start second grade. Well my first day in second grade was kind of cool. Because I had the same classmates and we were happy to see each other. Eliza walked in and she hugged me so tight and kissed me on the cheek. Twenty minutes later my second grade Teacher came into the classroom. She introduce herself and we got to know each other and we were better acquainted. And she took out her attendance sheet and called out our names and she was shock to see that our parents are in the big time and they had one thing in common other than their friendship, the fact is that they were after Vito Mancini. But she was scared to have Primo Mancini in her classroom. And it was finally lunchtime, Eliza and I went to walk around the playground and we went far away from everybody and we sat under a shade tree. I even brought my notebook and pencil and I wrote what I wanted to say to Eliza.

"How was my summer?" She read and smiled. "Well my summer was great, my mommy took me and my older brother to Miami, Florida. I met a lot of Cubans over there. And I was on the beach and as you can say. I'm sun burned but I had a lot of fun over there." She smiled. "What about you, Mauricio?" I wrote what I did on my summer and gave it to her. "Wow, you spent the whole summer with your dad in Washington D.C. and you met the President of the United States." She smiled and I wrote another thing and she read it. "Well I have an older brother and he's going to become a Teacher. My mommy works for the Socorro School District. And what about your parents?" She asked and I wrote it down and gave it to her and she read it. "You must be excited that your dad is an FBI Agent and your mom is a Police Officer and I know they are two Super Cops. And that's great that you have a baby sister and her name is Tania Marie." She gave me a huge smile and I nodded and I also smiled. And I picked up a yellow sunflower and gave it to her and she smelled it. Eliza looked at me and said, "Mauricio, I want to open up to you and I feel that I can trust you because we are very good friends. And I want to tell you everything about me and I hope you can tell me everything about yourself. I will love to hear your voice and I would be a happy camper. And as it turns out I never met my daddy. My mommy told me that he went away to the Army and he hasn't come back home. I hope I get to see him again and If I do see him I'm going to tell him that a made a special friend or I just tell him that you are my boyfriend and my future husband. The father of my kids!" She smiled and I touched her hand and smiled. "You're a good friend, Mauricio." She hugged me and kissed me on the cheek.

She was talking to me until the bell rang and it was time to go to class. I felt comfortable around Eliza and everybody else at school. I said to myself what can go wrong if I didn't talk at school. What's the worse thing could happen to me? Well my question was answered when my world was turned upside down with the things that were happening to me in school. I felt betrayed and used by the whole scenario. I never thought my shyness was going to cost me problems at school. And for instance my second grade Teacher kept asking me to read out loud in class and I didn't want to read. She started to mock me and embarrassed me in front of the classroom and everyone was laughing at me except for Eliza and the Pac Ten but Eliza was always defending me most of the time but the Teacher kept on mocking me until my friend Eliza finally stood up to her and said, "Is not funny! I cannot believe that you were Teacher of the year. You should be ashamed of yourself and it's not right to make fun of others!" She kept yelling at the Teacher and I got up and gave Eliza what I wrote down. She laughed at her. "Mrs. Martinez, I think you should look yourself in the mirror before you make fun of me. You are a fat four eyed Teacher and no wonder there are so many earthquakes around the world because your so fat and ugly! And farts a lot!" Eliza and I started laughing at her and we could tell that she was embarrassed and also the Pac ten also made fun of her. And I went up to the chalk board and wrote the word "pig" and I was imitating her with the way she walked in the hallways and making pig noises. She got mad at me and sent me to the Principal's office. She told the Principal that I was disrupting the whole classroom and she didn't mention to the Principal that she was making fun me and she made up stories so I can get into trouble. And Eliza also barged into the Principal's office and was defending me and started yelling at him. The Principal was upset with Eliza barging into his office and as it turns Eliza and I were suspended for a whole week and I knew my four eyed fat Teacher had the last laugh but she's not because she is going to pay for her actions.

As the year went on my grades started going down and everyone in class was getting upset with me because I didn't talk at all and I didn't want to read in front of the class. They were looking for anything little thing I did so I could get into some kind of trouble. Then there were a lot of monthly meetings and my mother was asked to come to those meetings. Everybody started to make a big deal out of it and they even asked me questions like "Why don't you talk? Is there someone threatening you if you talk? Will you get abused at home if you talk?" They came up with a lot of weird theories about my situation. And a couple of weeks went by, I was eating at the cafeteria and then I went running all the way to the playground. A couple of my friends were playing in the playground bus and they were playing tag. I climbed the bus and he tagged me, so I gently tagged him and it was like a powder puff tag and he made it look that I hit him so hard. Well he fell to the ground and everybody ganged up on me and said that I did it on purpose. And once again Eliza and the Pac Ten were there to protect me from everybody else. They took the boy to the Nurse's office and my Teacher yelled at me for supposedly injuring his arm. And I was expecting that my friend would say that it was an accident but he didn't and he even said that I wanted to hurt him because supposedly I was so violent after all my parents are Police Officers and they thought that's what they teach me at home.

And I cannot believe that he made up a story so I can get into trouble so I was given detention for a whole week. When I was at home my sister, my mother, Eliza, and the Pac Ten were telling me that everything was going to be okay and told me not worry. And at school was different from home. Everybody hated me so much and they stopped talking to me. And then I went to detention for a whole week straight and the following Friday I was on my way to detention and my Teacher and I ran into each other in the hallway. She asked me if I had learned my lesson from the accident. I said yes and she told me that I could go outside since my detention was complete. When I went outside everyone told me to go back to detention and at the same time they didn't know that my Teacher gave me the okay to go outside. But instead I started running to the playground bus.

When I reached the playground bus, I stopped right in front of it. And I was standing there for, I guess, three seconds and this girl fell down and hit her head and she was crying. They went up to her and told her if she was okay but she pointed at me and that made it worse for me. She blame everything on me. And everybody started yelling at me and they were punching me and they took the girl to the Nurse's office. And I received another yelling from my Teacher, and from my mother, and that year turned out to be a nightmare. I went from having five straight honor rolls into this mess and this was still the second grade. I wanted the school year to end and I hope that next year was going to be different. So, the school year ended and my mother took us to spend the whole summer with her family in Juarez. I was trying to enjoy the summer but I was so upset and I stayed away from everybody. My mother was trying to comfort me and she knew that those injuries were accidents and she told me not worry about it. And I started thinking about my best friends Eliza and the Pac Ten and I was wondering what they were doing this summer. And as always the summer has to end. I was going to enter the third grade.

Well the school year started and I started third grade and I had the same classmates and some of them were new and as always Eliza came in and she was happy to see me. I felt that everyone hated me so much because they were giving me a bad look all the time except for the Pac Ten they were cool with me. And will see how this year goes for me and my friends. Ten minutes later my new third Teacher came into the classroom and told us that her name is "Mrs. Martinez." That's great I had another Martinez and once again this year turned out to be a nightmare. And both Martinez's decided to team up and they agreed to sent me to see a Psychiatrist because they were fed up with me and they were looking for every little thing I did so I can get into trouble. They didn't help me they just sent me there just for the Hell of it. My third grade Teacher told my mother that she was responsible that I didn't talk and told her some more graphic things and my mother cried the entire night. I never seen my mother cry before and I hated my third Teacher so much and I wanted my mother to arrest that bitch and the other fat bitch too. So, my second grade Teacher was the one that took me to see the Psychiatrist. And the Psychiatrist wanted to talk to me in private.

"I want you tell me why don't you talk at school?" She asked and I looked at her and said, "That I didn't want to talk at all!" I exclaimed and I wanted to tell them that it wasn't their Goddamn business but I felt that they were going to make a bigger deal if I stood up for myself. And the Psychiatrist made me draw pictures, gave me tests, and put me through a lot of weird stuff for several months. I was getting frustrated with everything that was happening to me at school well I was getting abused at school and the Teachers were the real bullies not my parents. And there were more monthly meetings and both Martinez's were getting on my nerves. And I started thinking about how much they are getting paid by screwing with me. We all know that Teachers don't get paid that much but I'm sure they are going to get the big paycheck somewhere down the road.

And one good thing did happen that year when I entered the third grade spelling bee contest, and don't ask me why or how, but I ended up getting second place in the third grade spelling bee contest. And I remember Eliza and the Pac Ten giving me a huge hug and the rest of the school came up to congratulate me and it was my best memory that year. I was the best speller in third grade and maybe the whole school and I was on top of the world and I know that my two Teachers are going to screw me later on so bring it and will see who shits at the end. And also my third grade Teacher and the staff had no choice but to send me to Special Education and I knew somewhere after school they were drinking and celebrating that they are screwing with me. And summer came and the school year was finally over.

Well my father came home around the summer and we were together like one big happy family and we had a lot of cookouts in the backyard and at Marty Robbins Park. My father told me just hang on and just show them that you can do better and never give up. And I knew my mother and father didn't want me to worry about it but I let them do the worrying for me. But at the same time I was having fun pushing the envelope so much and I was pissing off everybody at school. Yes, I was frustrated but it was worth every minute of it and I felt that I would get the last laugh in this war. And of course the summer ended and I had to start school all over again. And I was excited that I had two years left in Elementary and the nightmare continued that same year.

Well I started fourth grade and I had the same classmates and they were pissed off to see me. But the only good thing was that Eliza and the Pac Ten and I were classmates all over again. Eliza really had changed during the summer. Her hair was a little bit longer and she was a lot more pettier than the rest of the girls at school. The word around school was that Eliza Caballero was the prettiest girl and all the guys wanted to go out with her. She ignored everyone and told all the boys at school that I was her boyfriend and I was honored that she pick me than some pretty boy at school. Well I was the envy of the school, I didn't talk and I was in Special Education but Eliza the prettiest and hottest girl at elementary school told everyone that I was her boyfriend. She chose me from the beginning until the end.

Well the first semester in the fourth grade started in a bizarre way. My fourth grade Teacher well I respected him for knowing History and everything else he knew about History of Spain and in Mexico. Well he got into trouble by his own students. They went to the Principal's office and told him everything that went on in the classroom. Eliza, the Pac Ten and I went to the playground because we didn't want to get him in trouble. Well the Martinez's return with vengeance and they wanted to recruit him so they can have their club together. But I guess he didn't want to join their, "I need a life club!" Then it was three weeks before Christmas vacation, my fourth grade Teacher was absent and we had a substitute Teacher. We were going to have a Christmas play and I told everyone that I was going to sing Christmas carols and I was so excited. We were getting ready to start and everyone told the substitute Teacher not let me sing because I didn't talk at all. They didn't want me in their group, but Eliza and the Pac Ten were defending me and the substitute Teacher took the other student's side and they went to the cafeteria to sing. They didn't even apologize and they just laughed at me and making fun of me.

Well things got out of control and there was another meeting and they asked me if I wanted to continue in that classroom or if I wanted to be in a another classroom. I wanted to leave because of the atmosphere. And I told the staff that I wanted a female Teacher and I was glad to get out of the classroom. I was sad to leave Eliza and the Pac Ten behind and especially my fourth grade teacher. But everyday they smiled and they were still talking to me. And Eliza still told me that I was still her boyfriend and I was happy and honored. And on that day Eliza and I went to Marty Robbins Park and we carved our names into a tree and I knew she was happy because she hugged me so tight and kissed me on the cheek. Then we had Christmas break and we came back on January and I started my first day in a new classroom. Everyone gave me warm welcome. So, one month later my new fourth grade Teacher told us that we have a guest speaker. She wanted all of us to be at our best behaviors.

So, the door open and the guest speaker came into the classroom. He looked like an Englishman and he looked to be smart and a scholar as well. He stood in front of the classroom and said, "My name is William Jones and I'm from London, England. I'm an Historian and I've been doing this for almost twenty years. Since I was a little kid I was fascinated with the history of Spain and other countries as well. Then one day I finally became an Historian well things worked out for me that I even became me a scholar. So, I was researching in one of the libraries of London but they didn't have any books that I was looking for, so I came to America and continued my research. And I couldn't

Jesus Morales

find anything that I was looking for. So, I went to Madrid, Spain and the Librarians over there gave me a lot of books about the history of Spain. I was reading one book that caught my interest, and I took the book home and read the book for about three hours and I found something that got my attention. So, I went back to the Library and asked the scholars about the book that I was reading and they told me that they have read it to and they prefer not to talk about the book. But they also did a lot of investigations and one of them gave me another book to read and when I read the book. It brought chills down my spine. And for a long time there was a catch in the history of Spain and it was more than a cover up." He smiled and drank some water and he started telling us more about the country of Spain. "Once upon a time in the early 1700's there was an honest to God King that ruled Spain for over thirty years. He was a respected and noble King that helped the poor people and he even took them into his Kingdom and fed them and they could stay in his castle for the rest of their lives. His name was Gregorio de la Vega." He smiled.

But everyone in the classroom looked at me and they said, "Mauricio, he's your relative!" And I didn't know what to believe.

The Historian smiled at me and continued, "You should be proud of your relative, Son!" And continued with his tale about King Gregorio de la Vega and the country of Spain. "The story goes that the Spaniards came to Mexico and became friends with the Aztecs, well they were learning from each other but there were half of the Aztecs that didn't like the Spaniards at all. Half of them left the tribe because they didn't want to be in the same place as them. Then all of the sudden the King of Spain fell in love with a woman well of course she was an Aztec, and she was so beautiful than the rest of the women of the tribe. You can say that it was love at first sight. She loved him and even though they were a different race. They got together on one night and they made love." He said and all the kids started giggling but he smiled. "Five months later the Spaniards were going back to Spain and the King suggested that his newly wed bride will come with him and see Spain and they can raise their kids over there in the Kingdom of Spain. She said yes but she wanted to stay one more night with her people and he agreed with her. So, on that night the Aztec woman was laying in bed with her husband. And all of the sudden this Witch Doctor came into the room and placed a curse on her unborn baby, the Witch Doctor hated the Spaniards so much that he wanted to see them die. He knew that the baby will die along with the parents and everyone in Spain would also die too. Then he was laughing as he left the room and the next day they went home to Spain." He said.

And one of the kids asked, "He killed her unborn baby?"

The Historian smiled and said, "No, Sweetie." So, the English Historian got everyone's attention with his side of the story. And I was kind of excited to hear about my relative being a good King to his people and he married a woman from a different race. And the Historian looked at us and continued, "The scholars told me what really happen and I couldn't believe it and I was in shocked when they told me the story. And I'm going to warn you kids, what I'm going to say next is not going to have a happy ending. So, twelve years later there was a serious of killings in Spain. The entire country of Spain were terrified of all the killings. They thought it was a plague that was spreading all over the country but it wasn't a plague at all. It was something else that was killing the people of Spain. But they began to notice that the people that were dying were the de la Vega family." He looked at me and everyone looked at me and they said, "Sorry, Mauricio." But the Historian continued. "And they found out that there was a serial killer on the loose in Spain and they didn't know if it was a man or a woman. Some say that it was a creature or a sick human being. The people began to described this serial killer as a Demonic figure with red evil eyes that was killing the de la Vega's. And also the people in the Kingdom remembered the King and his men went to Mexico and they knew that someone might have placed a curse on them and they thought that it was his wife that might have placed a curse on them but it wasn't her. Then the Aztec woman decided to send a messenger to Mexico so he can investigate the person that placed a curse on them. Then one day someone came to the King and Queen and they were describing this Dark Figure with red evil eyes as "The Aztec Conquistador." That's how they were calling him and they say that he had a sword and a spear, and it was also dressed as a Aztec, and dressed as a Conquistador, and they heard the creature laugh when he killed everyone in sight. But the King didn't believe in ghost stories but his wife believed in those tales. He told her not worry because they are very well protected. And all of the sudden The Aztec Conquistador entered the Kingdom and killed everyone in sight, and he killed the King of Spain and his wife, the Queen of Spain. The Aztec Conquistador went after the throne and became the new King of Spain and the people were terrified of the creature. The Aztec Conquistador told everyone that if they obey him that he was going to spare their lives and if they didn't obey him. He was going to chopped off their heads and feed their heads to the lions. Well everyone decided to take The Aztec Conquistador's side and their lives were spared so they were safe from the creature and they could live their lives in peace. Then The Aztec Conquistador ordered his new army to kill every de la Vega on sight well what was left of them. The new Army were spread all over the country and this psychotic killer also went and killed the entire de la Vega family. The Aztec Conquistador thought that there weren't any survivors left and there was one survivor that nearly escaped death, his name was Pedro de la Vega and he survived the attack." He said and one of the kids asked him something else.

"What about the Queen's messenger did he ever came back?"

The Historian responded. "The Queen's messenger did return to Spain and he was way too late to deliver the messenger that he had for the Queen and he saw their graves but someone who was loyal to the King and Queen told him that Pedro de la Vega survived the attack. And Pedro came to America to start another life. So, the Queen's messenger went to look for him and who knows if he delivered the message to Pedro de la Vega. The world is a big place. Thank you for your time." He smiled and everyone started clapping.

But someone else asked him. "What about the baby?"

"From what I read and from what they told me. The baby was born sick and he had a disfigured body but the parents still love their son."

"It was a boy?"

"Yes!" He looked at me and said, "His name was Mauricio de la Vega and he would have been the future King of Spain but he died due to health problems and right now you would have taken his place as the new King of Spain. You are Mauricio de la Vega the second." He smiled and took out something from his briefcase. "When the boy died, he left a letter saying that no one should take his rightful place as the King of Spain than his reincarnation. I figured that his parents had no choice but to accept it and even though this monster sat on the throne. Technically The Aztec Conquistador wasn't the King but he was just there to kill everyone in sight. But the throne belongs to someone else. And that makes you, Mauricio de la Vega, the second, the new future King of Spain. Your, Majesty!" The English scholar bowed down and everyone in class also bowed down as well. They were calling me your, Majesty and future King of Spain. And I couldn't believe that I'm next in line to become the new King of Spain. At the same time I was concerned because my family never once told us anything about The Aztec Conquistador and the fact that he killed our ancestors and they said that it was a plague but it was this monster that killed them. It looks to me that we may have a curse in our family and no one told me except this Historian.

And on that day the news were spread all over the world and my family found out that I was next in line to be new King of Spain. Not bad for someone that's in Special Education. Even my father called me and said that he is proud of me and he was encouraging me to go after the throne and to make the family proud of course. But my mother told me to be patient and as soon I was old enough, I can sit on the throne. And what bothered me the most is why my ancestor's name wasn't in the family's record book and the weird part is that no one talked about him. I didn't buy the fact that he left a note saying that no one would sit on the throne except him. But did the original Mauricio de la Vega hired The Aztec Conquistador to kill everyone else?

CHAPTER FOUR

THE BIRTH OF THE PACHUCO2K

It was three forty-five in the afternoon and it was time to go home. I was walking in the hallways and everyone was bowing down and I was thinking about my ancestor when I ran into Primo in the hallway. "Come to my house your, Majesty. There is something that I want to talk to you about. How about I give you a piggy back ride to my house your, Majesty." He smiled.

"Okay!" I smiled and I cannot believe that the son of the crime lord offered to give me piggy back ride but his house was ten blocks away from school and I out weight him over twenty pounds. And in about two hours later we finally arrived at his house and he opened the door and went straight to his room. "I'm listening."

"Well your, Royal Highness! We have one more year so we can finally leave elementary school and start middle school." Primo smiled and opened one of his drawers and took out his binder and gave it to me. "Look at it and read it."

I smiled and open Primo's binder and I was reading a bunch of articles and it was about twenty girls that were getting raped and tortured by that pervert. The Police Officers were calling him a dangerous serial rapist and the girls were recovering at Thomason Hospital. Because they bad bruises all over their body and broken bones along the way. Not to mention the girls had to see a Psychiatrist and I felt that they were traumatize from their awful experience with that serial rapist. "Well Primo, I feel bad about those girls that are getting rape and tortured and I hope the Police Officers arrest that pervert by the end of the week."

"I hope so too, Mauricio." Primo smiled and said, "And that's why I'm the pervert known as the serial rapist. You see I'm the one that's been raping all of those innocent little girls and don't worry they will recover from their experience they had with me and they will move on with their lives. Is that simple and no one dies. Oh, and by the way I'm really hoping to make my father proud of me and I want to become a legend just like him. But I cannot become a legend if I don't have friends to back me up."

I was shocked to learn that my best friend in the world is the serial rapist! "It was you that raped those innocent girls! You lucky dog and you are lucky that you're not in jail."

Primo was grinning from ear to ear and said. "Yes, your, Royal Highness! Guilty as charged. But you got to admit it. It was faith that brought all of us together. Eleven friends meet for the first time in elementary and it turns out that their parents are in the big time. Our parents have known each other since they were kids and they have a common goal, that they are after my father. Well Mauricio I have the ability to rape and torture girls and who knows what kind of abilities the others girls might posses. But I know you are going to become the future King of Spain and I don't know about your hidden talent. What if we worked together and try to become legends in own right."

"You mean having an alliance?" I asked and smiled.

"Of course and I don't know if people are going to get killed but we may be unstoppable if we work together." He smiled.

I looked at him and I was thinking about it for a couple of seconds and said. "Why not form a gang? You know like a cult and we can have a lot of missions together. We are going to be known as the *Pachuco2k*. We are going to be the new generation of gangsters. And another thing we need to be a secret gang. We're going to hit the city where it hurts the most and when the right time comes. We will let this city and the whole world know who we are."

Primo smiled and we shook hands. "It's a deal your, Majesty. The birth of the *Pachuco2k*. We are the co leaders, the cofounders and we should recruit the other nine girls."

"Okay! But make sure that you don't rape them because we are going to be one big happy family." I smiled.

"I promise and now let's recruit them." He said.

From there Primo made the phone calls and asked for the girls to come over to his house. And in about thirty minutes later the girls came to the house and I was sitting down on his chair and when the girls entered the room, they bowed down and called me your, "Royal Highness!" And they kissed my hand too. So, Primo started explaining everything to the girls and they also knew that it was faith that brought us together. Unlike our parents that they have been after Vito Mancini for a long time. Well we have formed an alliance with his son, Primo Mancini. And we could be legends in our own right. The girls were convinced and they respect the fact that Primo and I are the co leaders, the cofounders and we were going to be fair to one and another. This was my chance to learn to lead my new Army into action and like a good King, I will make sure that no one dies or gets arrested, not on my watch.

"I want to know is what kind of talent do you girls posses?" Primo asked them.

Christina Bobs raised her hand and said, "Well I'm in Karate and I can kick anybody's ass."

"That's good! And I know they told you not to fight with anyone else but we want you to start a fight with everybody that you see on the street. Kick their ass and send them to the Hospital!" Primo exclaimed and said, "Jennifer Callaway."

"Well I have the ability to kidnap. A month ago I kidnapped my neighbor's dog and I usually call them and tell them if you want to see your dog again. Well pay me the money and you will see your dog again. Well they left the money at the park and yesterday I brought the dog back to the neighbors. Well I just kidnapped and get paid but I don't do anything to them." She smiled.

"Mauricio de la Vega! The co leader and cofounder of the gang and the future King of Spain. He's going to lead us into action and if we get arrested, he's going to be there to bail us out." Primo smiled.

"I also want to be in the field taking charge." I smiled.

"Jessica Hernandez." Primo smiled.

"Well I can steal cars and my uncle taught me how to break into the car and steal it. I guess I can do that." She smiled.

"Lorraine!" Primo exclaimed.

"I like to race cars. And this one time I hopped into my mom's car and I raced against everyone and I won." Lorraine smiled.

"Erin Killins!" Primo said.

"I can steal someone's identity."

"Well you know about me. I'm a serial rapist, co leader, and cofounder of the gang." Primo smiled and said, "Cassandra Powell."

"I like to burn things and watch them explode." She smiled.

"Karina Reyes."

"I like to work on the computer and who knows I might be a computer hacker." She smiled.

"Sonia Rodriguez."

"I like to record people's conversation and I might put bugs in the offices and cars and we can hear their conversation." She smiled.

"Roxanne Sanderson."

"I can be a thief." She smiled.

"You see all of us have the talents and if we worked together, we are going to be unstoppable and become legends just like our parents. Now let's go see if we can do it on the streets." Primo smiled.

"Not so fast Primo! Karina, Sonia, Cassandra, and I need the proper equipment to do the things that we need and we need to stay here and at least strategize and tomorrow night you guys will start." I said.

"Fair enough." Primo said.

And on that day we were just chilling in Primo's room and every three seconds Primo and the girls asked me if I needed something, for instance something from the kitchen, a foot massage, a back rub, and they wanted to do my homework. I told them that I'm fine and we started watching a movie. I was actually sitting on Primo's bed and I was looking at my friends. Christina Bobs looks like a kung-fu fighter, she has long brown hair, brown eyes, and she weighs in ninety pounds. She loves to wear dresses and she loves to play with dolls, and she's very pretty. Jennifer Callaway has long blonde hair and blue eyes, she is sort of athletic, she weighs in eighty pounds and she's also very pretty. Jessica Hernandez has short black hair, brown eyes, she is she's also athletic, and also she's also going to be pretty very soon. Lorraine Hondo also has long blonde hair, with green eyes, she looks sort of innocent, she weighs in ninety pounds, and she's also pretty. Erin Killins has short brown hair, brown eyes, she looks very smart, she is also funny too, she weighs in eighty pounds, and also she's very pretty. Primo Mancini has black short hair and he has his hair comb back, he has an Italian accent, he's nice but sometimes he has the pervert look, and he weighs in one hundred and twelve pounds. You can say that he looks like a Greaser. Cassandra Powell, the new mad bomber, she has short blonde hair, blue eyes, she also looks every smart, she weighs in ninety-six pounds, and she's also very pretty. Karina Reyes has long brown hair, brown eyes, a genius on the computer, she might have a bright future with us like a Lieutenant and who knows maybe she can take over the "business." when we're not around anymore, she weighs in eighty-six pounds, and she's also very pretty too. Sonia Rodriguez has long brown hair, brown eyes, she looks much smarter than she looks, she weighs in ninety-six pounds and she's pretty too. Rosanne Sanderson has long blonde hair, blues eyes, she's also funny, she weighs in ninety-six pounds, and is also pretty. Well for me, I have short black hair, brown eyes, and I'm going to be a future psychotic serial killer, and I weigh in one hundred and forty-five pounds. Don't let our looks fool you, we are going to be dangerous. I was excited to have them in the gang and I knew we made a good decision to work together and we wanted to make our parents proud of us. Well I doubt that we are going to make them proud of us.

So, it was the end of May where school was finally out and my father came back from his business trip from Europe and the Middle East and I was already in summer vacation and my father had two surprises for me. Well my mother's birthday was coming up and mine too. And I wondered what my father and sister were going to give me and my mother for our birthdays. Well my father told me to pack up and I felt like I was going to like this surprise. I said goodbye to my mother and my baby sister, Tania. My father and I hopped on his private jet plane. We were sitting there talking and eating, and I was looking out the window and I noticed that everything looks small right from the sky. We arrive in some airport and three FBI Agents were waiting for us and my father introduce me to his colleagues and they were happy to meet me and they bowed down and kissed my hand. I accept people bowing down before me but I'm not going to tolerate them kissing my hand.

So, my father and I were tired from the long trip and we stayed in a Hotel for the night. And on that night my father and I were watching old cowboy movies and I was loving those parts when they were killing each other. I wanted to be like them and I wanted to ride a horse and shoot people, also I wanted to rob trains and rob banks. I wish I would do that in real life. And we finally fell asleep around three in the morning and we woke up around nine in the morning. My father and I were getting ready to leave the Hotel and I found out that we were in Washington D.C. We got into the black van and they took us to the Federal Bureau Investigation Headquarters. We got out of the van and walked into the front door and my father swiped his card and we went into the building. My father is very well respected FBI Agent and he is in command of everything on that building. Everyone said hi to him and shook his hand and they shook my hand too. So, my father took me all the way to the top floor where he has his business meetings. And I saw a secure door and he told me that's where they make the weapons for the FBI and some for the Army and Navy.

My father took me into his office and we sat down and served me a glass of water and he served himself a glass of whiskey. "You see all of this, Mauricio, when you grow up, everything you see in this building is going to be yours."

"Really!" I exclaimed.

"Yes. I want you to take over when I retire from the Federal Bureau Investigation. I see something special in you, Son. You have the ability of becoming a legend and make the de la Vega family proud along the way. And how about you become an FBI Agent and learn to command the team to action and you will have the experience when you become the new King of Spain. After all it's the de la Vega tradition."

"So, I have the ability to be someone important in life and become a legend in my own right?" I asked him and smiled.

"Well of course, Son. And I will personally train you and I know you are going to be a good FBI Agent and a good King in the near future. You might be better than me and I cannot wait for that day to come, Son." He said and smiled.

My father and I stayed in his office and we were talking for a couple of hours and he took me to the secure room and it turned out to be the Weapon Room. My father swipe his card and opened the door. I saw a man that was making weapons. "Hey, Pablo!" He said.

"How are you?" My father asked.

"I'm good. Just making weapons for the Navy and for the FBI." He responded.

"Look who I brought, Chris." My father said.

"My nephew and your, Majesty!" He exclaimed and hugged me.

Chris Farrell is a childhood friend of my father. Chris Farrell was born in Belfast, Ireland and he moved to America when he was just five years old. Well they grew up together and they are almost like brothers and they work together in this building. Chris is a nice man and he even treats me right.

"These are cool weapons!" I exclaimed.

"Yes, they are." He said.

Just then someone paged my father. "Well I'm going to have a conference. Mauricio you should stay with your uncle and you can learn from him."

"I will take care of him." He smiled and my father left.

I was looking around the room and I liked what I saw and asked him. "You work alone?"

"As the matter of fact I do. I work better alone and no one bothers you, just peace and quiet." Chris smiled and started drinking water. "So, your father told me that you have been in trouble at school. And the fact is that everyone hates you and they always ganged up on you and beat you up all the time. And I know you have suffered enough in your life." Chris said and smiled. "Have a seat, Son." We sat down and he said, "Now, Mauricio I'm going to tell you something and I know is going to change your life for the better and possibly for the best. How about we recruit a couple of your best friends so they can help you avenge everyone that has ever mistreated you in your entire life." Chris said and smiled. "I can teach you everything I know but it's up to you."

"Well I've been in trouble several times at school and everyone hates me. And I've been looking for a way to teach them a lesson." I said.

"I know you're a good kid and I know a way where you can teach them a lesson." Chris smiled and took out a briefcase and took out five Magnums guns and something else that he took out. He looked at me and started explaining. "Mauricio, this is a dart gun if you shoot someone with this, they will be paralyze for an hour." Chris showed me the dart guns. "I can give you a demonstration." He smiled and made a phone call and told somebody to bring an inmate into his office for a demonstration. Twenty minutes later they brought an inmate and he was scary looking. They gave him a file and he was reading it. "Mauricio, this is inmate Jason Columbus. Jason Columbus is a child murder and he is on death row and he volunteered for this experiment. Well actually they forced him to do a demonstration because he is going to die in the chair and why not use him for a demonstration. Jason Columbus rapes kids and then kills them so right now he is looking at you and he wants you so badly." He looked at him and said, "Jason Columbus, this boy is going to be the youngest King of Spain and how bad do you want him?"

I began to noticed that this freak was drooling all over me and I knew he was getting horny just by watching me. He was handcuffed from his legs and all over his body and they also had guns pointing at his head so he was just watching me and smiling and drooling all over me. "I'm ready for the demonstration." I said.

"Fair enough!" Chris smiled and started loading the dart gun and pointed at him. He shot him in the chest and he looked so weird. He was paralyze but his eyes were still moving around and it felt that he was still looking at me. "Mauricio, he cannot move but his eyes are still moving around. That will be your advantage. I can help you avenge those people that have been hurting you. You can shoot them with the dart gun. I'm also going to pay you for every person you want to paralyzed with the dart gun and confront them. And I'm going to open an account and when your old enough you can spend the money. This will be our little secret and I know your father and I have been best friends since we were little kids. It won't hurt to keep this from him."

"I accept but I want to ask you a couple of questions."

"Ask." He smiled.

"I have ten friends and it turns out that our parents are CIA Agents, FBI Agents, Police Officers and not to mention Primo's father is the crime lord. Well we formed a gang and I need to ask you if you have something that can make a bomb?"

"Bombs? Well I do and I am making bombs for the Army. Why? Who needs it?" He asked.

"Cassandra Powell. Also do you have bugs, recording equipment?" I asked.

"Yes, I do." He smiled.

"Can you teach a friend of mine how do hack into the computer system?" I asked.

"Yes, I do. Well I hope this could be a learning experience when you become the new King of Spain." Chris said and smiled and told the guys to take the prisoner back to his cell. And in about thirty minutes later my father came back from his business meeting and right after that, the three of us went out to eat. And from there my father took me back to El Paso, Texas. Where my father was going to give me another huge surprise. We got into the van and went to pick up my mother and sister. And my father took us to the Franklin Mountains to celebrate our birthdays. We finally arrived at the

Franklin Mountains and my father and I were putting the tents together and my mother and Tania were making sandwiches for us.

So, we were enjoying every minute together and we had a blast and there were a lot of families camping around in that area and we made friends with them. And we met another family and they recognize my father and my mother and they asked them for their autographs. Well my parents smiled at them and gave them their autographs and they were getting to know each other pretty well. Later on in the afternoon my father and I went walking around the mountain with another family and we saw Indians doing their ritual and I found it very interesting. We watched them for a couple of seconds and then my father grabbed my shoulder and took me back to the campsite and they didn't want us to bother the Indians. Actually I was kind of curious and I wanted to see more of the Indians. Then at midnight I decided to go back to see the Indians and I put on my clothes and grabbed my flashlight. And I went to the same trail and I got there just in time, and the Witch Doctor was sitting down in front of the fire and he was just staring into space. I went to his direction and I guess he was waiting for me. The Witch Doctor finally stood up and started talking to me in a language that I didn't understand at all. But the Tribe Chief was able to tell me what he was saying.

"He says welcome and he was expecting you."

I looked at him and said, "Thank you."

The Witch Doctor continued to speak to me and I was still standing in front of him and I was paying close attention to what he was saying to me. And the Tribe Chief said, "You have a lot of anger and you wish to let your anger out. You want revenge but you don't know how."

"I do have anger and I want revenge." I smiled.

The Witch Doctor continued to speak to me and I thought he was very wise person because everyone in the tribe respected him so much and they obeyed him too. And the Tribe Chief asked, "What is it that you seek here?"

Just for the Hell of it I said this, "I want you to help me and I'm tired of people picking on me. Like you guys said I want revenge and I want to let my anger out and teach them a lesson."

The Tribe Chief was telling the Witch Doctor what I wanted and the Witch Doctor smiled and was talking to me and the Tribe Chief said, "The Witch Doctor is willing to help you out, and he is going to do a ritual on you."

"That's fine with me." I said.

The Witch Doctor started doing his ritual and a couple of more Indians showed up to do the ritual and the Tribe Chief told me to stand in front of the fire and I kept watching them dance around me and they were also dancing around the fire. The Witch Doctor was also going around me and continue to speak me and the Tribe Chief said, "Don't think of anything and don't move at all because the ritual will go wrong." But I also disobeyed them because in my mind I started to picture an evil Cowboy that was killing people and during the ritual I began to notice that a Dark Shadow appeared in front the fire and I saw its red evil eyes and it called my name "Mauricio de la Vega! Your, Majesty! It's time for us to be united once again!" But I didn't move at all and I wasn't scared. And then it started to rain and there was a loud thunder and the lighting struck the mountain. They told me not think of anything because they also saw The Dark Shadow that kept going around everybody. The Dark Shadow stood in front of me and it growl at me. The Dark Shadow said, "We will have our revenge, Mauricio de la Vega, the second." Just like that The Dark Shadow entered my body. And I started feeling angry when The Dark Shadow entered my body. I was grabbing my head and I started having some kind of flashbacks. And in the flashbacks I kept seen this Dark Shadow killing a lot of people with a sword and was growling and the people were begging for their lives and I heard explosions. And I was loving this moment and then for some reason I started feeling dizzy and just like that I fell to the ground.

I found myself laying on the ground and I heard the Indians chattering and they were sort of disappointed because the ritual went bad and they didn't know what was going on and they couldn't explain why an evil Dark Shadow appeared in front of the fire and entered my body. And all of the sudden I started floating in the air and I open my eyes and I felt the evil presence that was going inside my body and it was like electricity. I started shaking and screaming and also I was growling. My voice was different and I think I might have been possessed by some Demon. And finally I was back on my feet and looked at the Indians. The Tribe Chief yelled, "His red evil eyes!" And I was laughing and growling and I could her the echoes of my laughter. And I went up to the Witch Doctor that was still standing there and he was loss for words and I went up to him and transformed into some kind of monster and said, "Thank you! Now I can have my revenge!"

Then everyone heard a loud thunder and lightning was striking everywhere in the mountain and it started to rain really hard. I was loving every minute of it. The Indians were stepping away from me because they were frightened. As I was laughing the thunder was even more louder and I heard a rock falling to the ground. I felt that someone followed me here, I turn around and I saw a boy. This boy was watching the ritual the whole time. I was pissed off and just like that a lightning struck where he was standing and he fell on his back. I went up to him and I was about to kill him with my own two fists. That's where the Indians interfered and they were protecting him from me. All of the Indians were grabbing me and the Witch Doctor started speaking to me but the Tribe Chief was saying, "Go back where you came from, Demon!" The Tribe Chief and the Witch Doctor were smoking the peace pipe and blew the smoke on my face and I fell down and I fell asleep and I had a dream.

I found myself walking in a strange place and I looked around and I was inside a huge cave. I continued to walk the cave when I saw someone or something that was coming out of the shadows. Someone was riding on a black horse and it looked to be a black stallion but the legs, arms, and face were missing. It was a Dark Figure and it's eyes were glowing red. The Dark Figure just stared at me and didn't talk to me at all and he jumped off of his horse and approached me very slowly. Well he was floating at my direction and I heard the wind blowing really hard and there was rain and thunder as well. And we were face to face, we were the same size and it was like staring at a mirror.

I asked him in the dream. "Who are you?"

The Dark Figure responded and his voice sounded like an echo, "I'm you, you are me, and we were once united! But for so many years you lived a great life and yet you keep wondering who you really are. And all this time you have been confused and also you have been unhappy all these years. You feel like you don't fit in with everybody else and you just feel like an outsider. And now you are back to the place where everything began and you are hungry to kill a lot of people and I know you are anxious to do it once again. Mauricio de la Vega your, Royal Highness. And I will show you the way and everything will come back to you and you need to learn to deal with everything that happened in the past. When the time is right, you will kill again and be legendary liked you always dreamed off."

"Who are you?" I asked him in the dream.

The Dark Figure was staring at me and just like that the Dark Figure transformed into somebody else. He looks just like me but he has a scar on his right side of his face and he started talking to me again. "My real name is Mauricio de la Vega the first, I was born in the year 1746, and in the year 1770, I killed my father the King of Spain and my mother the Queen of Spain. And I was only twenty four years old and I ruled the country of Spain until my natural caused of death. You can say that I was born disfigured. And I looked like a monster! But my parents loved me so much and they accepted me knowing that I was disfigured. But I died when I was just a baby, and thanks to the Aztec Witch Doctor's curse. A Dark Spirit entered my body and I rose from the grave and I became known as The Aztec Conquistador. I had incredible powers and I could do anything I wanted too and then I became an old man. I became sick and the Dark Spirit disappeared. My body died but my soul was still around and I was just waiting for the right time to enter someone else's body. I was waiting for my reincarnation." The Dark Figure looked at me with his red evil eyes. "And you are Mauricio de la Vega the second." He said in the dream.

"Where were you born?" I asked.

"You are a genius my, Master. You created me out of thin air." He was laughing in the dream and growled. "I will tell you where you recreated me. You loved watching cowboy movies and in your mind you started to create me and you wanted to do those things, and when our father took you right here in the Franklin Mountains. Well it was the Indians that did the ritual on you but it was your anger that created me once again, and in your mind you wanted revenge and as you can say I came out of the fire and went into your body. You see The Aztec Conquistador is long gone but we are something else and I just cannot explain the monster that we have inside our body. And let me show you everything from the beginning. Your Royal Highness." And once again I looked around the area and I noticed that we were still inside the large cave. "Don't be afraid, Mauricio de la Vega. Let everything come to you little by little." I just looked at him and I could feel everything going inside my body and I did felt all of my power that was going inside my body and I was screaming and making some weird noises along way. And I could hear the screams and the gunshots and the explosions. I also started yelling at top of my lungs. "I'm going to guide you ! Now let's have our revenge!"

The next day I woke up and I was feeling better than ever because I finally know a way to have my revenge on everyone that has every piss me off. I was laying there and I felt people will die to see the things that I can do. And later on in the afternoon my parents were making sandwiches and they were putting everything back into the truck and this was our last day on the Franklin Mountains. My parents saw how happy I was and I was also laughing and they felt that I enjoyed this summer with them well I did enjoyed it too. After we finished our sandwiches and I saw the same boy that followed me last night and he was scared to see. Well last night that boy was lucky that the lightning didn't kill him. But I will kill him sooner or later, if he decides to open his big mouth and tells everyone what he saw last night. Well maybe I'm going to have to kill him without thinking twice.

By three o'clock on the afternoon we finally went home and I went straight to my room and I saw the bags of dart guns laying on top of my bed. And I put them inside the closet and I went to the restroom and I was staring myself in the mirror and my eyes were glowing red and also my whole body transformed into some kind of hideous creature and I was growling. I looked like some kind of monster and I felt that I might have some kind of powers along the way and I couldn't wait to kill people.

Well the summer ended and I was going to start fifth grade and I was excited that I was going to leave elementary school and start middle school. I was in class when Eliza and the gang walked into the classroom and she was so happy to see me and we hugged so tight and she kissed me on the cheek. Everyone began to notice that I was happy and I was grinning from ear to ear and during the morning hours I was still smiling to everyone. Well things changed for me that year because the whole school decided to be nice to me and they bowed down and they called me, Sire and your, Majesty. Then the bell rang the gang and I went walking to Primo's house. Once again the son of the crime lord suggested to give me another piggy back ride to his house. And we finally arrived at his house and went to his room.

"What's with the smile?" Primo asked.

"You have been smiling all day long." Karina said.

I turn around and started laughing and my eyes were glowing red and my voice was different. I turn around and looked at them. "That's why I'm laughing because I have a huge surprise."

"What's wrong with your eyes?" Karina asked.

"My dad took me to Washington D.C. and he took me to a Weapon Room. My dad's friend makes weapons. His name is Chris Farrell, he gave me guns so I can have my revenge. Cassandra! Chris Farrell can give you all the supplies that you need so you can make your bombs. Karina! Chris can teach you how to hack on the computers. And Sonia! Chris can give you all recording equipment that you need and we have our gang completed." I said and I was growling.

"That's fine!" The girls exclaimed.

"That's great, Mauricio. Now can you explain to us what's wrong with your eyes and your voice?" Primo asked.

I laughed and started walking on the walls and I was standing at the ceiling and jumped down in front of them. I transformed into this hideous creature once again and said, "We went to the Franklin Mountains and I saw the Indians that were doing their ritual. So, at midnight I went back to see them and they did a ritual on me but I started imaging an evil Cowboy that was killing people. And there was a Dark Shadow that came out of the fire and went into my body and now I want to have my revenge in a bad way." I said and started laughing and I could tell they were afraid of me. They actually thought that I was going to kill them.

Primo and the girls were looking at me and they were kind of scared but Primo had the courage to ask, "What's your plan, Mauricio?"

"We're in this together and together we are going to become legends in our own right." Karina said.

"Will wait and see what happens and when the right moment comes we're going to see our uncle, Chris Farrell and he will help us out with our missions." I said and started laughing and we were hugging each other and I went back to normal. I looked at Karina and said, "As the matter of fact I'm going to make you Lieutenant of the gang. You see girls, you come to Karina when you have a problem and she comes to us for the final decision. Is that clear!"

"Yes! Your, Royal Highness." They all said.

We stayed in Primo's room and talked some more and later on in the evening we went home. So, this school year was kind of awkward for me because everyone at school was giving me gifts and they wanted to put food in my mouth. Also the media showed up at campus and they kept on asking me questions and there were so many phone calls from our family in Spain. But other than that the people were nicer to me and the Martinez's were also getting nicer to me but I told the kids at school to mistreat them and everyone obeyed my orders. And three months later my fifth grade Teacher was talking to us about joining the Cub Scouts of America and everyone was excited and we were talking about how much fun we were going to have on the summer. So, for the past couple of days we were doing all kinds of activities and we were preparing ourselves when we get our badges later on.

CHAPTER FIVE

DEATH IN THE FRANKLIN MOUNTAINS

It was the last two weeks of school and we were in the classroom and we were waiting for our Teacher because she was going to announce where we were going to camp this summer. And in about twenty minutes later our Teacher came into the classroom and she announced that we're going to go camping in the Franklin Mountains. And everyone started clapping, cheering, and hugging each other. Also five parents were also going to be there with us. And on that night I was in my room when the phone rang and I went to answer the phone and it was Chris Farrell. He told me that he was in town and he was going to be at his house. He actually gave me his home address and his phone number. After that I called Primo and told him to call the girls and I gave him Chris's address, and I also told him that I will meet them at Chris's house.

After I hung up, I was kind of curious about my hidden powers. I looked at my watch and it was eight-fifteen when I jumped out of the window and started running at the end of the block. I looked at my watch again and it was still eight-fifteen and now eight-sixteen. I was amazed that it didn't take that long to run down the block. I must be pretty fast so I ran all the way to Chris's house. When I arrived at his house, I saw Chris and the gang that were inside the garage and they were waiting for me. I looked at my watch and it was eight-twenty. A normal person would take half an hour to run at Chris's house but it took me a couple of minutes to get there. And I ran my way into the garage and went around them in circles and they thought the wind was blowing really hard. And they went to look outside until I startled them, "I found out that we are going to be at the Franklin Mountains for the Cub Scouts of America." I laughed and I scared everyone completely.

"Jesus Christ, Mauricio, you scared the living Hell out of me." Chris looked at me and noticed that my eyes were glowing red and asked me. "Mauricio, why are your eyes glowing red?"

"I want you to listen to me." I went up to Chris and the gang and asked him. "I want to know if you can help us with our operations?"

"Yes, of course but the other operations are easy to do. I know Sonia and Cassandra are going to learn how to do their own operations. I will show Karina everything I know about computer hacking. And I know you and Primo are going to lead the gang into action. And I hope you guys don't get caught because you will end up in the juvenile home and maybe in Boot Camp. But I will teach you guys everything I know." Chris looked at everybody and smiled.

"I finally figure it out." I was laughing and I was curious about my other hidden power, I started walking on the walls and I was standing on the ceiling of the garage. Primo quickly closed the garage door and they were looking up at me.

"What did you figure out, Mauricio?" Primo asked.

"That I finally figured a way to have my revenge. Chris gave me dart guns that can paralyzed them. But I want more than that. So, I decided to become a serial killer and I want to kill those two kids that turn the whole school against me." I laughed and growled.

"That will be great, Mauricio but I got to ask you something. What's wrong with your voice and why are your eyes are glowing red and why are you standing on the ceiling of my garage?" Chris asked.

Chris's question was answered when I turn into this hideous creature and jumped down and went up to everyone and I was growling and laughing. "You can say that, I created me myself in the Franklin Mountains just over a year ago. I'm a genius as the matter fact I am *Doctor Frankenstein* and that's all you need to know."

"Whatever Dark Spirit entered your body, Mauricio, it must have been an evil sprit from the past." Primo said.

"Well I'm planning to kill them on the Franklin Mountains and they will be a nice target practice." I laughed.

"What?" Everyone asked.

"Are you crazy?" Primo asked.

"How are you going to do this?" Chris asked.

I responded with this, "First I don't want the people to know that a hideous looking creature is killing people but I want you to get me a costume, a cowboy hat, spurs, black pants, black boots, a long black jacket, and a black stallion and that will be a nice cover up. I already have the dart guns and I want Magnum Guns. And this is my plan, I'm going to stay back and someone else is going to stay back as well. I'm going to catch a "fever" so I won't go and this girl will also stay back. And now tomorrow go and get me those things I asked for." I ordered Chris.

"Who else is going to stay behind, Mauricio?" Primo asked.

"Karina Reyes will stay back and hack on the computer. And I want to know everything that goes on the mountains and Sonia it's your job to put bugs on the mountains and we want to be able to hear everything."

"I can show Karina what to do and Sonia as well!" Chris said and smiled.

"And I may need the assistance from Jennifer because she can abduct people and Primo, so you can rape Deyna." I said and smiled.

"Let's hope this plan works and no one gets caught." Chris said.

"And if something else changes then one of you knows what to do and if something else happens, Primo is going to rape the girl. And on the last week of school we're going to come back here and strategize one last time." I smiled and they agreed with the plan.

"I'm also going to pay you guys." Chris smiled.

"That's a good boy and bring me the costume and the horse when they have left to the Franklin Mountains!" I laughed and I was the old me again and we stayed talking in the garage and we left home and I knew this plan was going to work and if everybody decides to work together.

Two weeks later school was out and I started coughing and sneezing and my mother took me to the Doctor and the Doctor told me that I have the "flue" and I cannot go to the Franklin Mountains because I was going to get worse. My mother called the school and told them that I have the flue and I couldn't go. And Karina's couldn't go either because her grandmother passed away from a heart failure and that wasn't part of the plan but it's a good thing that Karina stayed behind with me. So, the next day everyone read the newspaper and they were sad because I got sick and they even came to my house and brought me gifts so I can feel better. My mother brought me the newspaper and the headline was, "The future of King of Spain has the flue and we should pray for him!" I felt honored that the people showed their concern for me. Well I had other things in mind. So, on the night before everyone went camping to the Franklin Mountains. Primo and I gather the girls at Chris's house. We were sitting down in his living room when I stood in front of them.

I looked at them and smiled, "We all know what to do and what our mission is tomorrow night. There is no guarantee if we are going to be traumatized from what's going to happen tomorrow night in the Franklin Mountains. I know you girls are scared and Primo and I are also scared. And remember what our parents told us. There is going to be a day when all of us loose our virginities, at the beginning is going to hurt and as we keep on doing it, we wanted to do it again and again. So, what I'm trying to tell you, is going to hurt to do the things that we are destined to do and we keep on doing it we want to do it for the rest of our lives and from there we will become legends and we will have our names on the History books!" I exclaimed and smiled.

Everyone started clapping and Chris said, "Good luck to all of you!"

I couldn't believe that the girls got motivated by the weird speech I gave them well they started hugging each other. But Primo and Chris were staring at me and all I did was smile at them. "What? That's all I can think of." After that everyone went home and we started praying and hoped that the plan will work out and we all went to sleep. The next day all the kids went to school and waited for the bus to come. Chris and Karina told my mother that they will take care of me and Tania was going to spend the weekend at her friend's house. So, the three of us were alone at my house and Chris brought the equipment, so we can hear what was going on and he brought Karina the computer. Chris was showing her how to hack into the system and Karina was able to learn how to hack into the system. This was her chance to prove herself to the gang and to me especially. And she hacked into the system and found a lot of background information.

"I found some information on the parents of Armando Guerrero. They have a lot of money on the bank accounts and they have their accounts together."

"How much?" Chris asked.

"Forty-five thousand dollars on their bank accounts. They have two cars, and the house has been paid for and they have a Will. They have a lot stuff inside the house and who do we know that steals stuff?" Karina asked.

"Roxanne Sanderson!" I responded.

"After this! Are we going to steal their stuff?" She asked.

"No! We will wait for the right opportunity and besides everyone has their own talent, why not help Roxanne steal." I said.

"You are right!" She smiled.

And we heard the voice of Sonia through the radio. "Karina and Mauricio, we are waiting for the bus and everyone is talking about the Franklin Mountains and how much fun they are going to have. And I'm going to turn off the microphone because I'm going to pee. The bus should be here in a couple of minutes. Before I forget you should put bugs on the Police Station, so you guys can hear their conversation." Sonia said and turned off the microphone.

"Sonia is right, Chris!" Karina smiled and continued to hack into the system, "I'm also seen the information of Deyna's parents and they have a lot of money too."

"Well I'll come back because I'm going to put the bugs inside the Police Station. And I'm also going to stop by my house and bring you the outfit and the horse." Chris said and left.

"Leave the horse!" I exclaimed.

"How are you going to get there?" Chris asked.

"I'll run all the way to the Franklin Mountains." I smiled and Chris went to do his thing. Well let me tell you about Chris Farrell. He's six feet tall and three inches, he has blonde hair, blue eyes, he weighs in two hundred and twenty-two pounds, he was a great athlete in the Rugby league, and he has been a successful FBI Agent. Well I have a feeling that after this mission he's going to be a diabetic FBI Agent.

"What's it like to be that hideous creature?" Karina asked me.

I responded with a smile, "It's hard to explain and do you wan to find out?"

"I don't know and at the same time I'm kind of curious." She smiled and we continued to talk when we heard the voice of Sonia on the radio.

"Guys, can you hear me?" She asked.

"Yes!" Karina exclaimed.

"The bus is here, I'm going to turn on the volume. You will hear their conversation!" She said and went into the bus.

Karina and I sat there and we heard all the kids getting into the school bus and they waited for the parents and the Teachers to get into the bus and they were waiting for almost twenty minutes. And we were hearing the conversation they were having.

"I've never been to the Franklin Mountains." One of the kids said.

"I have and I had a great time." The boy said.

"It's just too bad that Mauricio, and Karina couldn't make it.' The other kid said.

"Why aren't they coming?" The boy asked.

"Karina's grandma passed away just three days ago. And his, Royal Highness, Mauricio has the flue and he's stuck in bed." The other kid responded.

"That's terrible." He said.

"We will miss them this summer." A girl said.

"Who are you going to miss the most, Eliza?" One of the kids asked.

"What do you mean?" Eliza asked.

"I know you're the only one that talks to Mauricio. If you like him so much you should have stayed with him and take care of him."

"Is there something going on with you two?" He asked.

"Yes. Apparently they played husband and wife and they go everywhere together. She loves him."

"I love him as a friend." She said.

"He doesn't talk, Eliza. He only writes what he wants to say in a piece of paper. He can't even defend himself. He's just pathetic and he's going to be the first retard to be the King of Spain."

"He doesn't talk?" He asked.

Before he was going to answer, the parents and the Teacher got into the bus. Then the Teacher said. "Ready for the adventure!"

They all answered "Yes!"

The bus driver started the engine and they left. During the road the new kid looked at Eliza. And he began to noticed that she was sad and he felt that she was embarrassed when they were picking on her. Well the new kid found out that two other Scouts Members weren't coming with them. Karina's grandmother passed away and his, Royal Highness has the "flue." Eliza was the only one that liked me and everyone was making fun of me. I have a disability for crying out loud and I probably haven't learn sign language, yes I, Mauricio de la Vega the second has a learning disability, Not. And the boy felt bad for me and even though he has never met me in person.

An hour later they finally arrived at the Franklin Mountains and all of them got off the bus. The Teachers and the parents wanted all the kids to stand in a straight line. Then a Scout Ranger came out to greet them and he came to help out the Teachers and the parents. They put their stuff on the ground and The Scout Ranger told them, "Welcome to the Franklin Mountains and we are going to have fun this summer." Right after that he took them to walk around the mountain. The Teachers and the parents stayed behind to set up camp. The new boy was walking behind the Scout Ranger and they stopped in front of a large hole and it looked to be burn.

He asked him. "What happened here?"

"Kid, a lightning struck in this part of the mountain."

"When was this?"

"A year ago." He responded.

"Really!" The boy exclaimed. Everyone couldn't believe that a lightning struck in this part of the mountain and made a hole along the way. I recognized the boy's voice and he's the one that followed me and saw me with the Indians. And the lightning almost killed the boy and if the lightning didn't kill him then I'm going to have to kill him myself. So, later on in the afternoon they went back to the campsite. The new kid ran into the boy that was making fun of Eliza and I and we were listening to everything they were saying about us.

"Hey, what's your name?" He asked.

"Mike Reyes. And what's yours?"

"Armando Guerrero. It's nice to meet you." He said.

"So, what's the story between Eliza and this Mauricio fella?" He asked.

"Mauricio is a freak. He doesn't talk and no one likes him. Except for Eliza and a couple of his freak friends." He responded.

"How come no one likes him?"

"We just don't like him."

"Are Mauricio's friends here?"

"Yes, they are. Do you see that guy that's hanging out with those girls?"

He looked at the guy. And he looked to be Italian and good looking kid. He was better looking than the rest of the boys. "Who is he?"

"That's Primo Mancini."

"By any chance is he the son of Vito Mancini, the crime lord?" He asked him.

"Yes!" He exclaimed. "There's a group of friends and they are eleven of them and two of them are not here."

"King Mauricio, and Karina." He said.

"You bet." They sat down and Armando started telling Mike everything about me and my beloved friends. "You already know about Primo Mancini's drug dealing father and his mom is actually a Detective. Jennifer Callaway's father is the Federal Bureau Investigation better known as the FBI. Karina Reyes's father is head of the Central Intelligence Agency and better known as the CIA Agent. Sonia Rodriguez's father also works for the CIA and her mother is a Police Officer. Mauricio de la Vega's father is in command of the Federal Bureau Investigation and his mother is a Police Officer and one of the good ones and not mention that Mauricio will soon be the future King of Spain. And I'll cut this story short. It turns that their parents are in law enforcement and very important and very powerful."

"Really! That's awesome!" He exclaimed.

"They think there better than us just because mommy and daddy are Police Officers, CIA Agents, FBI Agents and drug lords. Sometimes I want to go up to them and punch them right in the face and especially that retard, Mauricio." He said.

"Come on they are living their lives like us. If you guys get to know them better. You might like them." He said.

"Yeah, right!" He exclaimed and said. "I can't wait for this summer to end and it's a good thing that I'm going to go to a different middle school and in a different state." He said.

"By any chance is Eliza part of the group you hate so much?" He asked him.

"Eliza has her own friends but sometimes she hangs out with them. She always defends Mauricio. She's the only one that was defending him when me and this girl faked our injuries." He said.

"What do you mean?"

"We were playing tag in the playground bus. I was climbing the bus and he tagged me and I pretended that he pushed me really hard and I fell to the ground. Then the other girl was playing in the same playground bus. I was with her and I saw Mauricio standing in front of the playground bus and I told her to fall down and make it look that he pushed you. You should have seen the look on his face and the Teachers were yelling at him. It was funny." He smiled.

"That sucks."

"That's life. Mauricio got into trouble for it and I'm happy that he's not here." He said.

Mike Reyes couldn't believe what Armando was saying about me, Eliza and my beloved friends. He didn't like how they set me up and how I got into trouble. He felt that Armando was proud of himself. And he figured that Armando saw himself as a legend in his own time but he wasn't a legend at all and he was just a bully and a coward.

"What an asshole! I cannot believe that he disrespected you like that and us!" Karina exclaimed.

"Armando is an asshole but he is going to die tonight along with his girlfriend Deyna." I smiled and we kept on hearing their conversation for a couple of more hours. Then the sun was going down and everyone gathered around the campfire and they were singing songs and telling ghost stories. And it was ten thirty that night where Karina and I were eating Pizza and she already had on her pajamas and we heard someone pulling into the driveway. I looked out the window and it was Chris. Then my eyes were glowing red and I was ready for this operation and Karina looked at me and she was kind of scared to see me. Chris came into the room and brought me my new costume. And I went to the restroom and put on my new costume and when I came out of the restroom, they looked at me and I was laughing and growling. I was dressed as a Cowboy and I looked at them and said, "Check the traffic."

Karina started hacking into the computer and was checking the roads and said, "The roads are clear to go and good luck in your mission." The three of us went outside and we were standing in the middle of the road.

"Check on Sonia because we might miss something." I said.

"Mauricio, here's a radio, so you can listen to the conversation and you can also contact Karina and she will contact Sonia." Chris said.

"Thank you! Well I'm off to the Franklin Mountains," I laughed and ran all the way to the Franklin Mountains. I was listening to their conversation, and I heard Karina telling Sonia that I was on my way to the Franklin Mountains. And thirty minutes later I finally arrived at the Franklin Mountains and I was hiding in the shadows. And I saw everyone sitting around the campfire and they were still talking and laughing. They were eating marshmallows and were singing songs. And Primo was telling ghost stories. Well I got one ghost story, and it's about me killing those two kids and it's going to be a bloody mess. And then Armando gave me us a great idea.

"This is to the greatest summer of our lives and I really wish that Karina and his, Royal Highness, Mauricio de la Vega were here with us. We are going to miss them this summer and it's not the same without them."

"To our friends that couldn't be here with us!" Everyone cheered.

"I feel the same as you guys. And I know we're going to have fun this summer by doing outdoor activities and all that sentimental crap. And I know a way where we can all enjoy this lovely summer." He said.

"How?" One of them asked.

"We can make out with the girls. At midnight the grown ups are going to be sleeping. We can sneak out of here and go far away from campsite and we can make out with them and we will not be bothered at all." He said.

"That's your plan?" One of the girls asked.

"Yes!" He looked at the girls and said. "Any volunteers!"

One of the girls raised her hand and said. "Me!" Deyna smiled. And everyone knew that these two kids were going to get into some kind of trouble if they get caught kissing somewhere in the mountain or they might get lost or fall off the mountain or they are going to find them dead.

"You see! Deyna is willing to make out with me in the darkness." Armando said and smiled. "At midnight will leave together and we will make out far away from campsite." He smiled and Armando was kind of the leader of the group but they are known as the bullies.

"I'm looking forward to it." She smiled.

I got on the radio and said, "That's our chance, Karina and get Primo ready for this mission."

"You are right! I'm going to contact Sonia." Then I saw Sonia looking down when Karina contacted her. She got up and went into her tent and in three minutes later Sonia came back to the campfire eating a Banana. I was wondering about Chris giving me a walkie-talkie and I couldn't listen Karina giving orders to Sonia.

Then one of the parents told the kids that it was time to put the fire out and go to sleep. And the kids did put the fire out and went to sleep and Sonia told Primo to get ready and she told the girls to fall asleep. And it was around midnight where Armando kind of woke everyone up when he got up to put his clothes on. Also Deyna was putting her clothes on as well and they left somewhere to make out and I followed them in the shadows. Those two went somewhere in the mountain and they took their flashlights with them and they also took their sleeping bags with them. And Armando put both sleeping bags on the ground and they were just laying there kissing and looking up at the stars.

They were practicing kissing with a little tongue action and they were getting the hang of it. They were enjoying every minute together and they were about to take their clothes off until I decided to throw a couple of rocks at them and they got startled. Armando picked up the flashlight and went to see what was going on. They thought it was the parents or the kids that were trying to sneak up on them. I knew they were scared and I started walking around the shadows and they kept hearing the noise again. "I'm hearing the sounds of spurs!" Deyna exclaimed. And I was trying to sneak up on them but they were moving their flashlights way too fast and I figured that they might see me and they are going to be screaming like a couple of pansies and run back to the campsite. Well it's a good thing that they stayed in the same place and they were expecting a prank from their friends but they were too terrified. "This isn't funny you guys." I started walking a little bit more closer and they were hearing the footsteps. "Stop it!" Armando yelled and cried.

"Okay! You guys won, we're scared and guys you can hear the sound of our voices." She said and started sobbing. Then my heart starting beeping fast but it didn't hurt at all. And everything was going slow motion, Armando and Deyna were still standing there but they were walking very slowly. I was the only one that was moving around and the Dark Spirit got out of my body and it was standing in front of a large rock. The Dark Spirit put it's hands together and it's eyes were glowing red and then a large crystal ball appeared in his stomach. "Look at it!" I was staring at the crystal ball and there was an image of my room. I saw Karina sitting down and Chris went down to the kitchen to get something to eat. Karina stood up and looked straight at the door that leads to the hallway and to the kitchen. She sat down again and she got on the radio and whispered, "Sonia can you hear me!

Sonia responded, "Yes, I can hear you!"

And Karina whispered an order, "Sonia, send Primo over because Mauricio needs him to rape, Deyna."

And I heard Sonia on the radio and said, "Copy that! I'll send him over!" And I couldn't believe that Karina ordered Sonia to send Primo. And then The Dark Spirit entered my body once again.

Meanwhile Armando and Deyna decided to walk back to the campsite. Armando started rolling his sleeping bag and he had it in his hand and started walking away. And he turn around and saw his girlfriend Deyna having problems walking because she was way too terrified. And as soon Armando was going to turn around and helped her with the sleeping bag. I started laughing and growling and once again and they were startled. I continued to make some noises and I wanted to make sure that Karina was listening to this. Armando was pointing the flashlight to the direction where he heard the strange noise. "Let's go, Deyna we will be safe at campsite with everybody else. Come on!" They were walking away and Deyna's sleeping bag slip out of her hands. Armando was about to help her when he heard another strange noise, and he was moving the flashlight and he went to see who was coming when he ran into Primo and all three of them were screaming at the top of their lungs.

"Damn it, Primo, you scared me the living shit out of me and Deyna! Was it you that was making those strange noises?" Armando asked.

"No! I just got here! But do you realize that you two are going to get into trouble if you get caught kissing." Primo responded.

"Well Primo Mancini, if keep your mouth shut and you never saw us kissing at all. And besides you had your chance to kiss Deyna but it's too late. She's mine forever." He said and smiled.

Primo and Armando were still arguing and I began to notice that Deyna was having problems holding on to her sleeping bag and she was still shaken up. So, I started loading the dart gun. I steadied the dart gun and I shot her in the back and she just stood there and then she just fell to the ground. Armando and Primo finally turned around and saw her laying on the ground. Both of them went to see what was going on with her and they were trying to catch their breathe. Armando had her on his arms and said, "What's wrong? Come on we got to get back to the campsite." Armando and Primo couldn't figure out what was wrong with her. Both of them tried to pick her up and Armando saw a dart that was stuck on her back and their were trying to look at it and he still had her in his arms. They began to notice that she was looking at them with fear and she couldn't move at all but she was able to move her eyes. "No! We are going to get help and everything is going to be okay!" Armando cried and as soon Armando and Primo were going to get help, I shot Armando in the back with the dart gun and he also fell to the ground. And I came out of the shadows and I even saw Primo's reaction and I knew that he wasn't excepting this to happen.

Primo looked at me and he was loss for words. "Get a hold of yourself, Primo. These two are paralyzed and they won't feel a thing. I'm going to dig a hole and I'm going to put some lights and go and do your thing before everyone wakes up."

"Okay!" He exclaimed and he went up to Deyna and grabbed her hair and was dragging her into the darkness. Primo put the sleeping bag on the ground and he put her on top of the sleeping bag and he also got on top of her. He started taking off her clothes and he starting raping her.

Then I started digging a hole and planted three bright lights, so they can see my face. And I went back to grab Armando by his shoe and dragged him where the lights were. I grabbed him by his throat and sat him down on the ground and he was sitting up against five large rocks. And something else happened when I grabbed him by the throat and I was kind of shocked as well. I had a flashback and I started hearing a couple of voices. And everything looked so real.

I heard the voice of Armando. "Eliza, I need to talk to you about something!"

"About what?" She asked in the flashback.

He responded, "We have been friends since I can remember and we go to Church together. And as a friend I want you to listen to what I have to say. I want you to stay away from Mauricio because he's too dangerous."

Eliza exclaimed, "Mauricio, is not dangerous! He is a good person and I know you guys haven't gotten along! But at least try to get to know him!"

"I don't want to get to know him. I'm asking you to stay away from, Mauricio!"

"I love him as a friend. He hasn't done anything to me!"

"Everyone at Church is going to tell you the same thing just like me!"

I was staring at Armando and I couldn't believe that he told Eliza to stay away from me. That got me thinking, I'm killing him because he accused me of hurting him in the playground. Also because he told Eliza to stay away from me, well Eliza and I are best friends and there's going to be a lot people that don't want to see us together. Well that may be reason to take them out of my way for good. But I'm planning to keep this secret from everyone else. Well Armando was still looking at me with fear and his eyes were getting watery. And I sat in front of him and we were face to face. I took off my hat and I let him see my face and he couldn't believe that it was me and I wanted him to hear my voice. "Hey Armando, my best friend in the world. How's it going? Well this is the first time you are going to hear my voice and it will be the last time you're going to be able to hear it. So, I hope you enjoy this moment while you can and this conversation is just between us, Okay." I growled and grabbed him by his shirt and said. "You and I know have known each other since we were little kids, and we practically went everywhere together. You accepted me knowing that I didn't talk at all. Just like the coward that you are, you said so many nasty things behind my back. And remember in the second grade when you and I were playing tag in the playground bus and I gently tagged you and you just fell down just for the Hell of it. You blame everything on me and you were able to convince everyone that I was a bad guy and you turn the entire school against me. I will never forgive you. Also I heard that you were making fun of me earlier and that's not cool but I know that you were dying to hear my voice and I hope you enjoy our little conversation." I growled and spit at his face. I didn't mention anything to Karina about the flashback I had. Well I'm keeping my thoughts to myself and that will be my new reason to kill them. And I went to see how Primo was doing. "Are you finish?" I asked.

He looked at me and said, "I'm finished!"

"Well put Deyna's clothes back on and go back to campsite." I ordered him and Primo was putting Deyna's clothes back on and he also put his clothes back on too and he rolled their sleeping bags and left them there.

"I'm finished!" He exclaimed.

"Good and now go back to the campsite and don't let anybody see you. But report to Sonia. And good job." I smiled.

"Thanks!" Primo laughed and went back to the campsite and ten minutes later Karina radioed me and said, "Primo is back at campsite and everyone is now asleep."

"That's good to know!" And I went up to Deyna and I grabbed her hair and dragged her right next with her boyfriend. She looked at me with more fear and I had another flashback as well.

I heard the voice of Eliza. "Can you believe that Armando told me to stay away from Mauricio."

"I think you should listen to him because I'm telling you the same thing. Mauricio is way too dangerous. Please do it for us!"

"Why? Mauricio is our friend. He hasn't done anything to us. All of the things that happened on the playground were just a misunderstandings."

"Eliza just stay away from, Mauricio."

This bitch told Eliza to stay away from me but she didn't want to. Well I'm taking two people out of our way, so I can continue my friendship with Eliza. I looked at Deyna and said, "I met you on the second grade, you were friendly to me and then you turn the corner and hated me so much. Because I supposedly hurt his arm and I remember you threw rocks at me and you really hurt my feelings. And when our second grade Teacher gave me the okay to go outside and just like that everyone ganged up on me. I saw you playing with this jackass and as soon I was going to enter the playground bus. He told you to fall down and make it look that I pushed you down. And once again everyone ganged up on me and they were pushing me around, and they were spitting at my face and punching me. Then you guys were laughing about it and you turn the entire school against me, I hate what you guys did to me. I will never forgive you for that." I growled and started loading my Magnum guns and I saw the look of their faces and they wanted to cry like a couple of pansies. I loved every minute of it but it would have been better and they were screaming at the top of their lungs. I put on my cowboy hat and I pointed the gun at Armando and as soon I shot him all over his body, I heard something falling to the ground and I thought it was just rocks that were falling to the ground and I shot Deyna all over her body and both of them were now dead. Then I heard someone breathing heavily and was sobbing and I turn around and I saw someone laying on the ground. I didn't know who this person was but I stood in front of the lights and it was Eliza that was breathing heavily. My eyes were glowing red and I was growling but she remained on the ground and she couldn't move at all. Eliza was gasping for air and she was getting hysterical, and very slowly I approached her and all we could hear was the sound of my spurs and her breathing heavily. I started loading the guns and pointed at her head and started growling at her. Then she finally had the strength to yell at the top of her lungs when I fired the gunshots in the sky and I was laughing at her. I pointed the gun at her pretty face and yelled at her "Run and don't come back!" She quickly got up and ran away and as it turns out, the gunshots and Eliza's screaming woke everybody up and they saw the lights on the other side of the mountain and they went to see what was going on. They finally arrived when Eliza came running towards them and she was crying her eyes out.

"What happen?" The Scout Ranger asked.

"They're dead!" She yelled.

"Whose dead?" The Scout Ranger asked.

"Armando and Deyna are dead, someone killed them! It was some kind of a monster!" She was screaming hysterically.

The Scout Ranger went to see what she was talking about and they waited for him to come back. One of the parents was trying to calm Eliza down because she was getting hysterical and was crying a lot. The rest of the kids were also crying and a couple of girls were fainting because Eliza was loosing her mind. And minutes later the Scout Ranger came back and couldn't believe what he saw and didn't want them to see the massacre. Well I wanted to make things worse for everyone and I was standing on top of the mountain and I started laughing at them and growling. Everyone heard the evil laughter and they didn't know where the laughter was coming from. Then Primo saw me on top of the mountain. He was pointing at the mountain and yelled out, "The Dark Figure is laughing at us and his eyes are glowing red!" Everyone looked at the top of the mountain and they couldn't believe what they were staring at and it scared the living Hell of out of them. I was looking directly at them and was laughing at them because they were so scared of me. As I was laughing at them a thunder struck the mountain and I laughed even more and everyone continued to cry. Then I jumped away to the other side of the mountain and went running all the way to the house. And Karina radioed me, "What happen, Mauricio?"

I cannot believe that you gave that bogus order. "Well, Karina something else happen. Eliza was there when I killed Armando and Deyna but things worked like the way we planned. I saw the gang crying their eyes out and you better tell them to keep their composers." I ordered her and I kept on running to my house and I was hearing everything on the mountain.

"The monster disappeared!" The Teacher exclaimed.

"Okay, we need to call the Police!" The Scout Ranger exclaimed. "I'm going to get on the horn and call the Police."

"Okay! Let's go back to the campsite." One of the parents said.

The Scout Ranger got into the truck and got on the horn and told the Police what happen on that night. Everyone stayed together and the grown ups told the kids to get inside their tents. But the parents stayed outside the tents and they were guarding the kids.

This time I was able to hear Karina's orders. "Sonia, you guys need to get a hold of yourselves. As soon the Police arrive you need to put your things on your backpack. Chris already put the bugs inside the Police Station."

"Okay, I'll hide them. And I'm sorry, I guess their deaths really affected me!" Sonia sobbed and continued to bring information.

Half an hour later everyone heard the Police sirens, Ambulance, and they saw the helicopter chopper coming to the Franklin Mountains. The Police Officers, the Paramedics and two Detectives got out of their cars. Right of way they started to investigate the murder of the two kids. The Police Officers started questioning the parents, the Scout Ranger, and including the kids. The Paramedics put Armando and Deyna in body bags and put them inside the Ambulance. But at the same time the Police Officers couldn't investigate anything because it was way too dark even with the bright lights they were afraid that they might fall off the mountain.

"Okay. It's too dark to investigate the mountain. Take the kids and the parents to the Police Station and we're going to questioned them." The male Detective said.

Before they took the kids inside the bus everyone heard the female Detective say. "Go home and get some rest. Tomorrow at seven in the morning we're going to come back here to investigate."

They put the kids into the bus and drove off, and Sonia put her things inside her backpack and everyone were still crying. Then I finally arrived at my house and I went to the restroom and changed into my normal clothes. I wanted to punch Karina in the head but I kept my cool. I just gave Chris, the guns, and the outfit, so he can hide them at his house.

"What happen?" Chris asked.

"Everything was going fine according to the plan but somehow Eliza and Primo ended up where I was." I responded.

Right of away Karina changed the subject. "I'm sure by now everyone had stopped crying and they are going to question everyone at the Police Station. We will find out why Eliza left campsite. Also they are going to know that Deyna was raped."

"Don't worry about it, Karina, I already paid the Medical Examiner and she is in our pockets. Primo Mancini is going to make a living by raping girls and all the Doctors are right in our pockets." He said and smiled.

"Let's look on the bright side, everything went fine as plan but I'm sorry to say that Eliza had to see you kill Armando and Deyna." Karina said.

And we heard the Police Officers saying that they brought the kids to the Police Station and we started listening to their conversation. The Detectives and Police Officers couldn't believe what was going on. No one wants to see two kids dead and not even execution style.

"How are the kids?" The male Detective asked.

"Scared and traumatize. Their friends just died in a bad way." The Police Officer responded.

"We will questioned the parents and the Scout Ranger and the kids." The male Detective said.

"I think the kids and the parents already had a bad night." The Police Officer said.

"Separate the girls and the boys. Get a female Officer and a male Officer. You know anyone who dare to calm those kids down?" The male Detective asked.

"Yes. Officer de la Vega and Officer McFadden." One of the Police Officer said.

"Get those two in their with the kids and I'll questioned the parents and the Scout Ranger." He said.

They took the Scout Ranger to the Interrogation Room and the male Detective gave him a cup of coffee and both of them sat down. "My name is Detective Jim Nielsen. I'm going to ask you a couple of questions. So, how long have you been a Scout Ranger?" He asked.

"Twenty years." He responded.

"Just like me. I've been on the Police Force for twenty years. This is all I know." Both of them drank their coffee. "What happened when the kids arrived on the Franklin Mountains and did you see anybody suspicious?"

"I was there to welcome the kids to the Franklin Mountains and we all hoped to enjoy this summer. We plan to do a lot of fun activities and it was just your normal day." He said.

"What happened a couple of hours before the kids died?" He asked.

"We told the kids that it was time to go to sleep. I guess they went to sleep around midnight."

"Why did the kids left the campsite?" He asked.

"I don't know."

"Tell me what happened next."

"We heard gunshots and screaming. All of us got up to see what was going on and we saw bright lights. One of the girls came running toward us and she was saying that they're dead. And that's when I went to see what she was talking about and I saw the bodies of the two kids."

"There was another girl that left campsite?" He asked.

"I guess so. And we heard a laughter and something was on top of the mountain."

"You saw the one that did it!" He exclaimed.

"I don't know what it was. But it was laughing, it was a Dark Figure that was dressed as a Cowboy, and the Dark Figure's eyes were glowing red. And it just disappeared into the darkness."

"So, it was a Demonic Figure that came out to kill those kids? Was it the Boogeyman?"

"I know you don't believe me but we saw it."

Detective Jim Nielsen couldn't believe what the Scout Ranger told him and I guess he was loss for words. The Scout Ranger was free to go to his house. They also questioned the parents and it was the same thing. They were saying they saw this Demonic Figure killed the two kids and they heard Eliza screaming. And they also started questioning the kids. They had a different story than the grownups and all the kids said that they left campsite to make out and that was the last time they saw them alive. And they heard the gunshots and Eliza screaming, and not to mention they saw the Dark Figure on top of the mountain and it was laughing at them and disappeared into the darkness. And in twenty minutes later they gathered in the room.

"The kids said that they left campsite to make out and the same thing. They all claim that they saw the Dark Figure at the top of the mountain that was laughing at them and it disappeared." The female Detective said.

"We have one more to questioned."

"Who's left?" Jim asked.

"Eliza Caballero." The Police Officer said.

"Take her to the interrogation room." He said.

One of the Police Officers took Eliza to the interrogation room and she sat down. She was still shaken up and crying. The female Detective brought her cup of Apple Juice. "My name is Perla Mancini Fuentes and I know you've had a rough night." Perla smiled and started asking her questions and Eliza said that the kids wanted to make out and they fell asleep around midnight.

"What happened when you woke up?" She asked.

"I wanted to pee. Then I saw big bright lights and I thought that's where the restroom was." She responded.

"And what happened next?" She asked.

Her tears started to come down her face and was sobbing. "When I got there, the lights blinded me and I heard the gunshots and I fell down to the ground. And I finally looked up and my friends were murdered. I don't know how many times that thing fired at them. Then the Dark Figure turned it's attention to me and pointed the gun at my face."

"Can you describe the Dark Figure's face?" She asked.

"Just the red evil eyes and had an evil laughter in him, and it was some kind of creature. And I thought I was going to die, so I screamed at the top of my lungs and ran back to the campsite. Just then everyone came down to see what was going on and I told them what happened. And a couple of seconds later the Dark Figure was laughing at us and it disappeared into the darkness."

"You are lucky to be alive." She smiled and hugged her.

There was a dead end to this investigation. I doubt that the Detectives and the Police Officers didn't believed the story of the kids and the grown ups. Just then they all gathered in the room.

"A Dark Figure with no face kill those two kids and it disappeared into the darkness." Jim said.

"It could have been our kids." The Police Officer said.

"My son, Primo was there and I know he is pretty shaken up. But he is going to be okay." Perla smiled.

"By the way, Beatrice, wasn't your son supposed to be there with them?"

"Well my son is under the weather and another girl couldn't make it." My mother responded.

"What about the other girl?"

"Karina's grandmother passed away from heart failure." My mother said.

"That's awful. You might tell your son the news." Perla said.

"What about the dead kids?" The Police Officer said.

"Contact the parents, and these kids have been through enough. And I will call the parents and tell them that their kids have died." Jim said.

"What about the Medical Examiner?" The Police Officer said.

"There's no need to open them up. Get them to the morgue and let the parents identify their bodies. And get some rest because tomorrow we have a Hell of day." Jim said.

An hour later the parents came to pick up their kids and took them home and meanwhile down at the Morgue where the parents of the dead children arrived. The Detectives and the Doctor took them to see their kids. Very slowly the Doctor pulled the sheet off their heads and that's where the parents started crying.

"We're very sorry." Jim said.

"How did this happen to our kids?" The father asked.

"It was too dark to investigate the mountain but we will do it first thing in the morning." Perla said.

"Doctor, was happened to our kids?" The mother sobbed.

"There was a dart stuck on their backs. So, we don't know anything about the darts and all we know that they were shot to death. Execution style." The Doctor responded.

"I know how you must feel. My regards to you and your family." Perla smiled.

The Detectives took the parents away and the Doctor was getting ready to do the Medical report. And we looked at each other and said. "So the plan went well." Karina smiled.

"Yes, it did." Chris said.

"Do you think they were scared of me?" I asked.

"Yes, because you look freaky with your red evil eyes and when you transformed into that hideous looking creature." Karina responded.

And Chris brought two glasses of Apple Juice for Karina and I, and he pour himself a glass of whiskey and we made a toast. "I have a feeling that the Police Officers are still going to investigate the murder of the dead kids." Chris said.

"We got away with this one." I smiled.

"Let's just hope that our friends are okay and let's hope that they want to continue with the mission." Karina said.

"Now, I'm going to open an account for you guys and since I told you that I was going to pay you fifty bucks per person you kill. Well tomorrow I'm going to deposit one hundred dollars to your new bank account."

"That's great, Chris. And don't worry they don't know that it was me that killed them. I didn't leave a trail well I did leave a trail but it was a trail of their blood." I said and started laughing.

"Now let's not get cocky, Mauricio. Let's just hope that you don't become a suspect in this case."

"I'm not going to be a suspect but I have ten wonderful friends that are willing to risk their lives for me." I said and smiled. "How about we chill out for a while. And I will let you know when I want to strike next."

"I'll be here when you need me." He said.

"Thank you!" I said and I hugged them and the mission was successful. And we said, "Cheers!"

After that Chris took Karina home and I went to sleep. And the next day I woke up at seven o'clock in the morning. I took out my radio and I was hearing everyone going back to the Franklin Mountains to investigate. They were investigating for over five hours and found nothing at all. No fingerprints, footprints and they only found the blood of the two kids and that's too bad that they didn't find anything else. Everyone was frustrated and they felt that they let the families down. So, I put the radio away and started sneezing and coughing to make it look that I'm still sick. I was laying in bed when my mother came into the room and smiled. 'How are you feeling, Honey?" She asked.

"I'm feeling better." I smiled.

"Your uncle told me that you were sound asleep and you were also snoring." She said and her tears started coming down her face.

"What's wrong, Mom?" I asked.

"I don't know how to tell you this but something bad happen last night."

"Is dad okay and my sister and our family."

"They are doing fine." She said and cried. "Mauricio last night your friends were found dead on the Franklin Mountains."

I looked at her and asked, "Who?"

My mother responded and hugged me so tight. "Armando and Deyna. They were brutality murdered on the Franklin Mountains and no one knows who did it." My mother was sad and I was smiling on the inside. But my mother told me that everything was going to be okay, well my mother was hugging the one that killed them. Then at the end of the week they had the funeral service for them and they buried Armando and Deyna the very next day and everyone was throwing flowers on their casket as they were lowering it all the way to the ground. And we left the cemetery, the Detectives came by and we overheard what they had to say to the parents.

"What did you find, Detective?" One of the parents asked.

"Nothing just blood and no footprint or fingerprints." One of the Detectives said.

"You think the killer will strike again?" One of the parents asked.

"We don't know when the killer is going to strike next. And we hope that the killer won't strike at all."

After that we went home and my mother hugged me so tight and told me that everything is going to be okay. I gave her a smile and I stayed in my room while she went to the kitchen to make lunch for us. I called Primo and told them to meet me at Chris's house. I told my mother that I wanted to be with my friends at the park. So, I got on my bicycle and rode all the way to Chris's house. When I got there everyone was inside the garage and they were waiting for me.

"Now all of us are gathered here because we want to talk about the mission we did on the Franklin Mountains. You kids did well on your first assignment. What I saw on that night, is friends working together as the team and that's why Mauricio and Primo are good leaders." Chris smiled.

I stood up and looked at everyone and I said, "I know you guys weren't excepting this to happen. But you knew that I was going to kill them and everyone did their job. We did a good job and we did it well and we move on to the next mission."

Primo got up and said, "Mauricio is right. I know I cried and you girls cried and I hope God has mercy on their souls. We need to move on."

"I'm not walking away." Sonia said.

All the girls were saying that they are not going to walk away. "That's the spirit!" Chris smiled.

"We're willing to risk our lives for our leaders, Primo Mancini and his, Royal Highness, Mauricio de la Vega." Cassandra smiled.

"We are a team and we're not going to walk away. We're in this gang to the end." Karina said.

"Long live the King and the gang!" Primo smiled.

I looked at everyone and smiled. "Okay, it's time for Primo and you girls to have fun in the city. I'm going to let the Police forget about me and I know they are going to be distracted by other activities in the city." I smiled and transformed into the hideous creature and said, "Go and have some fun my friends!" Primo and the girls got up and we hugged each other and we said, "To the end!"

From there we went our separate ways and I know they were going to do great things out there on the streets and I knew the Police Department will be distracted by their activities. Then the next day my father came back around midnight and we hopped on his private jet plane and we went to Spain for vacation and it was a long summer at the beach. And even on the beach I started feeling depressed and I started thinking about my school problems. At the same time I felt relieved that I killed two kids that turn the school against me and they weren't going to interfere with my friendship with Eliza.

Then the people in Spain bowed down before me and they were proud to have me there in their country. On that afternoon a man came up to me and shook my hand, he told me that his name is Pedro Cortez and he requested that he should be my representative in the Kingdom so I said yes. I didn't want to sit on the throne not just yet but when I was old enough. After meeting Pedro, we went sailing around the Mediterranean Sea and I was having fun and I looked at my parents and my sister, Tania and I knew they are having fun too. And of course summer ended and I was excited to start sixth grade and I saw the name of my new school and it's called Walter E. Clarke Middle School. And as it turns out that all of us that were together in Myrtle Cooper Elementary School, started Clarke Middle School together and we were happy to see each other since the death of our friends in the Franklin Mountains. Most of us ran into each other on the hallway and started talking about what happened last year and we got very sad. Even though they were jerks to everyone, they were going to miss them so much. Then everyone got to know me and my friends that no one liked and we became best friends as well. Well of course they were nice to us because their leaders Armando and Deyna were dead thanks to me. So, my reputation as the future King grew even more in middle school, more and more people approached me and encouraged me to be the new King of Spain. But the worst part is when I walked to the cafeteria everyone stopped, so I can walk by and also they bowed down and kissed my hand. You can say that I was intimidating everybody but I wasn't a bully at all, I was just fair to everyone.

But the only person that we didn't see was Eliza and everyone felt that she was still shaken up from what happened last year in the Franklin Mountains. Everyday they kept asking me where Eliza was and I told them that I didn't know either and I was worried for her as well. Well everyone wondered that she probably ended up in the Psychiatrist Ward because she had an encounter with me. But we missed her a lot and we hope to see her very soon. Well Clarke Middle School started off well on the first semester and I received another honor roll and it was my sixth and final honor roll. I was so excited that I started running all over the school and I ran into a Teacher and she congratulated me for my accomplishment. Well this Teacher was the most respected Teacher in the whole city of El Paso, Texas and perhaps the whole world because she loved helping other kids plus she was Teacher of the year three times in a row. Well she said sorry for running into me and she bowed down too but I actually told her that it was my fault.

And on that year there were a lot of rumors going around. The rumor was that they were going to build a new high school. And it turns out that next year Walter E. Clarke Middle School was going to be full and half of the students were going to go to the new high school and they are going to call it Americas High School. They told me that I was going to remain at Clarke Middle School. And school was out and we stayed in El Paso and summer was here. I did a lot of things around the summer. I went around the neighborhoods cutting grass, painting houses and I was a paperboy and I did earn a lot of money along the way. Well most people were asking me why in the Hell would I do those things if I was going to be the future King of Spain and I responded by saying that I'm just a kid and I want to have fun in my life. Well on that summer I saw the newspaper and my friends were having fun in the city.

I sat on my bed and I was reading a bunch of articles of people that got beat up by a Ninja and they were bruised up and she sent ten people to the Hospital. I'm proud of Christina Bobs. I was reading another article of kids that were getting abducted in their own homes and somehow the kids managed to get back home to their families. Jennifer Callaway did an excellent job. There was another article of cars that have been reportedly stolen and good job by Jessica Hernandez. The same story with the stolen cars and most people speculate that the same car thief loves to race cars and the Police cannot catch up to them. Good job Lorraine Hondo. Another story is that someone is stealing the people's identity and Good job by Erin Killins. And on the other hand you have girls that are getting raped everyday by a dangerous serial rapist. Way to go Primo Mancini. And related story to the cars and it seems that the cars that get stolen and raced around the city are somehow exploding and waking up the neighbors. Good Job Cassandra Powell. Also there's a lot of people that are afraid to talk on the phone or have a conversation because they feel that someone else are listening to their conversations. Good job Sonia Rodriguez. Also there has been a lot reports about convenience stores that have been robbed around midnight. Good job Roxanne Sanderson, And at last some people are speculating that the reason that the Police haven't been able to arrest those criminals is because they are distracted by other things for example no one calls to reports missing kids, missing cars and so on. Well Karina Reyes is doing a good job blocking the phone calls and everything else. Not to mention that bogus order she gave back in the Franklin Mountains. But anyway I'm proud of my friends. And the last news is that the Police have yet to find the killer in the Franklin Mountains and they hoped to capture the killer before he strikes again. Well good luck with their investigation.

So, summer ended and I went to register at Clarke Middle School and in a couple of days later I started my seventh grade year. Well my first day in seventh grade started in a weird way. They told me that I wasn't supposed to be at Clarke Middle School and that all of my papers were at Americas High School. So, I ended up going only one day to Clarke Middle School. Plus I had two months of vacations, and I was so excited. And I continued to cut the grass, paint houses, and spent time with my family and my friends. I also started thinking about Eliza and I missed Eliza so much and I went to her house and her house was for sale. I figured that she moved away and she didn't tell me that she moved away. But I hope she is happy somewhere else and I will be happy if I see her again. And summer ended and I started my seventh grade year at Americas High School. And even though I was at Americas High School I still had to go to Special Education classes, and in the regular classes they would evaluate me to see how I was doing. I was passing all my subjects except for math. It was my "Achilles heel." Also there were more monthly meetings which in time I started calling them "my parole meetings." I felt like a prisoner in school and they should have put me into an orange jumpsuit.

CHAPTER SIX

THE DARK COWBOY IS BORN

It was Sunday afternoon where my mother and I went to the grocery store. When we went inside the grocery store everyone was standing still and bowed down and they didn't move until my mother and I went to find the food. The Manager of the store came up to us and said welcome to the grocery store and he was kissing my butt. And fifteen minutes later the Manager got to my last nerves and I told the Manager to drink water from the toilet and then report back to me if the water from the toilet taste better than normal water. Well I was surprised that the Manager actually went to the restroom and I was happy that he left us alone but my mother told me that it is normal for people to act like that when they see someone important.

Then I saw my old substitute Teacher from elementary school. Well she didn't see me and she was already on her way out of the store. And I was happy to see her because she may be the next one to die. Well my mother and I went to pay and went straight to my house. I went to my room and I called my friend Karina and I told her to meet me at Chris's house. And I also called Chris and told him that Karina was on her way to his house. I told my mother that I was going to meet some friends at Marty Robbins Park and she told me to be careful. I hopped on my bicycle and rode all the way to his house. When I got there Karina and Chris were inside the garage eating Pizza.

"How are you, Mauricio?" He asked.

"Good. I want you to do me favor." I said.

"What kind of favor?" He asked.

"I want you to investigate Melissa Owens." I responded.

"Who is she?" He asked.

I transformed into the hideous creature and I was walking on the walls and was growling. "She was my old substitute Teacher from the fourth grade. She didn't let me sing at the Christmas Play and made a fool out of me."

"I remember her." Karina said.

"I'm sorry to hear that she didn't let you sing at the Christmas Play but we will investigate her for you." Chris said and smiled and took us to his office. And I was the old me again. So, Chris went down to the kitchen to make coffee for himself. Karina and I were eating Pizza and we were drinking Pepsi. So, Karina hacked into the system and it took her three minutes to find Melissa's background. "I have information on Melissa Owens." Karina said.

"What did you found out about her?" I asked her.

"She graduated from the University Texas at El Paso. Her parents are wealthy and she is a spoil little princess. She has ninety-seven thousand dollars in her bank account courtesy of her parents. Her daddy paid for her house and her car. She is also a party animal plus she was in a sorority. And every weekend she goes to party at downtown El Paso and sometimes she goes to party at Juarez with her friends. She is a heavy drinker and smokes a lot, well she smokes cigarettes. And not to mention that she has "pretty boy friends" and she doesn't like the outcasts." Karina said.

"Party animal and she has favorites. It doesn't surprise me that she wants to fit in so badly." I said and laughed.

"This coming Friday she's going to be in the club of downtown El Paso. We don't know who is she going with. But there is going to be a lot of security and her friends are going to protect her."

"There's going to be a lot of drunk people. Well there's security inside the club but not outside."

"What's your plan?" Chris asked.

"The same thing as the last time but I want something dramatic when I'm done killing her." I said.

"How dramatic?" He asked.

"Be creative you know improvise." I said and was laughing. "Well I'm going to need to assistance of Karina, Sonia, Primo, Cassandra, and Erin. I need to have Primo at my side, so he can rape her. I want Karina to distract the Police, I need Erin to steal a reporter's identity, so she can tell the news about the psychotic killer in El Paso, Texas. And Cassandra you know for bombs. And Sonia I want her to listen to the phone calls for the whole week." I said.

"The bugs are still inside the Police Station." Chris said.

"Thank you." I said and started laughing.

"So, right after school the six of us are going to meet here at Chris's house." Karina said.

"Of course. I hope you guys are ready for this operation." I smiled and after that Karina and I went home. And on that night Karina called Cassandra, Sonia, Primo, and Erin and told them to get ready on Friday afternoon. And they said yes. And I'm wondering if she's going to have another stupid order.

And I was surprised how the week went by so fast and it was Friday afternoon where the six of us went to Chris's house. We started preparing ourselves for later on in the night. Sonia was listening to Melissa's phone calls for the whole week, Erin was preparing to organized a story about me and she was looking forward of been the anchorwoman. Karina was hacking into Melissa's profile, Cassandra and Chris finished making the bombs and they went inside three buildings and planted the bombs and went back to the house.

"Melissa is going to be at the club around nine thirty and there be might a chance that she might be late as well." Sonia said.

"That's good to know!" I smiled and we waited until the sun was going down and we all ate and it was a good meal. I went into the restroom and changed my clothes and I was now dressed as a Cowboy and I grabbed my guns and loaded them. Chris brought me the horse while Karina, Sonia and Erin stayed back on the fort and before we left Chris gave me a case and showed me what was inside the case.

"Mauricio, these are night vision goggles and you might need them to see in the night." He said.

"Thank you!" I smiled and put them back on the case. We all looked at each other and smiled.

"Ready!" Chris said.

"Yes!" We said.

Primo, Cassandra, and Chris went into the truck and drove off and I got on top of my horse and rode all the way to downtown El Paso. In about forty-five minutes later we finally arrived and I was hiding on the shadows and we were scouting the entire place very carefully. Cassandra and Chris stayed far away from the buildings that were going to explode. Primo and I saw the building that was in front of the club and that was the building that had the bombs inside. We went to back to the alley and I left my horse in the alley. Primo and I were climbing up the ladder until we were able to reach the rooftop. Karina radioed me and said, "Melissa should arriving pretty soon."

Primo and I were standing on the rooftop in that building and Primo was looking at the buildings and he was throwing pennies on the street and he was also spitting. And I took out the night vision goggles and I was looking down at the club. There were a lot of people that were entering the club and we heard them laughing and talking. We were waiting for Melissa to show up, and then half an hour later, she finally showed up at the club at exactly ten o'clock. Well Melissa Owens was so beautiful, she was twenty-six year old woman, she was around five feet tall and seven inches, hazel eyes, brownish hair, and she weighs in one hundred and two pounds, She was built to be a supermodel. Plus she loved to go out shopping and go to the beauty salon and she also loves to go out dancing with her friends and buys them round of beers. She had a lot of friends from high school and college friends too, she was very popular girl but she is going to be even more popular because when this night ends, she is going to go straight to Hell and they are going to give her a warm welcome and not to mention she is going to come out at tomorrow's obituary section.

And on this night she went out with her male friends and she actually thought that she was going to very well protected but she will be wrong. Then they went into the club and I have no idea for how long we were waiting for them to come out. And I could imagine what was going on inside the club. I felt that she was dancing with everyone in the club and they bought her drinks or she bought them drinks since she had a lot of money to spend. The night was going great for them. While we ware waiting for her, I took out the other case and I opened it. I took out the dart gun and the Magnum gun and I loaded them once again. And I had still had the night vision goggles and continued to look down at the club and also I had the dart gun in my other hand. Then the party ended at one o'clock in the morning and the substitute Teacher was so tired and drunk and her male friends decided to walk her to the car. We saw the front door open and I could hear them laughing and talking about how much fun they were having inside the club.

I gave Primo the night vision goggles and I put on my cowboy hat. And I also told him to duck and I began to notice that there were a couple of people from the club that were also getting ready to leave and they were going to open their cars. I was still standing there and I was watching them very closely and I had my eyes on that substitute Teacher. Then one of the people that came out of the club noticed something or someone was standing on the rooftop and I noticed that he was completely drunk and I knew no one would believe him that someone was standing on the rooftop of the building.

"What's that?" He said and pointed at the roof.

I got on my knees and everyone turn around and found nothing and they knew that he was way too drunk. I overheard the substitute Teacher saying that she forgot her purse inside the club and she convinced the guys to go back inside and get it. Her male friends opened the car door, so she can rest in the back while they go inside and get her purse. I saw her friends leaving. I put everything back on the case but I had the dart gun in my hand. I began to notice that Melissa got out of the car and started walking around.

I looked at Primo and told him, "Take the case and put them in your backpack. And do you remember the time you gave me a piggy back ride to your house?" I asked him.

"Yes, why!" Primo responded.

"Well I'm repaying the favor and get on my back." I said.

"That's good because I'm still tired when we were climbing up the ladder." Primo said and jumped on my back.

"Hold on tight. Now do you want me to walk, run, fly, or jump?" I asked him.

"Whatever makes you more comfortable, Mauricio. I'll just hold on to you." He said and smiled.

This building was fifty-seven stories high and I was walking to the stairs, but I started running and jumped off the rooftop and Primo started screaming like a little girl and I overheard Chris yelling on the radio, "What the!"

While we were floating on the air and my heart started beeping too fast and everything went into slow motion. I took out the dart gun and I steadied it. I heard the voice of The Dark Figure. "Look to your left! Now!" So, I look to my left and I saw someone standing next to the buildings. This person was recording everything that went on. And I could hear Sonia reporting to Karina. "Mauricio is floating in the sky and he's about to shoot Melissa."

Karina responded, "That's good because we have evidence! And keep recording!"

"Copy that!" Sonia said.

What did Karina meant by that and why in the Hell was Sonia recording this whole event. What are they up too? And that's where I shot Melissa in the back and she fell down and we landed in the middle of the sidewalk. I looked at Primo, "Are you okay?" I asked and we went walking to her car.

"Nice shot!" Primo said and was still dizzy from the fall.

"Thanks! She's all yours!" I laughed and Karina radioed me. "Don't worry! Chris paid a couple of girls to distract the guys and I'm pretty sure they are making out in the restrooms."

And Chris radioed me, "What was all the about, Mauricio?" He asked.

"I felt like jumping." I responded and grabbed Primo's backpack and put the dart gun inside and took out the Magnum Guns and I grabbed the keys and started the engine and rolled down the windows so they won't be moist. I waited for thirty minutes and finally I asked Primo, "Are you finish?"

"Give me a second, Mauricio!" Primo exclaimed and looked at me and said, "I'm finished."

"Put her clothes back on." I said.

Primo put Melissa's clothes back on and grabbed his clothes. And I gave him his backpack and he went running naked towards the truck but Chris made him put his clothes back on. So, I grabbed her hair and dragged her all the way to the wall. She was moving her eyes and her tears started coming out her face. She was scared to see me and I sat in front of her.

And suddenly I had another flashback. I heard Melissa's voice. "Mrs. Caballero I need you to convince your daughter, Eliza, to stay away from Mauricio de la Vega."

And Eliza's mother responded, "Why do you want my daughter to stay away from Mauricio de la Vega."

And she responded, "Because he's dangerous. Look what he did to Armando and Deyna at the playground. And I'm pretty sure that he murdered them on the Franklin Mountains."

"He wouldn't do that. His mom said that he had the flue."

"Maybe he had the flue but Mauricio probably sent a couple of hit man to do his dirty work."

"No he wouldn't do that."

I was standing there and I couldn't believe that another person said that Eliza should stay away from me. So, I took off my hat and Melissa saw my face and she was in shocked. "Hello, Melissa Owens. Do you remember me from the fourth grade? I know you are the daughter of the Librarian and just like your mom, you think your all that. I remember what you and everyone in class did to me and I won't forgive you ever again. You embarrassed me and I told everybody that I was going to sing in the Christmas play and as it turns out you guys didn't care about me and you didn't let me sing in the Christmas play. You were laughing at me and I have so much hatred towards you. And I found out something about you." I reached out into my pocket and took out a folder and showed it to her. "You are corrupted Teacher and you had done so many awful things in your life. But you also threw me to the wolves because I didn't talk at all. Now you are listening to my voice for the first time and for the very last time. And I hope you enjoyed our little chit chat. Now I'm going to send you to Hell and when you see your friends Armando and Deyna, tell them I said hi and I will be happy to know that you three are rotting in Hell." I laughed and started loading my Magnum guns and pointed them at her. "Class is dismissed you, Bitch!" I exclaimed and shot her all over her body and watched her die.

I called my horse and she went running towards me and I got on top of my faithful companion. And I saw the front door open and I heard her friends coming out of the club and they were looking for her and they found her laying on the ground. They thought that she was sound asleep and they touched her and they had blood all over their hands. Her friends were in the middle of the street screaming and calling for help and they were also crying their eyes out. And the people that came out with them, went back into the club to call the Police. Then her friends noticed that something was on top of the horse and I was staring at them, and I was laughing at them. I heard someone yelling, "His red evil eyes and it's true about The Dark Figure that killed those two kids back in the Franklin Mountains!" They were terrified and they thought that I was going to kill them. I told Karina to tell Cassandra to press the button and I was about to take off when the three buildings exploded and everyone covered themselves and I rode all the way into the darkness and Chris started the engine and we went home. During the road we kept hearing all the commotion and it's good thing that Sonia and Chris planted a couple of bugs in that part of the city.

"Is everyone okay." The owner of the club said.

"Yes! But she's dead! Somebody killed her." One of her friends yelled.

The owner of the club went inside to call the Police and in about twenty minutes later the Police, the Firefighters, and the Ambulance arrived at the crime scene. The Firefighters tried to take the fire out and the Ambulance came to take Melissa Owens to the Morgue. The Police Officers started questioning everyone at the crime scene and the same Detectives got out of the car and they began to notice that it was the same death as the two kids.

"The killer strikes again." Perla said.

"You bet. Execution style."

"Are there any witnesses?" Perla asked.

"Yes. These people that got out of the club and they all claim they saw everything." The Police Officer said.

"What about the other people that came out of the club?" Jim asked.

"They rushed out when they heard the buildings exploding." The Police Officer responded.

The Firefighters were able to put the fire out and a couple news vans arrived at the crime scene and started questions to everyone. "Take them to the Police Station! We will investigate tomorrow morning." Jim said.

Well we finally arrived at Chris's house and we were hugging each other and the plan actually worked. I went to the restroom and changed and we kept hearing everything inside the Police Station. And all the witnesses went to the Police Station and everyone gathered in the hallway. And one of the Police Officers brought Melissa's purse and showed it to the Detectives. "The killer didn't took anything at all. She has everything here and nothing seems to be missing."

"What was the girl's name?" Jim asked.

The Police Officer took out her Identification Card from her purse and read it, "Her name is Melissa Owens. She's twenty six years old."

"We should interrogate all the witnesses as quickly as possible." Jim said.

Detective Perla was the one that was doing the interrogation while everyone looked from the two way mirror. "What time did you arrived at the club?" She asked.

"Ten thirty."

"Did you see the girl?"

"Yes. I saw her there. She was sitting with their friends, they were laughing, drinking, and dancing."

"And what else happened."

"She danced like everyone else. All the guys wanted to dance with her and I asked her to dance."

"Did you see anybody that was suspicious at the club?" She asked.

"No"

"What time did the girl and her friends left the club?"

"They left around one o'clock in the morning and we were also getting ready to leave. So, we got out twenty minutes later. And I saw them at the parking lot, and they were still laughing and talking about how much fun they were having inside the club."

"What else happened?"

"I turn around and I saw someone or something on top of the rooftop in one of the buildings."

"What was it?"

"A Dark Shadowy figure with red evil eyes. The Dark Shadowy Figure was just standing there and it was looking at us. And I guess he was the one that killed the girl." He said and his tears started to come down his face and started yelling. "I cannot believe that this Dark Figure killed her. But she told us that she left her purse inside the club and we all went. We could have stayed and protected her from that monster!"

"After you guys got out of the club, what happen next?"

"We came out of the club and we saw someone on the top of the horse and his eyes were glowing red and he was laughing at us. And as soon The Dark Figure was getting ready to leave the buildings exploded." He had his hands on his head and started yelling. "She was just young! She didn't deserve to die!"

They took him away and they were going to interrogate her friends. This time Detective Jim Nielsen was going to ask the questions. "How long have you been friends with her?"

"Since we were little kids. We grew up together." He responded.

"Did you guys go to college together?"

"Of course. Melissa wanted to become a full time Teacher. Well she was just a substitute Teacher. She loved working with kids and she talked about getting married and having a lot of children."

"What happen inside the club?"

"The usual she danced with us and everyone else. We were drinking and enjoying the night. Everything was going okay inside the club. But all of us were tired and left at one in the morning."

"What happened when you went outside?" He asked.

"We were still laughing and we were talking about how much fun we had inside the club and we were going to eat somewhere." His tears were coming down his face. "Melissa forgot her purse and we went inside the club to get her bag. When we came back she was lying right next to the wall and we saw her face and we were covered in blood." He sobbed.

"I know this is difficult for you. But did she had enemies, an ex boyfriend maybe?"

"No. Everyone loved her."

The Detectives couldn't believe that the same killer had struck again and everyone described it as a Dark Figure that was dressed as a Cowboy was the one that killed her. They felt if they asked her other friends questions it will be the same thing. So, they let everyone go to their homes and they contacted Melissa's parents. "I want that club to be closed and that part of the street to be closed, so we could investigate tomorrow morning. Get a couple of Police Officers over there so they can close the entire block." Jim ordered.

The news reporters were outside the Police Station and they were waiting to get a story and taking pictures at all the witnesses that were coming out of the Police Station. And it was a circus outside and the Police Officers were guarding the door. Half an hour later the parents of Melissa arrived at the Morgue to identify her body. The Doctor very gently pulls the sheet off her face and they saw her face and the mother starting crying hysterically.

"I want to ask you guys some questions." Jim said and looked at them. "Did your daughter had enemies? An ex boyfriend, relative, or someone that wanted her dead."

"No. She got along with everyone." Her father responded.

"We could have protected her and made her stay at our house but she wanted to move out!" Her mother sobbed.

"Everyone loved her. She was our baby." Her father said.

"Do you know who killed her?" Her mother asked.

"We don't know yet. But we will catch him." Jim said.

The parents left the Morgue and they were crying and the Detectives and the Police Officers were still in disbelief with the story they were told. They were convince that it was an ex convict that killed the two kids and the substitute Teacher and not some Demonic Figure dressed as a Cowboy and with red glowing eyes. They didn't want to tell the press anything until they are able to catch this criminal.

We were excited and we were hugging each other until Chris said, "We are not out of the blues just yet. There is one more thing, Erin needs to send the story to the News Station and hoped they believe the story." He said.

"It will work and have faith, Chris." I smiled.

Well things couldn't get worse for them that the next day the murders of the three victims made the front page headlines and there was anchorwoman, Erin, that gave the city the news. "They call him "The Dark Cowboy" Erin also said, "That this Demonic Figure killed three people and everyone in the Police Department don't believe any of the witnesses." And they even had a picture of the now known Dark Cowboy. The Dark Persona Cowboy with red evil eyes holding a gun in his hand and the heads in a mantle. And Erin continued with the story, "The Police Department planned to keep this story from the people including the press and they didn't want to go public. They planned to keep this quiet and the Police knows who the killer really is."

And everyone in the city of El Paso, Texas were upset with the Police Officers. Even the parents of the dead children were upset that they went to the Police Station and started protesting against the Police Officers. "The Police Officers aren't doing anything to find this killer!" One of the parents yelled.

"They do not believe what our kids saw in the Franklin Mountains. They are just sitting down, stuffing their faces with Donuts."

"I cannot believe that they wanted to keep this quiet from everyone."

Well I was in my room listening to all of their commotions and I finally got up and went down to the kitchen and my mother was making breakfast. I sat down and she looked at me and she also sat down. "Mauricio, last night they found your old substitute Teacher dead in a night club." She said.

"Which one?" I asked.

"Melissa Owens." She responded.

"I remember Melissa Owens, she was the daughter of the Librarian and I cannot believe she is dead. Who kill her?"

"I don't know, Honey. But they are speculating that it was the same killer as the last time." She said.

"Mommy. I hope you can arrest this psychotic killer because you are the best Police Officers we have here in the city." I smiled and encouraged her.

"Honey, I know it will be difficult because this killer is very smart and he doesn't leave any footprints or fingerprints just a trail of blood." My mother said and hugged me so tight and she told me that everything is going to be okay.

Then later on in the afternoon there more protestors in front of the Police Station. Well the Commissioner of the Police Department ordered the Police Officers and everyone else to investigate the whole block and he was also going to speak in front of the media and they wanted to convinced the parents that they were doing everything they can to catch this killer. Well the investigation lasted for three whole hours where they finally discovered something well it wasn't the footprints or fingerprints. Well they did found her blood on the sidewalk of the club and they also found parts of the bombs laying around the buildings that exploded last night and they thought it was act of terrorist or the gangsters from Juarez. They took the evidence to the Police Station and they kept the whole block close for now.

And later on in the afternoon the Commissioner of the Police Department and the Mayor of El Paso, Texas teamed up to talk to the press. They were going to have it in front of City Hall and the press planned to asked them a lot of questions. The Commissioner stood in front of the press and said, "There's no such thing as a Demonic Figure that's killing people. This Dark Cowboy character is the act of some crazy convict that wants to seek revenge on our peaceful city. Earlier this morning they found parts of bombs laying inside the three buildings that exploded last night. This is an act of terrorist and the Mafia from Juarez and we will keep our eyes very closely on the borders and on the waters just in case they try to sneak into the city and try to harm us. We will keep the city and our citizens of El Paso, Texas safe and we will continue to live our lives. Thank you!" The Commissioner said.

But the media kept on asking questions and it was the Mayor's turn to talk and he looked at everyone and smiled. "I have an obligation to protect the citizens of El Paso, Texas. When you elected me as your new Mayor of the city of El Paso, Texas. I made a promise that I will bring the end of the crimes and the violence in this city. I hate looking at the newspaper and see people dying in car crashes, old ages and so on. I'm devastated to hear three people that were brutality murdered. Two of them were just kids and a twenty six year old woman and they didn't deserve to die that way. That I cannot have in the city, and I don't want to see the newspaper and find people getting murdered by a so called "Demonic Figure." I and along with the Police Officers will bring

Jesus Morales

this Dark Cowboy character to justice. I don't care if it's a Demonic Figure like some people describe it. We will bring you to justice! And when we do arrest The Dark Cowboy, we will give him the death penalty. May God have mercy on your soul." The Mayor said and went into City Hall.

So, at the end of the week there was a funeral service for Melissa Owens. Friends and family members went to pay their respects. Including the kids of the schools and they brought her a lovely poems. And it was Saturday afternoon where she was buried. Everyone was throwing flowers as they were lowering the casket to the ground. After she was buried, the gang and I went to Chris's house and we wanted to hear what the Police Officers planned to do next. Then later on in the evening the Commissioner gathered all the Police Officers and Detectives into his office and he looked at everyone in the room and said.

"I know we're getting criticize by the media and the people and we're not going to give up. We are going to catch this criminal and we swore that we will protect the citizens of El Paso from criminals and terrorist." He said.

"You've heard stories about this serial killer. They say that he can disappeared into thin air like he did on the Franklin Mountains, plus this serial killer has red evil eyes. It may be true what they say about this serial killer, he may be the Devil in person." One of the Police Officers said.

"We may be next to die. I'm going to start writing my Will and leave everything to my wife and kids. I think everyone should do the same thing." The other Police Officers said.

"We're Police Officers! We took an oath that we will protect innocent people and it doesn't matter from who. And I don't know about you but I'm willing to risk my life in order to protect the people of El Paso, Texas." Detective Perla said.

"We might need the help of the Federal Bureau Investigation." The Police Officer said.

Then my mother added and asked. "What would it take for the FBI to investigate these killings?"

"If we lose control of this situation they might come in and take over our investigation and we are going to look like fools. All we're going to do is clear the press for them." The Commissioner responded and said. "So, we must find a way to arrest this killer. Is that clear."

"Yes, sir!" Everyone said and they stayed in the office for another two hours. They were worried that they might loose control of all the killings and I hope that they are worried because there's plenty more where that came from. Plus I was wondering about Karina's plans. I'm going to keep my eye on her.

Well summer was just around the corner. The gang and I went to Marty Robbins Park and we were playing football. And Chris pulled into the parking lot, Primo and I went to help him with the grill and we started having a cook out. We even took out a huge blanket for us to sit. The food was ready and we were eating and I saw Chris smiled and we all gathered together.

"I liked the improve. Thank you." I smiled at everyone.

"You guys did great. Another fifty dollars will be added to your account, Mauricio and the rest of you. More money will be added in your account." He smiled.

"One hundred and fifty dollars. I'm happy." I smiled

"Well that's good." He said.

"But for now we need to chill for awhile. The next time we will catch them off guard once again." I said.

"There are building the case against The Dark Cowboy." Chris said.

"I'm planning to be controversial and it's going to be fun that way. Also the Police are getting criticize and they are going to loose control with this investigation and we are going to be happy and we're going to celebrate by drinking Chocolate Milk and it's on me." I said and smiled.

"If they do loose control of this investigation, that means the Federal Bureau Investigation is going to take over for good. Your father will be in charge and he is unpredictable." He said and looked worried.

"My loving father is going to have a Hell of a time dealing with my killings and my friends." I said and smiled. "Let's see how good he really is. I want to see the great Pablo de la Vega in action." I smiled.

Chris looked at us and smiled. "You guys are getting better at this. I've been reading the newspaper." He looked at Christina, "I've read about people getting beat up and that's good." He looked at, Jennifer, "Kids, are getting abducted and they are back at home with their parents. And Jessica stealing cars!" He looked at Lorraine, "And Lorraine racing against the Police Officers and that's good." Chris looked at the rest of us, "Erin is stealing people's identity. And Primo is raping girls, Cassandra making bombs when she needs to, Karina hacking into the system, Sonia putting bugs all over the city, Roxanne stealing everything from the stores, and his, Majesty, Mauricio killing people. You guys are great individual but when you guys come together you guys are unstoppable." He smiled.

"Yes, we are!" I said.

"Cheers!" We all exclaimed and smiled and hugged each other.

So, the whole week went by so fast and then summer was here and I did the usual routine. I was looking at the newspaper to see if there were any jobs available well they were jobs available. I continued cutting the grass, paining houses and I did earn a lot of money and I was happy to spend the money at *Cielo Vista Mall*. But the people kept on mentioning about this serial killer that's still on the loose in the city. They told me to be careful out there and they hope that my mother would arrest him. The truth is that we are unstoppable and nobody cannot touched us at all. But it backfire on us because two weeks later, I was in my room when the phone rang and it was Chris. And he told me that Primo was caught raping three girls and there was a witness and they were going to send him to the juvenile home or possibly boot camp. And all of us went to Chris's house and we heard what they were asking him.

Well we got there in time because they took him to the interrogation room. Detective Jim Nielsen came into the room and was asking him a lot of questions. "Why did you rape the girls?"

"Because I want to make my daddy to be proud of me." Primo responded and was laughing.

"Oh, yeah! Your father, the great Vito Mancini, he is a great mob leader. And your father has done a lot of good deeds over the years. I heard that he built a foundation for the fighting blindness and kids who have aids. That was wonderful of him. And did your daddy hire you to kill three people? You know Armando Guerrero, Deyna Alberts, and Melisa Owens. Did you raped them?" He asked.

"Yes, I did! I raped Deyna Alberts and Melissa Owens but I didn't kill them."

"Do you work for your father?" He asked.

"No I don't! But I work for someone else that killed the two kids and the substitute Teacher. And someone that you will never catch at all. I'm sure by now you have heard stories about The Dark Cowboy with red evil eyes that kills people." He responded.

"Did you kill them?" He asked.

"No! I told you that I raped Deyna Alberts and Melissa Owens." He responded.

His mother open the door and yelled at him. "Son, what's the killer's name!"

"What does he look like?" He asked.

"I never seen it's face just it's red evil eyes. We have an alliance, and I offered my services to him, so I rape girls and he asked me if I wanted to rape Deyna Alberts and Melissa Owens." Primo responded.

"Why did you do that?" His mother asked and sobbed.

"The Dark Cowboy asked me to help him out and I was glad to help him out. I'll do anything for The Dark Cowboy and he's my best friend." He smiled.

"Where can we find that so called Dark Cowboy?" He asked.

Primo responded and laughed, "Well The Dark Cowboy comes out of the darkness and he calls for me and I follow his orders. And the next time you see a woman murdered. Just make sure you check for my sperm. And that's all you need to know."

"Why are you doing this to me. I gave you all my love and I've done so much for you!" His mother was sobbing.

Primo responded to his mother with this, "The Dark Cowboy is a serial killer that takes lives away and I'm Primo Mancini that takes their virginities away, I'm not a serial killer or serial rapist, but I'm the "Virgin Killer!"

We heard what Primo had to say and I couldn't help it but to admire his sacrifice for the team. The girls looked at me and smiled. "We will also do anything for Primo and you too your, Royal Highness." Karina said and smiled. And from there Primo was sent to see a Psychiatrist for observation and he also went through Hell the whole summer. They also took him to see a Judge and he also sent him to do community service and see the Psychiatrists because they thought he was crazy and they thought that he was making up stories that he was working for The Dark Cowboy. And Primo had to be home schooled for awhile because they didn't want the "Virgin Killer" around campus.

Well summer ended and I was getting ready to start my eighth grade year in Americas High School. And this time I wanted to focus more on my school work and I was committed to study and learn math. And I usually stayed up late at night and I usually forgot to set the alarm clock and I was absent a lot. This went on until October when they sent me a letter that I needed to see a Judge for my absentees. They scheduled me for court around November. So, my mother and I went to court and it's a good thing it was at Americas.

We went there around seven or eight that night and we sat down and there were a lot of people. I think there were like thirty people. Then the Judge came and we had to wait for half an hour. There were like three people talking to the Judge and there was a girl and her mother. The girl was around thirteen or fourteen years old and she was wearing a red dress that you can see her legs and other stuff and I guess she was trying to impress the Judge. But I don't think the Judge was impressed with what she was wearing and I could tell that the girl's mother was giving the Judge her attitude problem. Then I heard the Judge slam his hand on the desk. The Judge started yelling at the girl and I was freaked out and he continued to yell at her until she burst into tears and he called the Police Officers to arrest her mother and her daughter too and everyone in that room was already freaking out.

The Judge finished with them and it was our turn. My legs were shaking and I could tell that my mother was also worried, even though she is Super Cop but she was still worried because she didn't know what will happen to me. Then the Judge asked me "Why don't you go to school?" And he also asked me if I was on the streets late at night doing drugs or having sex with women. The Judge went on and on with all of his weird theories about me. And the last thing he said to me was that I had to do community service for sixty hours and see a Physiatrist for fifty hours. I didn't like that and I was about to choke him in front of everybody because he just disrespected me and I could tell that the Police Officers didn't like the way the Judge was treating the Royal King but the Judge didn't care who I was.

So, the next day I started doing the community service. And I didn't mind doing it because it gave me something to do right after school. Then at night my mother and I went to see the Physiatrist and every single night the Psychiatrists started to judge me before asking me anything and they were accusing me the same way the Judge did and they also disrespected me. Well when my mother was around they were nice to me and they wanted to help me but when she wasn't around they were just criticizing me and making fun of me. This went on for a couple of months then I was allowed to go back to see the Judge. He asked me if I had learned my lesson and I told him "Yes!" The Judge dismissed us and he didn't apologize for insulting me well I guess I'm going to have to teach them a lesson. Then I rushed home and I jumped on top of the bed and I was happy because I thought that the nightmare was over.

Then the holidays came and we celebrated Thanksgiving, Christmas and New Years Eve. My friends and I celebrated because we were going to be in high school plus we were doing so many awful things to this city. We were excited and on the summer I did the same thing. I was working all summer long and I got paid good money as well. And I also had the time to have fun. My friends and I were having cook outs and going to parties and I also spent part of the summer having cook outs at the park with my mother and Tania. I was having a Hell of time with my friends and family.

Then Primo went to my house and my mother knew that he is still my best friend and she accepted him in her house. We went to our room and we started talking.

"I heard what you had to say." I said.

"Well they know that I'm friends with The Dark Cowboy and not the great King Mauricio de la Vega. You know that I will do anything for our friendship, and I am to willing to take the fault. And I meant what I said, that I was willing to do anything for you because you are a good leader and a great friend your, Majesty. You are like my brother to me." He said and we shook hands.

"We are one big happy family and don't forget about our sisters. But I don't like the idea of you taking the blame of the rapes and me killing the women. And I know you are doing this to make your father proud of you and I guess he is proud of you." I said and smiled, "What are we going to call you now? Primo "The Virgin Killer" Mancini."

"I was hoping Primo "The Sexual Predator" Mancini. The word "Virgin Killer" is what I'm going to use when I catch my prey." He said and smiled.

So, the gang and I continued to hang out during the summer and as always summer had to end and we were going to become freshman. But when I started high school, I was under a lot of pressure to keep my grades up, so I could join my friends in regular classes and not have to go to any of the Special Education classes but things were different, the Teacher Department didn't care if I was going to be King and they told me that I had to follow the rules or else they were also going to punish me if I didn't obey them. Well I started off well and the staff was impressed with my grades and everything else. They granted me the regular classes that I wanted, under the condition that I keep my grades up. I felt like a prisoner who was released from jail but was still under parole and I couldn't enjoy my freedom and again they should put me in a orange jumpsuit.

So, by the year 1999 my parents were turning forty-five years old. Both of them were doing great out on the streets and they hadn't lost a step. Over the years my parents arrested so many criminals there are in the world and I had a feeling that they were going to be challenged somewhere down the road. Then there were rumors going around the city and they were talking about that the FBI might come to El Paso, Texas. They were going to investigate the killings and among other things. Well they only care about the serial killer and not the rapes or the other things. But the people were counting on my parents to take out the serial killer before I kill once again. And let's see how tough my parents really are, when they meet and try to arrest The Dark Cowboy.

CHAPTER SEVEN

THE DEADLY STORMY NIGHT

It was Sunday morning where all of us went to Church and everyone were praying for the souls of Melissa Owens, Armando Guerrero, and Deyna Alberts. Everyone was praying and they were hoping that the psychotic killer would soon be arrested, well keep hoping ladies and gentlemen because I'm going to continue with my killings and no one will stop me from killing. So, we were in Church for three whole hours and finally I heard Pastor saying to everyone that service is over. We were walking outside when Chris stopped by to say hello to us. Chris told our parents that he was going to take us to get a Burger and they all said yes. And Chris took us to eat at *McDonalds*, and he pulled into the drive thru and order our food. And in about twenty minutes later they gave us the food and went to his house. We were in the kitchen eating.

"So, what's new?" I asked Chris.

"Just working and helping you guys out with your missions." Chris responded with a smile.

"Well you should be happy to know that I found someone else that I want to kill." I smiled and ate my Burger.

"How many people?" He asked.

"Three people." I responded and laughed, "I want to kill three people." I ate my Burger and drank my Coke and said, "Two Psychiatrist and a Judge."

"Really? You must be crazy? It will be suicide!" Karina exclaimed.

"I know I am crazy and I'm suicidal but I'm also going to increase my killings and along with my legacy and make the de la Vega family proud. And do you remember I was telling you about the two Psychiatrist that I went to see and the hanging Judge."

"Yes, I remember you told me what they did to you. Do you want me to investigate them?" Chris asked.

"Of course. And I want you to improvise the whole thing. I want to kill all three of them at the same time, the same day." I said and smiled.

"I'll see what we can do, Mauricio." Chris smiled and looked worried and thirty minutes later we finished eating our food. Karina hacked into the system and asked me, "What's are their names?"

"Doctor William James and he is the Psychiatrist that treated me from the time I was doing community service." I responded.

Karina put his name on the computer and found him right of away. "Well, Doctor William James has a lot of money in his bank account, and his house has been paid for. Wow, this guy looks to be wealthy. And what's the other Psychiatrist's name?'

"Doctor Erin Norton!" I responded.

Karina was looking for her information and found it right of away. "Doctor Erin Norton is also wealthy and I don't know why they have so much money in their accounts. And what's the Judge's name?"

"George Fuentes!" I said.

Karina was looking for his information and found it. "Judge George Fuentes has a lot of money too, and looks to me that all three of them are working for the mob. And it looks to me that Vito Mancini has them right in his pockets. So, no wonder Primo got off easy." She said and we looked at him.

"I'm also in shock and I didn't know that my dad has them in his pockets." Primo said.

"What's your plan?" Chris asked me.

"I need Sonia to put bugs in their office. I need Cassandra to explode the three buildings. Erin I need you to steal someone's identity and make sure that the people have abandon all three buildings and I need Karina to do her thing, and finally Primo I need you to rape Doctor Erin Norton and leave the scene."

"And I hope that you don't do anything stupid, Primo, like get caught and get arrested." Chris said.

"For your information, Chris, I'm willing to risk my life for my friends and I want to take the fall if I have too." Primo said and smiled, "It's a lot of fun to have people watching me rape and tortured innocent girls and they cannot do anything about it!"

I looked at Primo and transformed into the hideous creature and ran towards him and grabbed his throat and slammed him against the wall and yelled, "Not butts, Primo. Like I said before, nobody isn't getting arrested, not on my watch, Primo Mancini! When your doing my operation, I except each of you to follow my orders. That includes you, Primo and I expect that you to do your thing and leave the scene. I respect you and I know you want to take the fall but your not going to do it. And when your doing your own operation, you can do whatever the Hell you want. Is that clear!"

"That's fine with me! That's why you are a good leader, Mauricio." Primo smiled.

I let him go and I looked at everyone and said, "Karina and Sonia continue to monitor the Psychiatrist and the Judge and we will wait for the right moment. And in the meantime, Primo keep your penis to yourself because I need you for this operation."

"I'll be ready when you need me." Primo smiled and I was me once again.

After that we went home and during the week, Sonia and Chris went to put the bugs inside the Psychiatrist office and including the Judge's office and they were monitoring them for the whole week. And it was the beginning of September well I kind off took the day off from school. I was in my room and I started watching the news and they said that on Saturday afternoon it was going to be an ugly day. The weather man was saying that a thunderstorm was coming with a lot of hail, heavy wind, and a lot of rain and the weather man told us to be careful out there on the streets. And it was four o'clock on the afternoon when I called Primo, Erin, Cassandra, Sonia, and Karina and told them to meet me at Chris's house. So, I hopped on my bicycle and went to his house and they were waiting for me inside the garage.

"Guess what I find out?" I asked and smiled. "Guys, I found out that tomorrow there is going to be a horrible thunderstorm and it's going to be ugly afternoon. And that's our chance to do our operation." I said and smiled.

"What's the plan?" Karina asked.

"Karina and Sonia are going to stay back on the fort and monitor everything. Erin I want you to improvise everything and make sure that the people leave the building. Cassandra I want you to plant bombs in the buildings but plant them today. Primo and I are going to be together the whole time. Is that clear!" I ordered.

"Yes!" Everyone exclaimed and we left home while Chris and Cassandra were going to plant the bombs inside the buildings.

And the next day the six of us were together at Chris's house and we went outside to look up in the sky. And very slowly the clouds were coming their way into the city, the wind was blowing all over the place. By two o'clock on the afternoon it was getting cloudier and the wind was blowing harder. So, the storm was coming closer and it was beginning to sprinkle. Half an hour later everyone in the city heard a loud thunder that was knocking it's way into the city. The storm was going come into our city even if we didn't invite it into our city. Then it started to rain really hard and the hail was coming down harder and the hail were breaking the windows in most parts of the city. We were outside during those hours and those clouds looked freaky and the girls remained inside the house and they were monitoring everything.

Finally Primo and Chris decided to get back inside the house while I stayed outside for a couple of more minutes and I went back inside the house. And I looked at everyone and said, "It's time to play and have fun in the city!" I smiled and we heard another loud thunder and the rain was pouring down really hard. I went to the restroom and changed into my costume. I also loaded my guns. Primo looked at everyone and said, "We are ready, Mauricio!" We went outside and the girls said, "Good luck!" I looked at them and smiled, and ran off to find the two shrinks. Chris put the horse inside the trailer, and they got into the truck and drove off as well. And we arrived in time and we watched half of the people leaving the buildings and we felt that they listen to Erin's improve. I watched everything around me while the rain was pouring down really hard including the hail. Primo and I stayed together and Chris told us that he was going to be parked down the street. Primo and I went to that back of the building and climbed up the ladder and we were standing in one of the buildings that had a bomb inside. And I was staring down at the Psychiatrist building and Primo had an umbrella and I was waiting for the Psychiatrist to leave their offices. The storm didn't bother us at all and it our ally. And I was hearing everything from inside the building. The two Psychiatrist were in their offices putting their stuff together, so they can go home and call it a day. They were saying goodbye to everyone and Doctor William James was waiting for Doctor Erin Norton.

"Be careful out there it's going to get pretty ugly soon. The Secretary said.

"It is already getting ugly look at the rain and hail and the wind is blowing really hard." William said.

"At what time are you guys leaving?" Erin asked.

"Until nine o'clock." The Secretary responded.

The two Doctors said goodbye to everyone in the office and they went running to their cars. And I began to notice that Doctor William James's keys fell to the ground and Doctor Erin Norton was helping him find his keys. They were getting wet and getting hit by the hail and the wind was blowing really hard. Primo and I were staring at them from the rooftop of the other building and my eyes were glowing red and I was grinning from ear to ear. I took out my dart gun and steadied it and shot Doctor Erin Norton in the back and she fell to the ground. And Doctor William James thought that the wind and hail might have knock her to the ground. And he went to check up on her until I shot him in the back with the dart gun and he also fell to the ground.

I looked at Primo and said, "Get on my back!" Primo took a deep breath and jumped on my back and we jumped down and landed in the middle of the street. I grabbed Doctor William James and put him in the back seat of his car and Primo grabbed Doctor Erin Norton and put her in the back seat. We started the engine and drove on the other side of the building. Just then everything froze and I turn around to see if any of the disloyal members of the gang. But I heard Karina's voice, "Are you recording, Sonia?"

"Yes, I am! And I'm already inside the building and waiting for the get a away car." Sonia responded. And I heard Sonia's voice and it came from one of those buildings. What are they up too now?

So, anyway I got out of the car and went to Primo and said, "You know what to do!"

"Of course!" He smiled and started raping Doctor Norton.

I went to open the back seat door and I grabbed Doctor William James and sat him next to the wall. And that's where I had another flashback. I heard the voice of Doctor William James's that was saying, "Eliza, we have known each other for a long time and we go to Church together. But what can you tell me what happened on the Franklin Mountains."

Eliza responded and was sobbing. "I saw a monster that killed Armando and Deyna and it just disappeared into the darkness."

"It wasn't a monster that killed Armando and Deyna. There were rumors going around that it was Mauricio that killed them in the Franklin Mountains."

"That's not true. He wouldn't do that!"

"Mauricio was sent here so we can evaluate him and he almost killed us. I'm telling you that he's dangerous. But we have evidence on Mauricio and you can tell us what you know about him and we can take it to the Police and they can help him."

"No! He's my friend!"

I was just staring at Doctor William James and I couldn't believe that he has some kind of evidence pointed towards me. He was so sure that I killed all three of them. Well he may be right and his curiously is getting the better of him. And I went to see how Primo was doing and said, "Are you finish?" I asked.

"Yes! Should I put her clothes back on?" He asked.

"No! But I have an idea, take Doctor William James's car and put it back where it was parked earlier and come back to take her car too. And I grabbed Doctor Erin Norton and sat her down next to her colleague. Primo started the engine and put the car where it originally was and he came back to take her car back to the parking lot. Then he came back running and I said, "You did great and go with Chris." Primo smiled and went running into the truck.

And poor Doctor Erin Norton was complete naked and she had bruises all over her body and bite marks too. Well they were looking at me with fear. And I had another flashback. "Eliza, Sweetie. I was informed by Doctor William James that he told you something about Mauricio."

"He told me to stay away from, Mauricio!"

"Mauricio de la Vega is dangerous and we know it first hand. Because he tried to kill us right here in our office."

"It's not true!" Eliza yelled.

"We have evidence pointed towards him and we're going to help him. He's going to get the help that he needs!"

Well I thought it was all bullshit because they were criticizing me for no reason at all and I had a feeling that Karina was behind this. And I finally got on my knees and I took off my hat and I let them see my face and my eyes were glowing red and said. "Well good afternoon Doctor William James and Doctor Erin Norton. And it's been a long time since we have seen each other. How long has it been since we saw each other? Well I don't care about that because we don't have time to get reacquainted. Well you should by now that you guys are going to die in a couple of minutes." I growled and grabbed them by their throats and yelled at them. "You guys made a fool out of me in your office and I can seem to remember that you made up a story that I was so violent and that I almost killed you in your office. You described me as a borderline psycho path and I don't like it when people make up stories about me. You also disrespected a future King as well and that's not good either. You guys are corrupted Psychiatrist, and you work for Vito Mancini and you are a disgraced to the city of El Paso, Texas. That's not good! Don't worry I'm going to send you a check form Hell." I grabbed them by their hairs and I was dragging them back to their cars and they were laying motionless in the middle of the parking lot. And I pointed the guns at them and said, "This session is over!" And I shot them so many times and it was execution style and I was still standing there and I was laughing about it. Then the people that were inside the other buildings heard the gunshots and they went running outside to find their coworkers murdered. They also saw me standing over their dead corpse, and I radioed Chris and he open the trailer door and my horse came out. I called my horse and she came running towards at me and I got on top of her and we took off. I was heading where Chris was parked and we were hearing everything.

Then the other people from the other buildings also came out to the parking lot and found both Doctors dead and they called the Police. Their coworkers got on their knees and started crying their eyes out and they didn't care if they got wet. The other people were trying to get them inside the building because it was way too dangerous, because of the storm and they thought that I might want to come back and kill them. And this is where everything froze and everything went into slow motion. That's where I saw Sonia running with the crowd and there was a black car the pulled into the sidewalk. She quickly got into the car and they took off. And thirty minutes later the Police Officers and the Ambulance arrived and the same Detectives got out of the car and looked at the dead bodies.

"Damn it! He's killed again!" Jim yelled.

"Can you tell us, what happen here?" Perla asked.

The Secretary was crying and yelled. "The Dark Cowboy killed them!"

"There's another witness that claim that it was The Dark Cowboy that killed them." One of the Police Officers said.

"Take the coworkers to the Police Station for some questioning and call their families too. They need to identify their bodies down at the Morgue!" Detective Perla ordered the Police Officers.

I looked at Cassandra and said, "Now!"

Cassandra looked at me and smiled and pressed the button and just then the buildings behind them exploded and everyone fell to the ground and they were knocked out. That's where we took off to the next mission, I jumped down off the horse and Chris put the horse back into the trailer and I ordered the team to go home. Meanwhile back in the Eastside where it was pouring down rain and with a lot of hail and nobody couldn't see anything through the window. Well Judge George Fuentes was on his way home and he couldn't believe how ugly it was. He finally parked in the driveway and went running inside the house. And I was already on top of the roof of his house and I was waiting for him to come home and I was grinning from ear to ear. And just like that a thunder struck in one of the light post and the lights in the entire neighborhood went off and the entire block was completely dark. George and his wife, Mrs. Fuentes, were already lighting up the candles from all over the house. The family went to the kitchen and started playing board games, so the kids won't be scared at all. And I decided to jump down and landed in the middle of the driveway and I was standing in front of the door and kick it open well the door broke into splinters. The family heard the door breaking and Judge George Fuentes went to see what was going on.

His family heard him yell. "Take the kids, go upstairs and call the Police!" As soon he was going to say "Hurry!" I shot him in the back with the dart gun and he fell to the ground and Mrs. Fuentes and her kids ran upstairs to call the Police but they couldn't go through the line. I went over the Judge and picked him up and sat him down on the couch.

Once again I had another flashback. I heard the voice of Judge George Fuentes, "I need to talk to you about something important."

I heard the voice of Eliza. "About what?"

"That we need you to sign a petition."

"A petition for what?" She asked in the flashback.

"To give Mauricio the help that he needs because he's not well."

"He hasn't done anything to anybody."

"Everybody at Church are suspecting that he murdered Armando, Deyna, and Melissa!"

"Mauricio will never do anything like that!"

"Eliza!" Judge yelled.

I was staring at Judge George Fuentes and I was pissed off with what he was saying. So, I took off my hat and I got on my knees and I wanted him to see my face and he was shocked to see me and said, "Hello, Judge George Fuentes, I mean your, Honor. What a pleasant surprise. You remember me, don't you? Well I will make this short and sweet. You are a corrupted Judge, and I can see that you are in Vito's pocket and you let criminals remain on the streets and you are a disgraced to this great city. I want you to think about it when you are burning in Hell. You are not going to be alone there, your two friends, well you know Doctor William James and Doctor Erin Norton are going to keep you company. Here's a little personal note. I will never forgive you for falsely accusing me of doing drugs, having sex with women and you were saying that I was a crazy lunatic and you also described me as a borderline psycho path and you disrespected a future King of Spain. That's not nice your, Honor. Well I want you to think about it when you are burning in Hell and getting mistreated by the Demons." I started loading my guns and yelled. "This court is adjourned!"

And this is where the image froze, I was still standing there and I looked out the front door and I heard a car stopping in front of the sidewalk. Somebody was in the hurry to get there. And I heard the voice of Sonia, "It's a good thing that Mauricio broke the door, I can see what's going on inside."

Karina responded, "As soon he kills the Judge. I want you to get the Hell out of there! Because Mrs. Fuentes is calling the Police."

"Copy that!" Sonia exclaimed.

As soon I shot Judge George Fuentes I heard the car leaving the scene. And in the meantime Mrs. Fuentes finally got through the line and started talking to the Dispatch Operator until she heard the gunshots and she started yelling. "My husband has been shot!" She sobbed.

"Ma'am! You need to calm down. Do you know who shot your husband?" The Dispatch operator asked.

"Yes! It was The Dark Cowboy!" She yelled.

Well I couldn't imagine the reaction of the Dispatch Operator when Mrs. Fuentes told her that The Dark Cowboy shot her husband but she went to call for help. Meanwhile the Detectives and the Police Officers and everyone else were finally on their feet and they were making sure that everyone was okay. They Firefighters finally arrived and everyone were still upset with the killings of the two Psychiatrist and the buildings exploding.

"What else could go wrong?" Perla asked.

Finally the Dispatch Operator was finally able to reach them. "All units there's been another murder. The Dark Cowboy has struck again and this time he as killed a Judge!"

"Damn it!" The Police Officer yelled.

"We need another Ambulance and take them to the Morgue!" Detective Jim yelled.

The Firefighters were trying to put out the fire out and they had little help from the heavy rain. The Paramedics took the Psychiatrists to the morgue. And all the units went to the Judge's house and when they got there. They quickly got out of their cars and they all took out their guns and they running into the house. They found Judge George Fuentes dead on the couch and Mrs. Fuentes and her kids were still upstairs and they were crying hysterically. A couple of Police Officers went upstairs to bring them to the car and very slowly they went down the stairs to find her husband murdered. And all the Police Officers went all over the house to see if The Dark Cowboy was still there but I wasn't there.

"The house is clear." The Police Officer said.

"My husband is dead!" She sobbed.

The Paramedics arrived and went inside the house and they put the Judge in a body bag and put him inside the Ambulance and took him to the morgue.

"Three people died tonight." Detective Perla said.

"Yes. That's a total of six people that have been killed by this psychotic killer and we always arrived way to late. Detective Jim said.

"Okay, take Mrs. Fuentes and her kids to the Police Station for some questioning." Detective Perla said.

Everyone left the house and put Mrs. Fuentes and her kids inside the Police car. I was standing on top of their rooftop and everyone was getting into the car until one of the kids saw something me on top of the roof top of their own house. "Mommy! He's looking at us. I don't want to die. He's on the roof!"

"Who's on top of the roof!" The mother sobbed.

The boy pointed at the rooftop and everyone looked up at the roof. The

Police Officers and the Detectives couldn't believe what they were staring at. I started laughing at them, "He's laughing at us!" The Police Officer yelled.

"You think this is a joke!" Detective Jim yelled. "Open fire!"

Everyone started shooting at the me but I jumped to the other side of the street and went running to Chris's house. Everyone were just standing there and they finally were convinced that they were staring at the Demonic Figure now known as The Dark Cowboy. Well ten minutes later I finally arrived at Chris's house and I went to the restroom and changed.

"Everything worked out just like the way we planned!" Karina exclaimed.

"And now they believe in The Dark Cowboy." Primo said and smiled.

"Yes, they do." I smiled.

"Guys everyone arrived at the Police Station." Sonia said.

The Police Officers and everyone else arrived at the Police Station for some questioning. "What do we got?" The Commissioner asked

"Two Psychiatrist and the Judge. All three of them were found dead." Detective Jim responded.

One of the Police Officers brought a file on all three of them and gave it to the Detectives. "Doctor William James. Father of three kids and a wife of forty years. He's been a Psychiatrist for twenty-five years." Jim read and looked at the other file. "Doctor Erin Norton. Mother of five kids and a husband of thirty-four years. She's been a Psychiatrist for twenty-seven years."

"They've been helping out the kids with their problems and the inmates too. They're actually good and I don't know what drove The Dark Cowboy to kill them and they didn't have any enemies." Detective Perla said.

"They had families." Detective Jim said.

They were getting choked up about the killings. "What about the Judge?" The Commissioner asked.

Jim read the other profile. "Judge George Fuentes. Father of three kids and a wife of twenty years. He started out as a Lawyer for a couple of years before becoming a Judge. He was one of the best Judges this city has ever had. He was on his prime of his life and this Dark Cowboy killed them." Detective Jim said.

"You don't actually believe that there is such thing as a Demonic Figure dressed as a Dark Cowboy. Do you?" The Commissioner asked.

"We saw him standing on top of the rooftop of the Judge's house and The Dark Cowboy was laughing at us." Detective Perla responded."

"Three people have now died and they were important to the community. They did everything in their power to help other people. How are we going to stop this thing from killing more people and who knows when he's going to strike." Detective Jim said and looked at everyone.

"Okay, we need to keep our cool. And as for now we need to question the families and the coworkers. We need to move quicker on this one. Is already been bad enough that we're getting criticize by the people and the media. And when they hear about this, they're going to get even more pissed off at us." The Commissioner said.

"Okay. We're going to interrogate the families and the coworkers. And will see how it goes." Detective Jim said.

The storm was starting to calm down and the media was outside the Police Station with angry parents and they were protesting against them. The Police Officers were trying to calm them down and they were explaining the situation to everyone. And the Detectives started to questioned everyone. First things first they started to question the Psychiatrist coworkers. Well it was ten people that worked inside the building, so they plan to question everyone. Even if it took all night.

"How long have you worked there?" Detective Jim asked.

"About three years."

"How did the Psychiatrist treated you?"

"With respect."

"Did they had a lot of patients since you worked there?"

"Yes. They had a lot patients and they did a good job helping them out with their problems."

"Did they had problems with the patients?"

"No. They loved them"

"Did they had enemies outside the office? Maybe a patient that didn't want to get help?" He asked.

"Not, that I'm aware of, I just got back from my honeymoon. I left on September and came back on March."

"What happened when they left the office?"

"They were saying goodbye to everyone. And in about five minutes later we heard gunshots and we all ran outside and we saw The Dark Cowboy standing over their bodies and you know the rest." She started to sob.

Detective Jim told her that she was free to go home and they were interrogating the other eight coworkers and it was the same thing, and they didn't have any enemies and everyone loved them. And finally they called the tenth coworker and it was another female coworker. Detective Perla decided that she wanted to interrogate her.

"How long have you worked there?" She asked.

"Ten years." She responded.

"What can you tell me about the Psychiatrist?"

"They worked very hard. They always talked about their families and how much they love them. Also they were the most kind generous people you will ever meet."

"Did the patients gave them problems?"

"For the last ten years I've seen patients that have thank Doctor William James and Doctor Erin Norton for helping them out. Until there was an incident, and I think it was a couple of months ago on October." She said.

"What happen on October?" She asked.

"They told me that they are going to have another patient. And his parents are very important to this city. Anyway they said that he's a problem child and he was just in court and they were going send him to see a Psychiatrist. They thought he was on drugs or something like that." She said and was trying to remember. "He came in with his mother and she was wearing a uniform."

"What kind of uniform?" She asked.

"A Police uniform. She was too nice to be a Police Officer but her son didn't look that nice and I'm sorry to say that he is so scary looking."

"Do you remember the name of the Police Officer?" She asked.

"I forgot her first name but her last name is de la Vega."

And right there everyone in the other room looked at each other and they were in shock and including us. "What else happened on that night?" Perla asked.

"I don't know they never told anyone what happened during session. Except them, and the kid. The mother always stayed outside."

Detective Perla couldn't believe what was happening and she was excuse to go home. But all of us were looking at each other and Primo's mother went to the other room and they started talking.

"We have something now." The Commissioner said.

"What her son is mentally retarded. So, she took him to get help." Detective Perla said.

"I know you and Officer de la Vega are best friends but we need to questioned her too and we need to question Mrs. Fuentes and tomorrow morning will talk to his colleagues." The Commissioner ordered everyone. Detective Perla decided that she is going to interrogate Mrs. Fuentes. She was still in shock and sat down.

"How long have you and your husband have been together?" She asked.

"Since we were kids. We grew up together"

"Did he had enemies while you guys were growing up?"

"No. He got along with everyone."

"What about when he became a Judge. You think an ex convict might want him dead?"

"I don't think so. When the verdict was over, my husband always took the prisoners into his chambers and he started talking to them and consulting them and hoped that they get rehabilitated and start their lives over again. My husband always visited the prisons because he believed in second chances." She started to sob and remembered something. "My husband was chosen to be at a school. He told me that there were so many kids that are delinquents. He felt he was trying to help them, so he was the one that was sending the kids to do community service and see the Psychiatrist. But there was a boy that was different from the others."

"How different?" She asked.

"The boy was absent a lot and he was pissed off that he wanted to choke my husband and told him that he was going to kill him."

"Do you know the name of the kid, so we can talk to him?"

"My husband told me about the boy and I couldn't believe that the son of the FBI Agent and a Police Officer was a trouble maker. What was his name?" She was trying to remember. "De la Vega. Mauricio de la Vega. His mom was with him."

Everyone in the other room were in shock and they couldn't believe what was happening that night. The son of Officer de la Vega might be a suspect in this case. Well everyone was looking at me and I was loss for words. So, Mrs. Fuentes was excuse to go home. And yet they were looking at each other and looked at my mother that was doing some paper work.

"So, you think her son is the killer?" She asked.

"I'm not saying that. But we need to question her too and maybe we could be wrong about her son. We need to find out what she knows about those two kids that were killed on the Franklin Mountains and the substitute Teacher and these three." The Commissioner said.

"What about the boy?" Detective Jim asked.

"Will talk to him tomorrow." The Commissioner said.

"And what about City Hall?" Detective Perla asked.

"What about them?" The Commissioner asked.

"They're might be someone there that might wanted him dead. Who knows maybe someone in City Hall might be corrupted." Detective Perla said.

"I know Beatrice de la Vega is your friend since you were kids but we're professionals here. Get her to talk." The Commissioner said.

The Commissioner convinced Detective Perla to interrogate my mother, the great Beatrice de la Vega, but he felt that she wasn't going to get to the bottom line with his investigation. The Commissioner called a couple of Police Officers to tell her that they need to talk to her. All of the other Police Officers were worried for her. My mother was sitting down in the interrogation room and waited and wondered why is she's been investigated. The Commissioner picked Detective Jim Nielsen and he agreed to talk to her. Detective Jim Nielsen came into the room with a file and brought her a cup of coffee and he sat down.

"Why am I here?" She asked.

"We found a huge surprise on this investigation." He responded.

"And why am I been interrogated? She asked.

"We talked to the Psychiatrist coworkers and they told us that your son was a patient of theirs. Also Mrs. Fuentes mentioned that your son was about to choke her husband."

"Those stories are lies." She said.

"Is your son violent?" He asked.

"No. He's a good kid but he was problems learning. He has a learning disability, he just needs help." She said.

"We understand and you told us that before. But I want to start from the beginning. How does your son act around the house?"

"He talks a lot and he wants to go to college." She responded.

"How about at school. Do you have problems with him at school?"

"The Teachers have told me that he's a good kid but he has problems learning and among other things."

He looked at her and smiled. "What about those two kids that were murdered in the Franklin Mountains. Did he get along with them?"

"Yes!"

"You said that your son is not violent. Then why were those kids hurt in the playground?" He asked.

"It was an accident and we all know that." She said.

"The kids say that Mauricio pushed Armando out of the playground bus and fell on the ground. He was just lucky that his arm wasn't broken in three places but he had a sling on his hand and your son didn't apologize to him at all."

"Yes, he was lucky that his arm want broken but those kids are lying."

"Then you have the girl, Deyna. She was playing with her friends on the playground bus until Mauricio decides to play rough with her. And he decided to push her and she falls down and hits her head and she was lucky that she didn't die or had a concussion."

"Those stories are lies!" She yelled.

"A couple of years later they are found dead in the Franklin Mountains. Your son wasn't there." He said.

"He had the flue. That's why he couldn't go." She said.

"Also the kids say that Mauricio hated the substitute Teacher. What kind of lies did she say about Mauricio?"

"That I don't know but he liked her."

"But as you say he's different from everybody and she ignored him and that's why she was found dead." He said.

"My son didn't do it." She said

"Then you have Doctor William James and Doctor Erin Norton that wanted to help your son, Mauricio. He had an argument with them and boom they are found dead. Judge George Fuentes wanted to help your son and he's found dead. What can you tell me about that?"

"That there's a serial killer on the loose and my son is innocent!" She yelled.

"Don't you lie to me!" He yelled

The Commissioner barged inside the room and yelled at him. "That's enough, Detective Jim Nielsen!"

"My son is innocent!" She yelled.

"Cool it!" And the Commissioner ordered Detective Jim Nielsen to leave the room and he took my mother to his office.

"I told you my son is innocent. What we saw on the rooftop wasn't my son. It was some psychotic killer dress as a Dark Cowboy." She said.

"We understand but we need to talk to your son. Maybe he can help us with this case, and you said that your son is a shy kid and he knew them." He said.

"All your going to do is scare him." She said.

"Beatrice, your son's friend's are dead. The Teacher that he liked is dead, the Psychiatrist that wanted to help him were found dead. The Judge also wanted to help your son is also dead. Perhaps someone wants to see your son suffer and you never know that this Dark Cowboy is threatened to kill your son if he talks. We can protect him, Beatrice. Bring him here to the Police Station and he might know something." He said.

"No. I'm his mother it's my job to protect my kids. I rather take a leave of absence and protect my son and my family." She said.

"Beatrice!"

"He's my son and I will protect him even if I have to kill this Dark Cowboy myself. End of story, Commissioner."

The Commissioner couldn't convince my mother and all he could do is respect her decision. That night before everyone was going to go home, the Commissioner gave an order that they should investigate City Hall just like Detective Perla requested. And everyone was staring at me

Then Chris was yelling at me, "You are a suspect and a witness in this case, Mauricio!"

"Really?" I asked in a sarcastic way.

"Yes! You do realize that you are a suspect in this case and they are accusing you of all the killings!" He said.

"I know and you worry too much. And I earned one hundred and fifty dollars in my bank account."

"You are right, Mauricio. Tomorrow morning I'm going to deposit one hundred fifty dollars in the bank." He said.

"Now we need to chill out because I have a feeling that I might need your help by tomorrow. I will tell you who I have targeted."

"That's fine with me. But I want you to realize that you might be questioned sooner or later. And there is going to be a chance that the Federal Bureau Investigation is going to take over this investigation and your dad is going to throw everything at you and everyone will know that you are the one that's killing people!" He yelled.

"Guys, the Commissioner gave me a huge idea. He told my mom that someone is threatened to kill me if I talk and why not use that for an advantage. This is not over and we're not going to aboard this mission." I said and looked at everyone.

"Mauricio, is right we're not going to aboard the mission. So, Chris we're not giving up and if the great Pablo de la Vega decides to come well bring it and we will be ready for him." Primo said and smiled.

Chris looked at us and smiled and we hugged each other and after that we went home. The next day at seven o'clock in the morning, I grabbed the radio and was listening when the Police Officers marched into City Hall and asked everyone about Judge George Fuentes. And it was the same story as last night that everyone liked him and he will be missed forever. And on that morning there was more protestors in front of the Police Station. The Mayor of El Paso was watching the news in his office and saw the protestors in front of the Police Station and at City Hall. He started looking at the profile of the people that have died within the past couple of years. Six of them have died in a brutal way by the psychotic killer known as The Dark Cowboy. The Mayor was devastated and he was willing to stop The Dark Cowboy from killing anyone else and he was going to take a stand. Then on that morning the Mayor held a public press conference in front of City Hall, half of the people went and the other half saw it on the television. Everyone wanted to know what the Hell he was going to say in front everyone. And also the media was taking pictures and they were planning to ask the Mayor a lot questions.

But they made it clear to the press that the Mayor wasn't going to answer the media's questions. The Police Officers were securing the whole area just in case if The Dark Cowboy decided to appear or some crazy lunatic that might want of kill the Mayor in front of everyone and make a name for themselves. Finally in about twenty minutes later the Mayor came out and the media started taking pictures and as always they couldn't resist. The media started asking the Mayor a lot of questions but he ignored them.

"Ladies and gentlemen thank you for been here." The Mayor smiled and everyone started clapping and the media was taking more pictures. "We are living in tough times and for the past couple of years there's been a serious of murders. Six people have now died in a brutal way, they didn't have to die that way, and they were in their prime of their lives." The Mayor said and started drinking water. "The people elected me in the year 1995 and this my fourth year as your Mayor of El Paso, Texas. As I enter my fourth year as your Mayor and I don't know if I'm going to get reelected. This may be the last time I might be able to talk to the citizens of El Paso, Texas. Reelected or not elected, I came to the decision that I wasn't going to let the people down anymore, I'm planning to fight and to stop The Dark Cowboy from doing anymore crimes." He said and the people were wondering what he meant by that. "The first thing I plan to do is that starting today, I'm going to order a six o'clock curfew and no one is allowed to go outside during the night. The second thing is I'm going to take away all the second shifts from all the working places. And what does that mean? I want all the people that have second shifts to work directly from their homes and we will give you all the supplies that you need to work from home and to make you comfortable in your home. All the business will be closed at six o'clock. The third thing is that all the sports and outdoor activities will be canceled for now. And I want to clarify about the outdoor activities. No one cannot go to the mountains, camping, riding your bicycle, going to the park, and going swimming. No one is allowed to leave this city or enter the city. I want everyone to work with me on this one." The media kept on asking questions. "For the past couple of years I've been working with the Commissioner and the Police Officers with the investigation. I'll admit to you that we have failed to protect you from The Dark Cowboy. And the fourth thing is that I'm going to bring more reinforcements to help our Police Officers. So, everyone in the Police Department and I don't care what division they are in, they are going to come out and help out too. I've contacted the Border Patrol Agents and they agreed to help us out. I made a call to the Sheriff Department and they're going to help us out. I had a call last night and it was directly from the Federal Bureau Investigation and they offer to help us out. I want all the citizens of El Paso, Texas to be safe. We have all the help we can get and we hope to capture The Dark Cowboy and bring him to justice and we can live our lives in peace once more for old times. Thank you so much!" The Mayor smiled and left into his office. But the media kept on asking questions and taking pictures.

    The Mayor went to his office and had a drink. And the Commissioner came into the room and sat down. "That's your way of explaining the situation to everyone, that we have failed to protect them."

    "I did everything I could to save this city." He said.

"You don't care about this city, and all you care about is getting reelected and live the good life." The Commissioner said.

"Come on, John. Have a drink." He said.

"Matthew! You said that we are worse than the Los Angeles Police Department. Is not our fault that were dealing with a so called Demonic Figure." John said.

"The difference is that the Police from Los Angeles are not very good because of the violence they have over there. And half of them are corrupted and the other half could care less about people dying on the streets and here we are worse because we can't catch this "serial killer." Matthew said.

"How are we going to catch this serial killer?" John asked.

"Set up traps. Maybe you know something or someone that can help us catch this Dark Cowboy." Matthew said.

"I might know someone."

"Who?" Matthew asked.

"Mauricio de la Vega." He responded.

"Jesus Christ! Are you talking about the son of Police Officer Beatrice de la Vega and FBI Agent Pablo de la Vega? What makes you think that their son, Mauricio, might be involve in this case?" He asked.

"Because the two kids that died in the Franklin Mountains were his friends. He liked that substitute Teacher. Also those two Psychiatrist wanted to help him out and the Judge also wanted to help him. What do they have in common?

"They were murdered by The Dark Cowboy."

"Yes. We offered to help Mauricio and I was planning to ask him a lot of questions. But Beatrice didn't want too, and she didn't want to put her son in danger. Maybe you should talk to her and convince her."

"I can talk to her and I can put him in the witness protection program and we can ask him a lot of couple questions. Is that simple." Matthew said.

"Yes, it is." He said and smiled. "Now what can you tell me about the reinforcements?"

"Like I said, we need all the help we can get. We have the manpower to stop The Dark Cowboy." He said.

So, things were going to get a little bit more interesting around here and I was still in bed. And I went to the restroom and was drinking water. And I went back to bed and turned on the television and I was watching the news.

The anchorman was saying that last night the Two psychiatrist and a Judge were found dead. They were brutally murdered by The Dark Cowboy and that's how they were calling the serial killer that's still on the loose in the city. And I heard the front door open and my mother came into the room and saw me watching the news. "You had to find out by the news."

"I remember that they tried to help me. I cannot believe they were found dead." I said and was sad.

"I'm sorry, Honey." My mother said and hugged me.

"What time is it?" I asked.

"One o'clock in the afternoon." She said.

"I'm going to stay in my room and you know gather my thoughts." I said and my mother left to the kitchen to make lunch. So, during the evening I was in my room and was watching movies and I heard the doorbell ring. And I turn on the radio and I was listening to my mother's conversation.

"Mr. Mayor. What a pleasant surprise. Please come in." She smiled and they went to the living room and sat down. "So, what seams to be the occasion?"

"I wanted to talk to you about your son, Mauricio. I was looking at the Police report and I found something very interesting. I know your son has been suffering a lot the past couple of years. We all are."

"Yes. I'm more worried for him." She said.

"I wanted to ask you if we can help you and your son. I understand that this Dark Cowboy wants to hurt your son in a bad way. We can offer the witness protection program. No one cannot find him and we can protect him."

"I'm his mother it's my job to protect my kids. And I'm willing to put my life on the line for my son and daughter." She said and started sobbing.

"I know you're a mother and a loving mother and I know you will do everything in your power to protect your son and your daughter. But when it comes to your son you're not a Police Officer anymore. You're just a mother and you can be the greatest mother in the world but you heard stories of this psychotic killer. And tell me what do you think is going to happen when you kill The Dark Cowboy. You will end up in jail."

"I'll risk my life for my son and my daughter. I don't care what happens to me." She said.

"What about your kids? Where do you think they will end up? Think about your kids, Beatrice. Do it for them." He said.

"If I say yes, I'll go where my son goes." She said.

"I want you to think about it before you can make your toughest decision. Here's my card and call me." He said.

My mother walked the Mayor to the front door and said goodbye to him. She sat down on the kitchen and I heard my mother cry all night long. But I was proud of what I did to our enemies and I figured that sooner or later that I will be a wanted man and I figure that they might throw a huge reward on me. And I wanted to piss off a lot of people and I heard the news. They were talking about, how are they plan to stop me. So, all I could say to the Police Department and the FBI, is bring it on you sons of bitches and try to stop me from killing!

CHAPTER EIGHT

MY MOTHER'S BLESSING

The very next day the reinforcement arrived in El Paso, Texas and the Mayor and his staff welcomed them and gave them instructions on what to do in the city for later on in the night. Also on that morning my mother was making breakfast for us kids until a black van pulled into the driveway of our house. We opened the front door and the great FBI Agent de la Vega, got out of the black van, and he is my loving father. And we looked at each other and we hugged for a long time. After we finished hugging we went inside the house and sat down in the living room for a couple of hours. My father started telling us about the adventures he was having from all over the world and we were excited to hear his adventures in Europe and the Middle East. So, we spent the whole morning together and then my father took all of us to eat at *Chico's Tacos*. And that's where my mother broke the news to my father and she was telling him what the Mayor and the Commissioner had told her the other day. Well my father didn't liked the idea of getting me involve in the case and it would be way too dangerous for his beloved son. So, my father told my mother not to worry and he will talk to the Mayor and to the Commissioner of the Police Department. We finished eating and our parents took us to school. I started listening to what they were saying and later on in the afternoon my father decided to go to City Hall.

"Mr. Mayor. Agent de la Vega is here to talk to you."

"Oh, good bring Agent de la Vega in!" The Mayor smiled and my father came into the room and didn't look too happy with him. "Come in! Agent de la Vega. Make yourself comfortable. You want something to drink?"

"No, thank you. I came here to talk to you about something." My father responded.

"Ah, your wife told you about my plan. So, what do you think about my plan? We're going to have your son in the witness protection program!" The Mayor smiled.

My father responded, "Well Mr. Mayor. I think your plans sucks and it's not going to work at all. And there's no way in Hell that I'm going let my son get involve in this case. I won't allow it."

"I know you love your son and you don't want anything bad happening to him. But we're doing an investigation here. All we're going to do is ask him questions and he will be very well protected. Is that simple, Agent de la Vega. You can trust me!"

"We know every trick in the book, Mr. Mayor. That's not going to work on us. There's ninety percent that your plan is not going to work!" My father exclaimed.

The Mayor smiled and said. "Well I hope your team is ready for later on tonight. As the matter of fact I'm going to put you in charge of this operation because you are the best there is. I'm giving you my vote of confidence. Also I'm going to stay here and help you guys in anyway I can!"

"Well my team is ready for tonight and I thank you for putting me in charge of this operation. I wont let you down! As the matter of fact we're also going to keep you company. Just to make sure that The Dark Cowboy won't come after you!" My father looked serious.

Then at three forty-five in the afternoon where my mother dropped me off at Chris's house. They were just talking for awhile and my mother told me that she loves me a lot and she went to work. Chris looked at me and smiled.

"What do you want to eat?" He asked.

"Chris, I want you to call Karina and Cassandra because I'm going to kill two people tonight and that's going to be on tonight's menu and with a Cherry on top." I said and smiled.

"Mauricio, you are going to be the cost of my death. Do you realize that every law enforcement are going to protect the whole city and the people are going to be inside their homes. And not to mention that your dad is in charge of this operation. The Mayor put him in charge." He said and looked worried.

"I know that but I'm going after bigger fish here. And I'm going to need your help, Chris." I said.

"Okay, Mauricio you win. Who are you going to kill?" He asked.

I responded with a huge smile on my face. "The next two victims are going to be the Commissioner of the Police Department and the Mayor of El Paso, Texas."

Chris looked at me and started yelling at me at the top of his lungs. "Are you crazy, Mauricio! Your parents are going to protect the Mayor and who knows where the Commissioner is going to be at!"

"Well I want to risk everything on this mission. Now let's finish this conversation for later on and call Karina and Cassandra." Yeah, they are the disloyal friends that I have to deal with.

Chris had no choice but to accept this mission and he called Karina and Cassandra and he went to pick them up and they came back to the house in about half an hour later. I was sitting down on his couch and they came into the living room. "Let's get to work!" Karina smiled.

"Karina, I want you to stay back on the fort and block the radio calls and telephone calls. Since Sonia has the night off, I want you to listen to their phone calls too. I'm going to find the Commissioner of the Police Department and I also want to hear the conversation at City Hall."

"Well we put a lot of bugs in the city and we are going to hear everything. All Karina has to do is hacked into the bugs. So, we can hear their conversation." Chris smiled.

"And I want you to plant bombs at City Hall." I said.

"Well Mauricio and girls, I created something better than C4." Chris smiled and took out a case and showed it to us and it was two white gloves. "Cassandra this is an energy glove. You can use the Earth's energy and a bright energy beam comes out of the glove and that can destroy everything in sight. This makes the Atomic Bomb and all the bombs there are in the world looked like a school picnic compare with what comes out of the glove." Chris smiled and gave it to her.

Cassandra was putting the gloves. "Can I blow up something?"

"Yes!" Chris smiled and we went to the garage and there was at least thirty boxes on top of each other. "Target practice! And concentrate!"

Cassandra smiled and she put her hand in front of the boxes and was concentrating. Seconds later a large energy beam came out of the glove and destroyed the boxes. She loved the new invention. "Thank you, Chris!"

"Can you believe that the President of the United States didn't approve of this invention. Because it may be too dangerous for us to use it!" Chris said.

"Well these are cool!" Cassandra smiled and we went back to the living room.

Karina started hacking into the system at City Hall and we started hearing everything that went on that night. So, my father gathered all the troops in front of City Hall and my father and the Mayor wished everyone luck and to be safe on the streets and everyone went to their post. And for five hours straight, the reinforcement were standing guard in the entire city and they were waiting for me to come out and kill people. And back in City Hall where the Mayor was still in his office and Police Officers and FBI Agents were circulating the whole building. Then at nine o'clock that night everyone decided to eat something and luckily the Mayor ask a couple of people that worked in restaurants to come in at night and serve them food. Even they delivered the food wherever they we at and he was going to pay them a lot of money. And bonus if a Police Officer escorts them there.

The Mayor and company were also hungry and called for take out and one of the Police Officers brought them food. But no one at City Hall wanted to abandoned their post, so they ate wherever they standing at. There were a lot of Police Officers and FBI Agents that were in charged to secure the Mayor. And one of them was my mother, the great Beatrice de la Vega and my father, the great Pablo de la Vega. So, my mother called us every thirty minutes to see if we were doing okay. And everyone at City Hall started eating and talking to each other and some were resting. My parents haven't seen each other in more than two years. My father was telling my mother that he went to Italy, China, and the Middle East to capture terrorist and mobsters. My mother was happy to hear his adventures. But my father has yet to capture Vito Mancini.

"What about you, Honey?" He asked.

"Just working and taking care of our kids." She responded.

"You look sad." He said.

"It's been lonely without you. I missed you a lot." She said and smiled.

"Me too. I think about you everyday. I love you a lot." He said.

Chris looked at me and said, "Your parents really love each other."

"I know they do and I want to put their marriage to the test and let's see if my dad can fix the mistakes that he's about to make." I said and smiled.

My parents stayed together and they were talking and laughing and it felt that it was another date for them and they were happy to be together and it felt just like old times. And it was around midnight and there was no sign of The Dark Cowboy. Everyone in the city were getting exhausted and they were getting ready to fall asleep on the ground. There were at least six law enforcement standing post from all over the city and they agreed that one should stand guard while the others rested or fall asleep. That's how it was for the past couple of hours. Everyone was asleep while one was guarding everything.

I looked at Karina and said, "Karina find out where the Commissioner is at."

Karina smiled and was looking for him. "Ten minutes ago your dad made contact with him and right now the Commissioner is at Central El Paso and they're actually eating at *Chico's Tacos*."

"I know where they are. And now let's get ready." I smiled and I went to the restroom and changed. I also started loading my guns and I was ready to go and find him. All of us went outside and Karina brought her radio and she was hearing everything while she walked us outside. Chris gave me the walkie-talkie, so we can communicate with each other.

"Good luck!" Karina said and smiled.

Cassandra and Chris got on the truck and drove off and I took off to find the Commissioner of the Police Department. On the way there I was hearing everything in City Hall and I was glad that my parents were together and having fun. And in about fifteen minutes later I finally arrived at Central El Paso and I was hiding in the shadows. I noticed that every Police Officer and FBI Agents were resting in their cars and I know they were sleeping because I heard them snoring from where I was hiding. I even saw the Commissioner and he was standing in front of his car and he was still eating and he was talking to someone on his cell phone. He started smoking a cigarette and started looking up at the stars and I took out my dart gun and I steadied it and shot him in the back and he fell to the ground. Very slowly I walked up to him and I grabbed his hair and dragged him behind the restaurant. I sat him down and he was leaning against the wall.

And I had a flashback. I heard the voice of the Commissioner talking to someone. "I cannot believe that Beatrice de la Vega is working in our department. Most Police Officers are worried because she's actually good and making them feel bad in front of everybody. But I'm happy because she's going to take criminals right out the streets."

And I heard another voice. "With her reputation she can be promoted to Lieutenant and maybe even higher."

And the Commissioner asked, "How high?"

"If a couple of Police Officers die on the job and not to mention a Detective, Captain, and you."

"No matter what happens she's going to be something special in this department." The Commissioner said.

"And on a personal note! We have been trying to tell Eliza to stay away from Mauricio!"

"I told her the same thing but she doesn't want to listen to anybody!" The Commissioner said.

Well it looks to me if the Commissioner gets killed, they will promoted my mommy with a higher rank on the Police Force. And I'm actually going to help her move up the ranks and I'm no longer going to be on the suspect list by this punk. Not to mention that he wanted Eliza to stay away from me. And I finally got on my knees and I took off my hat and I wanted him to see my face. He looked at me with fear but I smiled. "Well, good evening Commissioner John Hancock. I haven't seen you in a while and I know you are beginning to wonder why I chose to kill you. I will tell you why I want to kill you so badly. I know everything about you and I know you are a corrupted son of a bitch. You thought that I was the psychotic killer and you were planning to kill me. Yes, you wanted to do that because you wanted to look good in front of your colleagues. And you were hoping that everyone in El Paso would worship you and respect you. I'm sorry to say this but I'm going to kill you. This one time you had me in your suspect in this case but not anymore. Before I kill you I want to know how loving my mother really is and her choice is going to affect our lives forever." I laughed and grabbed his cell phone and dialed City Hall.

Then at City Hall where the Mayor was still awake and was still working very hard and he was falling asleep in his office. My father was still circulating the whole area and found my mother sound asleep on the floor right next to the Mayor's office. My father took off his jacket and gave it to her, so she won't be cold. Then he got on the radio and wanted know how everyone was doing. Well everyone responded to him and they told him that they already ate and went to the restroom, and rested as well. My father went outside and all he could hear was the sound of the crickets. My father was standing there for about twenty minutes and he was enjoying the fresh breeze.

"What do you doing out here, Pablo?" My mother just woke up from her nap and kissed him.

"Getting some fresh air. How was your nap?" He asked.

"Good. Did you get some sleep?" She asked.

"No! I haven't. but I'll rest in the morning and remember I'm in charge, so I cannot fall asleep. I got on the radio and everyone is doing okay but The Dark Cowboy hasn't appeared." He said.

"That's a good sign." She said.

As I was calling them, I overheard the voice of the Mayor, "Agent de la Vega my phone is ringing!"

My parents went running into his office and both of them got on the radio and told everyone at City Hall to watch out because it was an unknown number. My father pushed the speaker and told the Mayor to answer.

"Hello!" The Mayor said and they could someone breathing on the other end of the line. "Hello. Who is this?" The breathing got even louder and spookier and it gave them chills down to their spines. "Hello who is this?"

"It's me." I responded.

"The Dark Cowboy!" The Mayor yelled.

"Yes, that's me. I'm the one that's been doing all the killings lately. Do you know how many people I've killed?" I asked them.

"Six people." The Mayor responded. "Why did you kill them?"

"Because it's fun. Now I know how they felt when they kill people." I said.

"Who?" He asked.

"All the mass murders that have killed people and I know how much fun they were having when they were killing people." I responded and laughed.

"Why are you tormenting us?" He asked.

"I love it. Killing is fun and later on I'm going love it even more. Because I'm going to send those six people some more company. And I already reserve two more graves for two special people and they are going to die tonight." I responded.

My father looked at my mother. "He has already targeted two more people. He's not going to get away with this."

"What's matter, Mr. Mayor. Why so quiet?" He asked.

"We're not going to let you do anymore killings! We are going to find you and arrest you!" The Mayor yelled.

"I don't like it when people raise their voice at me. It makes me angry and it makes me kill even more!" I also yelled and continued to breathe even harder.

"Are you what the people say you are? You know a Demon?" He asked.

"Maybe. Oh, by the way I want to thank the person that gave me that cool nick name "The Dark Cowboy" that's very clever. I never asked to be called that but I like it. But I don't see myself as a Demon but I do see myself as a psychotic serial killer not a Demon. You know how crazy serial killers are?"

"Yes, we know that. And do you work for Primo Mancini?" He asked.

"Primo Mancini works for me and he is my ally and my dear old friend and we work together and right now he has the night off because I wanted to have fun in the city." I growled and laughed. "Oh, by the way I want to say hi to Agent de la Vega and his lovely wife Officer de la Vega."

My parents looked at each other and they couldn't figure out how I knew that they were in the room with him. "How do you know that they are here in my office?" The Mayor asked.

"Because I know everything about them. Agent de la Vega a Super Cop travels all over the world and likes to catch killers like me. And Police Officer Beatrice de la Vega another Super Cop who has been anxious and waiting to arrest me and put me in jail. I also know they have two wonderful children, Tania de la Vega and Mauricio de la Vega. And how's Mauricio been handling the death of his loved ones." I said and started laughing.

My father got a hold of my mother and told her not to say anything. "Why are you doing this to him?" The Mayor asked.

"I no longer wish to talk to you, Mr. Mayor. But I want to talk to the great Beatrice de la Vega. Mauricio's mother." I said.

They couldn't believe what was going. The Mayor wanted my mother to talk but my father didn't want her to talk at all. But she insisted to talk to her son, the serial killer. "Hello! This is Beatrice de la Vega. Talk to me."

"Well, hello, Beatrice. It's nice to meet you and it is nice hear your voice." I said and laughed.

"Well is also nice to hear your voice too." She said.

"That's what I like a simple conversation. You're a better talker than that reject of a Mayor." I growled and I started laughing. "By the way how's your son? Is he still suffering that his friends died?"

"You stupid bastard. So, why are you doing this to my son? He hasn't done anything to you or anyone else. Why are you tormenting him?"

"I hate him because he's a nice boy and everyone loves him. It makes me sick to see him getting the love that he gets everyday from you guys. Every time I look in the mirror, I only see him and I just want to throw up and kill him right on the spot, so I won't have to see him ever again. I hate him!" I yelled.

"Why do you hate him!" She also yelled.

"You don't know your son like I do. Your beloved son did something to me and I won't forgive him ever again. He turn his back on me. As you can say that we have known each other since we were little kids. We made a pact that we will be friends forever and then just like that he just turn his back on me. He left me for dead. That's where I decided and started thinking about how to get my revenge on him. Let's see what can I do to hurt him, oh, that's right by attacking his heart. By killing the people that he's loved over the years." I said and laughed even more.

"You son of!" My mother yelled and her tears started to come down her face. My father wanted my mother to stop talking but she did fought him off. "You won't get away from this, you're not going to hurt my son or my daughter. You are going to get through me first. And I will do everything in my power to protect my son even if I have to kill you myself and spend the rest of my life in jail. As long my kids are safe from you!" My mother continued to yell.

"Beatrice, you are indeed a loving mother but it will be simple. If I wanted to I can go to your friend's house, break the door open and I'll just point the gun at his head and kill him. Piece of cake, Beatrice." I laughed and breathed even more harder and louder. "We can make a deal. You have two choices. I know everyone is going to like it. Since, I like you Beatrice and I wish I had a loving mother like you that can love me no matter what and accept me as a psychotic killer. And I will make you promise, Beatrice, that I'm not going to hunt down Mauricio and smash your door and kill him in your lovely home. How about you bring your son, Mauricio, to me and I can kill him and all the citizens of El Paso, Texas will be alive and live a normal life like nothing bad happen. It will be like the Garden of Eden a peaceful city. I won't come back ever again." I said and laughed. " But the second choice is if you don't bring me, Mauricio, then I will be forced to kill two more people tonight and kill more people forever. So, what do you say Beatrice the ball is in your court."

Everyone was staring at my loving mother and her choice will affect her life and everyone's life of course. It took her a minute to think about it while everyone waited for her tough decision. "I came to the decision." My mother's tears started to come down her face and yelled out. "Fuck you! I'm keeping my son! I don't care how many people you kill just as long is not my son and my daughter! Do whatever the Hell you want in the city! I don't care what you do!" She started sobbing and looked at the Mayor and at my father and said. "Please forgive me."

"It's your call, Beatrice de la Vega." And I looked at the Commissioner and he wanted to cry. "My mother loves me so much that she gave me permission to kill more people for the rest of my life." And I pointed the guns at his head and I shot him so many times and the gunshots were heard on the speaker. They were wondering who was the one that died tonight and then I got back on the phone and said, "Hi, Beatrice and remember I told you about the two graves that I have reserve for tonight. Well it was the reserve for the Commissioner of the Police Department, he's now dead and it was execution style just like the next victim. And the Mayor is next on the hit list. And I forgot to mention that the reason I wanted to kill the Commissioner and the Mayor is that they wanted to help your son, Mauricio, and put him in the witness protection program. Well Beatrice I'm sorry to say but I'm going to continue to torture your son and by killing everyone that he loves and everyone that wants to help him. Oh, and by the way you should protect the Mayor of El Paso, Texas because I will be there very shortly." I laughed and hanged up the phone. I threw the phone on the sidewalk. Once again my heart was beeping fast and everything was going slow motion. I turn around and I saw the same black car parked down the street. And I heard the voice of Sonia. "Mauricio just shot the Commissioner!"

"Record it everything for evidence!" Karina exclaimed.

What the Hell are these two bitches talking about. I cannot believe that they were doing their own mission. Curse them to Hell. And she turn on the engine and drove off and I was hearing the Police Officers and FBI Agents moving around the area and I ran away into the darkness and went straight to City Hall.

On my way to City Hall, I was hearing everything that went on. My loving mother couldn't believe that the Commissioner of the Police Department was murdered that night. And my mother got on her knees and started crying her eyes out. "Get up we need to protect the, Mayor!" My father yelled.

My mother was on her knees crying and she knew that a lot of people were going to die because of her tough decision. "It's my fault!" She sobbed.

My father got on the horn and called for more back up and everyone that was inside the building went to protect the Mayor. There were at least thirty-four law enforcement protecting the Mayor and that was not enough. My father called for more back up but everyone were half an hour away, and he felt that they would arrive way too late. Then someone radioed my father. "Come in, Agent de la Vega!" One of the Police Officers said.

"This is, Agent de la Vega, over."

"We have a problem, Sir. The Commissioner of the Police Department has been murdered by The Dark Cowboy."

"We already know that. The Dark Cowboy already told us. The Mayor is next on his hit list and I want everyone to abandon their post and come to City Hall. We need all the help we can get."

"We will be there, Sir."

Everyone was sticking together and they were trying to protect the Mayor while my loving mother was still on her knees and she was crying her eyes out. They were telling her to get up. "Beatrice, get up we need to protect the Mayor!" My father exclaimed.

"It's my fault." She continued to sob.

"Officer de la Vega get up! That's an order!" My father was yelling at her to get up. "Officer get up!" He yelled at her and grabbed her and was trying to knock some sense into her. "I'm going to suspend you from the Police Department! Do you understand!" He continued to yell.

While he was yelling at her, well Karina was doing her thing and made all the lights go off and all of them took out their flashlights. All they could hear is my loving mother sobbing and finally my father slapped her as hard he could and that might have knock some sense into her. "It's not your fault. You didn't kill the Commissioner, you did your job as a mother. You wanted to protect your son from that psychotic killer but we need to protect the Mayor. Now, I'm ordering you to protect the Mayor!" My father ordered her and slap her again.

And finally my mother took out her gun and was angry with The Dark Cowboy. "We should take the Mayor into his office." One of the Agents said.

"No! That's what he wants us to do!" My mother said angrily and she was so pissed off.

They were waiting for backup to arrive and once again my father got on the radio and was calling for back up. And there was no answer. Then I threw a smoke bomb in the hallway and everyone started coughing. My mother and my father held their breathe while everyone was coughing and they fell to the ground. My parents felt that they couldn't protect the Mayor in a smoky hallway. So, they grabbed the Mayor and took him to a safer place just then one of the offices exploded and even knocked the great Pablo de la Vega out and he was down for the count. It was up to my mother to protect the Mayor. "Get up!" My mother yelled and she also got on the radio and was calling for back up and still there was no answer.

They went inside in one of the offices when all of the sudden I appeared before them. I was standing behind them and finally my mother looked at me and she was scared to see me. They saw my red evil eyes and I was laughing at them and she pointed the gun at my head. And I grabbed her hand so tight that the gun fell to the ground. And very quickly I got her handcuffs and handcuffed her to the desk. My mother was screaming for help but I knocked her out, and the Mayor was still standing there and he was scare for his life and I punched him in the face and he fell to the ground. I took out the dart gun and shot him in the back of his spinal cord. I went up to him and flip him over.

I had another flashback. "Well, John I've been impressed with Beatrice's work. She's a tough Police Officer. And I was thinking of promoting her to Commissioner and you can take my place as the Mayor. Besides you have done a good job."

"I know but on a personal note. We have been trying to convince Eliza to stay away from Mauricio and she doesn't want to."

"I told her the same thing. If she doesn't want to listen to us well maybe she's going to have to see it for herself. And she's going to realize that Mauricio is very dangerous."

So, these two knew Eliza and they want to promote my mommy to Commissioner of the Police Department. Well there wish is going to come true. And I finally got on my knees and took my hat off and he saw my face and I was laughing at him. "Hello, Mayor Matthew Sheppard. You are beginning to wonder why I want to kill you. You see! You have done so many awful things in your life and now ugly things as the Mayor of this peaceful city. And I'm not going to let you be naughty anymore and I know you are corrupted and you will pay for your actions. And don't be afraid, Matthew, because you are going to see your best friend the Commissioner very soon and tell him that I said hi when you see him in Hell. And a little personal note and I know you work for Vito

Mancini and that's not good either." I growled and started loading my guns and started shooting at him so many times. I put my hat on and my mother was just waking up and she saw the Mayor getting murdered right in front her.

"No!" My mother yelled. "Help. Somebody help us!" My mother continued to yell and I turned my attention to my loving mother and started laughing at her. It was a satanic laughter. "You bastard! Someday I'm going to kill you!"

"We will see each other soon!" I said and laughed.

I left the office and my mother started crying and screaming and then my father was getting up and he heard my mother screaming. My father took out his gun and went to the direction of my mother's screams. I was standing in the middle of the street and my father open the door and we saw each other. I said goodbye to him and winked at him and jumped into the darkness. Chris also started the engine and also went home. And that's where I was hearing Karina's conversation with Sonia. "What do you think it's going to happen now?" Sonia asked.

"I don't know but I have a feeling that somewhere down the road. Mauricio's mom and Primo's mom are going to get promoted. And I cannot believe that Mauricio is doing this just for kicks. He's helping out his mom move up the ranks." Karina responded.

"I don't think he's doing this just for kicks. He's doing this because they worked for the mob." Sonia said.

"Don't think, Sonia! There's got more to the story. And we're going to find out!" Karina said.

And on the way home I heard everything that was happening at City Hall, I was still hearing my mother screaming at the top of her lungs. My father open the door and the Mayor was already dead and my mother was handcuffed to the desk. She was still crying and screaming. My father got the keys and took the handcuffs away and she was hugging him very tight. "The Mayor is dead! I'm sorry, Pablo, I have failed as a Police Officer." She sobbed and hugged him tight.

"You did your job, Beatrice, but I guess it wasn't enough to stop that psychotic killer from killing the Mayor." He said.

"Now there's eight people that have died and all were trying to help and befriend our son, Mauricio." She sobbed and asked him. "What are we going to do?"

"I don't know, Honey." My father said and the smoke in the hallway finally cleared and they radioed my father. And everyone went to the room and found the Mayor dead. "We were too late." My father said and he also got on the radio and was calling everyone in the city. "We have bad news, the Mayor and the Commissioner are dead." He said.

We finally arrived at the house, and I went to the restroom and changed and we started celebrating and hugging each other. "Mission accomplished!" Karina smiled.

"Hold on. This is not over!" I said.

"You really done it, Mauricio. I'm proud of you and I know you did what you had to do but your mom is a tough Police Officer." Chris said.

"Chris take the girls back to their house and we will see each other tomorrow." I said and hugged them and kissed the girls in the cheek. So, Chris took the girls home while I stayed and I heard the Police sirens on the radio. Six Police cars pulled into the parking lot of City Hall and they came running into City Hall. Well everyone went outside to greet them and they were too late. "The Mayor is also dead." He said.

"Are you kidding me?" One of the Police Officers ask.

"I was calling for back up and there was no answer. I guess The Dark Cowboy must have block it out." He said.

"Call the ambulance."

"And call the Firefighters." One of the Agent said.

They were waiting for half an hour and the cavalry just arrived at City Hall. They saw my father's reaction when they arrived way too late. My father gave them a bad look and he was so pissed off. "Send someone to the Commissioner's family and the Mayor's. And take them to the Morgue and in the morning and we will let the families see their bodies. And go home and get some rest and at eight in the morning will meet at the Police Station. We're going to have a meeting before we go public." My father said.

Everyone agreed to go home and call it a night. They went home and told their families that they have failed that night. The Police Officers and FBI Agents told the families of the Mayor and Commissioner that they were murdered by The Dark Cowboy and they were crying their eyes out. My parents went to pick us up and they didn't want us to sleep alone, so they took us to their room and we fell asleep together like one big happy family. I saw my parents reaction and I knew they had a rough night dealing with me and so much for two Super Cops.

CHAPTER NINE

THREE NIGHTS OF HELL

The next day I woke up and I couldn't believe that it was Monday morning. I was getting ready for school after I got dressed. I went down to the kitchen and my mother was making me breakfast and I saw the bump on her head. All my mother could do is smile and she kissed me on my forehead. My mother served me eggs and we sat down and started eating and we had a great conversation on that morning, and it was better than the night before we talked on the phone. My mother and I finished eating our breakfast and I told my mother that I was going to take the bus. I grabbed my backpack and my mother gave me a huge hug and she told me that loves me a lot. I told her that I also loved her so much. And I felt that she loved me no matter what. Even if I'm the psychotic killer known as The Dark Cowboy.

My mother was also getting ready to go to work, so I walked my mother to her car and saw her leave and I went to catch the bus. Karina was already waiting for the bus and we were the only ones there. We waited for ten minutes and the damn bus has yet to show up until Chris came by and he offered to give us a ride. Karina and I hopped into his truck and we were happy to see him again. On the way to school we didn't talk but I wanted to have a conversation.

"So, are you impressed with my killings?" I asked him and smiled.

Chris looked at me and smiled "Yes, I am, Mauricio, and as the matter of fact I'm proud of you guys. And Mauricio actually took out the two top dogs in this city. Now one hundred dollars will be added in your account and of course everyone is going to have more money in their accounts."

"I just hope that Mauricio is no longer a suspect in this case." Karina said.

"Before I forget. I want to kill more people before the week finishes." I smiled.

Chris and Karina looked worried and they were afraid to ask. "Okay, Mauricio de la Vega. How many people do you want to kill?" Chris asked.

"Well I was thinking a couple of people like ten and I want to kill all of them by the end of the week. And we will start on Friday."

"Are you crazy?" He asked.

"Yes, I am. Now we need plan everything." I smiled.

"Well how about on Friday morning will have a ditch party. And we all go to your house and strategize everything." Karina said and smiled.

"That sounds like a good plan.' Chris gave us a grin and we arrived at school and we said goodbye to him and went into the school. During the morning hours I was wondering what Karina and the girls were up too. Well I'm keeping my eye on them. So, during class I had my radio with me and we were hearing everything that was going on while the Teachers were giving us work.

And on that morning the Police and the FBI brought the loved ones of the Mayor and the Commissioner to the Morgue to identify their bodies. Everyone were offering their regards to their families. But the families knew that they did everything in their power to protect them on that night. Also on that day half of the people of El Paso were so upset with the Police Officers and with the FBI and they started putting a mob together and started protesting in front of the Police Station.

My father decided to close City Hall and they were planning to remodel the whole building because of the explosion and the bullets holes and of course the blood of the beloved Mayor of El Paso, Texas. Also there were rumors going around the city that they started comparing us to Detroit, Michigan and we she should be honored for it because that's how bad it was getting around here. And it was courtesy of the gang and myself. Then at lunchtime I called Chris and told him to pick me up from school, so we can spy on my parents and their team. Then the bell rang at thirty forty-five and it was time to go home. Chris was waiting for us in the parking lot and we hopped into the truck and went to his house. Chris already had lunch for us and we started eating together and we were listening to everything that went on.

So, the gang started doing their homework and we kept on listening to the conversations on the radio. And it was around five o'clock in the afternoon where my father gathered everyone at the Police Station. They were planning to stay there for the rest of the night if they have too. So, my dear sweet old father was standing in front of them and everyone was looking at him and they were wondering what he was going to say. "Okay! I believe that we all have some explaining to do about last night!" My father exclaimed and looked at everyone. "I want to know is why you didn't responded when I radioed you!" He yelled and kicked the chair. "I'm waiting!"

One of the Border Patrol Agents stood up and said. "Sir, we waited for your orders and we didn't hear from you and we all thought that everything went okay last night."

"That's right, Agent de la Vega. We finally heard from you when you told us that the Commissioner and the Mayor were killed. Perhaps The Dark Cowboy was able to use his power to block the CB radio sequence."

"The Dark Cowboy is not a Wizard or the Devil. He's a crazy psychotic serial killer that's toying with us and he is doing a pretty job messing around with us!" My father exclaimed and sat down and looked at everyone. "Last night we failed to protect the Commissioner and the Mayor."

"Thanks to Officer de la Vega's decision. You should have done the right thing and gave him your son. The Dark Cowboy promised as soon he was going to kill your son, he wasn't going to come back ever again. And now he killed the Mayor and the Commissioner and who knows whose going to be next on the hit list." One of the Agents said.

"Do me a favor, shut up and we will never know if The Dark Cowboy would stick to his word!" My father yelled and was walking back and forth while everyone was staring at him. "Mayor Matthew Sheppard put me in charge of this operation and damn it I will not let him down. We will do everything in our power to stop The Dark Cowboy from killing ever again! Our top priority is The Dark Cowboy and that's it. I don't want to hear people getting beat up on the streets, people that have been abducted in their owns homes, and girls getting rape. The Dark Cowboy is our top priority. And I don't care if we have to spend the night in the streets or in the offices. I don't care if you get divorced or I get divorce. We will work together and catch this serial killer!" He addressed everyone in the room.

Well I got a kick out of it and I loved my father's speech. I was planning to congratulate on his famous speech. So, I picked up the phone and started dialing the Police Station and suddenly the phone rang and one of the Police Officers put the phone on the speaker. "Who is it?" One of the Police Officers asked.

They heard someone laughing at the other end of the line and I said. "Bravo! Bravo!" I could tell that they were having chills down their spines when they heard my evil voice. "Your speech was incredible, Agent de la Vega. And I have tears coming down my face and my red eyes are getting watery."

"What do you want now?" My father asked.

"I admire you, Agent de la Vega. See I have respect for authority. I want to know is how are you going to stop me from killing innocent people. I hear and see everything that goes on in this city. You cannot stop me, no one cannot stop me. I'm unstoppable, immortal, a legend. That's it, I want to become a legend, and I want to be known as the world's greatest serial killer of all time." I said and laughed. "You're also a legend Agent de la Vega. You've arrested and killed so many killers like me, you're a Super Cop."

My father responded, "I've seen serial killers like you. You make a wrong move and boom you'll be arrested or get killed right on the spot. I'm not proud of killing them, I'm more proud of them rotting in prison just like you are going to. I'm also a legend and as far your so call "legacy" goes, it will be cut short. No one will ever remember who you are, you'll become old news. All of us will live our lives in peace."

I laughed and breathed even harder. "You are impressive, Agent de la Vega. I'm going to have fun with you. You may be a Super Cop but Super Cops also have weakness. I will like to see your reaction when you find out that ten innocent people are going to be dead by the end of the week."

"You wouldn't." He looked at everyone and he was angry.

"Ten people are going to die before the week finishes and I guarantee that ten people will die and there is nothing you can do about it. You might want to have the Ambulance and the Firefighters on call just in case you see a fire on the neighborhood and a dead body laying around the street. Let my legacy begin, bye." I laughed and hang up the phone. Everyone saw me laughing and they were staring at me.

Everyone in the Police Station couldn't believe that I made a promise that I was going to kill more people by the end of the week. And then my father threw the phone to the wall and started kicking the chairs and he started cursing me all the way to Hell. "The Dark Cowboy is not going to get away with this!" My father yelled at everyone and said "I want everyone to guard every house in the city and I want you to be inside with the people and protect them and if The Dark Cowboy tries to break in. I want you to kill The Dark Cowboy! Is that clear!" My father yelled.

"Yes, Agent de la Vega." Everyone said.

And on that night my father pulled some strings and brought the Army for moral support. Everyone were guarding the people from inside their homes and it was like that in the entire city of El Paso, Texas and the people that were been guarded brought them food. And nothing bad happen during the past couple of days.

THE FIRST NIGHT OF HELL

It was Friday afternoon where my friends and I ditch school and Chris took us to his house. We started planning everything for later in the night. Karina hacked into the bugs that were spread all over the city. So, when the phone rings we hear a loud beep. That's where Karina press the button and the phone number pops out in the screen and it also gives us the address of the place where the phone rang or if someone from out of town calls, we have their information saved on the system. So, we heard a loud beep and Karina pressed the button. A number that we didn't recognize appeared on the screen and also my home phone number appeared too. Karina hacked into the system and my father answered the phone. It turns out that my father received a call from the Mayor's Lawyer. He told him that he needed to see him and my mother as soon as possible. They were going to meet at the Mayor's house and they were planning to read his Will. And Karina hacked into the bugs from the Mayor's house, so we can hear their conversation. An hour later my mother and my father went to his house and the Mayor's family gave my parents a warm welcome. They were in the living room talking and drinking coffee. Finally the Lawyer and his assistant came into the living room. Mrs. Sheppard brought them a small table for them to put their papers.

"So, what's this about?" My mother asked.

"Well we gathered everyone here so we can read the Mayor's Will. Matthew Sheppard wrote his Will all over again and he asked for the two of you to be present with his family." The Lawyer smiled and started reading the Mayor's Will. And for almost two hours the Lawyer read his Will and it turns out that Matthew Sheppard left his money and his belongings to his whole family. "Okay, Beatrice and Pablo, I know you guys aren't looking for medals and money."

"No were not." My father responded.

The Lawyer took out a video tape from his briefcase and put it inside the VCR and played it. Everyone was sitting down and they were wondering what the Mayor was up to. "My name is Matthew Sheppard and I'm a father of four wonderful children and I have a beautiful wife. You all know by now that I leave everything to my family because I want them to have a better life and I knew that it was the right thing to do. I love the city of El Paso, Texas and when I found out that The Dark Cowboy started killing people and a lot of bad things were happening to the city. Well I was worried for my safety and my family's safety too, and I was also concerned for the safety of the people of El Paso, Texas. And that's why I made this tape and a new Will and it says if I ended up getting killed by The Dark Cowboy that someone else would take my place as the new Mayor of El Paso, Texas. Who better to take my place as the Mayor than Pablo de la Vega also known as Agent de la Vega. I picked you to be in charge of this operation. Now Pablo it's your duty to capture The Dark Cowboy because you're the best there is. So, Mayor de la Vega I wish you nothing but best of luck. And I know you are the right man for the job." He said and smiled.

The video tape finished and no one couldn't believe it and neither could we. Yes, we were loss for words. And everyone saw my father's reaction and my mother's reaction as well. The Lawyer turned off the television and the VCR and waited for my father to speak. "Congratulations, Mayor de la Vega."

My father was speechless and said, "I don't know what to say. I wasn't expecting to become a Mayor of this great city. I'm also worried because The Dark Cowboy promised to kill ten people by the end of the week."

"But you're Agent de la Vega and you have captured mobsters and terrorist from Russia, Italy, and the Middle East. You can do anything." The Lawyer said.

"Just give it a try. And you never know that you may be the one that ends up arresting this killer." Mrs. Sheppard encouraged my father.

"Okay, but I'm not going to guarantee you that I'm going to arrest him by tomorrow or the next day. It's going to take a long time because we don't know where he is." My father said and looked everyone that was counting on him. "But for years I've arrested some of the worst criminals in the world and I've hunt them down and threw them in jail. So, I don't mind doing it again. You can count me in. And I know The Dark Cowboy is no match for me."

My father, the great Pablo de la Vega accepted his new position as the new Mayor of El Paso, Texas and everyone went up to congratulated him and they were hugging him. My father saw the reaction from my mother and they knew that they will never captured me at all. All my mother could do is just smile and hugged him so tight and kissed him in the cheek. Half an hour later my parents left and went back to the house and they were in the living room talking.

Meanwhile Chris was talking to Karina and Primo about the mission, Primo was going to have somewhere down the road. The girls were also curious with Chris's demonstration, so they went to see what Chris was talking about but I wasn't paying attention to what he was saying to them. I was too wrapped up in my own world and I overheard Chris telling everyone about white pills and red pills that he created in his laboratory and a new radio. Well I guess I had other things in my mind and I felt that they were impressed about the pills and the new radio he made . So, finally Primo asked me. "What's your plan, Mauricio?"

I looked at everyone and said, "Karina is going to stay back on the fort and do what you do best. Cassandra is coming with me, Primo, and Chris and the rest of you stay with Karina." I smiled and went to the restroom and changed into my costume and I came back to the living room. "Cassandra, I want you to blow up a building in downtown and I'm sorry for the people that are going to be inside the building."

"Good luck!" The girls encouraged.

We noticed that Primo brought his backpack with him and we didn't ask him what was inside the backpack. We went outside and I took off and Cassandra, Primo, and Chris got into the truck and they also took off. And on the way there I was listening to my parent's conversation. So, my father knew that Monday morning he was going to be inaugurated to become officially the new Mayor of El Paso, Texas. My mother went to the kitchen to make lunch and she was in the kitchen making Hamburgers for themselves. Tania was with her girlfriend's and they were going to have a sleepover. So, it was just my mother and my father alone in the house. And in twenty minutes later we finally arrived in downtown El Paso. I got on the radio and told Karina to call my parents. Cassandra was putting on her gloves and we heard the phone ringing and my father picked up the phone and answered. "Hello!"

Karina yelled, "Bombs away!" And Cassandra stood up and was standing in front of the building and a energy beam came out and hit the building and we heard a loud explosion and I felt that everyone took cover from the loud explosion.

I was still listening to my parents. "Stay here!" My father yelled.

"I'm coming with you!" My mother also yelled

Someone radioed my father. "Agent de la Vega, The Dark Cowboy has struck again! We will go to the burning building!"

"Roger that, We're on our way there." My parents went running into the car and took off to the burning building.

And I looked at the team, "You guys need to leave the area! Meet me at the other side of the block." Chris started the engine and went to the side of the street to hide. Then my parents arrived at the crime scene and they were watching the building burning down and the cavalry arrived just in time and they came running towards my father. My father ordered everyone to scout the entire neighborhood and they were looking for me but they couldn't find me anywhere in the area. Twenty minutes later everyone went back to my father and the Firefighters arrived in time to take the fire out. The people were running away from the burning building and they were screaming and crying their eyes out. My father decided to have a second search and sent everyone in groups.

I was on the rooftop in one of the buildings when I saw Detective Jim Nielsen and his men that were circulating the entire whole block and found nothing at all. And I had my eyes on Detective Jim Nielsen. And I was smiling from ear to ear.

Detective Jim Nielsen got on the radio and said, "There's nothing, Agent de la Vega. Just a building burning and a empty alley and us." Detective Jim Nielsen said and looked at everyone. "I got to take a piss, you guys go ahead and meet up with Agent de la Vega."

"Yes, Sir!" They said.

Detective Jim Nielsen was all alone in the alley and stood in front of the wall and started peeing and he was writing his name on the wall. Detective Jim

Nielsen started whistling and singing and I knew that he was singing, peeing, and writing his name on the wall for the very last time. Enjoy this moment while you can, Detective Jim Nielsen. I took out my dart gun and I shot him in the back and he fell on his knees and he didn't make any noise at all. I jumped off the roof and landed right next to him. I went up to him and turn him around and sat him next to the wall where he peed. That's where I had a flashback.

I heard the voice of Detective Jim Nielsen. "I cannot believe that I'm going to get promoted to Lieutenant Detective. And I hope that I move higher than everybody else here in the Police Department. Detective Perla Mancini was going to get that promotion but her son got into trouble. And there is no way that she's going to get that promotion. I'm the King around here."

And I heard another voice, "How can you say that. The Commissioner is dead and the Mayor is dead. It will be a long time for any of us can get promoted. Because were caught up with The Dark Cowboy and that's important than moving up the ranks. And I cannot believe that psychotic killer nearly killed Eliza back in the Franklin Mountains."

"I heard that too. We all have been telling her that it was Mauricio that killed them. And she doesn't believe us." Detective Nielsen said.

"If only Beatrice handed Mauricio to The Dark Cowboy. And all of this would be over."

"What are you talking about? Mauricio is The Dark Cowboy!" Detective Jim Nielsen exclaimed in the flashback.

I was staring at Detective Jim Nielsen and there more allegations point towards me, and the problem was they told Eliza to stay away from me. Well with Detective Jim Nielsen going to Hell. Primo's mother might get that promotion and I cannot wait to kill him. So, I got on my knees, and took off my hat and I let him see my face. He was shocked to see me. I smiled and winked at him. "Well good evening, Detective Jim Nielsen. I've been expecting you. I know you and your friend the Commissioner John Hancock were so anxious to talk to me. I'm here and I'm ready to talk and your not asking me anything and that's rude of you." I said and laughed. "You and everyone else were so sure that I was the psychotic killer known as The Dark Cowboy. But I'm going to confess to all my killings to you. Yes, Detective Jim Nielsen I did killed those innocent people and guess what you are next on the hit list. And I will give you an explanation of why I'm going to kill you so badly. You are corrupted Detective and you were planning to kill me and my loving mother too. I don't like that at all and I'm going to defend my family's honor from people like you. With you gone and I am pretty sure that my loving mom will be giving the rank of Detective and with my loving mother's blessing I can kill anyone I want too. And I want you think about it while you are rotting in Hell." I smiled and I took out my guns and I pointed them at his head and shot him so many times. So, everyone heard the gunshots and they went running towards the back of the alley. I saw them running and I jumped on top of the rooftop. And my heart was beeping too fast and everything went into slow motion. I turn around and saw the same black car and it was park across the street.

I heard the voice of Karina, "Did you get that, Sonia?"

"Yes, I got that!"

"Leave the scene and wait for my orders!"

Someone turn on the engine and took off pretty past. And I heard the Police Offices yelling when they found Detective Jim Nielsen laying on the ground and he was already dead and they heard my laughter and I was loving it. They looked up and saw me staring a them.

"You bastard!" My mother yelled and sobbed.

"Shoot him!" My father yelled.

Everyone started shooting at me and I jumped to the other side of the street. And I radioed Chris and he told where he was parked. I ran into this direction and we waited for the right opportunity. The Police Officers called the Ambulance and the Firefighters were able to take the fire out. And in about twenty minutes later the Ambulance arrived in time and took Detective Jim Nielsen to the Morgue. They couldn't believe that another person died and five news van arrived and they started asking my father a lot of questions.

I looked at Cassandra and said, "Cassandra, you know what to do." Cassandra smiled and put her glove on. And I yelled. "Now, Cassandra!"

As soon the Police Officers were going to pull my father away from the press, another building exploded. And everyone took cover and they knew somewhere in that part of area I would be around. "I will see you soon, Chris!"

"Okay, we are going to hide somewhere else." Chris smiled and took off. And I went to the other alley and I jumped to the other rooftop.

"Everyone get in the car! Load your weapons." My father yelled.

Everybody including the news reporters got into the van and went straight towards the burning building. On the way there they called for another set of

Firefighters while the other team rested. They arrived in time and got out of their cars and they went to search for any signs of The Dark Cowboy. Then they heard the sirens of the Firefighters and they came out and did their routine.

"Any signs of him?" My mother asked.

"No! Everything is clear."

They continue to search for me while the rest of the team tried to tell the news reporters to leave the crime scene. The Captain of the Police Department and his team were circulating the whole area and found nothing at all. Just over the rooftop I was standing there and I was watching everyone move around the area and I was grinning from ear to ear. All of the sudden they saw something moving and they took out their guns and saw five dogs walking around. They looked to be hungry and they were looking for food in the trash cans and one of the Police Officers saw four people that were walking around the area and they looked to be suspicious.

"Hold it right there!" The Police Officers yelled.

They looked at them and started running and they threw something on the ground. The Police Officers and the FBI Agents were running after those thugs. And the Captain stayed behind to pickup ten bags of cocaine and weed and four knives. The Captain got on the radio and said. "Don't worry, Agent de la Vega. We found some thugs and my team arrested them over."

I was wondering why were those thugs walking around the alley. This might be the work of Karina. And the Captain was walking away but he stopped and he started to sniff the cocaine. While he was sniffing the cocaine, I took out my dart gun and shot him in the back and he fell to the ground. Then the dogs started barking and they were radioing the Captain of the Police Department. I jumped down and turned him around and I was dragging him next to the wall and I got on my knees.

And I had another flashback. I heard the voice of the Captain. "I've been on the Police Force for thirty-five years. And now our jobs are in jeopardy because Beatrice de la Vega's reputation. One distraction and she will end up becoming our General of the Police Department."

"She has a great reputation and a lot of criminals are behind bars. But she should have handed her son to The Dark Cowboy."

"Yeah, but I'm speculating that her son killed all of those innocent people. And he almost killed Eliza back in the Franklin Mountains. He deserves to die."

The Captain of the Police Department was staring at me and I also took off my hat. "Hello, Captain of the Police Department you are wondering why I chose to kill you. I will tell you why and the reason is that you a dirty Police Officer. And I know who you work for and the fact is that you were also planning to kill me and my parents and my baby sister. I'm not going to allow that to happen because I am planning to kill every corrupted Police Officers and person that wants to work for Vito Mancini. You are not going to be alone in Hell, you are going to have some good company." I was laughing at him and started loading my guns and shot him in the head and all over his body. And I heard the Police Officers and the FBI coming back with the thugs and they saw me jumping to the rooftop. I was looking down and there was a large trash can and I could see a hand. And I turn around and saw the same black car that was parked at the other side of the street.

"You think he saw me?"

Karina responded, "No! He was in a hurry! And Sonia leave the scene and Erin I want you to stay there. As soon the Police and the FBI leave. I want you to leave the area."

"Copy that!" And I radioed Chris and he told me where he was at, and I ran into his direction and of course we waited for the next opportunity.

The Police Officers and FBI Agents found the Captain of the Police Department laying in a pool of his own blood and they radioed my father and they came running. "The Captain is dead." My father said angrily.

"At least we got witnesses." My mother said.

"Take them away! We will questioned them in the morning! But for now take them to the holding cell until we are able to capture The Dark Cowboy." My father ordered.

Four Police Officers took the thugs away to the Police Station and they were going to be in a holding cell for the night. And the Ambulance arrived and all they did is put the Captain in a body bag and took him to the Morgue. And finally my father had enough of the press and made a couple of his FBI Agents to tell the press to go back to the news station. The FBI Agents took out their guns and told the reporters to leave for their own safety. So, the three FBI Agents forced the reporters into the van and told them to leave. But they made sure they went back to the news station. And they did escorted them along the way. My father went to see how the Firefighters were doing and the Firefighters put the fire out.

I got on the radio and said, "Karina find out where Lacey Jones lives."

"The female reporter?" Primo asked.

"This is where you come in, Primo." I smiled.

Karina told us where Lacey Jones lives and Chris wrote down the address. "I have an idea. Cassandra, You see that Hotel?" I asked and pointed at the Hotel.

"Yes!" She responded.

"That's a big Hotel." Primo said.

"What are you going to do?" Chris asked.

"We're going to play a game. "Which way did The Dark Cowboy go!" And I'm going to trick my father." I smiled.

"Here we go!" Cassandra smiled and minutes later there was another explosion and it was the third building that exploded that night. Everyone got into their cars and took off to the burning building. On the way there they called for another set Firefighters and the Ambulance just in case is there any dead bodies in the area. They arrived along with the Firefighters and everyone was standing in front of the burning building. And on the way to Lacey Jones's house, we could hear my father yelling at the team. "We're not going anywhere and we're not going to separate! That's what The Dark Cowboy wants! We're going to stick together and keep our eyes on the roofs!" My father commanded the team.

This time they went to together to see if I was there waiting for them from the rooftop and that's a smart move, Daddy. Keep making mistakes. "Show yourself!" My mother yelled.

Meanwhile the news van arrived at the news station and the FBI Agents went back to the burning building. The Chief Editor told everyone to go home and called it a night. So, Lacey Jones was getting ready to go home and she was on her way home and she was watching the burning building just a couple of blocks away from her house. She knew that no one would fall asleep and it was going to be a long night for every law enforcement. So, Lacey Jones finally parked in the driveway and went inside the house. And we parked a couple of houses away from hers.

Primo got out of the truck and I said, "Knock on the door, Primo!" Well Primo smiled and went walking towards her house and she was outside checking her mail box. Primo stopped by to say hi to her and she recognized him because she did a story on him a few months back. Lacey Jones was freaked out and went running into the house. She locked the door and looked out the window. I snuck into her house and I was behind her and covered her mouth. I sat her down on the couch and I unlocked the door and Primo went into the house. "She's all yours and take your time. Torture her, do whatever the Hell you want with her!" I smiled and I was looking for any information she has on me. While Primo was raping her I started checking her purse and found nothing. Well she had a police file on the table, and I also found three disks on her desk and I turn on the computer and put the disks inside. Well as it turns out that she was writing a story about me and Primo too.

I radioed Chris and we took her computer away and I even gave Chris the police file and the three disks. And I went to her room and found nothing, so I went back to the living room. And I noticed that Primo took out his toys from his backpack, for example handcuffs, ropes, you named it. "So, that's what you have inside your backpack when you rape girls?"

"Yes!" Primo exclaimed and tapped her mouth and tied her up with a rope and handcuffed her arms and legs.

"Take your time! And I'm giving you two whole hours!" I smiled and went outside to get a fresh air. That was my excuse if I see that damn black car was parked on the sidewalk. And I radioed Karina, "When we get home I want you to check out the computer and the disks that we took from her house."

"Yes!" Karina said.

"And how's Primo doing?" I asked.

"It's sad to see Primo torture somebody but we are professionals here." Karina responded.

"Well in two hours it will be over and I can kill her."

And Chris radioed me too. "I cannot believe that you gave Primo two hours. You realize that most of us have a squeamish stomach to hear someone getting tortured."

"Deal with it, Chris, and I'm giving him some space. What can go wrong in my mission?" I asked.

And in about forty minutes later, I heard Karina screaming at the top of her lungs. "Mauricio! There's a little girl crying in the living room. Primo it's letting himself been seen again!"

"You got to be kidding me!" I exclaimed and transformed into the hideous creature and broke the door. And Primo was raping Lacey in front her only daughter. "What the Hell are you doing?"

"I'm raping Lacey Jones in front of her lovely daughter and she won't do a damn thing to stop me. Look at her she's crying like a little bitch!" Primo responded with a smile.

I grabbed him by the throat and slammed him against the wall, "You allowed yourself to be seen again and this is the second time I tell you. Now put your back clothes on and leave." And I noticed that Lacey's fingers were broken and I looked at Primo and I also broke his hand in three places. "This is a warning not to be seen."

Primo grabbed his clothes and went outside. I turn around and I couldn't help feeling bad for Lacey's daughter. I'm sorry that she had to see this but I came here to do my mission. I grabbed Lacey and untied her and took the tape from her mouth and she was sobbing and she was hugging her mother so tight. "Please don't kill my mommy! I love her a lot."

"Take everything you want!" Lacey sobbed. And I also began to notice that her hands were broken and toes were also broken and she couldn't walk at all. I picked her up and took her to the kitchen and sat her down and her daughter was hugging her mother so tight. I went to get a glass of water and she was drinking the water while I had the glass in my hand. "Thank you!" She said softly.

"You know why I'm here?" I asked.

"Yes! I may be next on your list." She responded.

"Well Lacey Jones, I wish things would have been differently and I really don't care if you put the story on tomorrows paper. I can imagine what the people are going to say about me. They can say that the future King is the one that's been doing all the killings and it doesn't matter to me. What are they going to do to me? Nothing." And I went back to normal and continued. "But I'm sorry that your daughter had to see this. She's a beautiful little girl and a innocent child that didn't deserve to see this. She didn't deserve to see her mom getting raped and she doesn't deserve to see her mom getting killed right before her very eyes. Your daughter wasn't on my hit list but you are on my list. I'm pretty sure that you have a husband or family member that can take care of your daughter or she can live with me and I promise you that she will have a good education. Your daughter will grow up to be a college student and grow up to be a beautiful woman and she will have a great life."

Lacey Jones looked at me and was still sobbing, "I don't care what you do to me just as long my daughter will be safe from the likes of your friend and yourself. You have been causing terror in this city but sooner or later you will pay for your actions."

"Fair enough! While you are looking up from Hell or looking down from Heaven. I will continue to bring peace to this peaceful city. But tell your daughter to go to her room because I don't want her to have nightmares. You think what she saw earlier scared her completely just imagine when sees what I'm about to do next." I looked at her daughter and asked, "What's your daughter's name?"

"Her name is Samantha Jones! And, baby, go to your room. This nice young man has offered to send you to the best schools in the country. I love you a lot and now go to your room!" Her daughter ran to her room and closed the door.

When the door slammed I had another flashback. I heard Lacey's voice. "Eliza I'm writing the story on Mauricio and he's the one that has been killing over the years. He's dangerous."

Eliza responded. "Mauricio is innocent! I don't know why people hate him. He's a nice boy!"

"Eliza stay away from, Mauricio!"

Lacey Jones looked at me with her sad eyes and I transformed and I grabbed her neck and said, "Hello, my name is Mauricio de la Vega also known as "The Dark Cowboy" and I know you are writing a story about me and you have me as a suspect in this case and I am the killer just to give you more information about me. What kind of lies are you going to say to me, well it turns out that you no longer going to write a story about me. In fact I'm going to take all the evidence away and I'm going to burn it. Well here's a news flash you are going to die and you will be another dead person that came out on the yesterday's news." I took out my guns and shot her so many times. After I was done killing Lacey Jones, I could hear Samantha breathing heavily in the hallway. "Don't come to the kitchen!" I went to the hallway and she was crying her eyes out. "Don't worry your mom is in a better place. You are coming with me and I will treat you like a Princess. And let me help you pack your things." She tried to smile and we went to her room and very quickly I packed everything into her suitcase and I heard Karina on the radio, "We have company! Someone is pulling into the driveway!" And I looked at Samantha and said, "Hold tight!" She was able to hold on to me and we jumped out the window and landed on the other side of the street.

"That's my daddy parking in the driveway but he is mean to us."

"You are going to be safe with us." I smiled and we went to Chris.

"What's with the girl?" Cassandra asked.

"Samantha Jones needs a place to stay and I couldn't leave her alone." I responded and put her inside the truck and Cassandra had in her arms. And Primo looked at me and I said, "Will talk later on and we need to go to the club in downtown." I smiled and we took off. Meanwhile Samantha's father went inside the house and tried to call the Police but there was no response at all and he kept on calling the Police. And back in the burning building where the Firefighters were finally able to put the fire out and they couldn't find me.

"He's not in the rooftop. The damn Dark Cowboy is playing with us!" My mother said angrily.

"We're sticking together and we're going to the rooftops. Will catch him off guard." My father ordered.

We finally arrived at downtown and we could see them on top of the rooftop. I looked around and saw another building. "Cassandra that's the one that I want you to take out." I said.

"Okay!" Cassandra exclaimed and everyone were getting ready to go to the other rooftop when another building exploded and it was the fourth building that exploded night.

I looked at Samantha and said, "Sweetie, they are going to take you to a safer place and I will be there very shortly. And it's time for you guys to go back to the house and I'm going around the club and I'll see you guys later."

Chris smiled and started the engine and took off to the house, while I ran around the streets to find the club. And I overheard my mother yelling. "Damn it! Not another one!"

"Let's move it!" My father yelled.

They got into the cars and went to the burning building. On the way their my father got on the horn and called for another set of Firefighters while the others rested. They arrive in ten minutes and the Firefighters also arrived and were trying to put the fire out. Everyone was climbing up the ladders and they found nothing at all.

"The roof is empty." One of the Police Officers said.

"Keep looking." My father said.

One of the FBI Agents took out their night vision goggles and put them on and was looking for me. "He's not up here, sir."

"This is a long night." My mother said.

"Yes, it is." My father said.

"Sir, he is not here." One of then FBI Agents said.

They continued their search on the roofs. And just around the block the owner of the club was ordered to lock the place down. He was closing the place where I just happened to be on top of the rooftop of some other building. The owner of the club was talking to himself, he was cursing and started whistling. He decided to pee, so he was standing in front the wall of his club and started peeing. When he finished peeing, I shot him in the back with the dart gun and he fell to the ground. And I jumped off the roof top and landed in front of him. I grabbed his fat ass and sat him next to the wall.

I had another flashback and I heard the voice of the owner of the club. "Mrs. Caballero what are we going to do, so we can convince Eliza to stay away from Mauricio. Because I've been hearing that he's The Dark Cowboy!"

Eliza's mother responded, "Mauricio is innocent and he hasn't done anything at all. Why are so many people telling us to stay away from, Mauricio!"

"I care about you guys because we go to Church together. But I hope you guys think about it."

I got on my knees and took off my hat and said, "Hello, you fat bastard. I'm going to make this short and sweet. I know what happens inside this club. You and your men sell drugs and among other things. You also rape young girls in the restrooms and now I am here to kill you. And everybody is going to live their lives in peace. Because they are not going to remember you at all. So, I want you to think about it when the worms are eating your body and your soul is rotting in Hell." I started laughing and took out my guns and started shooting at him. And I left the area until one of the Police Officers heard the gunshots.

"Sir, I heard gunshots and I think it came from around the corner."

"Where?" My father asked.

"I heard them too and it did came from around the corner." My mother said.

"Okay let's go." My father said.

Everyone got off the rooftop and went running around the corner of the buildings. They found the owner of the club laying there and he was already dead. "That's the third person that died tonight." My mother said.

"Four buildings exploded tonight and who knows where the fourth person might be at." One of the FBI Agents said.

"He's right. We could have been the ones that might have died tonight but we stayed together." My father said.

"We did stick together and we should be proud of that." My mother said.

"And call the Ambulance, so they can take him to the morgue." My father ordered his men.

I overheard the siren of the Ambulance and they arrived at the crime scene. They took the owner of the club to the morgue. Then my father and his team went to see how the Firefighters were doing. They saw them drinking water and resting.

"What a night!" They said.

"Three people died." My mother said.

And I decided to go back to Lacey Jones's house and I had a feeling that Samantha's father is still having problems calling the Police. And I radioed Karina, "Karina let him through the line." I ordered her and it looks like Sonia put so many bugs in all the houses that we have targeted. And meanwhile everyone were sitting down and drinking water and they were tired and they were getting sleepy. My father and everyone were enjoying a good twenty minutes of rest when the Dispatch Operator was calling them. "What can I do you for?" One of the Police Officers asked.

"All units there's been another murder."

They quickly got up and went inside the car and took off to the house. On the way their they asked the Dispatch Operator for the address. "Could it be the fifth person that died tonight?" My mother asked.

"No. I have a feeling that this may be the fourth person because the other building was a decoy, a distraction for us." My father responded.

They finally arrived at the house and went running into the house and they found Lacey Jones dead in the kitchen. "How long has she been dead?" My mother asked.

"My wife has been dead for over three hours and I have been calling you guys and there was no response until now." He responded.

"You couldn't get threw the line?" My mother asked.

"No!" He yelled.

"That's great. You see the burning building was a distraction. So, The Dark Cowboy comes in and kills this woman." My father said.

"She looks so familiar." My mother said.

"That's Lacey Jones, the news reporter. She was there before Agent de la Vega ordered us to take them away." One of the Agents said.

"I was worried for their safety. And I thought they would be safer back at the news station." My father said.

"Call the Ambulance." My mother said.

"Agent de la Vega, my daughter is also missing and my ex wife was raped and someone killed her!" The man exclaimed and everyone looked at Perla.

"Primo is at home sleeping, and he promised me that he wasn't going to rape anymore women." Perla sobbed.

"I want to press charges and I hope he goes to jail for the rest of his life." The man said.

"Sir, right now we're dealing with this psychotic killer and all we can do is arrest her son for raping your wife. And I don't want you to worry because Primo Mancini and The Dark Cowboy are going to pay for their crimes." My father said and looked at Perla. "Your son and his friend have gone too far."

"We're sorry for your loss." My mother said.

"Will also find your daughter and I have a feeling that Primo has her somewhere." My father said.

"What happens if he's raping my daughter?"

And Chris and the girls looked at Primo and said, "Sorry, Primo it looks like they're going to arrest you."

"I'm going to turn myself in." He said.

I radioed Chris and I addressed everyone. "I told you that nobody is getting arrested, not on my watch. You got that, Primo. And we have a mission to do and they are not going to worry about you until I finished killing the others and I promise that you will not get arrested."

And half an hour later the Ambulance arrived at the crime scene and took Lacey Jones away to the morgue. My father and everyone else were coming outside when they saw me standing in the middle of the street and I was laughing at them. "What's the matter, Agent de la Vega can't keep up with me!" I was laughing at my father.

"You stupid bastard! You're not going to get away with this!" My mother yelled at me.

"This was suppose to be a lovely night, ladies and gentlemen. But this night turned out to be black Friday. Four buildings exploding and four people were found dead and the Police and the FBI arrived way too late. So, much for the great Agent de la Vega that couldn't keep up with me. Perhaps you are getting too old for this job. So, let's call it a night and will continue with this adventure tomorrow night." I smiled and started running on the streets.

"Everybody get in your cars and we're going to follow him!" My father ordered his team.

Everyone got into their cars and started pursuing me and they were right on my tail. And I noticed that there was a Police car that was on my backside and I turn around and kicked the Police car and it landed on top of the other cars and they exploded. I was still on the air when I noticed the same black car that was parked on the street. And everything went into slow motion once again.

"Mauricio just saved a little girls' life!" Sonia said.

Karina responded, "You are right! I wasn't expecting this! Maybe he's good after all but you girls are doing my mission. And we need to continue with this!"

And I jumped away into the darkness and everyone got out of their cars. "Is everyone okay?" My father asked.

"Yes!" Everyone said.

"The Dark Cowboy jumped away into the darkness." My mother was loss for words.

"What are we going to do now?" One of the Agents asked.

They heard the sirens of the Ambulance and the Firefighters. "The Dark Cowboy called it a night." My father looked at everyone and said. "Go home and get some rest because tomorrow we have a long night."

"You heard Agent de la Vega, go home and get some rest." My mother said and yawned.

My parents stayed there and went to help their falling colleagues while everyone else went to their house. And I arrived at Chris's house and I went to change and I went to the living room and I saw Samantha and she was still crying. I picked her up and sat down her down on the table. "Your mom is in Heaven and she wants you to have a better education and a better life."

She looked at me and said, "You are too nice to be a serial killer!" She said and looked at us, "You guys are too nice to be evil people."

"You are right. How old are you?" I asked.

"Six years old." She responded.

The girls went up to hug her and they started playing around with her. And I could tell Chris wasn't too happy with Primo's action. Well he was putting his hand on ice. "You want to explain your actions to me." Chris said.

"I did my job!" Primo yelled.

"Bullshit! This is not a game, Primo! When you rape girls, rape them and leave the scene! Don't get carried away by allowing yourself to be seen by other people! You are this close to go to jail for the rest of your life but I guess your father has everyone in his pockets and you are going getting off that easy! And we know that you want your dad to be proud of you and you are jeopardizing your mission and everyone else's mission!" Chris yelled at him.

"It was my fault, Chris. I was responsible for this. I should have scouted the whole house and if I knew Samantha was there I would have taken her to you guys in the first place. I'm responsible for this incident, blame me and not Primo because he was doing his job. I know he got carried away and it won't happen again." I said and looked at Primo, "Hang in there and stay strong for the team!" I said.

Primo looked at me and smiled. "Mission accomplished!"

Chris was still upset and said, "Okay, you guys, Mauricio's parents are going to come home soon. So, I need to take all off you back home as quickly as possible." I was hearing the sirens of the Ambulance and the sirens of the Firefighters arriving and together they took out the fire from the cars that exploded and there was no more dead bodies for tonight. Most of them had burns and injuries but they are going to be okay.

Thirty minutes later Chris came back to the house and we just looked at each other and smiled. Samantha was sleeping like an Angel and Chris looked at me, "What are we going to do with her?"

"Find her a good education. Far away from this place. You know like a boarding school. I want her to have a better life and I made her mom a promise and I'm going to keep my promise. And Monday morning you will take her to the boarding school." I said.

"That's fine!" Chris said.

Then my parents came to pick us up and we went home. My mother put Tania in her bed and she put me in my bed and she said goodnight to us and my parents went to their room and they tried to get some rest because they were going to need it.

THE SECOND NIGHT OF HELL

The next day everyone in the city woke up all depress and tired from first night of terror well I have a feeling that the second night is going to be even worse from last night. My parents spent the morning with us and they tried to smile and they wanted to be with us. We ate and watched television together like one big happy family. And all morning long I began to notice that my father was staring at me and in his mind. He felt that I might know something about my alter ego. I guess my father was remembering what The Dark Cowboy told him about his adorable son. My father began to wonder what was the secret between me and The Dark Cowboy. Why is there was so much "hatred" between us? My father felt that I might be the key to this investigation and sooner or later my father might start asking me questions. Well if my father decides to stick his nose in my business. Well I'm sorry to say this but my father is going to be on the hit list just as soon I was done killing everyone.

Then later on in the afternoon my mother left Tania at her friend's house and she left me with Chris. My mother said to goodbye to me and told me that she loves me a lot. Chris and I went inside the house and we heard everything that went on the radio. Samantha came running at me and sat in my lap.

"What's the plan?" Chris asked.

"Call Primo, Karina, and Cassandra and bring them here, so we can be ready for tonight." I said and smiled and continued to play with little Samantha. And Chris went to pick them up. And during that time Samantha and I were overhearing everything on the radio.

My father and his team were going to meet at the Police Station and down the road where my father wanted to ask my mother something. "I wanted to ask you something for awhile." He said.

"Tell me." She said.

"What if it's true what The Dark Cowboy said a while back."

"What do you mean?" She asked.

"That our son, Mauricio, turn his back on him when they were little kids and left him for dead. You think they might know each other. Do you remember Mauricio having a weird friend?"

"No, I think so. You know Mauricio was always alone when we were living in California and in Mexico until he started having friends here." She said.

"You remember The Dark Cowboy saying that every time he looks in the mirror, he sees Mauricio." He said.

"We all know that The Dark Cowboy is a borderline psycho path. He never got the love that he needed from his family and that's why he envies our son, Mauricio, and Tania because we gave them all the love that they need. And Mauricio probably knew him in summer camp and maybe they talked. But I would hate to be The Dark Cowboy's mother right now." She said and smiled.

"You think we should ask him questions?" He asked.

"No. I don't want to put our kids at risk." She responded.

"Mauricio may know something. We got to ask him someday." He said and they arrived at the Police Station and they parked. "Do you want to see more people die or more buildings exploding like last night?" He asked.

"No!" She exclaimed.

"I want you to think about it." He said and my parents went inside the Police Station and everyone were waiting for them. They all sat down and started discussing about the events of last night. "I want to talk about what happen last night." He said.

"We're listening." Everyone said.

"We did everything we could to protect the people but The Dark Cowboy is one step ahead of us. We had four deaths last night. The Captain of the Police Department, Detective Jim Nielsen, Lacey Jones the news reporter, and the owner of the club."

"All of us tried to protect them, Sir. Maybe we should try harder but we did failed." One of the Police Officers said.

"There were burning buildings and."

My mother interrupted and said, "The burning buildings were a just distraction. Don't forget The Dark Cowboy blocked the call from the news reporter and that's why we couldn't get there in time."

"How are we going to stop The Dark Cowboy from doing anymore crimes?" One of the Police Officers asked.

"We need to stick together and to be honest we don't know when he's going to strike and we don't know how to stop him." My father said and looked worried.

"This might be the serial killer that we will never catch at all and he might be the Devil in person." One of the Police Officers said.

"Who knows whose going to die next." One of the Agents said.

"We're not giving up and we need to try harder and maybe who knows we might catch him tonight." My father said and smiled to everyone. They stayed in the office for a couple of hours and they went home to get some rest. They were going to get back together around five o'clock in the Police Station and they were going to be spread all over the city. The teams were spread in ten groups and all of them had walkie-talkies so they were communicating with each other every thirty seconds. So, on that night they were on top of the roof top of the buildings of downtown El Paso and found nothing. Then at seven o'clock that night everyone were on their break and they were eating and others were sleeping inside their cars. My mother fell asleep inside the Police car while my father and his team were waiting.

Well we were listening to them and we were also eating and at the same time we also knew that they were loosing their minds. "What are we going to do?" Karina asked me.

"Find out where Mike Reyes lives." I smiled and looked at them. "Primo I might need you for tonight, so ride along with Cassandra and Chris."

"Okay." He smiled.

"I found him. Mike Reyes lives three blocks from here." She said and wrote down the address and gave me the address.

"Let's get ready." I smiled and hugged little Samantha and went to the restroom and changed. Karina had Samantha in her arms and they walked us outside and they wished us a lot of luck. They got into the truck and we took off to his house.

Let's recap I think we all remembered good old Mike Reyes the same kid that went to the Franklin Mountains and saw the two kids murdered and also he got struck by lightning when he saw me talking to the Indians well this is sudden death. We were listening to what he was doing in his room and he was in his room playing Play Station and he was having a good time. His parents were sound asleep and I landed on the rooftop of his house and I was smiling from ear to ear. But the dogs were barking loudly and he looked out the window and noticed that the dogs were barking at the rooftop. He went outside to see what was going on and it was too dark to see what the dogs were barking at. He went back inside to turn on the lights from the backyard and that wasn't enough for him. And he went to his room to bring his flashlight and I'm guessing that this moron is afraid of the dark or he cannot see in the dark. Meanwhile I threw a couple of bags of Pork Chops and the dogs didn't barked anymore. Mike went back to the backyard and noticed that that dogs were eating something and that's where I shot him in the back with the dart gun and he falls to the ground. The dogs were barking even loudly but I threw eight more bags of Pork Chops and the dogs were eating them but they finished the Pork Chops and I did the smart thing and I open the gate and they went running outside and I closed the gate. So, I went up to him and I was dragging him into the room and sat him down in his bed. I also closed the door and locked the door so we won't be bothered.

I was standing in front of him and I had another flashback. I heard Mike's voice, "Eliza, I saw Mauricio talking to the Indians a year before the kids were murdered on the Franklin Mountains."

And she asked, "What were they talking about?"

"They were doing a ritual on him and a Demon went into his body. And this Demon has control of him. And he's the one that killed them and he nearly killed me too."

"That's not true!"

I kept hearing Eliza's screaming at him and I was happy that she was defending me from those sons of bitches. And I took off my hat and gave him a nice smile. "Good evening, Mike Reyes what's happening. I haven't seen you since the day you saw me talking to the Indians and I almost killed you on that night. And I have every reason to kill you. One of the reasons I want to kill you, is that you followed me and you saw me talking to the Indians and that's how I was born. You were lucky that the lightning didn't kill you. And you are the key witness to this investigation and you went to Detective Jim Nielsen and you told him everything you saw on that night. But he is now dead and there is no more evidence pointed towards me. And the second reason I want to kill you is that you are doing drugs and that's not cool either. What are your parents going to think when they find out that their only son is a drug dealer. As the matter of fact you are going to die and I will live on, for a long time." I was laughing and started loading my guns and shot him so many times. I unlocked the door and jumped out the window.

The gunshots woke his parents up and a couple of neighbors also woke up. His parents went running into his room and found his son dead. His father looked out the window and saw me and I said goodbye to him and disappeared into the darkness and he called the Police. His mother got on her knees and started crying her eyes out and his father was trying to calm her down. And finally the Dispatch Operator called one of the Police Officers.

"Come in, Agent de la Vega." He said.

"What is it Officer?" My father asked.

"There's been another killing. We're on our way to the crime scene."

"Roger that." My father said and got on the horn and called for back up. He went to the car and said, "Wake up, Honey."

"What is it?" My mother asked.

"There's been another murder!" He exclaimed.

"Not again."

Everyone got inside their cars and arrived at the house in time and found the door close. My father was knocking on the door and Mike's father opened the door and everyone went inside the house to see if I was still inside. Then they went to the room to find the boy dead and the Ambulance arrived and went straight inside his room. They put him in a body bag and put him into the Ambulance and my father was able to identify the boy.

"I know this kid. We met a year before those two kids were murdered on the Franklin Mountains." He said.

"That's right Pablo we have met before. We ran into each other on the mountains." He said and cried.

"I'm sorry for your loss. Take him away." My father said.

My parents were sad to see another person murdered and they were about to leave. But the boy's mother was still crying and my mother wanted to stay with her until she was able to calm down. My father suggested that they stayed in a Hotel, so they can get some rest and the Police Officers and the FBI closed the house down. My mother took Mike's parents to the Hotel and stayed with them for the night.

I radioed Chris and he told me where he is at and I went running to this direction and we waited for the right moment. "Do you want me to blow up another building?" Cassandra asked.

"No!" I said.

I radioed Karina, "Where's John Parker?" I asked.

Karina responded right of away, "John Parker is back at the news station and I'm going to find out what he's typing on his computer and if he decides to put a hard drive. I'll make sure to disable the system." She said.

"Wait for my orders." I said.

"Copy that." Karina sad.

"What now?" Chris asked.

"We're going to the news station." I said and we left.

Then back at the news station where news reporter John Parker was working late in his office and he was writing a story about me and my friends. And again another person had me as a suspect in this case and he was going to put the story on tomorrow's paper, so the people can read it. He was able to finish his story and all he needed is to print out the whole story.

We just got there and I radioed Karina, "What's is he doing?" I asked.

She responded. "He's about to print the story, and I'm going to disabled the printer." Karina did her thing and we heard John complaining about the printer breaking down at the last moment and Karina said, "Well say goodbye to your story, John Parker." The computer was getting crazy on him and it turned off by itself. He was standing there and turned on the computer and all the information he had about me was gone. "He's putting the disk drive well again say goodbye to your story." John put the disk inside the computer and just like that the disk drive was empty. There was no more information about The Dark Cowboy and I was no longer a suspect in this case, and he was wondering what went wrong, so he called it a night and he was getting ready to go home. "Mauricio he's clocking out."

I was hiding on the shadows when he came out and he was still confused and he was cursing as well. I took out my dart gun and shot him in the back. He fell to the ground, I grabbed him and sat him next to the wall.

And I had another flashback and I was hearing him talk to Lacey. "Lacey we keep telling Eliza to stay away from this Mauricio but she won't listen at all."

"She needs to know that he's dangerous. We need to have more evidence, so she could be more convince."

"I don't want her to be hurt again."

John Parker was staring at me with fear and I got on my knees and took off my hat and I let him see my face. "Good evening, John Parker. Well we have a special bulletin. In a couple of minutes you are going to be dead. And you are wondering about this situation. I will tell you why I want to kill you so badly. And I know you are doing Lacey Jones's dirty job. You two have worked so damn hard on the story and as it turns out the story won't come out at all. But there is a story that will come out tomorrow. You are going to come out at the obituary section. You are going to be missed and you will go straight to Hell.

And here's a news flash, this is where you die, John Parker." I started loading my guns and I started shooting at him so many times and left the scene. And Chris radioed me and I went to his direction and we heard what was going on.

The coworkers ran outside to find John Parker dead in the middle of the parking lot and they called the Police. So, the Police and the FBI Agents were on their way back to the restaurant when they received the call from the Dispatch Operator. "All units there's been another murder and it was on the news station!"

"Copy that and we're on our way." My father said.

Everyone did a u-turn and drove all the way to the news station. They got there in ten minutes and they found the male reporter dead and his coworkers were crying their eyes out. "We got here too late." One of the Police Officers said.

Everyone stood in front of John Parker's body and they couldn't do anything to protect him from The Dark Cowboy. The Ambulance arrived and took him away to the Morgue and they were upset and the great Pablo de la Vega started kicking the tires and was cursing me all the way to Hell. The Police Officers and FBI Agents were trying to calm him down and they took him into the car and drove away.

We were in the same place and we watched them leave. "My dad is going to have a nervous breakdown." I smiled.

"Yes, he is." Chris said.

"So, what now?" Primo asked.

"We have two more to kill and I'm sorry Primo but I'm not going to need your service tonight, you have the night off." I smiled and got the radio and asked Karina, "Where does Pastor John Wilkinson live?"

"He's a Holy Man, Mauricio." Cassandra said.

Karina responded right of away and gave me the address. "Let's go to this house. I'm going to need you to explode something just in case something bad happens at his house." I smiled and we took off to his house.

And it was nine o'clock and it was almost an hour since two people were murdered and my father and his team were still together and they were waiting for any calls. Just then my mother left the Hotel and went to see their Pastor at his home.

"Hi, Pastor sorry to visit you this late." She said.

"That's okay, Sister. Please come in."

They went into the kitchen and sat down and he made coffee. "What brings you here, Beatrice?"

"Well I'm sure by know you've seen or heard the murders of innocent people." She said.

"Yes, I've heard about the killings. God bless their souls." He said.

"I'm worried what if we cannot stop this Dark Cowboy from killing innocent people?" She asked.

"The Dark Cowboy will pay for his actions." He smiled.

We arrived at his house and we were listening to my mother talking to Pastor. "Mauricio, your mom is there." Chris said.

"Cassandra I need you to have a light explosion." I smiled and looked at Chris. "I guess I'm going to have to knock her out once again and leave right away."

I went to the front door and I was listening to my mother and Pastor talking and I kicked the door open and they got up to see what was going. They saw me standing in front of the living room and my eyes were glowing red. "You!" My mother yelled and took out her gun but she left her gun back in the Hotel. But she was train to take down criminals. Pastor started praying.

"That's not going to work on me. You think praying is going to help, Pastor." I said and was laughing.

"Stay away from us!" She yelled.

"It's your fault, Beatrice, that people are dying because of your decision. I'm not after you, Beatrice. I'm after him." I said.

"Stay back, Pastor. I'll handle this." She said.

"Don't test me. You think your Police training is going to help. You and I have so much in common, we both have heard the sound of bang before." I laughed and there was an explosion in the backyard. I was able to knock my mother out and Pastor was still staring at me and was praying. I shot him with the dart gun and grabbed him and sat him down on his couch.

And I had another flashback. I heard the voice of Pastor, "We gathered here in our Church because we have a situation."

"What kind of situation?"

Pastor responded, "That Mauricio may be the one that's behind all of the killings. Someone told me that Mauricio was possessed by a Demon and he's forcing him to kill innocent people. And Eliza doesn't want to accept the fact that Mauricio is dangerous."

"What are going to do?"

Pastor responded, "We need to do an exorcism on him without his parent's permission."

I was laughing at his bullshit and I got on my knees and took off my hat and smiled, "Hello, Pastor. I haven't seen you since Sunday morning. And you are wondering why I chose to kill you. Well I kept my eyes on your for a long time and the fact that you are a child molester and you have a lot of videos of child pornography inside your closet. Not to mention a drug addict and you work for the mob. You are corrupted son of a bitch. I'm not going to allow you to ruin people's lives anymore. Service is over." I started loading my guns, and I pointed the guns at his head and my mother was recovering and she still was loopy. She heard me say, "Maybe God have mercy on your soul when you are rotting in Hell!" I yelled and shot him so many times and killed the Pastor right in front her.

"No!" My mother yelled.

"Tell Mauricio that I said hi." I laughed and left the scene and I went to Chris's direction. We went to a safer place so the Police Officers and the FBI won't see us. And we heard everything.

My mother was crawling and she grabbed the phone and called the Dispatch Operator and the Dispatch Operator was able to call my father. "What now?" My father asked.

"There's been another killing! This time a Pastor."

"We will be there!" He yelled.

Everyone got in their cars and went to Pastor's home and on the way there they called the Ambulance and the Firefighters. They arrived in twenty minutes and found the door broken and saw Pastor dead and my mother was also on the ground.

"Are you okay?" He asked.

"Yes. Just a bump in my head." She responded.

"Let me guess Dark Cowboy?" He asked.

She started crying and yelled! "That bastard killed our Pastor!"

"It's okay."

The Ambulance arrived and put Pastor in a body bag and took him to the Morgue. They also took my mother to the Hospital for further testing. The Firefighters also arrived and took out the fire from outside. My father started yelling at everyone and started kicking the furniture and everything else. His team was able to calm him down and took him outside and left the crime scene. They took him to eat at a restaurant because they were tired and hungry.

"Your mother went to the Hospital." Chris said.

"Yes, but she is going to recover." I said.

"What's next?" Primo asked.

"They went to the Northeast to eat at Chico's Tacos. I want you guys to be parked behind the restaurant. And I want to kill Officer McFadden." I smiled and we took off to the Northeast.

Then it was around eleven thirty where they were outside the restaurant resting and eating. My father was still laying inside the Police car and was trying to calm down because he was so upset with three more killings and my mother was in the Hospital for the night. And Officer McFadden decided to go to the restroom and he went inside the restaurant. And the employees went outside to get some fresh air and they were talking to the FBI Agents and to the Police Officers. And I saw him entered the restaurant and I quickly went around and open the back door. So, Officer McFadden found the restroom and noticed that the back door was wide open. He took out his gun and checked it out and he heard a strange noise but it was a dog that was looking for food. I was standing behind the Police Officer and shot him in the back with the dart gun and he fell to the ground. I turn around and he was staring at me.

And I had a flashback, "I was the top Police Officer in the city of El Paso, Texas until Beatrice came along and took my spotlight away. I should be Lieutenant."

"You will be one!"

"But I'm also upset that Eliza wants to be with Mauricio. And we keep on telling her not to see him but she won't listen to us."

I took off my hat and smiled, "Good evening, Officer McFadden. My name is Mauricio de la Vega also known as The Dark Cowboy. Well isn't this a lovely night don't you think. Well I'm going to tell you why I want to kill you. I have pictures of you buying drugs from crime lords and you are corrupted and you were planning to plant drugs in my room, so they can arrest me and kill me. I put everything together in one night, yes, I am so smart. And now you are going to die and I'm going to plant so many bullets in your body and you are going to be buried fifty feet below the ground and you will be worm food." I started loading my guns and shot him so many times. And everyone heard the gunshots and went inside the restaurant and saw the back door open. They found the Police Officer dead and they heard a laughter that was coming from the roof top.

Everyone looked up. "What's the matter Agent de la Vega can't stand the heat." I laughed and six more buildings exploded and everyone fell on the ground. I jumped the other side of the restaurant and landed on the sidewalk and I was standing in the middle of the parking lot. And I was waiting for my daddy to come out and confront me like a man. Well my father finally got up and went running inside the restaurant, and to the parking lot and found me laughing even more. He saw me standing there and my eyes were glowing red.

"You've gone too far!" My father yelled.

"Yes, I have Agent de la Vega but don't worry because one of these days you get to see them again. You will join your friends later on, just as soon I finish killing your other friends." I laughed and jumped into the darkness.

My father stood in the middle of the parking lot, and he was so angry with me and went back to see his team. They were still recovering. "Are you guys okay?"

"Yes."

"Call the Firefighters. And go home and get some rest." He said.

One of the Police Officers called the Firefighters and they arrived in thirty minutes and took out the fire and the Ambulance came to take the Police Officer away. My father was upset and he was so worried that he might be next on the hit list. My father couldn't figure out why The Dark Cowboy has him targeted but after all he is the father of Mauricio and he hates him so much that he wants to see him suffer for the rest of his life. My father didn't tell anyone that he was next on The Dark Cowboy's hit list. So, my father and the FBI Agents went back to the Police Station for awhile.

Meanwhile we arrived at Chris's house, and I went to the restroom and changed. We hugged each other and were cheering and we hugged Samantha Jones. "Okay you guys. You need to go home because my dad is on his way here." I said and smiled. Chris took them back to their homes and he came back in twenty minutes. My father finally called him and said that he was on his way to pick me up. My father pulled into the driveway and I came outside and he hugged me and we also pick up Tania and we went home.

THE THIRD NIGHT OF HELL

So, the next day my father took us to the Hospital to see our mother and he was talking to the Doctor. "You're wife has a concussion but she's fine. And she's been through a lot of stress lately."

"We all are." My father said.

"I know how you must feel. If she continues with this investigation she's going to loose her mind and end up in the Psychiatric Ward. She needs to be at home resting comfortably and she needs to quit her job before she looses her mind." The Doctor said.

"This was her dream job since she was a little girl."

"I understand but this is going to kill her." He said.

"I'll talk to her." My father said.

The Doctor smiled and took us to her room and she was sound asleep and woke up and smiled. "Hi"

"How are you feeling?" He asked.

"Better. And I'm ready to go back out there and try to catch this killer."

"Honey, you're not well enough." He said.

"What's wrong with me?" She asked.

"You have been under a lot of stress lately and this might cost you to lose your mind and also you have depression." The Doctor explained to her.

"Good, Heavens I thought I had something else. So, I can walk around and live a normal life?"

"Yes. You need to be at home resting and quit your job." The Doctor said.

"Doctor, will you please leave us alone." My father said.

"Yes!" The Doctor said and left the room.

"You heard what the Doctor said. You need to go home because of your nerves." He said.

"The Hell with the Doctor. I'm ready to go back out there and for now I'll rest and tomorrow I will come back and try to stop this monster from killing innocent people. I won't let you down anymore. I want to risk my life for my kids and the people of El Paso, Texas." She said.

"I never doubt it you for second. I'm not going to like it but I will let continue with this investigation until we are able to catch this psychotic killer." My father said and smiled.

We stayed with my mother for a while and then we went home, and at the same time I felt bad for my mother but I know she is going to recover pretty soon because she's a tough Police Officer. Then my father left my sister Tania with her friends house and left me with Chris. They wanted to start early and they stood in their post and waited for something to happen. And it was eight o'clock that night and nothing happened and they couldn't figure out where The

Dark Cowboy was. An hour later they decided to rest and they were going to eat, so they called for take out.

Well Chris brought Primo, Cassandra, and Karina to the house. "What's the plan?" Karina asked.

"We have two more people to kill." I said.

"And tomorrow I'm going to turn myself in to the Police." Primo said.

Samantha started to like all of us because we were too nice to her and she hugged Primo and said, "No! Don't turn yourself in!"

"I have too!" Primo smiled and hugged her so tight.

We looked at him and smiled, "I hope it's the right decision and I'm not going to like it." I smiled and looked at everyone. "Let's get ready." I went to the restroom and changed and I started loading up the guns.

Karina and Samantha walked us outside, "Find out where Steve Johnson lives. He's the Mayor's Lawyer." I smiled and we took off to his house. During the road Karina told me where he lives and we went to the Westside. And we arrived at his house and we watched him through the window and we saw him doing all kinds of paper work. He decided to take a break and eat something and his wife was sound asleep.

And I went to the front door, and I kicked the door open and Steve went to see what was going on. And he saw me standing there and I was staring at him and the Lawyer was about to run upstairs when I shot him in the back with the dart gun and he falls to the ground. I grabbed him and sat him down on the couch.

I had a flashback. "Are you crazy, Matthew?"

"Yes, The Dark Cowboy is killing people and if I die, I want someone to take my place as the Mayor. I want Pablo de la Vega to take my place."

"Is that what you really want and that's fine with me."

"Work on that. And we should talk about Eliza. He's running out of patience and He wants us to convince Eliza to stay away from Mauricio."

"He's putting more pressure on us and she's not listening to us."

So, I got on my knees and took off my hat and said, "Hello, Steve Johnson. I know you get paid four hundred dollars per hour and I will make this short and sweet. Well I know you were one of Vito's henchmen and you were getting ready to steal the money of this great city. And you were going to use it to buy the mob and kill innocent people along the way. But don't worry you will join your best friend, Matthew Sheppard and tell him I said hi." I started loading my guns and before I was going to shoot him. I looked at his paper work and it was for my father's inauguration. Well I shot him anyway and killed him and left out the front door.

The gunshots woke his wife up and started calling the Police and then his wife runs down the stairs to find her husband dead and she was crying her eyes out. And the Dispatch Operator was able to get threw my father and told him what happen and he ordered his team to go to that house. On the way there he called the Ambulance and he even ordered that the Firefighters would be on call just in case if there's a fire on the area. They arrived at the Lawyer's house to find him dead and they saw his wife crying and she was getting hysterical. The Paramedics arrived to take him away to the Morgue and they took the Lawyer's wife to the Police Station for some protection.

We saw them leave and I gave Cassandra the signal and as soon they were going to leave another building exploded and the noise was loud enough and it woke up all the neighbors. And we took off and we heard my father yelling. "The Firefighters are handling it!"

"What are we going to do?" One of the Police Officers asked.

"We need to keep our cool and don't give up." My father responded.

Then my father and his team got on their cars and went straight to the burning building. All the teams arrived in time to take the fire out and they were circulating the rooftops and nothing no sign of The Dark Cowboy.

"Where are you?" My father asked. "We know your hiding!"

"He's hiding but we cannot find him anywhere!" One of the Agents exclaimed.

"Yes, he is." He said.

They were searching for me on the roof tops of the buildings and found nothing. But somewhere back in the Eastside there was my old second grade Teacher that was in the kitchen and she was checking out the kids assignments and she was grading them. She was tired and she was getting ready to go to sleep. And I kicked the front door open but I didn't break it this time. Mrs. Martinez went to the living room and saw me standing there looking at her. She started screaming and she was about to run to her room when I shot her in the back and she falls to the ground. Primo walked in and closed the door.

"Primo she's all yours and take your time to torture her but I'm going to see who else is here and I'm giving you two hours and good luck." I smiled and looked everywhere and there wasn't anybody there with her. Primo grabbed her and took her to her bedroom and started raping her while I was fixing myself a nice dinner. I was eating her food and I was looking at her papers. And I decided to take it with me. So, Primo was raping her for two whole hours and I was hearing her moan and she begging him to let her go.

"Are you finished?" I asked.

"Yes, I am." Primo smiled and he was catching his breathe and he put his clothes back on. And I gave him the plate of chicken and the bag with her papers. "See you in Hell you fat bitch." Primo said and left.

I grabbed my second grade Teacher and dragged her to the living room and sat her down on the couch and I shot her again so she won't scream at all. I got on my knees and I took off my hat and I let her see my face.

I had another flashback, "I cannot believe that He's putting pressure on us."

"Why?'

"He's wants us to convince Eliza to stay away from Mauricio. And we are suspecting that Mauricio is the serial killer. But she wont listen to us."

I was wondering who He was and is He putting pressure on the people that I killed and He doesn't want to see us together. So, anyway Rebecca Martinez was staring at me, "Hi, Rebecca Martinez. It's been a long time since we seen each other. You are that stupid fat bitch that was making fun off me and was screwing with me. You, Armando, Deyna wanted to see me get hurt and you got me in trouble for everything that I didn't do. You should be ashamed of yourself and you are going to see them again and this time you guys will suffer together and I will be laughing for a long time. I'm not going to forgive you at all and now you can rot in Hell." I started loading my guns and shot her so many times and left out the back door. The neighbors heard the gunshots and called the Police and the FBI and the Dispatch Operator called the team and told them the news. They went straight to her house to find the Rebecca Martinez dead on her living room and she was still naked and she had bruises all over her body. My father started kicking the walls and was cursing me to Hell. And the Ambulance arrived and took her away to the Morgue.

"That was my son's Teacher." One of the Police Officers said.

"You're right." He said.

"She was even raped." One of the Agents said.

My father looked at Primo's mother and Perla noticed that she was raped and then murdered and she started crying. "Your son raped this poor defenseless Teacher and his friend The Dark Cowboy killed her. We're going to arrest your son for this and we need to know what your son knows about The Dark Cowboy!" My father exclaimed.

His mother cried and said, "Send him to the juvenile home, so he can get the help that he needs!"

"When you go home I want to hug your son, Primo Mancini because you are not going to see him again for a long time." My father said and hugged Perla.

"How could The Dark Cowboy do this to everyone that has died?" One of the Agents asked.

"That I don't know. No one deserves to die this way." My father said.

We saw him leave the house and I gave Cassandra the signal and as soon they were going to leave, another building exploded. And everyone went to the direction of the burning building. The Firefighters were the first ones to arrive and they were taking out the fire and my father and his team also arrived. All they did was stare at the burning building and they felt helpless that night.

"Ten people died this past weekend." One of the Agents said.

"That's a total of eighteen people. The Dark Cowboy promised that he was going to kill ten people by the end of the week." My father said and looked at his watch. "It's twelve o'clock and we couldn't stop the killings."

"What are we going to do now?" One of the Agents asked.

"We need to go home and rest because tomorrow we have a long day. The families need to identify the bodies down at the Morgue." He said.

"We're not going to question them?" One of the Police Officers asked.

"No. Because we all know why The Dark Cowboy has been killing everyone. And that's because he hates my son so much that he wants to see him suffer for the rest of his life." My father said.

"Are you saying that your son may be a key witness in this case?" One of the Agents asked.

"We don't know that because Beatrice doesn't want him to get involve in this case. We need to respect her decision. Is that clear for everyone, nobody is going to question my son. Whoever decides to question him or do something to him, you will find yourself unemployed and I will personally kill you, is that clear." My father said and looked at everyone. "Go home and get some rest because we have a long day tomorrow. Good night to all of you and drive home safe. The Firefighters were able to put the fire out and everyone went home.

And on that night all of us said goodbye to little Samantha Jones because she was going away to a boarding school and she gave us a hug and we wished her a lot of luck in her future and we gave her our address. Samantha told us that she was going to write to us every single day. And I was wondering if Karina and the girls were recording me right after I saved Samantha's life.

CHAPTER TEN

DESPERATE MEN DO DESPERATE THINGS

The next day my father, Tania and I woke up at seven o'clock in the morning. I was getting ready to go to school. While my father went to the Hospital to pick up my mother and she was clear to go home. And I was in my room and I was listening to what my parents had to say.

"Ten people died the past three days?" My mother was worried.

"Yes. And who knows what's going to happen tonight or tomorrow night. This may take along time to arrest The Dark Cowboy." He said.

"I'm ready to work tonight." My mother smiled.

"I know you are ready and knowing how you are. You would want to die by protecting the kids and everyone else in the city. That's why you're a good mother and a very good Police Officer." My father smiled and they finally arrived at the house. My father parked in the driveway and went into the house.

"I'm home!" My mother smiled.

Tania and I went up to hug our loving mother and we stayed together in the living room. We were talking and laughing and my father made us breakfast and we had a good meal and we were one big happy family. So, my parents took us to school and I said goodbye to them and my mommy gave me a hug and told me that she loves a lot. So, the gang were waiting for me in front of the school and we stayed outside talking.

"Guys, there is a chance that Primo might be arrested today or tonight." I said.

The girls were crying, "Why?" They asked.

"I'm taking one for the team and whatever happens to me. I want you guys to know that I love you a lot. And I'm never going to tell them about your identity, Mauricio. Your secret is safe with me." Primo smiled and we hugged each other.

"I looked at Primo and asked, "Are you sure about this? Because I can call off the dogs."

"Yes, I'm sure about this! Well I want to pay the consequences and don't try to rescue me, Okay." He smiled and hugged me.

"Fair enough!" I smiled.

Then the bell rang and it was time to go class and during the morning class. We were hearing everything that was happening on that day. An hour later my father called his team and told them to meet him at the Police Department and later on my parents arrived at the Police Department. When they went inside the office everyone started clapping and they were happy to see my mother again. And that's where my father broke the news to everyone.

"I want all of you to know that on Friday afternoon we went to the Mayor's house. And the Matthew's Lawyer read the Will and played a video tape. It turns out that the late Mayor Matthew Sheppard requested that I'd take his place as the new Mayor of El Paso, Texas."

"You should take it, Sir." One of the Police Officers said.

"You are the right man for the job and we know that The Dark Cowboy is no match for you, Sir." One of the Agents said.

"I was ready to start my new position as the new Mayor of El Paso but after what happen the past three night, I couldn't accept the position as the new Mayor of El Paso." He said and looked worried.

"You should take it, Sir. You're the perfect man for the job." One of the Police Officers encouraged.

"You should take it." One of the Agents said. "We know you can bring that psychotic killer down."

"Come on, Honey. Everyone wants you to accept it. I do want you to accept your new position." My mother also encouraged.

"If I accept my new position that means that you guys are going to protect me at all times." My father said and smiled. "Since you guys insist of me becoming the new Mayor of El Paso, Texas well I accept. But I'm going to miss the action and I'm going to stay back in the fort and continue to give commands and I hope that will be enough to bring this psychotic killer to justice. I'm still going to be in charge of you guys and write your paychecks." My father smiled and looked at Perla and said, "After I get inaugurated I'm ordering you guys to arrest Primo Mancini also known as the "Sexual Predator," also known as the "Virgin Killer." Primo has been raping a lot of women and he's been helping out his friend The Dark Cowboy with all of his killings. Primo Mancini is The Dark Cowboy's Lieutenant, his partner in crime, and he has helped him in many ways. And I hope Perla that you gave your son a hug and spent the last night together. And I'm sorry Perla and I hope that you can understand and we need to question your son and give him the help that he needs. Primo is going to pay for his actions!" My father hugged her and everyone started cheering for him and they went up to him and congratulated him. They were hugging him while my mother was hugging Perla and they were crying their eyes out. So, we heard what was going to happen and we went to lunch and made a toast to our friend Primo Mancini. I didn't want him to take the fall but that's what he wants well I'm not going to have him hostage. Then later on in the afternoon we were in the middle of class when they made the announcement and they wanted us to turn on the television.

The whole school and along with the city were watching my father's inauguration and it was at City Hall where the people were excited to meet the new Mayor of El Paso, Texas and they were cheering on. A new Judge came out and presented the people the new Mayor.

"Please give a warm welcome to the new Mayor of El Paso, Texas. His name is Pablo de la Vega!" He exclaimed.

Everyone started cheering for him because they knew that he was going to be a good Mayor. My father came out and he was officially inaugurated and hugged the Judge and smiled to the people. He then started speaking to the public. "Citizens of El Paso, Texas. I want to thank you for this warm applause and I'm deeply honored to be your new Mayor. I also want to thank the late Mayor Matthew Sheppard for hand picking me to become your new Mayor. I was born in Madrid, Spain and I grew up in Mexico City, Redwood City California, and now here in El Paso, Texas. I always felt that El Paso was my home. And everyone knows that I became an FBI Agent. I traveled all over the world catching some of the most dangerous criminals in Europe and the Middle

East. And now I come back home to find out that there's a serial killer on the loose in the city that I love so much. I want to address this to you that ten people were murdered within the past three days and you know by now that a lot of buildings exploded. And eighteen people have now died and those families that lost their loved ones these past three days, my sympathy to everyone." My father said and drank some water and continued. "We've been working very hard to catch this Dark Cowboy and I'm sorry to say this but he's always been one step ahead of us. This will not happen ever again, I cannot guarantee you that we will catch The Dark Cowboy by tonight or tomorrow night. But I do have a couple announcements to make this afternoon. My colleagues have been asking me what's going to happen to my old position as an FBI Agent and who's going to command the team? The answer is that I'm resigning from the Federal Bureau Investigation and I'm going to appoint someone that's going to lead the team into capturing The Dark Cowboy. Who better to do it than my lovely wife, Beatrice de la Vega." He smiled and my mother went to my father and shook her hand and everyone started clapping. My mother was happy and wondering what my father was up too. The people were excited but my mother and the team didn't know what was going on. But she smiled in front of the people. "Thank you, FBI Agent Beatrice de la Vega." My father smiled and shook her hand. "Now I have another announcement to make. Starting tonight I'm going to order the Police Officers, and the FBI Agents to guard the people from inside their homes. I want the people to be safer in their own homes. Also the Border Patrol Agents and the Customs will be on call, the Paramedics will be on call, the Firefighters will also be on call. We will work together in order to keep the city safer from The Dark Cowboy. Also the third and final announcement. I'm ordering the Police Officers and the FBI Agents to march down to Americas High School and arrest Primo Mancini, he his the son of the mob leader Vito Mancini. Primo Mancini and The Dark Cowboy are working together and they have formed a deadly alliance and they are using their deadly alliance to harm all the citizens of El Paso, Texas. So, right now I'm asking the FBI Agents and the Police Officers to go to that school and arrest him, so he can get the help that he needs. Thank you very much." He said and smiled.

The people were clapping for the new Mayor of El Paso, Texas. My father went inside City Hall and went to his office and then my mother also went to his office. And the FBI Agents and the Police Officers got into the van and went to arrest Primo Mancini.

"What was that about?" She asked.

"I'm the new Mayor." He responded.

"You put me as the FBI Agent. Are you nuts?" She asked.

"No. I haven't resign from the Federal Bureau Investigation, I'm still the FBI Agent. All of this is part of an act, and this is for The Dark Cowboy. I want him to think that he's in control but he's not, I'm in control of this situation. That's why during daytime I'm the "Mayor" and during the night I'm the super FBI Agent. We will catch him off guard and just like today we are going to arrest his partner in crime Primo Mancini." He smiled.

"Wow! You should have told me about the plan or your team."

"Now they know. I want you to trust me on this, Okay." My father said and kissed her.

"I do trust you. That's why I married you." She said and they kissed again. "What's next?"

"You and I are going to go to meet the families down at the Morgue, so they can identify their bodies. And then make funeral arrangements for the families." He said.

"What about Perla? Primo is her only son." She asked.

"Like I said we're going to help him because he was under the influence of The Dark Cowboy's spell." He said.

"I hope you are right." She smiled.

So, Primo and I were in the same class together and we looked at each other and we just smiled. "Don't worry, I will see you soon." Primo smiled and we saw the FBI Agents and Police Officers knocking on the door. The Teacher went to open the door.

"Primo Mancini you are under arrest!" But Primo smiled and got up and they arrested him right on the spot.

And I got up and said, "Stop!" And all the kids in the classrooms step aside and they also bowed down. The FBI Agents and the Police Officers also bowed down and they made Primo bowed down too. "I want to see your faces." I said and read their tags, "Agent Williams, Agent Russell, Agent Rodriguez. I want you three clowns to treat Primo with respect and if I find out that he got mistreated on the way to the Hospital or wherever is you're taking him. You guys will be responsible and I will order someone to chop off your heads. Is that clear!"

They looked scared, "Yes! Your, Majesty." They grabbed my hand and started kissing my hand. "As the matter of fact I'm going to order for them to cut off your penis and your balls. Now get out of my sight!" They left the school grounds and I looked at everyone. And I went up to the Teacher and she bowed down, "Teach us something! For crying out loud!"

"Yes! Your, Royal Highness!" She smiled.

I went back to my seat and I was upset with my father but I didn't want him to know that I was upset. Well I'm just going to cost more problems in their marriage and his job as well. Meanwhile my parents went to the Morgue to meet up with the families. The Doctor showed them the ten bodies and the families were crying their eyes out. "We're deeply sorry your loses." My mother said.

"The city will cover the funeral service and everything else." My father said and smiled.

"Bless you, Mayor." They hugged him and left home crying.

My father may had a great idea earlier this afternoon and he was smiling to everyone but deep down inside, he felt like crying because his friends were getting killed and there was nothing he could do to protect them. At the same time he was going to regret the order he gave, so Primo could get arrested and all he did is put his arm around his wife and said. "I love you."

"Me too." She said.

Then the bell rang and it was time to go to school, I saw the girls crying in front of the school. I went to hug them and told them that everything is going to be okay. We heard someone honking and it was Chris and we hopped into the his truck and went to his house. And on the way home he grabbed Chinese Food and took us home. We were in the living room eating and the girls didn't want to eat anything because they were still crying.

"I'm sure that you saw the news?" Chris asked.

"Yes, my beloved father is the new Mayor of El Paso and he made my mom the new FBI Agent. And he also made the FBI Agents come to the school and arrest my best friend Primo. That's great news and we should celebrate by killing more people." I smiled and laughed.

"Mauricio, they are going to guard the people from inside their homes! Now your father is the new Mayor and we don't know what kind of orders he's going to give. Like I said your father is unpredictable and today you saw it for yourself and who knows what's going to happen to Primo. I wasn't excepting this to happen." He said.

"You worry too much, Chris. And I'm no longer a suspect in this case. All the people that had me as a suspect in this case are dead and they are worm food. And besides my dad doesn't have the balls to question me because my loving mommy doesn't want me to get involved in this case."

"I hope you are right." Karina said and sobbed.

I looked at Chris and smiled, "Well I earned five hundred dollars for killing ten people over the weekend and I have the total of nine hundred dollars."

"You are right, Mauricio. Tomorrow before I leave and I will deposit five hundred dollars in your bank account." Chris looked worried.

"Well I want to know what my father is planning to do. Let's chill out for awhile and take a vacation and let's see what he's capable of." I said.

"Fair enough." He said.

"So, how unpredictable my father really is and I mean besides arresting my best friend in the world?" I asked.

"You don't want to know!" Chris said and the phone rang and before he was going to answer it, he told me, "But we need to abort this mission for awhile. I'm going back to Ireland just for a couple of months. Promise me that you are not going to do anything stupid like Primo."

"I promise." I smiled and he went to answer the phone.

"What's your plan?" Karina sobbed.

"You will find out about my plan!" I yelled and Chris heard me. And then Chris came back and looked at me and I asked him. "You want to know about my plan?"

"Fine I want to hear about your plan, Mauricio." Chris responded and looked worried.

"I want to drive a wedge in my parent's marriage and I want to know how much my parents love each other. I'm going to drive my dad crazy for the rest of his life." I said and smiled.

"Mauricio you are upset because your friend got arrested." Chris said.

"I am pissed off but let's see how unpredictable my father really is." I said and looked at Karina. She smiled and hacked on the computer and we were hearing all the commotions inside the Police Department. I looked at the girls and said, "Girls, maybe you do your homework!" I smiled and hugged them and told them I love them.

Then at six o'clock that night Chris and all of us were still eating the Chinese Food and just then my parents gathered the team in the Police Department and they started discussing about tonight's festivity. My mother started talking to everyone. "Ten people died over the weekend and that's the total of eighteen. I know all of us are doing our jobs the best way we can and we are tired and exhausted. But we're not giving up and you heard what the Mayor said. All of you are going to do is guard the people from inside their homes, so they won't be anymore killings. I don't know how long it's going to take for us to arrest The Dark Cowboy. We're not giving up!" My mother said and her tears started coming down her face.

"Guys, this is the only shot we got. I had a great time being around you guys and now I've past the torched to my wife, Beatrice de la Vega. And I know it hurts when people die and when our colleagues die it hurts even more. Because you're used to seen him everyday and there is a brotherhood in law enforcement. And I feel honored that they risk their lives for this city and for all of us and for their families. We will miss them and now we need to move on and try to stop The Dark Cowboy from killing. That's why I'm going to stay back in the fort and hope that you guys are able to capture him. You're in good hands."

"Now let's get out there and protect everyone." My mother said.

Karina looked at me and asked me, "Who are you going to kill?"

I responded with a smile, "No one. I just want to drive my parents crazy. After all I'm a teenager."

Well the team started clapping and at exactly thirty minutes later, the team were protecting the people from inside their homes. The Firefighters were in the Fire Station and they were waiting for the building burning and the Paramedics were also prepared for any dead bodies in the area. My parents were alone in their house and we were listening to their conversation.

"I never thought of you protecting me, Beatrice. I promised your parents that I was going to protect you." He said.

"I know but I promised everyone that I was going to protect you. I love you a lot." She said.

"Me too. I don't know what to do without you or the kids." He said and kissed her.

My parents continued to talk until I decided to call them and the phone rang. My mother thought it was us kids and she press the speaker. "Hello!" She said.

"Hello, Beatrice." I growled and was breathing heavily.

"What do you want?" She asked.

"Just to speak to you guys and to congratulate the new Mayor of El Paso, Texas and I know Beatrice that you have failed to protect someone in the past. As the matter of fact you've failed twice. But I still respect the two of you." I said.

"What is it that you want?" He asked.

"You think your plan is going to work?" I also asked.

"Yes, it is. Because I thought about that plan and I didn't consult it with anyone else. And I can come up with any plan I want too and you won't even know about it. I can give you an example. Today, I sent my men to arrest your best friend, Primo Mancini, and he is going to get tortured at the Psychiatric Ward and what are you going to do about it? And right now I can come up with another plan and my men will follow it." He said.

I was laughing at him, "Will get to Primo later on in our conversation, and just because your men are guarding the people from inside their homes. It doesn't mean that they're going to be safe." I said.

"Five law enforcement are guarding each house and if you break in. They will kill you right on the spot and it will be the happiest day of our lives. As the matter of fact tomorrow I'm going to speak in front of the people and my wife or anyone else doesn't know what's I'm going to say." My father laughed and grabbed my mother's walkie-talkie. "I want you to listen to what I'm going to say Dark Cowboy." My father had the walkie-talkie in his hand and said, "This is the Mayor speaking and I want everyone to know that there's been a bounty on The Dark Cowboy. Ten thousands dollars whoever brings him alive and thirty thousand dollars for whoever brings him dead. Is that clear."

"Yes." Everyone on the radio said.

"You see Dark Cowboy I have the power to bring you down. I can snap my finger and I can bring anyone I choose to take you out." He said.

"Very clever. I'm so scared and this is your way of protecting the people of El Paso, Texas. Your team is going to go outside and try to catch me and they are going to leave the people alone in their homes and they are going to be helpless and defenseless. And more people are going to die insides in their homes. Unless all the people heard you and they probably are going to march down the streets at night with torches and try to catch me and more people are going die out in the open. You and your wife are good negotiators." I said and laughed.

My father whispered something to my loving mother. "That bastard thinks he's won."

"What's the matter, Mayor de la Vega! Cat has your tongue? Don't worry very soon you will get the chance to see your friends again and when you meet them, tell them that I said hi. And on a little personal note. Primo Mancini sacrificed himself for the team and I will give him a huge reward for his loyalty to us and he is going to suffer but the pain would be worth for the alliance that we have. Until now I will see you later on and please make the announcement tomorrow morning. I can't wait to kill more people out in the open. Since, I feel bad that I'm killing people and the buildings are exploding and people are loosing their jobs. And Beatrice has been under a lot of stress lately and she is depress. And since this is her first night commanding the team and making sure that the Mayor is safe, maybe we should take a break and regroup, you know recharge our batteries. I want to give you more time to strategize and plan how you are going to convince the people to come after me at night. We will see each other very soon and I will send you a sign and you will know that it's me coming back to piss you off." I growled and hang up the phone and I was laughing.

"Pablo! Don't tell me that you're going to put a price on The Dark Cowboy's head?" My mother asked him.

"Yes, I am. And if that doesn't work, I will have Plan B ready." My father responded and smiled.

Chris looked at me and said, "You are getting into his head and he is loosing his mind."

"Of course and there is more where that came from." I smiled.

"You lucky dog!" Karina smiled.

Well my mother and all of us were wondering what Plan B was and she knew that he's putting everyone and including her in the dark about his plans to stop The Dark Cowboy. And both of them wondered if I was going to strike tonight. Well the next day my father wanted to speak in front of the press and the people gathered in front of City Hall. He stood in front of everyone and said,

"I've been receiving threading calls from The Dark Cowboy. The Dark Cowboy thinks that he's going to get away from all the crimes, he's been committing over the years. Last night he threatened to kill me and he's not going to get away with this anymore. As for today I'm going issuing an order and it will help the people of El Paso, Texas. I'm ordering a bounty on The Dark Cowboy, ten thousand dollars for the one that brings The Dark Cowboy alive and thirty thousand dollars for whoever brings him dead. The bounty starts tonight and that will show that we're not afraid of this Dark Cowboy." He said.

My father was smiling in front of the crowd and the people were cheering for him. My mother thought that he was abusing his power as the Mayor. She looked at her colleagues and they also thought that he was hungry for power and he was anxious to catch The Dark Cowboy. And on that night the people joined my mother and her team and it was more like the mob scene. The people were carrying blow torches and they were saying, "Kill The Dark Cowboy! Kill The Dark Cowboy!" The people exclaimed and my mother and her team were so upset with my father and they waited of me to arrived but I didn't showed up that night. I was at home with my baby sister, Tania and my father. And I was laughing at them and I was turning red along the way. Then my mother got on the speaker and ordered all the people to go home and get some rest. She was shocked that they actually listen to her. She was excited that nothing bad happen on that night, and she was more worried for the mob than me. My mother felt that it was going to get worse if the people continue to show up and put themselves in danger and they might have gotten killed out in the open.

Well my friends and I were excited that the school year ended and another summer of working hard in the yards and earning a lot of money. And I was spending more time with my friends than my family and we had a good time together. But the problem was they had the curfew and no one was allowed to go outside during the night. We had to be indoors at exactly six o'clock. But I looked on the bright side that we were going to be a sophomores. And it was the end of July where my father finally ordered my mother and her team and the angry mob to stop looking for The Dark Cowboy. My father told everyone to rest because they were going to need it and he so was sure that The Dark Cowboy would leave him a sign. My father said to himself when I was going to strike and all the people were sleeping at night and they were also wondering when I was going to strike next. Well you guys can now sleep at night. And from there the people were getting crazy because they couldn't come outside at night and go out on vacations and go out clubbing and it was driving them insane and they wanted to enjoy their summer. So, my father went through a lot of expense that he gave away free arcade games and everything was for free, so the people won't lose their minds in their own homes.

And on that afternoon my father had a special visitor. "Mister Mayor, you have a visitor." She said.

"Who is it?" He asked.

"Me! Your darling wife." She responded and sat down and they were alone.

"Hey, Honey. What are you doing here?" He asked.

"Are you insane? You are giving stuff away for free and it's the summer for crying out loud and at least let them have fun during the night." She said.

"I don't want them to loose their minds in their own home. Besides it was the other Mayor's plan to keep the people safe from The Dark Cowboy. It is also my job to make them feel comfortable at their own homes." He responded.

"You must be the worst Mayor in the history of El Paso, Texas. I knew that you were going to drop the ball. You swore to protect the people and you ordered a bounty. And you saw what I had to deal with. One night with the angry mob was a year for me, and I don't want to deal with the mob every single night. You're not out there because of the decision you made. You are putting me in a horrible position."

"I didn't mean to put you in that kind of position. I didn't expect the people to go outside at night. I don't want you to be upset with me because I'm trying to be a good Mayor and we're trying to catch this psychotic killer. I know you and the team are upset with me. That what he wants."

"Who?" She asked.

"The Dark Cowboy is driving us crazy and he wants us to turn on each other. One false move and one person dies out in the street. We need to stick together in order to kill this guy. I want you to trust me."

"I do trust you but not as the Mayor and now you are hungry for power and if you keep leaving us in the dark about the wrong decisions you make. Well you're going to have a lot of people that are going to be angry with you and maybe they want to kill you. And perhaps you should resign as the Mayor and go back what you do best. You were a good FBI Agent and don't ruin your reputation."

"I was good FBI Agent, and I remember I used to arrest some of the most dangerous killers in Europe and the Middle East. I also remember risking my life trying to protect this country from terrorist."

"Don't you miss those days?" She asked.

"I do miss those days but I'm the Mayor now. My job is to protect the people of El Paso, Texas. And I'm still respected and I will keep on giving orders until The Dark Cowboy is finally dead and he will be buried fifty below the ground. And we all can live our lives in peace. Beatrice we're not giving up." My father said and grabbed her hand. "I said from the beginning that I don't care if I get divorce or the Police Officers get divorce, and what's more important is stop this serial killer from doing more crimes."

My mother sat there and looked at my father very seriously. "You're right. You care about catching this serial killer than our marriage and when this is over so are we. I'm also going to stick around and try to stop this Dark Cowboy from doing anymore crimes." My mother was upset and got up and looked at him again. "I raised my kids without you. I did everything I could to protect them and damn it like I told The Dark Cowboy, that I would do anything to protect my kids. Even if you take me to court and I will fight for them." She said and left the office.

"Beatrice!" My father yelled at my mother. "You see what The Dark Cowboy has done to our marriage."

My mother turn around and looked at him. "Our marriage fell apart when you ran away and became an FBI Agent."

My father sat there and he couldn't believe what was going on and he was blaming The Dark Cowboy for his problems in his marriage. The truth behind this, it was my father's ego and his pride. My father wanted to become a legend because he was a Super Cop and he thought being the Mayor of El Paso, Texas was going to increase his legacy but it didn't and he wasn't that great at all. My father was now power hungry and he is making the wrong decisions in the city but my friends and I couldn't stop laughing at my father for his mistakes.

And on that night my father had to sleep on the couch because he knew that my mother would be mad at him. Tania was wondering why my father was sleeping on the couch but I was smiling from the inside and I knew that I was driving my parents insane. And later on in the night my mother went down to the kitchen to get something to drink and she knew that my father was cold and she brought him a blanket.

"Thank you!" He said.

"You're welcome. We need to get along for our kids sake." She said.

"I'm sorry for the way I've been acting." He said.

"I know. And you said it you don't care if you get divorce but I do care. You came home every three months to visit us and we never get to spend one moment together. I was angry because you left us."

"Remember when we were kids and we talked about what we wanted to become when we became grown ups. I wanted to become an FBI Agent and I was a pretty good Police Officer."

"You were a good one."

"I wanted you guys to have a better life. And that's why I risked my life by capturing mobsters, killers and rapist, so they wouldn't come here to hurt you guys. And what I said to those guys about not caring if they get divorce or we getting divorce, I was just saying that to motivate them. You use terms like that to motivate someone and I know it hasn't work because were trying to capture this freak from doing anymore crimes." My father got up and hugged her and kissed her. "I don't want to loose you, I love you a lot."

"Me too!" My mother smiled and her tears started to come down her face. "I'm so damn scared. What happens if we never capture The Dark Cowboy. We are losing our friends that we grew up with and our kids friends are dying."

"I know and it hurts me too. We are alive and we will capture him and as soon he gives us his sign that he's going to come back. But I will make more calls and bring more reinforcement and when he does comes back we will be ready for him and he will be arrested on the spot."

"You promise." She said and sobbed.

"I promise." My father said and they kissed.

Then months went by and it was now three weeks before Christmas and my father made the wise decision to let Primo out of the Psychiatric Ward, so he can spend the holidays with his mother and his friends. The gang and I were united all over again and we went to Chris's house and we started talking.

"What's this about, Mauricio?" Primo asked.

I looked at them and smiled, "I wanted to tell you guys that how about we do one last job together and we need to make a promise that were not going to do anything else to the city. Because I feel when we graduate from high school we're going to have a lot of money to spend."

"We're sophomores and we have two years left. Let's enjoy our last two years in school." Karina said.

"I think we've done a lot of damage to this city." Sonia said.

"But why, Mauricio?" Primo asked.

"We have them right where we want them, Primo. My father and everyone else are scratching their heads and my father is loosing control of this investigation. And we are winning the war and this city is now ours." I smiled and looked at everyone and asked, "Christina Bobs what's your opinion?"

She smiled, "I agree and I had fun the past couple of years."

"Jennifer!" I said.

"I had fun too and I also agree." She smiled.

"Well Mauricio we all agreed to have one more last job together." Karina said and smiled.

"What's your plan?" Primo asked.

"New Years Eve. Ten buildings exploding and after that we can continue to live our lives in peace." I said and smiled.

"I also want to move on and I hope to start my life over." Primo said and smiled, "I wanted my father to be proud of me. I think he's proud of me."

"He is!" I said.

"Well one lat job together and I know what to do!" Cassandra smiled.

"I'll do it, you guys have fun with your families." Chris said

"Also, I'm getting tired of people kissing my ass. So, Erin I need you to steal a reporter's identity and make up a story. And I want the people to know that it was bullshit that I'm going to be the future King of Spain. I want the people to know that it was just a hoax. So, I'm retiring from killing and I hope to have a normal life." I smiled and we all hugged each other.

"Merry Christmas to you guys and a happy New Year too." Chris smiled. Then it was now the countdown to the year 2000 where we were watching television and we were seen the countries celebrating the New Year. And it was our turn to celebrate and the clock struck at midnight and we were hugging each other.

I radioed Chris and said, 'Now!"

While we were hugging each other there was a loud bang in the city. My parents went outside and saw the ten buildings burning down. They heard the sirens of the Firefighters and they were trying to take the fire out. Then I radioed my father well I was in my room and said, "Happy New Year! Pablo de la Vega" I growled and breathed harder.

"You son of a bitch!" My father yelled.

"Well I'm actually celebrating the New Year and I hope you saw the firecrackers. I'm going to make the New Year's resolution, so you can live your life in peace. I'm not going to kill anymore people and since I'm having fun with you, Mayor de la Vega, why not keep pissing you off with our great conversation that we are having. And we can do this for the rest of our lives. I've enjoyed watching you drop the ball in your marriage and professionally as well." I laughed and disconnected and I went to the living room and my parents were outside looking up at the smoke. Tania was in the living room and she was crying her eyes out and I was hugging her so tight. I told her, "Happy New Year! My little munchkin."

CHAPTER ELEVEN

I SEE A BEAUTIFUL ANGEL

By now it was the year 2000 my beloved parents were already turning forty-six years old and they have been on the Police Force for over twenty-eight years. And now the Police Officers and the FBI Agents were getting younger and they had to be out on the streets taking orders from my parents and the rest of the veterans. So, the rookies had to be ready right from the start but the FBI Agents were the ones that were doing all the training, so the rookies can be prepared for anything. Well the great Mayor Pablo de la Vega was still in charge of this operation and still he hasn't made any progress in arresting me and he has yet to ask me a lot of question. And I want to know who wears the pants in this marriage? The answer was my sweet old mother. She was the one that called the shots in the marriage and she didn't want us to be in any kind of danger and she was willing to die for us. And on that morning my mother made me breakfast and I ate scrambled eggs and there were so delicious. My mother is a good cook and it would be nice if she becomes a Chef when she retires from the Police Force. Also on that morning I received a letter from little Samantha Jones but she changed her name, so they won't know that she's hiding in a boarding school. And I was happy to know that she's doing fine at school and she's growing up so fast. After that I grabbed my backpack and my mother dropped me off at school and I went straight to the cafeteria. I went to the Pepsi machine and took out a Pepsi and I was in a good mood to eat another set of scrambled eggs and I grabbed my plate and sat down with my new two friends and they were eating and talking.

"Hey, Mauricio! How was your weekend?" Joe asked.

"I was studying for the Geometry test and you know the usual the damn curfew. And I was in my room listening to music and watching a lot of movies." I responded.

"I know I was doing the same thing as you and I think everybody in the city is doing the same thing. I'm also starting to hate the curfew so damn much and I hope they arrest that psychotic killer soon before I hung myself in the restroom." Joe said.

"Well I also hate the curfew like everybody else but the worst part is that today I have my annual meeting. In other words I have my parole."

"Why do you keep on saying that?" Miguel asked.

"That's how I have been feeling all these years and sometimes school reminds me of prison. Look at the food they serve us! And we have to ask permission to go to the restroom! And then there are my annual meetings which I can say that I hate so much. And I hate high school and I cannot wait to graduate from this place and go to college." I responded.

"I know it's hard for you since you're in Special Education and you might be stuck in that department. My sympathy to you." Joe said.

The bell rang and we got to put the food in the trash can and left the tray on the table. "Hang in there, Mauricio. Soon it will be all over and no more Special Education just college where no one makes a big deal and drunk college girls." Joe smiled and we went to our classrooms.

During the morning class, I kept thinking about the Geometry quiz and my annual meeting that I'm going to have in the afternoon. Well I had History in the morning and I wasn't paying attention to my Teacher was saying because I was too busy day dreaming. Then the bell rang for third period and when I got to Geometry class, Mr. Caballero was already handing out the Geometry quiz to everyone and he told us to start and said good luck to all of us. I had a tough time with the Geometry quiz and I had no choice but to start guessing and I didn't care if I get a good grade or a bad grade. I know I've worked so hard for the Geometry quiz and still I didn't know the damn answer. Then the bell rang and all of us handed in the Geometry quiz to Mr. Caballero and I guess he saw me guess the entire time and he didn't look too happy but he smiled.

Joe and Miguel were outside the classroom and they were waiting for me. "How did it go in the Geometry quiz?" Joe asked me.

"Awful! I had to start guessing." I responded.

"That was your only regular class." Miguel said.

"Mauricio, you always wanted to get out of Special Education." Joe said.

"They told you in the annual meetings that you need to have good grades in order to be in regular classes." Miguel said.

"That's what they say in all the annual meetings but I guess my grades are never good enough for them. It's the same thing in every meeting I had over the years. I bet you that they are not going to grant me regular classes and they are going to keep me in Special Education." I said.

"If you work extra hard in Geometry they might give you regular classes. And if you asked them nicely they might give you regular classes." Joe said.

"That's what I've been doing and I play the nice guy all the time and it doesn't work at all. Plus I worked so damn extra hard to have good grades but they don't see it that way, and they think of me as a mentally retarded!" I yelled and everyone looked at me.

"What a great speech, Mauricio! You might want to be emotional when you tell them that." Miguel said.

"Maybe I should cry and get on my knees and beg them to put me in regular classes with everybody else!" I yelled and smiled. And we went to eat lunch and as always the lunch line is always full but it's a good thing that we have *Subway*, *Little Ceasers*, and *Sonic* inside the school because we don't have open campus. The line from Sonic was not that full. I was going to pay for Joe and Miguel and the Teacher asked me what I wanted. "Well three Conies and three Cheeseburgers!" I smiled and I gave Joe and Miguel their Conies and we went outside to eat lunch. We sat down and we talked about my situation I'm going to have this afternoon with the annual meeting. And just like that lunch was over and it was time to go to class and I was in the classroom when they call me for the annual meeting. I was so nervous because I didn't know what they were going to say to me. For some reason the Campus Police were waiting for me outside the classroom and they were going to escort me all the way to the annual meeting. Since they found out about the bogus story that I'm no longer going to be the future King of Spain they have been acting like this. They were hoping that the story wasn't true. The Campus Police wanted to escort me for my own safety, yeah someone is going to kidnap me or I'm going to trip against the trash can. It would be best if they hold my hand while I cross the damn street. But they don't know that I was the serial killer on the loose. And I can defend myself as well.

And on my way to the annual meeting I started feeling like the prisoners feel when they have to report to their Parole Officers. When I opened the door to the meeting room, I saw my Counselor, my English Teacher and all the others who were there waiting for me and they bowed down and I sat down. And I was waiting to get evaluated for at least half an hour. They were already going over my grades and my conduct in class and they were doing paper work and they were whispering.

Finally my Counselor looked at me and said, "Most of your grades are acceptable but your grades in Geometry are not good enough."

I began to notice that my Counselor was scared to talk to me but I smiled, "I'm doing the best that I can."

"We understand, Mauricio but." My Teacher said nervously.

And I interrupted her. "Since, I'm doing okay can I have regular classes now. Please."

My Counselor look worried and I knew she didn't want to respond to my question. "Mauricio, we're not sure if you're ready to have regular classes."

Then my Teacher had the guts to say this. "It would be better for you to continue in the same Special Education classes. We're very sorry, Mauricio, but regular classes would be too hard for you. We're very sorry your, Majesty."

I got up and started to yell at them, "So, I'm stuck in Special Education forever! And I've been working so damn hard to have good grades! And this is getting ridiculous and you are guys have been a thorn on my side for a very long time! All I want to have regular classes!" I continued to yell at them and they told me to calm down because I was going to spend the whole week in solitary. And just like the prisoners I was rejected and I was so frustrated with everything they told me but The Powers of B didn't hear my voice at all. But they were scared of me, "You know what I'm not going to spend the week in solitary." I turn around and called the Campus Police and told them to bring me the Principal to the meeting room. Seconds later the Principal came into the room and he was announced, "Well I want to make announcement I want these people to get suspended without pay until I tell them to come back to work."

"Thanks!" I smiled and I felt a lot better. Boy, I sure do miss been King de la Vega but I chose this other road.

The Principal had no choice but to agree with me of course and he suspended everyone until I tell them when to come to work. All I did is smile and left the room and slam the door on the way out. I went back to the classroom and the bell the rang and it was three forty-five. I was upstairs and I was walking on the hallway and everyone saw the look on my face and they bowed down and got out of my way. I went down the stairs and I heard someone yelled out "Make way for the future King of Spain!" Geez, someone is kissing my ass. Well everyone looked at me and bowed down and I was on my way to the library until Mr. Caballero stopped me in the hallway. I heard one of the students that were telling him to bowed down.

"Allow him to speak his mind!" I smiled.

"Mauricio, I've been noticing that you are having problems in my class. I also noticed that you like to guess in the pop quizzes and the test." He said and everyone was telling him to shut up.

"Yes, Mr. Caballero. For a long time I've been having problems with Geometry. Well you know it's my weakest point."

"Do you want me to tutor you?" He asked.

"That will be great, Mr. Caballero. When can I start?"

"Tomorrow right after school."

"I'll be there." I smiled and we shook hands. And I turn around and looked at everyone. "I want everyone to look at me!" I exclaimed and everyone looked at me, "As you were!" And I went inside the library and also the people also bowed down. "As you were!" So, Joe and Miguel and I started going over our homework and we were talking about what are we going to do on Saturday night and the problem I had earlier.

"So, how did it go in your parole? We're you emotional in there?" Joe asked me.

"Well the same thing as the last time I went, they are going to keep me in Special Education forever and forever. And I was angry and they told me to calm because I was about to spend a week in solitary. So, I was pissed off and they are going to get suspended until I tell them to come back to work." I said.

"Sorry, to hear that." Miguel said.

"So, what are you going to do about your situation in Geometry?" Joe asked me.

"I got that covered. Mr. Caballero is going to tutor me."

"You are in good hands, Mauricio. Mr. Caballero is an excellent Teacher and he cares about his students." Joe said.

"Of course he is an excellent Teacher. He may be the best Teacher I ever had in my entire life." I smiled and we stayed in the library to do our homework and we left home around five o'clock that afternoon.

And the next day couldn't have been worse for me. I had four pop quizzes and I wasn't prepared to do any of the pop quizzes. I wanted the day to end because I was having my first migraine and I guess my blood pressure was sky high and not to mention that I wanted to kill all the Teachers but I kept my cool. And I looked at my watch and it was three-forty five when I entered Mr. Caballero's classroom. As I walked into his classroom I saw a girl sitting down with her friends and they were doing their homework and I heard them giggling and they were whispering about something. Well the girl is a brunette. I wanted to go over to get a closer look at this pretty girl but I felt that she might get uncomfortable with me staring at her. And I knew that she would get up and leave because I would be drooling all over her. From a short distance all I could see was her long hair and that she was wearing a white blouse, blue pants and flip flops. And I figured that she might be around feet tall and probably one hundred and three pounds. As I was standing there, she turned around and said hi to me and smiled and I said hi as well. She was very pretty and she had brown eyes, light skin and a nice smile. I felt like that I was staring at "Angel." I could even hear the "Halleluiah" song! And I began to notice that Karina and the girls were sitting with her and they even said hi to me and smiled but I told them not to bow down.

Mr. Caballero was in the hallway talking to one of the Teachers and they were in front of the coke machine and then Mr. Caballero came into the classroom. And right of away he started giving me a couple of assignments. And the girls got up, and the "Angel" smiled at me and I smiled back at her and they all left somewhere. I couldn't keep my eyes off her as she walked out of the room. She was so pretty and I think I was in love with her. And later on when Mr. Caballero was checking my assignments, the "Angel" came back to the classroom and we continued to stare each other with a big smile on our faces.

"I brought you guy's chips and cokes and I thought you two guys might be hungry." She said and smiled.

"Thanks, Honey. Oh, by the way, Mauricio, I want you to meet Eliza."

"Nice to meet you, Mauricio. I'm so happy to meet you." She smiled.

"Pleasure is all mine, Eliza." We were still staring at each other and smiling for a very longtime. And I could see stars and a light surrounding Eliza but maybe it was love at first sight and I was drooling all over her.

Karina and her friends got her attention and she looked at us and said, "Well goodbye and I hope to see you later, Mauricio." Eliza smiled and winked at me and she left with her friends and I heard them giggling in the hallway.

Eliza looked so familiar and I thought I had seen her somewhere before. I had a tingly sensation when we were staring at each other. Then my mother came for me around five-thirty. And I spent the whole evening thinking about Eliza "The Angel." And the next day my sister, Tania and I were eating scrambled eggs for breakfast.

"I met a girl yesterday." I said.

"That's great! What's her name?" Tania asked me.

"Her name is Eliza."

"Is she pretty?"

"Oh, Yes! She looks like Angel!" I exclaimed.

"Did you guys talk?" She asked me.

"Mr. Caballero introduced us and all we did was stare at each other for a long time but I hope to see her today."

"Talk to her! I'm sure you guys will have something in common." Tania said and smiled.

"I hope she likes you, Mauricio." My mother said.

"So, are we still going to have the curfew, Mommy?" Tania asked.

"I'm sorry to say but I don't know when they are going to take the curfew away but for now we need to live with it." My mother smiled and kisser us on the cheek.

"How about if I stand in front of City Hall and take the curfew away. They might listen to the future King of Spain." I smiled.

"That will be great!" Tania smiled.

"You're so funny, Mauricio! But you are going to school and get a good education and maybe someday you can sit on the throne. But the story wasn't real." My mother smiled and hugged me.

Tania and I finished eating our breakfast and my mother dropped me off at school and I saw my two best friends Karina and Sonia walking toward the cafeteria and I caught up with them. "Hey, Karina and hey, Sonia!"

"Hey, Mauricio, how are you?" Karina asked.

"Good, I want to talk to you about something." I said.

"Ahh, you want to talk about Eliza?" Karina asked me.

"Yes, I sort of like her." I responded with a smile.

"Oh, really!" Sonia exclaimed.

"I saw the look on your faces. You guys were smiting with each other!" Karina said and smiled.

"What?" I asked.

"That means you must have fallen in love and were drooling with each other!" Karina responded.

"Do you know where she is?" I asked.

"Eliza comes to school on the bus and she should be here in a minute." Sonia smiled.

"They changed her schedule and she's going to have Physical Education with us." Karina said.

"Thanks! And I'll see you at Physical Education." I smiled and left. And I was wondering if the girls knew that I was in love with her. And I was surprised how fast the morning went by and I was already entering the locker room when a bunch of guys that were in their underwear bowed down to me and I told them to put some clothes on for crying out loud. Well all of us got dressed and went into the gym. The Physical Education Coach told us that we were going to run to day but I suggested to him that we should do whatever the Hell we wanted and of course he agreed with me. So, I played basketball with my friends and then I turned around and Eliza was there talking to her friends and she was looking at me and she was giving me a smile.

"Who is she?" Joe asked me.

"Her name is Eliza." I responded.

"What are you waiting for?" Miguel asked me.

"Go and talk to her!" Joe said

"Okay." I said nervously.

I started walking towards Eliza and my friends were cheering me on. There were a couple of girls that were also playing basketball and they bowed down and I could tell that she was waiting for me. "Hi Eliza!" I smiled.

"Hi, Mauricio!" She smiled.

"Oh, we were just leaving." Karina said.

"We're going to shoot some hoops with the guys." Sonia said.

"How you been, Mauricio? It's been a long time since I've seen you. What's new?" Eliza asked me.

"Then we have met before, because when I saw you yesterday I felt like I had seen you somewhere before."

"We've known each other since elementary. I was always the one that was talking to you and smiling at you." Eliza smiled and said. "It's nice to hear your voice."

"Thanks!" I smiled and said, "Where have you been since elementary?"

"I went to Clarke Middle School but I guess we missed each other over there."

"Yeah, it's true!" I exclaimed.

"So, what's new with you?" She asked.

"Well I've had a good time on summer vacations, but here at school I've been miserable, and I'm in Special Education. I'm also having a hard time in Geometry but the Teacher who introduced us yesterday, is helping me out." I answered.

"That Teacher is my brother and you're in good hands! My brother is an excellent Teacher." She smiled.

"Oh, really!" I exclaimed. "So, do you have plans for Saturday?"

"The girls and I are going to hang out at Marty Robbins Park. We're probably going to run around the park and play softball."

"Is it okay if my friends and I hang out with you guys at the park?" I asked her.

"Yes, that will be great and I hope we get to hang out just like old times. I hope our tree is still there, you know the one we carved our names when we were little kids! Your, Majesty!" She smiled and she wanted to kiss me.

"I do remember. And how could I forget. I think about you everyday and I just wanted to see you again and I wanted you to hear my voice for the first time." I smiled.

Just then Joe, Miguel and the girls showed up to make fun of us. "What are you two lovebirds talking about?" Joe asked us.

"I hope it was about love." Sonia said and Eliza and I must have blushed.

CHAPTER TWELVE

ADVICE FROM MY MOTHER

And we talked for a while and it was time for Physical Education to end. Eliza and I didn't want the day to end and we just wanted to be together at all times. And we were in the locker room changing and everyone saw the look on my face.

"Someone is happy."

"Can you tell?" I asked them.

"Did you lose your innocence?" They asked.

"No! I'm happy that I was talking to a girl."

"We saw you talking to Mr. Caballero's sister. Are you trying to have an A in his class?" One of them asked me.

"That has nothing to do with me having an A in his class." I responded.

"Do us a favor, Mauricio. Sleep with Eliza and you will feel a lot better." One of them said and laughed at me.

"I'm not going to sleep with her." I responded.

"Mauricio, you're the laughing stock at Americas High School. It's bad enough that you're in Special Education, but you're also the only guy in high school that has never had sex with anyone. And as the matter of fact you're the only guy in the entire world that has never had sex. So, much for the future virgin King of Spain." He smiled.

"He didn't mean that!" One of them said.

And I went up to that jackass and he was now afraid of me. "You want me to kick your ass?"

"No, Sir. I mean I'm sorry, Sir. I was just playing around." He was about to cry and I looked at everyone and they quickly were putting their clothes back on. I got dressed up and I went to put water on my face because I had the sensation that I wanted to kill him right on the spot but I need to keep cool. I wanted to change my ways. Then the bell rang and it was time to go home and I was walking down the hallway and I was thinking about what the guys in the locker room had said to me when Eliza and her friends bumped into me. "We're sorry we didn't mean to bump into you!"

"That's okay!" I smiled and looked at Eliza and she smiled. Eliza gave me her new address and she also gave me a kiss on the cheek. I was so excited and I didn't want to stay after school for tutoring so I went home. I was in my room and I started thinking about Eliza for the rest of the night.

Then it was on a Saturday afternoon where Joe and I were hanging out at *Peter Piper Pizza* and we started playing Arcades and started eating Pizza. "I can't stop thinking about Eliza." I said.

"When are you going to ask her out, Mauricio?" Joe asked me.

"I don't know but I have an idea."

"What kind of idea?" He asked me.

"I want Eliza to like me, so I'm going to impress her. And I hope that will be enough for her to like me and let's go to my house after we're done eating." I smiled and we ate a couple more slices of Pizza and left the restaurant. When we got to my house Joe and I took out my bicycles and we rode them all the way to Marty Robbins Park. Eliza and the girls were playing softball. And I was waiting in the parking lot and Joe went up to them and told Eliza that I wanted to show her something. When I got Eliza's attention, I started doing my infamous bicycle "tricks." I started jumping on boards and everything I could jump on. Eliza didn't seem to be that impressed but she was smiling.

I was doing great until I bumped into a rock and fell down and landed on my ass. Eliza and her friends started laughing at me and they continued to play softball. And I got up and looked at Eliza, well she gave me a smile and winked at me. So, Joe and I went back to my house and we stayed outside talking.

"Well you are 0 for 1." He said.

"I know."

"Well I'm going to go to my house because I made a promise to my parents that I was going to cut the grass and clean my room. And I hope you find another way to impress Eliza. Just make sure you don't fall down." He said and left. "Good luck!"

"Thanks!" I yelled.

I put the bikes back into the garage and went to my room and I wanted to work hard and find a way for Eliza to go out with me. And I spent the whole weekend in my room since we had the damn curfew and we couldn't go outside because it was too dangerous. So, I started looking at my sister's magazines. At that time "pretty boys" were the talk of the school and also in the movie industry. And I saw a lot of pretty boy celebrities and I figured that was the kind of guy Eliza might go out with and not some retard like me or a serial killer. And I knew I wouldn't stand a chance to be like those guys. I'd have to pluck my eyebrows and then use my mother's eyelash curler! And I probably would have to color my hair. Not me! But I think she will be impressed if I come to her house dressed up as The Dark Cowboy and I hope it won't be that bad like the last time I saw her on the Franklin Mountains. So, I decided to see her, I jumped out the window and I ran all the way to her house. And I was hiding in the shadows and she was in her room. Eliza was listening to music and she was dancing in her room and she is so pretty and she has a gorgeous body as well. After that I ran back to my house and I stayed in my room and fell asleep.

Then on Monday morning I woke up and my mother made breakfast and she sat down next to me. "How's school?" She asked.

"Good! Mr. Caballero is helping me out with Geometry and I'm getting good at it. I'm happy that I have two years left in high school. And I'm thinking about going to The University of Missouri." I said.

"I hope so too. Just keep trying and we know that you are working very hard in school." My mother smiled and I finished eating breakfast. She took me to school and I went to straight to the cafeteria. I saw Joe and Miguel were sitting down eating and they were going over their homework and I sat down with them and said, "Guys, I don't think it will be a good idea for me to ask Eliza out." I said.

"Why not?" Miguel asked me.

"You should have seen him on Saturday. Mauricio wanted to impress Eliza with his bicycle skills and he fell down and landed on his ass!" Joe laughed.

"Ouch, so I guess you're 0 for 1 and still stranded on first base and as the matter of fact you're still sitting on the bench waiting to swing the ball." Miguel laughed.

"Yeah, but someday I will make a homerun." I smiled and looked at them. "But someday I'm going to go down the field and score the winning touchdown and you guys are using baseball talk and I'm using football terminology it's a lot easier." I said it in a sarcastic way.

"So, why do you want to impress Eliza?" Joe asked me.

"You know how girls are. They like "pretty boys." I said.

"I know they do." Joe said.

"Did you see the 2000 Calendar? It's supposed to feature the hottest guys in school and a lot of girls went crazy over it." Miguel said.

"That was ridiculous and all the guys had plucked eyebrows and they looked gay and I don't know what they see in them." I said.

"That's why you're worried?" Joe asked me.

And Miguel added, "What about the day you saw Eliza again? There was a sparkle in your eyes. And you guys have even known each other since you were little kids. I remember you two played husband and wife back in elementary school. And not only that but she always smiles and talks to you. I think you were the first one to have a girlfriend and we did envy you."

"You're just overreacting. You should ask her out and maybe something good might happen." Joe said.

"You guys are right. Thanks." I smiled and I saw Eliza and her friends coming into the cafeteria, they got their food and went to another table on the other side of the room. They didn't see us and I saw them talking and laughing. Then I noticed Joe had his guitar with him.

"Can I borrow your guitar?" I asked Joe.

"I didn't know you played the guitar." He said.

"I don't know how but it will be worth it and trust me." I said.

Joe and Miguel looked at Eliza and then they looked at me. They thought I was going to embarrass myself once again. "Don't tell me, you're going to impress her again?" Joe asked.

"No, I'm not going to impress Eliza. I'm better than that. I'm going to sing her a song and she will love it."

"This should be good." Joe said.

"We're going to be at the library." I said.

"Are you going to sing to her in the library?" Joe asked me.

"Sure, why not. Eliza is going to like the song and all the girls will want to be with me because I have a good singing voice." I said and smiled.

The bell rang and it was time to go to class. And during the morning class, I kept thinking about the song I wanted to sing for Eliza. Well time passed quickly and before I knew it, we were in the library. Eliza was sitting with her friends a couple of tables away from us, so I grabbed Joe's guitar, and went up to her and said "Hello, I'm Mauricio de la Cash!" and started singing "It Ain't me, Baby!" I followed that with "Jackson" and "Cocaine Blues." During the song I began to realized that everyone in the library were staring at me and some were mad and some were happy, and they wanted to hear more from me and the rest of them wanted me to shut up but they didn't say anything. And I had no idea that Mr. Caballero's class were also there and they were mad because I was interrupting them and I saw the look on their faces. When I stopped singing, Eliza was still smiling like she wanted to hear more from me and I looked around and everyone started clapping and they were saying "Encore, Encore!" As soon I was going to sing another song, Mr. Caballero and the Librarian escorted me to the Principal's office. I was in the office and waited while they were talking, and then the Principal approached me.

"Mauricio de la Vega I made a decision that I'm going to suspend you for three whole weeks. I hope that's okay with you, Sir." He said and looked worried.

"Why?" I asked.

"Because you were disrupting the library and the library is not a place to sing. And I know everything about you, Mauricio. I have your school file and it doesn't look too good. Perhaps I should send you to the juvenile center with Primo Mancini and you have good company."

"That won't be necessary, Sir." Mr. Caballero intervened and smiled. "I will handle the punishment and I will take full responsibility for Mauricio. If he does it again you can fire me and suspended him and even send him to the juvenile center, so he can fool around with Primo Mancini. But I will promise you that Mauricio learned his lesson from this experience and he is not going to do it again." Mr. Caballero looked at me and said, "Right, Mauricio."

"Yes, it won't happen again!" I said.

"Okay, Mike. I trust you enough. This is a warning for the both of you."

"Thank you!" We both said and smiled.

"Now get out of my office!" The Principal yelled and I looked at him and he said, "I'm sorry I just having problems with my wife and I don't mean to yell at you!"

"I want you to bring back my Counselor and everyone else that was suspended and I want them to come back by next year." I said.

"Sure! I will make the phone call." He said.

Mr. Caballero and I left the office and we were walking in the hallway. "Thank you so much." I said.

"You are welcome. But that was a good concert, Mauricio, and the next time you want to sing to my sister, do it at the house and bring the Mariachis where it's more romantic than the library." He smiled and took me to his classroom. Mr. Caballero actually saved my ass from getting suspended for three whole weeks and he had me write on the board "I will not disrupt the library." I wrote it like one hundred times and my hand was killing me. While he was checking the grades on his computer, Eliza came into the classroom to see how I was doing. She winked and gave me a big smile. Then my mother came into the classroom and she had her Police uniform and she wasn't in a good mood.

"What happened, Mauricio?" My mother asked me.

"Mrs. De la Vega,, I mean Officer de la Vega, your son got in trouble because he was disrupting the library with a concert." Mr. Caballero said.

"Mom." I said.

"We'll talk at home, now get in the car and I will be there shortly." She said and looked at Mr. Caballero. "How is he doing in Geometry?"

"He is improving and he is talking about having regular classes and I have a good feeling that he might have the regular classes by next year." He said and smiled.

My mother smiled and we got into the car and drove to home in silence. We went into the kitchen and sat down. "Why did you get into trouble at school, Mauricio?" She asked me.

"I'm sorry, Mom. There's a girl that I like and I started singing to her in the library."

"So, you were trying to impress her?" She asked me.

"I want her to like me."

"Mauricio, you are trying to impress a girl and is not the right thing to do and there are other ways to get a girl to like you." She said.

"How do I get Eliza to like me?" I asked her.

"You can be yourself at all times. You don't have to show-off like the other guys at school. You're better than this, Mauricio." My mother smiled and laughed. "So, tell me who is the girl that you like?" She asked.

"Eliza Caballero, you remember her?" I asked her. "As it turns out that we've known each other since we were little kids. She was the one who was always talking to me and was always smiling at me."

"Oh, yes, I remember her and I always wanted for the two of you to get together and get married and you guys looked cute together and it will great to see you guys get married and have a lot of children." My mother smiled. "Promise me that you're going to be yourself when you talk to her. Please."

"I promise, Mom." I smiled and I was about to go to my room and I turn around and looked at her. "What about the locker room talk. They want me to sleep with her because everyone else is doing it."

"Mauricio, I'm going to tell you the same thing my father once told me when I was your age. Don't be a bloody chicken, you don't have to listen to those jackasses. Just because everyone is doing, it doesn't mean that you have to do what they do. Well your grandfather said a lot more graphic things than that but I love you so much to see get manipulated. Mauricio, if you like Eliza you should ask her out and who knows you two may end up getting married and I want to be a grandmother and I also want to spoil my grandkids." She smiled.

"You are right, Mom. I should talk to Eliza and will see how it goes." I said and was about to go to my room.

"Mauricio de la Cash?" She said and smiled. "It fits you."

I also smiled and I went to my room. And on that night I was thinking about Eliza and what I had been doing lately. I was embarrassing myself all the time. When I did my bicycles tricks, I fell down and landed on my ass, and what was I thinking about singing to her in the library? All this because of the pressure in the locker room! So, I decided to stay away from Eliza for a while because I was really embarrassed and maybe I should follow my mother's advice and talk to her.

Then on Friday night my friends and I were at a party and we ignored the curfew and did the party anyway and I was outside looking up at the stars when Joe went outside and was kind of drunk. "Are you thinking about Eliza?" He asked me.

"What's the point, I'm too embarrassed to talk to her." I responded.

"Mauricio, why are you afraid to ask her out?"

"Sometimes I think about what's the point of having a girlfriend? Didn't you hear what those guys in the locker room said to me?" I asked.

"Yes, I heard them, I was there with you and I heard what they told you. And is that the real reason you don't want to have a girlfriend?" He asked me.

"I don't want a girlfriend just to have sex with her. I just want to have a normal relationship and I want a special girl. Sex is the last thing I'm thinking about." I responded.

"Mauricio, I hate to say this but every couple in this school is having sex. One of the reasons they stay together is because they are having sex all the time."

"They're also getting pregnant and the guy ends up leaving the girl." I said.

"Mauricio, those guys in the locker room may be right! You're probably not ready for a serious relationship with Eliza and you really want to have sex with Eliza. We both know that's what you really want. Trust me, Mauricio, you will feel a lot better once you get Eliza into bed."

Joe was completely drunk when he told me to sleep with Eliza and he went back into the house and I stayed outside. And I was thinking about what he said to me and even though I didn't want to listen to a drunk. Well I ended up going to my house to sleep it off. And the next day I had the courage to go to Eliza's house and rang the doorbell. Her mother opened the door. "Good afternoon, Mrs. Caballero." I said.

"Good afternoon to you, Mauricio, but please call me, Rachel. It's nice to see you again. I haven't seen you since you were a little kid." She smiled and she invited me into the living room and we sat down on the couch. I was nervous because I didn't know what her mother wanted to talk about. "Eliza told me that my son is tutoring you, is that right?" She asked me.

"Yes, I'm doing my best to keep my grades up."

"That's good to know, Mauricio. Well Eliza is in her room putting her clothes away."

Just then Eliza came into the living room and she was glad to see me. "Well, I've got to go." Her mother said and went to her bedroom to get her purse and she came back to the living room and gave Eliza and I a kiss on the cheek and left.

"Does your mom work today?' I asked.

"Not today. She has to run an errand." Eliza said

"Perhaps, I should apologize to you."

"Apologize for what?" Eliza asked me.

"For not speaking to you during those couple of days and also I should apologize for singing to you at the library and when I fell down at the park." I said.

"That's okay, don't worry about it. That's what every guy does when they like a girl." She smiled.

"I want to tell you the truth, Eliza. I'm a little shy when it comes to girls and I didn't know how to talk to you."

"You don't have to be nervous around me. All I want from you is for you to be yourself and be honest." She said.

"So, what do you say if we start over?" I asked her.

"I would like that."

"Hi, I'm, Mauricio."

"Well, I'm Eliza, nice to meet you. And it's nice to finally hear your voice."

We shook hands and Eliza gave me a kiss on the cheek and we stayed in the living room talking and laughing for hours and hours. And on that day I got to know Eliza much better than the first time we met in elementary school. Eliza was born in El Paso, Texas and her mother is Mexican and her father might also be Mexican but she hadn't seen her father for so many years and I knew she was sad but at the same time she didn't know what race her father really is. And her sense of humor was great. She was a bit timid when she talked to everyone. Most of the girls in high school were into sports but not Eliza. During the time we talked I kept bringing up football and wrestling but I could tell she wasn't that interested and it's a good thing that I didn't tell her that I'm The Dark Cowboy. But Eliza was a *girly* girl and not the tomboy type and she was really into make up, dresses and going to the beauty salon for a perm and getting her nails done. She loved to dance and sing in the choir of her Church and at school. Most of the time she was with her girlfriends and they had a lot of slumber parties and they like going to the mall. And Eliza wasn't like most of the girls in high school who fooled around with the boys and got pregnant right of away. I was so sure that Eliza might be the one for me. And one of the things that really surprised me was that even though she is so beautiful, she'd never had a boyfriend at all. She could have any guy she wanted but she chose me right from the beginning and to the end. At the same time she was different from the last time I saw her when we were kids. I was wondering if she was still traumatize when she saw me back on the Franklin Mountains.

We talked for a couple of hours and finally I went home around five o'clock that afternoon and I fell asleep around midnight. And the next day Miguel and I were hanging out at Joe's garage and we were drinking water and talking.

"So, Mauricio, have you asked Eliza out?" Joe asked me.

"Not yet but I will ask her sooner or later." I responded.

"Mauricio, you're the only one in high school that hasn't scored with anybody. You know how many times Joe and I have scored." Miguel said.

"This isn't a sex contest, Miguel." Joe said and looked at me. "What did you do yesterday then?" Joe asked me.

"I spent the entire afternoon talking with Eliza. We were listening to music and she has a great sense of humor."

"That's what every guy in high school wants from a girl, a great sense of humor and listen to music." Miguel said. "That's hot!"

"Guys, I really like her and I think she's starting to like me too." I said.

"Are you going to ask her out anytime soon?" Joe asked me.

"I want to get to know her a little bit better."

"Well on Saturday night I'm going to have a party at my house and we are going to be alone, you can invite her and maybe you can ask her to be your girlfriend." Joe said.

"I'll ask her if she can come to the party and I will ask her to be my girlfriend and you will see that we are going to be the perfect couple at school and the envy of the school once again." I smiled and I was feeling the pressure from my friends and I didn't know why all the guys at school kept talking about sex. And I didn't want to be like them and again I should follow my mother's advice. Then I went home around eleven o'clock that night and went to sleep.

The next day my friends and I were on our way to eat breakfast and we bumped into Eliza and her friends in the hallway. We were glad to see each other and as always everyone bowed down in the hallway.

"We'll leave you two love birds alone." Sonia said.

"We're going to be eating outside." Joe said.

I looked at everyone and said, "Leave us alone! Now!" And everyone ran away from the hallway and Eliza and I stayed by ourselves in the hallway and we were glad to be alone. "Eliza, I've got to ask you something." I said.

"What are you going to ask me?" She wanted to know.

"There's going to be a party on Saturday night at Joe's house and I was wondering if you want to go with me. So we can talk."

"Yes, I would like to go with you! Maybe we can dance and hang out." She exclaimed and smiled.

"I can't wait for Saturday!" I said.

We smiled and went to the cafeteria to get our breakfast and went to eat outside with our friends. I didn't want the day to end, I wanted to stay with Eliza forever but the bell rang and we had to go to class. Then at three forty-five I went to get tutored by Mr. Caballero. He gave me couple of assignments and checked my grades on the computer. Eliza and her friends showed up to do their homework. Eliza and I kept looking at each other and we were unable to do our homework and all we were doing was smiling and winking at each other and I wanted to get up and give her a kiss on the mouth but I didn't. I kept my cool.

At five o'clock that afternoon we went home and I was in my room and I was thinking about was Eliza and the party and everything I had to do that week. Well there wasn't anything on my agenda. All I wanted to do is kill someone and I would have been a happy camper. Then it was Saturday night and I was getting ready to go to the party and I snuck out of the window. Joe's house twelve blocks away from my house, so I ran all the away to Joe's house. When I got there, my friends were already waiting for me and we shook hands and talked for awhile. We decided to stay outside and wait for the girls to show up and twenty minutes later, Eliza and her friends showed up at the party. Eliza looked different that night. She was wearing a white blouse and black silk pants and high heels and she looked so beautiful that night.

Eliza gave me a kiss on the cheek and I wanted to grab her by the waist and kiss her all night long. But we looked at each other and smiled and she was about to kiss me too. Then we went into the house and everyone was dancing and I grabbed Eliza's hand and we started dancing. Eliza and I were in our own world while everybody else was getting drunk and doing other stuff. We ignored them and kept on dancing. And later on in the night Eliza and I decided to walk around the block.

"What a great night." I said.

"Yes, it is a beautiful night." She responded.

"Mauricio!" We turned around and Joe was calling me and I went back to see what Joe wanted. "Well, have you asked her out?" He asked.

"Not yet, I have everything under control and when I do ask her out you will be the first one to know."

I went back to Eliza and she was looking up at the stars and gave me a huge smile. "What did Joe want?" She asked.

"Oh, nothing, don't worry about it." I said.

"I feel like our friends are spying on us." She said.

"Eliza, I've wanted to ask you something for a while."

"What, Mauricio?" She asked.

"I don't know how to say this." I took a long breather. "Will you be my girlfriend?"

Eliza took a minute to think about it and she was teasing me for a couple of seconds and finally she smiled and said. "Of course, Mauricio!"

She looked at me and gave me a huge smile and then we hugged and we kissed for a while and it was a little tongue action and we were excited. We looked at each other and smiled and kiss some more. Then we went back into the house and everyone saw us holding hands and they were happy for us and they started clapping for us.

Eliza and I went back outside and we were kissing under the moonlight and we were together for a couple of more hours just holding on to each other. And it was around eleven o'clock that night when I walked Eliza to her house and we were holding hands and talking. Eliza was worried that were going to be alone on the street and she felt that The Dark Cowboy would show up and try to kill us. I told Eliza that there's nothing to worry about and I will protect her from that psychotic killer. Well we finally got to her house, when we got there we kissed once again and she went inside the window and blew me kiss. She closed the window and I walked around the corner and ran to my house and fell asleep right of away.

And the next day I woke up all excited. My mother was in the kitchen making breakfast and Tania was in the kitchen with her.

"What's with the smile?" My mother asked.

"Did something happen between you and Eliza?" Tania asked.

"Yes, yesterday I asked her to be my girlfriend and she said yes! We also kissed for awhile!" I smiled.

"I'm so happy for you, Mauricio!" Tania exclaimed.

"I'm really proud of you, Honey." My mother and Tania went to hug me and we were all excited.

"This is the happiest day of my life!" I exclaimed.

CHAPTER THIRTEEN

TROUBLED IN PARADISE

On Monday morning my mother dropped me off at school and Eliza was waiting for me in front of the school. As soon I got out of the Police car, Eliza dropped her books and ran towards me and hugged me and kissed me as hard she could. I was holding her so tight and we were kissing for awhile with a tongue action. We were glad to see each other and I picked up her books and went inside to eat at the cafeteria. Well of course everyone got out of our way and they were clapping for us and cheering as well. We grabbed our food and we sat down with our friends and they were happy for us. And as it turns out the day went by so fast and I went to get tutored by Mr. Caballero. Ten minutes later Eliza and her friends showed up to do their homework. And all Eliza and I did was stare at each other with a huge smile on our faces and she blew me a kiss and I also blew her a kiss as well. By five o'clock in the afternoon we left home. And I called Eliza and we talked for hours and hours, and all we said to each other that we missed each other and we couldn't wait to be together and kiss all the time. We said goodnight and hanged up the phone around eight o'clock and I went to sleep.

The next day I woke up and I wasn't feeling to good. So, I got dressed up and went down to the kitchen. My mother was making breakfast and she looked at me and she told me that I shouldn't go to school. My mother called the school and told them that I got sick. I went back to bed and my mother told me that she was going to work but she didn't want me to be home alone, so she called Chris and it's a good thing that he was back in town. Half in hour later Chris came to the house and he also saw the look on my face. So, my mother told me that she loves me and went to work.

Chris and I stayed alone in my room and he said, "Let's go to my house! There is something that I want to show you."

"Okay!" I tried to smile.

We went outside and I locked the door and we hopped into the his truck and drove to his home. And we arrived at his house and he open the garage and saw a nice car.

"Who's car is it?" I asked.

"The car belongs to Primo Mancini! It's Lamborghini and it's custom made but he calls it the Primoghini. Primo asked me to make him a custom made car and he wanted to impress the girls. But I cannot say how we got this car because it's a top secret!" Chris smiled.

"Well it's a nice car." I smiled and again I started feeling uneasy. I was grabbing my head for a couple of seconds.

"Mauricio, are you okay?" He asked.

"I'm fine. I just need a glass of water and some aspirins." I said.

Chris closed the garage and we went inside the kitchen and he gave me glass of water and some aspirins. I put the aspirins on my mouth and drank the water and I was sitting down in the kitchen and there was a knock on the front door. Chris opened the front door and it was Primo and he came into the house. He smiled and said, "How are you, Mauricio?"

"I'm good!" I responded.

"The girls told me that you are dating Eliza." He said.

"Yes, I am. And what's new you with you?" I asked.

"I can see that you saw my custom made car. I call it the Primoghini and I met someone." He smiled.

"How old is she?" I asked.

"Well she's twelve years old, I met her in the bowling alley and she's so beautiful." He said.

"What's her name?" I asked.

"Her name is Madelyn Van Der AA and she is so pretty and hot as well. And don't worry I'm going to respect her and I want to change my ways.

Madelyn accepted me knowing that I was once a rapist! I think her aunt is a famous world wide Psychiatrist!"

"That's good to know and I'm glad that you are changing your ways! And I hope we can double date someday!" I smiled and drank the glass of water and I took another aspirin. I thought I was going to feel better by later on in the afternoon and I was beginning to wonder what the Hell was wrong with me but I guess since I haven't killed anyone in the last couple of weeks. I figured that I should kill somebody, so I can feel a lot better or maybe I was really sick that day. So, the three of us stayed in the kitchen for thirty minutes and we went back to the garage and continued to talk some more. Primo and Chris were doing all the talking and they were laughing while I was feeling crappy. And I was just sitting down drinking more water and gathering my thoughts. And then something weird happen to me on that day and I thought I was the bad guy that was killing people and pissing off my father but somehow that wasn't the case at all. I couldn't explain what I was feeling on that day. Until it was four o'clock on the afternoon where Primo and Chris were still fixing the remains parts of the Primoghini. And they finally took a break and started drinking water and I overheard Chris saying that Samantha wrote to him and she misses us like crazy. And once again I started feeling uneasy, and it got worse by the second and by the minute and then I couldn't take it anymore.

I started yelling at the top of my lungs and transformed into the monster and I was breathing heavily and my eyes were glowing red. Chris closed the garage door and they were asking me if I was alright but I ignored them and continued to breathe heavily and I went inside the house to put on my outfit and grabbed the Magnum guns. And I came back to the garage and I was gasping for air and my eyes continued to glow red. They were looking at me and they were scared of me. I started loading my guns and I broke the garage door and I was standing in the middle of the driveway and I ran to the place where I felt uneasy feeling that I couldn't explain on that afternoon. I also could hear Primo and Chris yelling at me. "You are going to get arrested, Mauricio! Be careful out there!" But I didn't care if it was the daylight.

I was running faster and then I found myself at Marty Robbins Park. And I was standing in the middle of the park and I saw a black van parked on the parking lot and I could hear someone screaming. And the screams came from inside the van and I ran towards the van. When I got there I slammed my guns into the van and it almost like a loud bang from the inside. And I could feel that the girl was calling for help and she was trying to make a lot of noise. And once again I slammed my guns into the van and I was waiting for them to come outside. Five minutes later I saw the side door open and a man went outside. The man was going around the van, where all of the sudden he saw me, and he screamed like a little girl. "What the!" I took out my guns and shot him all over his face and body. I wanted to scare everyone and I continued to bang the van with the guns. And I open the back doors, and I saw a couple men, and a defenseless little girl. I couldn't believe that they had her tied up and they were raping and punching her and she was in pain. The men were frightened because they were staring at my red evil eyes and I was laughing at them. And the little girl lifted her head just for a couple of seconds and saw me staring at them and she also saw my eyes that were glowing red. The man in the suit was about to turn on the engine when I shot him in the head and the blood was spilled all over the window and including their faces. Three men were left and they nearly peed on themselves. I took out my other guns and shot two of them. And the little girl noticed that the side doors were still open, so with all of her strength she had left, she crawled her way out and landed hard on the sidewalk.

There was one man left and the man was crying his eyes out, "Please, don't kill me! I'll do anything but please don't kill me!"

"Anything!" I was laughing at him and I shot him in the head and killed him. Then I turned around and saw the little girl laying in the middle of the sidewalk. And I could hear her breathing and was sobbing because she was so much in pain. And I turn around and saw my mother and this other woman that were running to my direction and they saw the little girl laying in the middle of the sidewalk.

"What did you do to my daughter!" The woman yelled.

My mother took out her gun and said, "Freeze do not move. You are under arrest!"

I was holding something and threw it to my mother "Those are drugs these men were raping her and drugging her!" I exclaimed and went up to the little girl and got on my knees.

"I said don't move! They may be drug dealers but you are still under arrest for the murder of eighteen people! And now twenty-three!" My mother continued to yell. "Dark Cowboy I want you to step away from the girl!"

I took off the tape from her mouth and the little girl started crying. My mother told the woman not to move and both of them saw the little girl crying her eyes out. And I guessed that she was her daughter and just then the cavalry arrived and many Police Officer and FBI Agents got out of their cars and pointed the guns at me. My mother went to the van and found bags of weed and cocaine and a lot of weapons they had inside the van. I picked up the little girl and she was in pain and she said. "Help me."

"Put the girl down!" One of the Agents said.

"Hold your fire!" My mother exclaimed and looked at them. "The Dark Cowboy saved her life from these drug dealers. So, hold your fire!"

And very gently I picked her up and had her in my arms and I looked at my mother and said, "We need to get the little girl to the Hospital and I'm going to need your help, Beatrice."

"Fine!" My mother exclaimed and looked at her team. "Half of you come with me and the rest of you take the drugs and the van back to the Police Station. Call the Ambulance, so they can take them to the morgue. Is that clear?"

Everyone nodded and half of them stayed behind and they were collecting evidence. The other half planned to escort me to the Hospital. My mother looked at me and asked, "How are you going to get there?"

I responded, "I'm going to run and I hope you can drive fast enough to get to the Hospital." The girl's mother rode along with my mother and they turned on their Police sirens. I ran way and I made sure that they were following me and I noticed that a lot of people were moving away when they saw me running like the wind. And in about twenty minutes later we arrived at Thomson Hospital.

I was in the middle of the parking lot of the Emergency Room and my mother and the girl's mother got out of the car and they went running into the Emergency Room. I still had her in my arms and I also went inside the Emergency Room. My mother was talking to the Security Guard when he saw me enter the room. He took out his gun and my mother also took her gun.

"Put the gun down! We need a Doctor for this girl. She was beaten and rape." My mother said.

"My daughter needs help." She said.

I began to notice that the fat Security Guard was still standing there and he wasn't cooperating with my mother, and I gave the woman her daughter. "Hold her for a second!" I exclaimed and took out my two Magnums guns and the people inside took cover. I shot at the door and kicked it open. I went inside to find a Doctor, the woman took her daughter inside and my mother went inside and was looking for a Doctor. I took out my guns and yelled out, "We need a Goddamn Doctor for this girl because she was rape and beaten!" And the Doctors were finally cooperating and decided to treat the little girl. They put her in a bed and she was still in pain. I grabbed her hand and said. "You're going to recover."

She squeezed my hand so tight and said. "Thank you!" She tried to smile.

I looked at the Doctor and said, "You better take care of her and if anything happens to her, I'm holding you responsible!" I exclaimed and left the Emergency Room and my mother followed me all the way outside. When they saw my mother that was behind me and they took out their guns.

"Put your guns down! That's an order." She yelled and looked at me. "So what now?"

"Just because I saved a girl's life doesn't mean that it's over." I said.

"You don't have to kill people."

"You left me with no choice. You should have handed me your son. This would not be over, I hate your son, Mauricio de la Vega. You already know that and someday we will face each other and settle the score."

"So, this will never end between you and my son?" She asked.

"No! Whenever you are ready to give up your son, so we can finally face each other. The fight to the death and just tell your son that I will see him soon!" I exclaimed and ran back to Chris's house and I had my radio with me as well.

"Okay. The show is over. You guys go home and will meet tomorrow in the afternoon at the Police Station." My mother said and went back inside the Emergency Room to check up on the little girl. And twenty minutes later I finally arrived at Chris's house and I went to the restroom and changed. And I went to the kitchen and sat down and started drinking water. Primo and Chris sat down with me.'

"What happen?" Chris asked.

"Well earlier I killed five drug dealers and I saved a little girl and that's what happen on today's agenda. Boy, am I glad that I killed people and now I can sleep at night!" I got up and looked at them, "I'm going home goodnight and I feel a lot better, because I gave my father another reason to loose his mind." I smiled and I could tell that Primo and Chris were loss for words. So, the next day I tried to put on a brave face for everyone's sake. I went to school and Eliza and I were hanging out with our friends. And I began to notice that the girls were looking at me and they were asking me about the other day. I just smiled and told them that it was good to kill more people. I have a feeling that a big mouth, Primo told them what I did at the park.

So, after school we went home around five o'clock in the afternoon. Karina and I went to Chris's house and she hacked into the system, and it's a good thing that Sonia also put bugs and hidden cameras with audio on the Hospitals and on that day my mother and Tania went to Thomason Hospital to visit the little girl. When my sister and the little girl saw each other they cried and tried to smile.

"How are you feeling? Tania asked.

"Better." She said slowly.

"It was my fault. I shouldn't left you alone at the park." Her mom said.

"Come on, Alma. You didn't know what was going to happen. She's fine now, she's going to be back on her feet and we all can go out just like old times." My mother said.

"We can have a lot of slumber parties." Tania said.

"That will be fun. And we can talk about guys and our plans for the future." She said.

"I can't wait!" Tania smiled.

"That's how we were! Remember, Beatrice."

"Yes, but that was a long time ago. And we married our Prince Charming."

"You did but I didn't." She said.

"Don't say that, Mommy. Someday you'll meet the man of your dreams." Her daughter smiled.

"Don't give up you'll find someone else. You deserve someone better than that Irish Leprechaun. No offense, Sweetie." My mother said.

"That's okay." She smiled.

They stayed talking for almost two more hours and the Doctor came into the room and told them that she needs to rest. Tania and my mother gave her a kiss on her forehead and left the room. The girl's mother went outside to walk them to their car.

"So, is she going to recover?" Tania asked.

"Yes." She responded.

"I've seen that look before. Come on what did the Doctor really told you?" My mother asked.

"Is not good. My daughter has internal injury and she cannot have any babies. I haven't told her and I know she's going to be crushed. Because she talked about getting married and having a lot of children." She said.

"She's going to be devastated. I love her and I don't want to see her suffer." Tania said.

"You never know there might be a miracle and someday she's going to have a lot of babies and marry the man of her dreams." My mother said.

"I hope so." She smiled and walked them to the car and they said goodbye to my mother and sister. So, she went back inside to be with her daughter.

And Karina looked at me and asked. "Is that the girl you saved the other day at the park?"

"Yes! I cannot believe that Tania is friends with her." I smiled and we saw that Chris had tears coming down his face. "What's wrong with you?" I asked.

"Nothing! I just have allergies." He responded.

"I have a strong feeling that your dad is going to question you or they might forgive The Dark Cowboy because you saved the girl's life from those drug dealers." Karina said.

"If my father wants to talk to me well let him talk to me and let him ask me anything he wants to ask." I smiled and Karina turned off the computer and we home to do our homework. And the next day I went to school and I had a feeling that my mother was going to tell my father about the other day. So, I was in class and I was listening to their conversation. My father woke up around eleven o'clock in the morning and went to the kitchen and saw my mother cooking him breakfast and he sat in the kitchen and they started talking.

"We had a problem yesterday." My mother said.

"What happened now?" My father asked.

"Luz was beaten and rape." She responded.

"How is she and how's Alma?" He asked.

"Alma is sad and Luz is going to recover but she has internal injury and she may not have any kids." She responded.

"Poor girl. How did Tania took it."

"I took Tania to see her and they were happy to see each other. I hope you can go and visit her."

"I'll go in the afternoon. Luz is like our daughter and we love her a lot."

"That's not all." My mother said and sat down. "The Dark Cowboy actually saved her life from those drug dealers."

What!" My father yelled at her. "You mean that psychotic killer saved her life and killed more people along the way?"

"Five men were raping Luz and The Dark Cowboy saved her life and killed them. Well it was execution style." My mother said.

"Are you serious?" He asked.

"They were drug dealers and they had a lot of weapons inside the van. I ordered that half of my team stayed back and collect the evidence while me and the other half escorted The Dark Cowboy to the Hospital."

"And what happened next."

"The Dark Cowboy kicked the door open and the Doctors started caring for her. And he left and I followed him and confronted him."

"What did you told him?" He asked.

"When is the hatred between Mauricio and The Dark Cowboy going to end. And he responded when he and our son, Mauricio confront one and another. You know he doesn't like him and wants to see him dead." She said.

"You know what I had enough of this! Beatrice it is time to question our son Mauricio, and this has got to stop because I had enough of The Dark Cowboy. You and I need to question Mauricio and we need to know what he knows about Primo and The Dark Cowboy. Why did Mauricio left The Dark Cowboy for dead and walked away from him." My father said.

"I told you that I don't want to put our kids in danger and especially our son." My mother said.

"Stop it, Beatrice! I don't want to see another person dead at the Morgue. When our son comes back from school, I'm going to question him! Even if I have to resign as the Mayor of El Paso and go back being the FBI agent that I once was!"

My mother was thinking about it and said. "Okay, Pablo. You win but I'm warning you if anything bad happens to Mauricio. I'm holding you responsible and I know The Dark Cowboy has threatened to kill you. But I will be the one that kills you if something bad happens to our son." She said.

My parents agreed to wait for me to come home. Meanwhile I was in class when the bell rang and the gang and I went to Chris's house and we were in the living room.

"Your dad wants to question you, Mauricio." Chris said.

"I know and I was listening to their conversation all morning long." I smiled.

"What are you going to do?" He asked.

"Improvise the whole damn thing." I responded.

"What's your plan?" Primo asked.

I got up and looked at them and smiled, "If my father wants to talk to me well let him talk to me and he can ask me anything he wants. And something else is going to happen."

"What do you have in mind?" Karina asked.

"My father is going to ask me a lot of questions and he is going to ask me about The Dark Cowboy and he thinks that I'm him. Well my parents and my sister are going to have a huge surprise on their hands. When they see that The Dark Cowboy breaks into my own home and attacks me right in front of them. He will be convince that I'm not The Dark Cowboy!" I smiled.

"Any volunteers?" Chris asked.

"Me!" I smiled and showed them what I was talking about. I grabbed my outfit and put it on the couch. My eyes were glowing and I put my hands on the outfit and then two dark hands came out of the sleeves and dark legs came out of the pants and the eyes were glowing red and it was growling at everyone. "What's your mission?" I asked and The Dark Figure responded. "To kill Mauricio de la Vega!" And it was floating in the air and found the guns and pointed the guns at me and everyone started screaming and they took cover. "Guys, I'm in control and relax. My father is the only one that thinks that I'm The Dark Cowboy and when he sees us fighting in the living room, he's going to know that I'm not the psychotic killer and I'm no longer going to be a suspect in this case. Once again I will make a fool out of him!" I smiled and looked at everyone, "I should we going home and I hope you can listen to our conversation."

Everyone smiled and I ran to my house and I stopped on the corner of the block and walked into my house. I put my backpack on the couch and I saw the look on their faces.

"What's wrong?" I asked.

"We need to talk, son." My father said.

I sat with them in the kitchen and asked them, "What's this about?"

"We need to talk about something serious." My father said and asked me, "What can you tell us about The Dark Cowboy?"

"What about that jackass!" I exclaimed.

"Just tell us what you know about him?" My mother said.

"What did he told you about me?" I asked.

"Just tell us!" My father yelled.

I looked at them and said. "I hate him. We met when we were little kids he became a trouble maker. He made fun of me and that's why I left him for dead. He was begging me to be his friend." I said.

"Did you guys fought?" My father asked.

"Yes, we did. Even now I try to fight him and every time I look in the mirror I see him staring at me. I hate him so much. I wanted to come to you guys about this but I thought you were not going to believe me." I said.

"Why wouldn't we believe you?" My mother asked.

"We're your parents, Mauricio. You should have come to us and we could arrested him when he was just a kid." My father said.

"I don't like him! I hate what he's been doing! I hope we face each other and fight to the death." I said.

"No, Mauricio. That's what he wants. He wanted me to give you up, so he can face you and kill you." My mother said.

"I'm going to find him tonight and get this over with." I said.

"No, we're not going to let you do this alone. We love too much to see you get hurt. It's our job to protect you." My mother said.

"I don't want him to hurt you guys and he's already hurt the people that I loved. If he wants me and I will go and find him." I said.

"We can help you, Mauricio." My father said. "Just tell us where he is and we will catch him."

"The Dark Cowboy is everywhere. I cannot look in the mirror because I know he's there looking at me. Sometimes I see him in the backyard staring at me or in my dreams." I said and they knew that I was scared to talk about him.

"Tell us where he is!" My father yelled.

"You will find out soon enough." I said and just then my sister, Tania came downstairs and she could hear us yelling at each other. Then the phone rang and my mother put it on a the speaker. "Hello!"

"It's me." It was The Dark Figure that was talking on the other end of the line and was breathing heavily.

"What now?" My father asked.

"I saw you guys going to Thomason Hospital to see the little girl that I saved at Marty Robbins Park and how is she?" The Dark Figured asked.

"She's going to recover." My mother responded.

"It's good to know. Now we got that sentimental crap out of the way. It's time for business." The Dark Figure growled and laughed. "I enjoyed listening to Mauricio's speech and he's my best friend in the world. I love the fact that he wants to take me out, I'm so scared."

And I responded. "I did it before and I'm willing to do it again. Remember I left you for dead."

"Don't worry, Mauricio. I'm still alive and still breathing and I'm going to leave you for dead when I point my Magnum guns on your head and boom your dead and you will be worm food. That sounds good." The Dark Figure said.

"It's going to sound good when you fail to kill me. And I know everything about you and I know how you think." I said.

"Yes, I know about you too very well. It's like looking in the mirror and see the same person. I feel honored that we think alike and act alike." The Dark Figure laughed.

"You two need to workout your differences. How about you guys sit together and talk about your problems and after that we arrest you, Dark Cowboy for all the murders!" My mother yelled.

"That sounds a good idea, Beatrice de la Vega, and you are in fact a very smart lady and once again you have dropped the ball on protecting someone. So, Mauricio, how about we workout our differences right here, right now. At this moment I'm standing on the rooftop of your house." The Dark Figured said and growled.

I grabbed the kitchen knife and said. "Well bring it!"

"It's your funeral, Mauricio de la Vega." The Dark Figured laughed and hanged up the phone.

"Mom, dad and Tania. I'm going to collect the thirty thousand dolly bounty on The Dark Cowboy. Stay back and watch a de la Vega in action. The King will take the serial killer down for the count!" I smiled.

My parents and Tania were freaked out and they wanted to protect me. So, The Dark Figure kicked the door open and looked at me and started laughing. "We meet again, Mauricio de la Vega. Round two."

"I left you for dead and this time I will make sure you die." I said.

The Dark Figure put his guns away and I put the knife down and we started fighting the old fashion way. We were tangled and we were throwing each other on to the walls and breaking stuff while my parents and my sister were watching us fight and they were worried for me and Tania started crying her eyes out. My mother got on the phone and called for backup and this would be their chance to finally arrest The Dark Cowboy and The Dark Figure knocked me on the floor and grabbed his Magnum guns.

"Any last words?" The Dark Figure asked.

"Yes. You can go to Hell." I responded.

"Please don't kill my son." My mother begged.

"You don't know your son like I do." The Dark Figure said and pointed the gun at my head. And we heard the Police sirens and they parked in the driveway. "We should continue with this some other time when were alone."

"I agree." I smiled.

My mother picked up her gun and shot The Dark Figure on the arm and just like that the Dark Figure disappeared into thin air and my parents went to pick up me and asked. "Are you okay?"

"Yes. I'm fine." I said.

"You want us to take you to the Hospital?" My father asked.

"No, I'm fine I just need to rest." Mauricio said.

The Police and the FBI Agents came running into the house to find The Dark Cowboy but he was gone and at least no one died. "Where is he?"

"He's gone." My father said.

"Are you guys okay?"

"Yes. But we need a new door and everything is fine." My mother said.

"Go home and get some rest. Because tomorrow I'm going to talk in front everyone." My father said.

"Your heard the Mayor." My mother ordered and the Police left to their homes to get some rest. But the FBI Agents and my father decided to get a new door, so they went to buy a new one while my mother and Tania took me to my room. And they went to the kitchen to make something to eat and I was laying in bed when the Dark Figure reentered my body once again. My eyes were glowing red and I radioed Karina, "What did you think?"

"Very clever and they actually bought it. And you're no longer a suspect in this case!" She responded and laughed.

"Well I'll see you tomorrow at school." I laughed and stayed in bed and I was so happy that my parents and sister bought it.

Then at midnight where my mother and my father couldn't not fall asleep. "We drop the ball, Honey." He said.

"Big time. We've been getting chances to arrest The Dark Cowboy but we failed to do so. And I hope your decision will be for the better. I want to go back to be the same Police Officer and you as an FBI Agent."

"I thought I would be a good as a Mayor but it wasn't for me. I'm better off as an FBI Agent. I'm going to stick around and try to catch The Dark Cowboy. And then I can go back to my post and try to chase another criminal. You know who I'm talking about."

"Vito Mancini. I haven't thought of him in a long time. Vito Mancini and The Dark Cowboy have been giving us problems." She said.

"First will arrest The Dark Cowboy and then I'll go and try to arrest Vito Mancini." He said and smiled, "Get some sleep, Honey."

Well I started laughing and I knew that I got them right where I want them. And at the same time I planned to continue my relationship with Eliza and continue with my education. Then it was on a Saturday afternoon where I was following my mother and Alma and they went to pick up the little girl from the Hospital. Well I was waiting in the parking lot and three hours later they came out and I saw the girl smiling. And I followed them to their house and I already know where the girl lives, I will see you tonight, young lady.

And on that afternoon my parents and Tania decided to throw a party at Alma's house and they were in the backyard. The little girl was happy that she was back at home and she was devastated because she found out that she couldn't not have babies but she continued to smile for her mother and her best friend in the world Tania. Then Tania gave her a surprise and she opened her present and it was make up kit. So, the girls went inside the house to put their make up on.

"So, you're no longer Mayor." Alma said.

"No. I'm excited to go back to my old position." He said.

"You must be thrilled of getting back out there. That's what you do best." Alma said.

"I'm also excited of returning as a Police Officer. It was driving me crazy being an FBI Agent. That wasn't my style." She said

"But you did great out there." Alma smiled and asked. "So, where's Mauricio?"

"He's with his friends. You know him he doesn't like parties." He said.

"I haven't seen him since middle school." She said.

"Alma we need to talk about something important! Well Pablo and I need to tell you that we must protect our kids from The Dark Cowboy because he's getting dangerous." My mother said.

"Beatrice is right, Alma. Last week The Dark Cowboy attacked Mauricio and nearly killed him in our own home." My father said.

"We know that The Dark Cowboy saved your daughter's life but there is a chance that he might want to kill her too." My mother said.

"That won't be a problem because my daughter keeps talking about him all day long. She says that she wants to thank him in person because he saved her life. Well you know Luz, she loves fairy tales and she actually thinks that The Dark Cowboy is her Prince Charming." Alma smiled. "That's how my daughter is, she's very generous and kind."

"Well she reminds me of you, Alma. You helped our kids and everyone else's kids. You love helping people and you are also generous and kind. Like mother and daughter." My father said.

"It runs in the family." My mother smiled.

"But don't worry. And you know that I will protect my daughter and I'm willing die for my daughter and for Tania and also for Mauricio." Alma smiled. And I was hearing what they were saying and they are worried that I was going to kill the little girl that I saved in the park. So, my parents were now convinced that I'm not The Dark Cowboy after all and they decided to move on with the investigation and they were now convinced that they were dealing with a Demonic Figure. Well they stayed at Alma's house until it was getting dark and they finally went home. My parents were in the kitchen and my father was talking to my mother about something important.

"This might be the sign from The Dark Cowboy." He said.

"Which one." She said.

"He's now targeting our son. There's a chance that they might see each other again and this time he's going to kill him." He said.

"He better not. I'm going to protect my son for the rest of my life." She said.

"Honey, our son is growing up and he's in high school. We cannot protect him forever. We need to take control of this situation. Now I'm in charge again and we need to move quicker and be smarter than The Dark Cowboy." He said.

"How are we going to do that?" She asked.

"I don't know but we need to do something or by the time we know it we're planning our son's funeral." He said.

"You may be right. The Dark Cowboy might get him alone when he's in college. He might find him there and right now he's just toying with us because he knows that were protecting him." My mother wanted to cry and my father hugged her so tight. So, my parents went to my room said goodnight to me and went to sleep.

And I was getting curious about the hidden powers that I have inside me. I started thinking about the night I killed Armando and Deyna. I ran so fast and I felt that I was faster than a speeding bullet and on the night I killed Melissa. I jumped off the rooftop and somehow I was able to hit the target while I was floating in the air and I am able to separate myself and I also I can walk on the walls and stand on the ceilings. My new powers are sensing when someone is in danger. And I was wondering, how come I couldn't sense anything when Samantha was seen her mom getting rape, well maybe if Primo would have gotten his hands on her. I would have felt it right of away. And that's why I was feeling crappy on the day I saved the girl's life. What's the next hidden power I might have? My answer was I have a heart after all and I do care about others and I must be a good guy after all. So, I decided to go undercover and see the girl I saved and I ran to Chris's house and he was still in his garage fixing Primo's car.

I was behind him and I said, "Good evening!"

And I startled him. "Hey, Mauricio!" Chris smiled and looked at me and asked, "How did you get here?"

"I ran here!" I responded.

"Well you got here pretty fast!" Chris closed the car door and looked at me and I was floating in the air, "What the?"

"I wanted to ask you if I was floating in the air when I shot Melissa?" I asked.

"Yes, you were!" He was shocked.

"Well I came here because I wanted to spy on somebody and this is not an operation and I'm not going to kill anyone." I smiled and went inside the house to put on my outfit and when I went outside, Chris had the horse with him. I got on top of the horse and said goodbye to Chris and I took off all the way to her house. Before I went to her house, I decided to stop by the grocery store and ran trough the doors and the doors broke. And I heard the alarms going off and I went to get a get well card and some roses and I got back on the horse and went to her house and I could hear the Police sirens. And I arrived at her house and I looked at my watch and it was eleven o'clock at night.

I had my night vision goggles and I saw the little girl and her mother in the living room. They were watching television together and her mother started yawning and her daughter walked her to the room. I went to the backyard and I went into the little girl's room. I was looking around her room, and I can tell that she loves horses and she has a lot of stuffed animals and she has a lot of pictures in her wall. There was a picture of her hugging my sister, Tania and I'm guessing that Tania and this girl are best friends maybe closer than sisters. She also had the newspaper article on top of her bed and this girl made the front page and there was the picture when she was in my arms. Finally I heard the door open and the little girl came into the room, she looked at me and smiled and closed the door. I was shocked that she wasn't scared at all.

The little girl went to turn on the lamp and she whispered to me. "Hi, it's nice to see you again."

"How are you feeling" I asked quietly.

"Better but the Doctor told me that I have internal injury and I cannot have any babies. I also have a broken arm and bruises in my body." She looked at sad.

"Don't worry I already took care of them and they paid for their actions. There buried fifty feet below and there are now worm food." I looked at her and I touched her face and said, "Chin up and you never know there might be a miracle on the way and you are going to have a lot of babies in the future." I smiled.

"Why did you save my life?" She asked.

"I felt like killing people, so I went to the direction where I could felt the presence of someone being in danger and I was in the middle of the park and you were calling for help. But I was happy that I killed five more people and increased my killings. And I'm happy to know that you were safe and sound. I also brought you roses and a get well card." I responded.

She smelled the roses and smiled, "Thank you again for saving me. But why do you kill people?"

I responded, "I wanted revenge and all of those people that I killed and they called me so many horrible names. That's all you need to know for know and I'm glad that you're doing okay but there was a problem when I got there."

"What kind of problem?" She asked.

"I counted six drug dealers that were inside the van and I only shot five. I'm guessing one got away and right now I'm looking for him." I said.

"I only saw five of them and they drugged me." She said.

"They are drug dealers and right now I'm going to hunt him down and kill him." I said and I was going out the window. And I'm know who the sixth person might be. I have a feeling that they were sponsored by Vito Mancini.

"Wait! I never got your name but I know your name is The Dark Cowboy but do you have a real name?" She asked.

"The Dark Cowboy and what's your name?" I asked.

"My name is Luz Maria Fitzgerald Estrada. I'm half Irish and half Cuban, I'm twelve years old and I just got back from Ireland and on my first day back in El Paso, Texas. I was rescued from a pack of drug dealers! And I always hope that my Prince Charming would rescue me from a pack of wolves and you're the one that saved me from those drug dealers!" She smiled and went up to me and grabbed my hand and said. "I know there's good in you because you saved my life and let the Police handle them. Don't kill anymore people and you must forgive this person that you hate. Will you do it for me."

"I'll be thinking about it." I said.

She looked at me and hugged me so tight and said, "A Princess gets attack by a pack of drug dealers and gets rescued by her Prince Charming. And a Princess always receives a kiss from her rescuer." She smiled and took off my bandana.

"Wait! Are you sure you want to kiss a monster?" I asked.

She smiled, "Yes, and I will always remember that The Dark Cowboy saved my life." She put her feet on my boots and I put my arms around her waist and hold her tight and I picked her up and we kissed for a couple of minutes with a little tongue action. And she looked at me and blushed and started giggling and she hid her face on my chest "My first real kiss!" She smiled and said, "And if you need anyone to talk too. I will always be here for you. I'm here as a friend. Even if I go back to Ireland, I would love for you to visit me there!"

"Okay. I like that idea." I said and shook her hand. "I'll try not to kill people and I might forgive this person that I hate so much." I said and went out the window.

My new friend Luz Maria Estrada watched me from the window and I was standing in the middle of the sidewalk and said goodbye to her and hopped on my horse and took off. After I left her house I went to my house and my mother was outside and she getting some fresh. And I went up to sneak up on her.

"Good evening, Officer de la Vega." I said.

My mother was startled when she saw me and asked, "It's you! What are you doing here?"

"Wait. I'm not here to start another fight with your son." I said.

"Then why are you here?" She asked.

"I came here to ask you about those drug dealers that I killed. I counted six of them and I killed five." I responded.

"So, one got away from you. My team already took the van for evidence. We know that they were drug dealers and there was more than fifty pounds of weed and cocaine. They were working for Vito Mancini."

"Well, Agent de la Vega, you should lead your team and try to find these drug dealers and arrest them. And I hope you can find their sponsor!" I said.

"Well I'm no longer in charge of this operation and don't you watch the news, my husband was forced to resigned as the Mayor and went back to his old position of being an FBI Agent." She smiled and said, "But we will find them later on just as soon we try to arrest you."

"Just because I kill people doesn't mean that I'm the villain, but after all I saved Luz Maria Fitzgerald Estrada's life remember? And earlier I went to her room and she thanked me in person. She made me promise not to hurt other anymore people, so I be will be thinking about it. And later on I will tell you the reason why I killed those people. And I know you guys are going to take a long time to find them and that's why I decided to hunt them down and kill them for you guys. I'll also gong to hunt down, the great Vito Mancini."

"I'm speculating that he hired you to murder all of those people that you killed over the years?" My mother said.

"I don't work for him, Officer de la Vega. Well I'm going to turn over a new leaf and maybe my new friend Luz and you were right along that it's time to put my hatred towards Mauricio aside and forgive and forget. I want to have a clear conscience when I enter the Gates of Saint Peter. I'll be away for awhile and catch those drug dealers and Vito Mancini."

"But even though you bring Vito. You're still under arrest!" My mother said.

"I've known you for quite a while, Beatrice. I'm sensing that there's more in your depression. You have regrets in life?"

My mother looked at me and said, "As a mother I don't have ay regrets. But as a Police Officer I have a lot of regrets. For instance I've killed twenty criminals. They had families and I was devastated for that. And I made a promise that I wasn't going to kill but I should have arrest them, so they can get the rehabilitation."

"You did your job! You're a great Police Officer and a great mother too. You don't need to regret anything. So, good night, Officer de la Vega." I said and disappeared into the darkness. Then I was walking around the roof tops of the houses and I was looking for the crime lord. Well I bet he's hiding somewhere and I was looking around and saw an empty city. So, I went back to my room and I was thinking about Luz Maria and how could a beautiful twelve year old girl had the guts to kiss a monster like me but then again another beautiful girl like Eliza is also kissing the monster that kills people. Well nobody is perfect, so I finally went to sleep.

The next day I was walking around the block when Chris parked in the sidewalk and he was calling to me. I turned around and went to see what he wanted. "Where are you going?" He asked.

"I'm going to Eliza's house." I responded.

"Are you feeling okay?"

"Yes, why."

"You should have seen the look on your face when you storm out and went to the park. I was worried for you and you are lucky that they didn't arrest you."

"Yes, I'm so lucky."

"Well since this wasn't part of our agreement and I want to say congratulations, two hundred and fifty dollars are going to be added in your back account. Wow, Mauricio that's one thousand, one hundred and fifty dollars. Now I'm impressed and I know you are going to be the greatest serial killer of all time. And a little personal note, you want to tell me what was that all about because you have been acting strange lately."

"I don't know but I want to be alone and lived my life in peace. I want to start my relationship with Eliza. As for now will be in touch." I said.

"You're saying that you want out of the gang. You know that you cannot do that to us. Think about what your doing?"

"I didn't sign a contract, so I'm free to do what I want to do with my life. It's a free country, Chris!" I said and left to her house.

I heard him yell! "Think about it!" Well I am thinking about it, Chris, and all I could think about was the kiss I gave to Luz. But what am I thinking about her. She is a twelve years old girl for crying out loud and I'm going out with Eliza, she is my girlfriend and the love of my life. Well I wanted to move on with Eliza.

Three months later Eliza and I started dating more and more. Eliza and I spent those times kissing and holding on to each other. We were in our world and we wanted to be together at all time. We went to the park and we saw our tree. We were kissing under our tree. But we had a test on Monday morning and Eliza and I decided to study for a test at my house and we kissed and it was a little tongue action as well and we looked at each other and smiled. I decided to walk Eliza home and we finally reached her house and once again we kissed. She went inside her house and I went to my house and fell asleep. And the next day I woke up all happy, I was laying in bed and I was still thinking about the kiss I gave to Luz. Once again I'm still thinking about that twelve year old girl. So, I went to take a nice hot shower and after that I went to the kitchen and saw my mother making breakfast.

"I'm going to school." I responded with a smile.

"Mauricio it's Saturday. You don't go to school on Saturday or Sunday." She said and continued to make breakfast.

"What are you talking about, Mom?" I asked her and at the same time I didn't paid attention to what my mother was telling me.

My mother looked at me and said, "I know what this is about, Mauricio. You are too busy kissing Luz Maria Estrada that you don't remember what day it is. And I remember those days and it seems it was just yesterday when your father and I couldn't stay away from each other." She smiled and serve me breakfast and continued, "Luz Maria should be here in twenty minutes because you guys are going to kiss and I trust you that you are going to kiss her all afternoon long and take advantage of a twelve year old girl."

I looked at her and asked, "What did you say?"

"I said that you are too busy kissing Eliza that you don't remember what day it is. And don't forget that Eliza is going to be here, so you guys can study for the test. I trust you guys to be alone." She smiled.

"You can trust me, Mom." I said and I think that I'm loosing my mind.

"I'm going to work at nine o'clock and I won't be in your way but I want you to look out for your sister while I'm gone." She said.

"You know that I will protect my baby sister." I smiled and started eating my scrambled eggs and after that I went back to my room and I was wondering what the Hell is happening to me today. And twenty minutes later my mother opened the door and said. "Mauricio, Luz Maria is here to see you and she wants to kiss you!"

"Excuse me!" I said.

"Eliza is here, Mauricio!" She said.

"Good send her in." I said and I was turning on the computer when she came into the room and put her backpack on the bed and I turned around and saw her and she was so pretty. Her hair was a little bit longer and I think she went to the beauty salon. "Good morning, Sunshine." She smiled and she was different.

"Your hair." I said.

"What about my hair?" She asked.

"It's longer." I said and went up to her and she thought that I wanted to kiss her and I was looking at her. I saw Luz's face and she was smiling at me and she wanted to kiss me.

She kissed me and said, "Ha, Ha, You are so funny, Sweetie. Now let's study because we have a test on Monday!" She sat down on my bed and started going over the test. "Guess what we're going to do later on at night."

"Party."

"No, but you are getting close."

"Kiss, hug like we always do." I said.

"No!"

"I don't know." And I once again I heard Luz's voice that said, "A Princess gets rescued by a pack of drugs dealers. And a Princess receives a kiss from her rescuer." Suddenly I started thinking about the kiss that I gave her.

And Eliza got my attention. "Mauricio are you listening to me? Did you hear what I said."

"Something about a Princess that gets rescued by a pack of drug dealers." I responded.

"No, Mauricio! It's our three month anniversary!" She smiled.

I stayed quiet for awhile and I didn't want to stir up more anymore problems between us and all I did was hug Eliza and told her "Happy three month anniversary!" And all I care is to make Eliza happy for the rest of my life. And I looked at her and she smiled and we kissed and continued to study for the

Jesus Morales

test. And later on in the night we celebrated our three month anniversary. Eliza was happy and I was concerned because why am I thinking about a twelve year old girl. Well I made a decision that it was now time to forget about Luz and move on with my life. Eliza is my girlfriend and my future wife.

Well as it turns Eliza and I spent the next three months together but at the same time those three months were really hard for us. All I heard from the guys in the locker room is, "When are you going to sleep with, Eliza." And a lot for crap and I had to deal with from those guys. And it came to a point that I stopped talking to my friends and I ignored most the boys in the locker room and they actually stopped making fun of me and they started treating me like an adult. And also I kept thinking about Luz and the kiss I gave her and I heard her laughter and again I tried not think about her.

Then Eliza was about to turn seventeen years old on March 14 and I was going to turn seventeen years old on June 17, so we celebrated our birthdays together at *Chico's Tacos*. Then the school year ended and we became juniors. Eliza and I were excited about spending the summer together and we wanted to be together at all times. And I wanted to forget about the locker room talk, my school problems, and also I wanted to forget about Luz Maria Estrada and moved on with my life. All I wanted to do is enjoy the summer with Eliza. But as it turns out I hardly got to see Eliza. She always had something else to do, instead of seeing me. She always told me that she had to spend time with her family from out of town and when I called her house, her mother said that she was washing her hair, taking a nap or doing other things. I think one time she had the flue and she didn't want to answer the phone at all. Before the summer was going end I went to her house, and knocked on the door, and her mother opened the door.

"Is Eliza here?" I asked.

"Yes, she's here."

"Can I talk to her, Please?"

"Come in, Mauricio."

"I'd rather wait outside." I said.

Her mother smiled and went inside to get Eliza. And I was standing there for a couple of minutes when Eliza came outside and I was upset to look at her. She looked like she still had the flue or something else was wrong with her because she didn't wasn't herself. She was about to kiss me but I didn't let her.

"What's wrong?" She asked.

"What's wrong you ask. I will tell you what is wrong. I've called you so many damn times and you didn't have the decency to call me back. You never even answer the phone and you have better things to do than to see me and spend the summer together like we planned."

"I was busy. I had the flue. My family came to visit us and there are a lot of things going on with my life right now. You know about my family problems and I'm dealing with our friends that died in a horrible way and the people that I went to Church with were also killed by The Dark Cowboy. How do you think I feel about that?"

I was angry with her and she began to realized that I was about to lose my temper. And I wanted to punch the wall so badly.

"Mauricio, you don't have to worry, I'm not cheating on you and I wanted to be with you too but my family came to visit us and I was helping my mom with her work. Remember when we were kids I was telling you that I was having problems with my family. You know everything about me and I know everything about you."

"So, why didn't you call me back?" I asked her.

"I'm sorry. I wasn't avoiding you. Sweetheart, I care about you. I always had a crush on you since we were little kids and I don't know if you had a crush for me when we were little kids. When I was a little girl I had a dream that we got married and had a lot of children together." She smiled and her tears started to come down her face and she put her arms around my neck and we kissed for a while.

"I love you, Eliza."

She kissed me as hard as she could. "Me too."

"I'm sorry for acting this way. I just don't want to loose you." I said.

"I don't want to loose you either and I really hated this summer because of my family's problems. If I was living alone I would love to spent all my time with you." She said and smiled.

"To answer your question. I felt something about you when we were kids and I'm glad to have you in my arms. I was also dreaming that you and I got married and had a lot of children and I've been in love with you for a very long time. And I want to marry you when we graduate from high school." I said.

"Me too. I want to have babies with you."

We kissed again and held each other for a while. So, the next day we decided to go to the movies and all we did was kiss during the whole movie and we were glad to be with each other. We had a goodtime on the last day of our summer vacation. And we went to the park and went under the shade tree and we saw our names carved into it. We were happy to see our tree.

"Do you think about them?" She asked.

"Who?" I also asked.

"Our friends that died and everyone else we knew."

"I do miss them."

"Armando and Deyna two friends that we grew up with. They just died in a brutal way." She said.

"I know it could have been me that would have died that way or you. And I cannot imagine what you went through on the mountain." I said.

"And it's weird that they accused you of hurting them and they were found dead in the mountain."

"We both know that they were lying and I don't hurt people."

"Melissa Owens our fourth grade substitute Teacher. She was found dead in a nightclub in downtown El Paso. It's sad how she died."

"I ran into her at the store and a couple of days later she was found dead."

"I met Doctor William James and his family at Church, and I also met Doctor Erin Norton and her family, and my mom knew Judge George Fuentes and his family and they started going to Church with us. They became friends with my mom and we always went to a retreat together and they were found dead outside in their working place but George Fuentes was found dead at his house."

"I heard about it on the television." I responded and I felt this was going somewhere.

"The Commissioner was a close friend of my mom's and your mom. I forgot to tell you that he was my Godfather. He loved me a lot and he was like my father to me. The Mayor was also a close friend of my mom and a good friend to this city. The Commissioner was found dead in a alley and the Mayor was found dead in his office while your parents were protecting them."

"Are you kidding me?" I asked and I wanted to make it look that I didn't know either.

"Detective Jim Nielsen well he was my mom's second cousin. Well he was found dead in another alley. The Captain of the Police Department was also a close friend of our mom's and he was found dead in another alley. A female reporter and the owner of the club were found dead and her daughter has been missing for so many years. The new kid that came into the classroom. Do you remember Mike Reyes? He was also found dead at his home. And a male reporter was also found dead. Our Pastor was found dead at his house. And a Police Officer was also found dead. The Mayor's lawyer and Mrs. Martinez were found dead." She said and sobbed and hugged me so tight.

"I'm also sad, Eliza, and I miss them so much. And don't worry my parents are going arrest that psychotic killer and he will pay for his actions. I don't want to see you sad." I said and kissed her and hugged her.

"I'm so scared what happens if The Dark Cowboy comes out and tries to kill us. And I know The Dark Cowboy is after you and he almost killed you in your own home and I don't know what to do without you. I love so damn much!" Eliza sobbed.

"I'm still alive Eliza and I will protect you at all times and I'm willing to risk my life by protecting you and making sure you are safe. I love you a lot and I don't want you to worry." I said.

"I love you more." She tried to smile and we hugged so tight. And I know Eliza is devastated by the loss of everyone but we need to move on and she was hopping that my parents make progress in arresting that psychotic killer well good luck with that one. If Eliza knew that she was hugging the psychotic killer known as The Dark Cowboy. I don't know how she would react to that surprise.

Right after that I took Eliza to her house and I walked her to the front door and we kissed and she went inside the house and I went to my house. Eliza called me around eight o'clock that night and we talked for a long time and she was happy again. She happened to mention that she wasn't going to let her family problems come between us ever again. She also told me that she loves me a lot and I told her that I love her too.

Then summer ended and school started. I walked around Americas High School and it really had changed a lot from last year. Most of the new students were from out of town and there were a lot of lesbians and pregnant girls walking around the school campus and I felt that I was living in San Francisco, California. So, anyway Eliza and I checked our new schedules and I couldn't believe it. All of my classes were in Special Education! I was upset but Eliza tried to cheer me up and kissed me on the cheek.

I decided to be more aggressive in the annual meetings. I would work harder and study a lot. So, I saw the annual meeting schedule and mine was set for October 23rd. I planned to be prepared for that day. And the first day of school went well for me and it went by so fast and the bell rang at thirty forty-five and it was time to go home.

My mother came for us and we took Eliza home. I walked Eliza to the front door and we kissed and she went into the house and blew me a kiss and closed the door. I stayed quiet on the way home and went straight to my room. Around seven o'clock that night my mother came into my room.

"What's wrong?" She asked.

"Well mom, I took one look at my schedule and I'm still in Special Education." I responded.

"I'm sorry, Mauricio. I know you've worked very hard to get out of Special Education. But your dad and I know that you're doing your best. Don't give up. Just keep showing them that you can do better."

"My little parole is going to be in October 23rd and I wonder what they're going to say to me." I said.

"Hang in there, Mauricio, it will all work out."

"You know, Mom. How important it is to me to have a diploma and I want to become someone important in life. You know a legend like you and my dad." I said and smiled.

"Don't worry, Son. You still have the people who loves you a lot and now you have Eliza supporting you. I can tell she loves you a lot and I hope that you guys end up getting married. And now dinner is ready!"

"Good because I'm starving." I said and I told my mother that I wanted to be a legend like them but I'm already a legend and they don't even know it but they have seen live it live in person. My mother and I went to have dinner and I tried to enjoy the meal and it was so delicious. So, I went through the first semester with really good grades. Eliza and her brother, Mr. Caballero were helping me out with math. And I believe that year Eliza and I were drawn closer than ever before. We went to the movies together and we went to Marty Robbins Park and we spent those times kissing under the shade tree. Eliza and I wanted to be together all the time and we spent those times holding on to each other and kissing as well with a tongue action. The two of us were happy and in love. And Saturday afternoon we went to *Cielo Vista Mall* and took some pictures. I made faces but Eliza was smiling in all the pictures and she has a wonderful smile.

And October 23rd was around the corner and it was time for my annual meeting well actually it was my parole. I was in class when they called me to go to the conference room. And in my imagination I could hear them saying, "Bring in Inmate Number 453242." I also felt that I should wear that orange jump suit and I should be handcuffed from all over my body and I felt that a guard would escort me to the room. Well the Campus Police did escort me for my own safety just in case if The Dark Cowboy would showed up and attack me. And I opened the door and there were six or seven of them sitting behind long tables and they smiled and bowed down when I came into the room. I approached my Counselor and I felt very uneasy when they all looked up at me and they told me to sit down. My Counselor opened my thick file.

"How are you doing in your classrooms?" She asked.

"Good, I have good grades."

"That's good to know." She said.

"I've asked all off my Teachers for regular classes and they all said yes. So, I'm asking you for regular classes because I have good grades and I'm improving in everything." I said.

"So, you think you're ready to have regular classes?" My Counselor asked.

"They are going to be hard your, Majesty." The Principal said.

"Yes, I'm ready to have regular classes and I've been asking for regular classes for at least two years!" I yelled.

"Mauricio we understand that you have good grades and you want to have regular classes but the regular classes are going to be hard for you." My Counselor looked worried.

"What they teach me in Special Education is what they're going to teach me in regular classes." I said.

"Mauricio, we know that you want to have regular classes and to be honest with you, you're not ready. We are sorry, Mauricio and please don't be mad at us." My counselor said and I sat there and I was upset with them. I couldn't believe that I was going to spend another year in Special Education and I wanted to yell at them but I was holding back all off my of anger.

Then the bell rang and it was time to go to lunch and every peasant at school bowed before me and I bumped into Eliza in the hallway and she smiled and I grabbed her hand and we went to the cafeteria and of course everyone saw the look on my face and they got out of my way and took our food outside to eat at the tennis court. I was pacing back and forth while Eliza was sitting down staring up at me.

"What happened? Why are you mad?" She asked.

I looked at her and said. "I'm still going to be in Special Education. All my hard work was for nothing. The worst part is that you have to go through this with me."

"What do you mean?" She asked.

"I don't know why you're with me. I'm in Special Education and you are the prettiest girl in the school and you can have any normal guy you want." I threw the milk carton at the fence. "And not some retard like me."

"I can't believe you are saying that to me!"

"All I want to know is why are you still with me?" I yelled.

"You want to know why?" Eliza said and she put the tray down and said, "Because I love you a lot and you and I are in this together. You suffer and I suffer. We're supposed to be there for each other. Don't take your problems out on our relationship."

"It's all God's fault, And He's sitting down on His throne and He's laughing at me." I said.

"Don't take this out on God!" Eliza yelled and got up and started yelling at me. "It's your fault! You got yourself into Special Education! Because you didn't want to talk at all! I can seem to remember that everyone tried to help you. But you didn't let anyone help you! And now no one cannot help you because they're dead!" She continued to yell at me.

"I hate everybody in this world and now you're just like them and you can all go straight to Hell!"

"Now that you've said that to me, I could say a lot of bad things to you about how you're acting now, but I'm a Christian. You can figure out what I want to say to you."

"You're not a Christian, Eliza!" I was face to face with Eliza. "I think you're a Devil worshiper and a tramp!" I said.

"Don't you dare call me that!" She yelled at me and her tears started to come down her face and she slapped me as hard as she could and the worst part is that I didn't feel a thing but Eliza started screaming and she was holding on to her hand.

And I came to my senses and I realized that everyone who was outside was staring us. The Campus Police thought there was a fight going on in the tennis court and they came running down all the way to the tennis court. Eliza was holding her hand and she ran into the school. And I followed her inside and everyone saw me and they bowed down and Eliza was in the hallway and she was running like a crazy person. And I ran into Joe and Miguel in the hallway. Just then the bell rang and we all went to class. I felt that everyone kept on looking at me because I had Eliza's hand marked in my face but it didn't hurt at all and I don't know why it didn't hurt. And I knew that I messed everything up because I was upset with what they told me in the annual meeting. Then the bell rang at three-forty five and I went to get tutored by Mr. Caballero.

But Mr. Caballero and I didn't speak to each other. He just gave me a couple of assignments and then I went to take a break. I was standing in front of the coke machine when Joe and Miguel came up to me.

"What happened between you and Eliza?" Joe asked.

"Nothing."

"You want to talk about it?" Joe asked.

"No, that's okay." I said.

Joe and Miguel were about to leave when I decided to take everything out. "Why do these things always happen to me?" I said.

"What do you mean?" Joe asked.

"I've worked so damn hard to get good grades and I'm still in Special Education." I said.

"We heard about your parole. You took out your frustrations and you blame everything on Eliza."

"Yes, I did. And I made a complete mess out of it! I'm just tired of being a nice guy."

"Where are you going with this?" Miguel asked.

"I have a girlfriend and I can have sex with her anytime I want to." I said.

"So, what you're saying is?" Joe asked.

"What I'm saying is that you guys were right all along. I am going to do everything I can to get Eliza into bed." I said

"Are you serious?" Joe asked.

"Oh, yeah, I'm serious."

"Mauricio is growing up." Joe said.

"What are you going to do for Eliza to forgive you?" Miguel asked.

"I will apologize to her and she will see my sensitive side and I bet that's how all the guys were able to get the girls into bed." I said.

"Don't forget to tell her that you love her." Joe said.

"So, Mauricio, does this mean that you're not mad at us anymore?" Miguel asked.

"Nah, that was a long time ago. Forget about it. This time I want to go the down the field and score the winning touchdown and I don't care if it takes fifteen plays to score but I will score sooner or later and even if I have to go for it on fourth down and score." I laughed and went back to finish tutoring and at five o'clock in the afternoon I went to my house.

That night I decided to go to Eliza's house well I snuck out of the window and once again I broke into the grocery store and I broke the curfew for the second time and grabbed the red roses and ran to her house. Yes, I broke the curfew and I still went to her house and I showed Eliza Caballero and her mother that I wasn't afraid of the psychotic killer known as The Dark Cowboy. And if Eliza says something I will tell her that The Dark Cowboy can kiss my ass and go to Hell along the way. And I wanted Eliza to forgive me, so I bought her some of her favorite red roses and I could hear the Police sirens. I rang the doorbell and she opened the door. I could tell she had been crying since we left school grounds. I noticed that she had a band aid around her hand. I gave her the roses and we sat down on the bench.

She was smelling the roses. "They're beautiful and they smell wonderful!"

"I'm sorry, Eliza, for the way I acted today."

"You should be! You acted like a jerk and you really hurt my feelings."

"I was upset about what they told me in the annual meeting. I didn't mean to hurt your feelings." I said and touched her hand. "Let me make it up to you, I want to change my ways. I want to go to Church with you. I want to have a clear conscience about our relationship." I touched her face and her tears were coming down her face and I wiped them with my fingers and I kissed her. "I want to spend my life with you and marry you and have kids with you."

"I love you a lot." She hugged me very tight and kissed me as hard she could and she was crying on my arms and I told her everything would be okay in our relationship. We stayed outside talking for awhile and as soon I was going to leave, she told me that loves me a lot and I went home. And on my way to the house, I started thinking about what I had accomplished tonight. I wondered when would it be a good time to ask Eliza if we could have sex.

Then holidays came Eliza and I spent a lot of time together and at the same time we were happy to be with each other at all times. I was beginning to wonder when Eliza wanted to go to bed with me and I hope that it was very soon. I was doing what my "Teachers" Joe and Miguel were telling me to do. Then our one-year anniversary was in a couple of days away. I wanted to give Eliza a present. And Friday afternoon Tania and I were jogging at Marty Robbins Park and we stopped to rest.

"Tomorrow Eliza and I celebrate our one-year anniversary." I said.

"What are you going to get her?" She asked.

"Probably a doll or a necklace." I said.

"Are you serious, Mauricio?" Tania asked.

"I don't know what to get her. Do you have any ideas?"

"Well yesterday, Madelyn's dog had puppies. Maybe you can give her a puppy." She said.

"You mean a Chihuahua?" I was about to laugh. "Those things look like rats."

"Hey, they're cute and trust me, Eliza will like her new puppy." Tania smiled and we went to her friend's house to pick up the puppy.

And the next day my mother took me to Eliza's house around three o'clock that afternoon. "Happy one-year anniversary." I said.

"Thanks, Baby!" She exclaimed.

"I have a surprise for you."

"Really!"

My mother got out of the car and she had the puppy in her arms. When Eliza saw the puppy, she was so excited that she gave me a huge bear hug. "Happy one-year anniversary!" My mother said as she gave her the puppy.

"Thanks, Mrs. De la Vega!" Eliza said.

"What are you going name her?" I asked.

"Princess!" She exclaimed.

"What a great name." My mother said.

"I have another surprise." I said.

"What is it?" She asked.

"Be patient, now get into the house and change your clothes." I said.

"Okay." Eliza said.

Eliza invited us into her house and my mother and I sat on the couch while she went to change. Eliza's mother and my mother were talking and in about thirty minutes later. Eliza came downstairs and she was so beautiful. She was wearing black silk pants, a red blouse and boots. I was drooling all over her and I blindfolded her and my mother took us to *Applebee's* and drove off and there were five FBI Agents that were guarding the restaurant just in case if The Dark Cowboy decided to show up to ruin the party. Eliza and I walked inside the restaurant and I asked for a table. Then I took off Eliza's blindfold and she was very surprised. The workers at *Applebee's* brought a cake and started to sing to us "Happy one-year anniversary!" Eliza was excited and we blew out the candles.

"You did all this?" She asked.

"Yes, only because I love you a lot."

"I love you, too."

She was so happy that her tears started coming down her face and she wanted to cry. If she only knew that I was only interested in getting her into bed and I felt that all the things I was doing, she would want to make love anytime soon. Around nine o'clock that night I called my mother to pick us up. And we took Eliza home, and she gave me a kiss and went into her house. My mother was happy for us.

The next day I went to see Eliza and found her home alone and she was still in her pajamas well she had shorts and a white tank top. She took me to her room. She sat on the chair and I sat on the beanbag.

"I had fun last night." She said.

"Me, too." I said.

"That was the happiest night of my life!" She exclaimed.

"You deserved it." We stared at each other for a while and I got up to kiss her and I was touching her legs and she didn't mind me touching her body. I was excited that she let me touch her legs and she pulled away, and she also smiled. She grabbed my hand and we laid in bed and we were making out and again she was letting me touch her butt and legs and her whole body. So, we stayed in her room kissing for almost half an hour. She pulled away once again and we went back to the kitchen to make some sandwiches. I stayed all afternoon with Eliza and we talked all the time and I grabbed her by the waist and we were kissing. I started to tickle her and she was laughing and we continued to kiss. And finally after spending five whole hours with her, I could tell that Eliza was getting tired and I was also tired too, so we kissed and she told me that she loves me a lot and I told her that I love her too and I went home. I went to my room and looked at the calendar.

Time passed by so quickly and we celebrated Valentine's Day, her birthday, my birthday together and then summer came and we hoped to be together at all times. Eliza wanted to spend the summer with her grandparents in Albuquerque, New Mexico and she invited me to go with her. So, I asked my parents permission and they said yes and wish me a lot of luck in the summer with her and with her grandparents. Eliza's mother took us to their house but we were escorted by a couple of FBI Agents and then she parked in the driveway and her grandparents came out to greet us and they were happy to see Eliza and they were honored to meet me and her grandparents actually bowed down to me and they kissed my hand but I was happy to see them again. And Eliza's mother said hi to them and kissed them on the cheek and she went home, and the FBI Agents also left with her. Eliza and I spent the entire afternoon talking in the living room with her grandparents..

"How old are you, Mario?" Her grandfather asked.

"His name is "Mauricio." Grandpa." Eliza corrected him.

"I'm seventeen years old." I said

"So, you guys have been together for almost a year, is that right?" Her grandmother asked.

"Yes, grandma and we're in love." Eliza said.

"Mauricio, what are your plans when you graduate and for the future?" He asked.

"I'm sure he's going to be the King of Spain and make good decisions. And be kind to the people of Spain!" Her grandma smiled.

"Actually I want to go to the University of Missouri and study law and will see how it goes in the future with Eliza. You never know we might be married when we finish school." I responded.

"That's good, Mauricio. And I was like you once and I wanted to finish school and I had a lot of dreams. And I gave up a scholarship to Harvard Law and I sacrificed everything when I married the love of my life. I don't regret it at all. I hope you two make the right decision about your future. You need to take a risk in life in order to get what you want. I hope you guys make the right decision but make the decision together." He said and smiled.

"You have our blessing, Mauricio." Her grandma said.

"Thank you and I really love Eliza. She is the love of my life and I don't what to do without her." I said and smiled and it was fun getting to know Eliza's grandparents and I have met them before when I was little kid and I usually smiled at them but this time I was able to tell them that I was truly in love with Eliza. By ten o'clock that night her grandparents had gone to their room for the night. Eliza and I were outside and we were laying in the hammock, and we were looking up at the stars and we started kissing. We were glad to be with each other.

"This is the best summer I've had in years. I love you a lot." I said.

"I love you more than you love me." She said and smiled and we were still kissing and cuddling.

"Eliza, can I ask you something?" I asked.

"You can ask me anything."

"We've been together for about a year. Don't you think it's time to take our relationship to the next level?" I asked.

"What do you mean?" She asked.

"We love each other and I want to spend the rest of my life with you. Don't you think it's time for us to make love?" I said.

"I don't know what to say."

"I want to marry you when we graduate from high school and start a family together. I thought about what your grandpa said to me in the living room. I want to risk everything for you. All I want to do is to make you happy and I don't care if I get some miserable job just as long I get the chance to marry you and have a lot of children together. I don't want to continue with school. When I graduate from high school I'm going to be the new King of Spain. We can live there and you can have anything you want. We can raise our kids and bring peace to the world." I said and now I want that stupid position once again..

"Oh, Mauricio but you know the laws that you have to marry someone that's royalty." She said.

"I want to make you happy and I'll respect you and I want us to stay together forever and I'm willing to break the laws of royalty and marry someone that I truly love." I went on and on and Eliza looked at me and her eyes were getting watery and she was about to cry. I wanted her to give me an answer. "What do you say, Eliza, do you want to make love?"

"Yes, of course! I really love you a lot and I'll make love to you. I'm offering my body to you. But not here at my grandparent's house because we might wake them wake up and they will get mad at us."

"I understand and I will respect your decision." I said and kissed her. On that night I had gotten the response that I wanted from Eliza. And I knew that she would want to make "love" to me later on but when will that day come. We stayed at her grandparent's house until the summer ended and we had fun and it was time to go home and start our senior year at Americas High School.

On the first day of school and I looked at my new schedule. I was still in Special Education but I could have cared less and I had no desire to fight in the annual meeting the Hell with my parole and my orange jump suit. And I wanted to suck it up and try to enjoy my final year in high school and will see how it goes at the end of the year. I already know what I'm going to do in my life. I'll get a miserable job or I can continue to kill more people and get paid along the way. So, anyway my annual meeting was on September 11th but it was canceled and moved to October 23rd because of what happened on 9/11. All of us paid our respects to the people who died on that day and risk their lives for their country they love.

And on October 23rd I went to my annual meeting. I had been doing well in all my classes for the past two months. Well the same thing happened. They turned down my request for regular classes and I stayed in Special Education. I just smiled at them and left the room. Then the bell rang at three forty-five and Eliza and I walked into Mr. Caballero's classroom. "How did it go in the meeting my love?" She asked.

"I said everything and my voice wasn't heard."

"Cheer up, Mauricio! At least you're passing all of your classes. I still love you a lot and I still want to marry you." She smiled.

"All these years that we've known each other. You always find a way to make me happy. That's why I love you more than ever." I said.

"I love you more than you love me." Eliza exclaimed and we were about to enter Mr. Caballero's classroom when she looked at me and said. "Mauricio, I want to tell you something."

"Tell me." I said.

"My mom is going out of town and she's coming back in February. So, I'm going to be alone the past couple of months. I was wondering if you can come over to my house and protect me and it would be great if we made love on our two-year anniversary. It will be special for the two of us."

"I'll be there and I cannot believe that we are finally going to make love. I remembered when we played husband and wife and pretended to have a baby. I hope that day comes when we finally get married and have a baby together." I hugged her tight and I saw her smile and we kissed.

CHAPTER FOURTEEN

ELIZA'S FINAL DAYS

So, I was waiting for two months, so Eliza and I could finally celebrated our two-year anniversary, so we can be together and we can finally make love all night long like we planned to do. And it was finally January 10, 2002 and I was in my room getting ready to go to Eliza's house. She called me and said to come over to her house and for the third time I broke into the grocery store and the curfew and picked up the red roses. And I ran to her house and I was standing in front of her door and rang the doorbell. Very slowly Eliza opened the door and she was smiling and I kissed her and I gave her the red roses and she was smelling them. We were walking in the kitchen and we were holding hands and I could tell that she was nervous or scared because she looked so strange when she opened the door. And I figured that she was nervous because we were going to loose our virginities. Finally we went to her room and we sat on the bed and she closed the door and locked it. She sat on the bed and I sat next to her and we looked at each other and we started kissing for awhile and then she pulled away.

"What's wrong?" I asked.

"I'm nervous and I want this to be perfect." She said.

"I'm also nervous, Eliza. It will be perfect because we love each other." I said and smiled and I ran down to the kitchen and grabbed two Cokes from the refrigerator. I wanted to make a toast to our love and I went running back to her room and sat on the bed with her. And I opened the Cokes and gave one to Eliza and we pretended that it was Champagne and we began making a toast.

"Eliza, I want you to make me a promise."

"What kind of promise?" She asked.

"Promise me we're going to be together forever." I said.

"I promise." She said and smiled. We both said. "I love you and we said happy two-year anniversary." We drank our Cokes and put them on top of her dresser and we started kissing and it was a night that Eliza and I will never forget.

And on that night I was dreaming about something that was so weird. I saw myself kissing a girl but it wasn't Eliza it was someone else. "Hi, Mauricio it's me Luz Maria. The girl that you saved at the park." She smiled in the dream.

I remember saying to her in the dream. "We cannot be together because you are too young for me. I'm a monster!"

She responded, "I'm fourteen years old. I love you a lot and I want us to be together forever."

And suddenly I heard a voice of a Priest that was saying, "Do you Luz Maria Fitzgerald Estrada take King Mauricio de la Vega as your husband?"

"Yes!" She responded.

"I also take Luz to be my wife." We smiled and started kissing and all of the sudden Luz and I were in our honeymoon at the Virgin Islands. The two of us were happy together and I was holding on to her and we were kissing. We were outside and we were laying on the hammock and we were staring the stars and making love all over the place. And we started dancing and this dream turned really ugly in a hurry. While we were dancing and I began to notice that something was coming out of the shadows. It was a Dark Figure that was riding a dark horse and had a sword and a spear and it was laughing at us. The Dark Figure jumped off the horse and came up to me, his eyes were also glowing red and I didn't know who this dark figure was.

"Stay back, Luz." I said in the dream.

"You think you are going to protect her?" The Dark Figure asked.

"Yes. Do you know who I am?" I asked.

"No."

"I am the legend King Mauricio de la Vega also known as The Dark Cowboy." I yelled at this figure.

"I'm so terrified but that's nothing. I've wiped out the entire population of Spain. And do you know who I am?" He asked.

"I'm afraid not."

"I am the legendary Aztec Conquistador." He said and started laughing.

"I've heard of you and I know you killed all of my ancestors and you are going to pay for your actions."

"I've also heard of you Dark Cowboy but your story is not legendary just yet." He said and started laughing at me. "Come on, King Mauricio de la Vega your girlfriend knows that you cannot kill me because I am far better than you."

I was in positioned to fight him and he had the sword in his hand and had the spear in the horse and he threw his sword on the ground. We started fighting and he threw me to the ground and I fell against the tree broke in two places and The Aztec Conquistador started running towards me and I told Luz to run. And I turn around and this freak punched me in the face and I fell to the ground I couldn't move at all. I was the punching bag of my own dream. The Aztec Conquistador threw me on the ground and to the trees and also kicked me so hard. I could feel the pain all over my body. I could hear Luz screaming and crying for help and yet I couldn't protect her in my own dream and I couldn't defended myself. Then the Aztec Conquistador picked up his sword but somehow I had my own guns and finally I was able to transformed into the hideous creature and I could hear Luz screaming at the top of her lungs. I also heard the gunshots and the explosions.

And that's where I woke up to the sound of someone breaking into Eliza's house. I got up to see what was going on and Eliza also got up and she hugged me so tight and started crying. I told Eliza to call the Police and luckily Eliza had a baseball bat inside her closet. I grabbed the baseball bat and went to the hallway and the robbers were already coming upstairs. I was in position to hit them with the baseball bat but they all had all kinds of weapons. And I had no choice but to put the bat down.

They came up to me and hit me with a gun but somehow I fell on my back. I don't how for how long I was laying on the ground and I was having a hard time moving around and I could hear the screams of Eliza and I was still loopy from the bump on my head. She was yelling at them to let her go. Then they grabbed me and dragged me into the room. I only saw a glimpse of Eliza and she was in the middle of the room, she was crying and begging them to let her go. They were rapping her and they were beating her and I could feel her pain. She was screaming hysterically and gasping for breath. And I wanted to save her and I was willing to risk my life for her. I got up and grabbed the lamp and smashed it on one of the robber's heads and I kick one of them on the face. Then I started to choke one of the other robbers but something whacked me in the head and knocked me out cold.

Then the next day I woke up and I was laying in a Hospital bed and I heard my mother saying, "How are you feeling?" She asked.

"I'm bruised up. How's Eliza?"

"She's doing good." Mr. Caballero said..

"Mauricio, I want to know what happen last night. What can you tell us about last night?" My father asked.

"Well on October, Eliza told me that her mother was going be out of town and if I can come over to her house. So, we can celebrate our two-year anniversary and yesterday she called me around five o'clock and she told me to come over to her house." I said.

"What happen next?" My mother asked me.

"Half an hour later, I went to her house and she took me to her room and we started having sex. We were nervous that we were going to take our relationship to the next level. I'm sorry for letting you down." I said.

"Don't be you guys are in love." Mr. Caballero said.

"What happen next?" My father asked.

"We fell asleep and I woke up around three o'clock in the morning and I heard noises and it was coming from downstairs. Eliza was scared and I wanted to protect her from those intruders. It's a good thing that she had a baseball bat inside her closet and I took it out. And that's where the front door broke and they were breaking everything in the house. I told Eliza to call the Police and I went to the hallway and that's where six men were coming upstairs. And one of them knocked me out and I could hear Eliza screaming. They dragged me into the room and I could see her suffer and they started to rape her. I love her so much that I was willing to risk my life to protect her. I grabbed her lamp and smashed it into their heads and kicked one of them in his face. But it was to many of them and they knocked me out."

"You told Eliza to call the Police?" Mr. Caballero asked.

"At what time did you get there, Mike?" My mother asked.

"I got there half an hour later and that's where I called you." He responded.

"Mauricio told Eliza to call the Police and she couldn't go through the line but Mike was able to get trough the line and that's where we arrived." My father said.

"Perhaps, The Dark Cowboy was too chicken to come after me and that's why he sent those men to come after us." I said and at the same time I wanted to know what they were going to say.

"It wasn't The Dark Cowboy, Mauricio. Now I'm convinced that it wasn't him. A bunch of robbers break into the house and decided to rape a girl and knock you out. You guys are lucky to be alive." My mother said.

"I want to see Eliza." Mauricio said.

"You, can see her tomorrow, Mauricio. Right now you need to rest." My mother said.

"Your mother is right." My father said.

"I hope my new buddy The Dark Cowboy finds them and kills them like he did to all my friends." I said.

Please, Mauricio. Let's us find them and arrest them." My mother said.

"No. When I get out of here I'm going to find them and I will personally kill them. Because I'm not going to allow anyone lay a hand on my girlfriend ever again!" I yelled.

"That's enough, Mauricio, you need to rest." My father said.

I was worried about Eliza. I wanted to see her but they told me to rest. I was concerned about last night. How come I was knocked out and I didn't seem to sense that Eliza was in danger well something was wrong and there were a lot of questions that needed answers. So, the next day the Doctor said that I could go and see her. I got a volunteer to take me to the gift shop. I bought some balloons and I wrote her poem and I knew that she will like it. That afternoon my parents took me to see Eliza and she was in the Intensive Care Unit. When she saw me coming I could see her smile. She had a broken arm and still had bruises on her face and her body, she also had a bandied around her head and she had the oxygen mask on.

"Here's a present." I said.

"Thank you, Mauricio!" She whispered and smiled. I kissed her forehead. I stayed with her for about half an hour and the Doctor told me that she needed to rest and I can see her tomorrow morning. And my parents took me back to my room and I knew that she would recover from this. A week later the Doctor cleared me to go home well he said that I was healthy to walk again but Eliza remained in the Hospital for further testing.

I was in my room and I started remembering the dream I had. And I started remember when Historian mentioned The Aztec Conquistador and I cannot believe that I was dreaming about him. I got my ass kicked in the dream and if he was alive I would personally kill him and I know he will rot in Hell. But I'd rather think about Eliza, the real love of my life and not some twelve year old little girl that I saved at the park or my ancestor. So, I went to the restroom and I transformed into the hideous creature well I still have my powers but I was able to sense when Luz was in trouble and how come I didn't sense when Eliza was in trouble. Well I knew Eliza was going to get better but I was wrong. As the days were passing she got worse. And I had double duties, one was to graduate from high school and the other one was taking care of Eliza. Because she was getting pale and she slept a lot and she was getting worse by the hour.

The next day I was on my way to the kitchen and my father was on the phone for three hours and no ones knows who he was talking to because he was outside talking for a long time. And he didn't want anyone to hear his conversation. My mother also woke up and went to the kitchen to make breakfast and she served me scrambled eggs and she sat down to drink her coffee and my father came back inside and made coffee.

"Who were you talking too?" She asked.

"My boss. He wants to know when I'm going to be back on board. I told him that we haven't arrested The Dark Cowboy. My boss said that it was okay and there was no rush in coming back." My father said and looked at my mother and saw her sad. "We're doing our best, Beatrice. And I came to the decision that it's time to move on with our lives. We are going to let the seniors graduate from high school, so they can move on with their lives. We cannot have the people hostages in their own homes anymore. Tomorrow I will announced it and also the people can now go out at night because The Dark Cowboy hasn't showed up and he saved someone's life. I'm going to pardoned him from the crimes he committed. But half of it." He said.

"You are right, Pablo! It's time for all of us to move on because he is turning good." My mother said.

"If it makes you feel better, Mauricio, we have captured those men that broke into Eliza's house and I swear to you that they will get life in prison." My father smiled.

"When did you arrest them?" My mother asked.

"Three days ago!" My father smiled.

My mother and I were loss for words and just like that my father said that him and his men were able to arrest those men that broke into Eliza's house. It's been more than three years and my father couldn't arrest me but somehow he was able to arrest those criminals in seventy-two hours. Way to go daddy and we're proud of you. So, my father was about to make his decision that we all can now move on with our lives. And he was going to announce it tomorrow but I wasn't concerned about his speech. I was more concerned with Eliza and I didn't give a damn about my father's announcement. And I was really worried for Eliza because I didn't know why she was getting worse and no one told me what was wrong with her but she remained in the Hospital for further evaluation.

A month went by Eliza's mother came back from her vacation and went to the Hospital to see her daughter. And I spent Valentine's Day with Eliza at the Hospital. I bought her more balloons and her favorite red roses and I gave her a kiss on the mouth. We were talking and it was like old times and her mother and brother were there along with my parents and my sister.

"I'm glad that you're going to recover." My mother smiled.

"Soon, you'll be on your feet and I hope you end up marrying my brother and having a lot of children." Tania said.

"I hope you feel better, Eliza, so we can go to the prom together." I smiled.

"I would like to go with you, Mauricio. And I hope the Doctor lets me go to the prom." She tried to smile.

"You remember when we played husband and wife?" I asked.

"How could I forget, Mauricio?" She smiled and said softly. "I always dreamed of marrying you and having a lot of children. I hope that day comes."

"When you recover we will get married and we're going to have a lot of children. I'm going to make you happy and like I told you before that I was willing to risk everything for our love." I smiled and I could tell that Eliza was a little bit tired and she was kind of sleepy. Then the Doctor came into the room to check up on her. "We are going to leave so you can rest, Eliza." I said.

"I feel fine. Stay here with me." She said.

"I'm sorry, Eliza, but I've got to leave and do my homework. I'll come back tomorrow. We will talk some more and I will promise that I'll stay longer and we can talk all night long." I said and kissed her and we went home.

And it was seven o'clock that night when her mother came to my house. We were in the living room and I saw the look in her eyes. "What's the news of those scumbags? Are they going to get the chair? And if they are I want to get a front row seat and I hope my buddy The Dark Cowboy ends up killing them."

"Mauricio." My mother said.

"They don't deserve to live they deserve death row."

"Mauricio!" My mother got my attention.

"I have to talk to you about Eliza." She said.

"What's wrong?" I asked.

"She was diagnosed with a heart disease."

"How can she have a heart disease?" I asked her.

"From what the Doctor told me, her heart is not working anymore and she's going to die very soon." Her mother looked at me and was sad. "It was on the night when the robbers broke into the house and raped her, and beat her up. That might have caused her state of shock and plus Eliza has been seen a Psychiatric since she was little a little girl, I'm sorry, Mauricio, that she didn't told you. That's why she has been acting strange lately because she was traumatized when she was face to face with The Dark Cowboy and that might have scared her completely. She was heart broken when her friends were dying and the people that she went to Church with were also killed by The Dark Cowboy." She said and her tears started to come down her face. "Mauricio you got to understand that Eliza is not well and she hasn't been well for a long time and right now she needs our love. We should make her happy because that's what she needs form us."

I was sitting there and I couldn't believe what was happening and I started crying. "Is all my fault!" I suddenly yelled.

"It's not your fault, Mauricio. You didn't do anything wrong." She said.

"That's what I get! I wanted to get her into bed and then leave her and now she's dying because of my actions! Not to mention that I should have protected her on that night from those bastards. It should be me dying not her. I'm sorry that she's dying. I'm really sorry that she is dying!"

"Mauricio, it's not your fault. You don't need to feel guilty. The important thing is we need to make Eliza happy and love her a lot." She wanted to hug me but I ran to my room. After a while my father came to my room.

"Mauricio, what's wrong?" He asked.

"Eliza has a heart disease and she's going to die in any day!" I yelled.

"Son, calm down." He said.

"Dad, I don't know what I'll do if she dies." I said.

"It's not easy for a father to tell his son what to do and especially when a love one is dying. But I want you to know that your mother and I will always be there for you and will always love you. Everything is going to be okay."

"I'm sorry that she is dying. I made the wrong decision to hurt her. I'm sorry, dad." I said and I hugged my father very tight and he was telling me that it was going to be okay. I spent Valentine's Day crying because I found out that Eliza, the love of life was dying and I couldn't do anything to protect her that night and all I had to do is watch her die right in front my eyes. Perhaps I am human being after all and maybe I could sense when someone is in danger and not when they are dying. And everyone at school showed their concern for Eliza and they sent her flowers and get well cards. That was enough to make her happy.

And Eliza spent most of her days sleeping and sometimes she ate but she usually slept a lot. Her birthday was coming up and we decided to celebrate her birthday at the Hospital and we gave her a huge party and we tried to make her feel happy. She spent the day in her Hospital bed. She tried to smile when her mother opened her gifts and showed them to her. Eliza had always had a contagious smile but now her smile was gone. At eight o'clock that night her mother and my mother left to take her presents to the car. I stayed with her.

"Did you enjoy your birthday?" I asked.

"Yes." Eliza responded with a weak voice.

"I'm glad you had fun." I said and smiled. "Have I told you that I love you?"

"Yes, a lot. I love you more than ever." She said softly.

The Nurse came into the room to take her tray away and the Doctor came to check up on her. I went to the restroom to wipe my nose and I could hear what Eliza told the Doctor. "Doctor, you know what I want for my birthday?" Eliza spoke slowly.

"I'm afraid not. Why don't you tell me?" He smiled.

"I want to go to the prom with, Mauricio."

"Eliza, you know you aren't well enough just yet and I'm sorry but I can't let you go. You have to understand that you need to rest."

"Doctor, I'm only asking you for this one thing before I die and I know I'm going to die anytime. All I want is to go to the prom with my boyfriend and I want to look pretty for him at least one more time before I die."

"Okay. I'm not going to like it, Eliza but I will let you go to the prom with Mauricio. And at the same time you need to rest because you don't have any strength left in your body. But like I said, I will let you go to your house and I know you are going to recover from this."

I heard what they had to say and I came back to see how she was doing and I gave her a smile. Her contagious smile returned for a second and she looked at me and I kissed her forehead. I left the Hospital and I was scared that she might die in anytime. I didn't want her to die and I really wanted to marry her and spend the rest of my life with her. Them the following week the Doctor finally made decision that Eliza could now go home and be with her family because there wasn't anything they could do for her in the Hospital and they felt that she needed her family and she could be comfortable at her home. Eliza had to use a wheel chair because she was too weak to walk and her mother took care of her and fed her most of the time. She had to quit her job to be with her daughter at all times. She stayed strong for her daughter's sake and she was trying to make her happy. It was enough happiness for the whole week that she had left to live.

Finally my father had to postponed his speech because he was also worried for Eliza. And on that week my father decided to talk in front of City Hall and he gave the okay that all the seniors had the right to enjoy their final year and they were free to go to the prom and the FBI Agents would be there just in case if The Dark Cowboy tried to interfere and kill somebody at the prom. Also he gave the okay that the people could now live their lives all over again. And my parents went through a lot of expense and rented a limousine for us to go to the prom.

Then on Saturday night I was all dressed up for the big night and my parents took me to Eliza's house. And I waited for Eliza in her living room and I was talking to her brother and we were sad and we were wondering how long does she have left to live. My mother and her mother helped Eliza down the stairs and carefully put her in the wheelchair.

I took one look at her and said, "You look beautiful!"

She blushed. "I wanted to look pretty for you."

I gave her the corsage and her mother took a picture of us and I could tell that she was happy. I pushed her all the way to the limousine and then my father and I picked her up and very gently put her inside on the seat of the limousine. The driver put the wheelchair in the truck of the limousine and we said goodbye to our parents. My father told me that there were going to be a lot of FBI Agents around the prom and they wanted to make sure that The Dark Cowboy won't show up and try to come after me or everyone else at the prom. Well my parents were going to be at the Police Station because they were going to strategize how are they going to capture The Dark Cowboy if he ever shows up again.

We finally arrived at the prom, the driver took out the wheelchair from the trunk of the limousine and I got out and picked up Eliza, very gently I put her into the wheelchair. As soon as we got inside the prom everyone bowed down and we had to pose for our picture, then I pushed Eliza into the big room where they were holding the dance. We went to say hi! to our friends and they were really happy to see us together again especially they were more excited to see Eliza again and she was smiling to everyone. They started clapping and cheering for us. Everyone came over to Eliza and they wanted to know how she was doing and she tried to smile and she able to talk to everyone that came up to her. I left Eliza with her girlfriends and I heard them laugh and I was glad that she was happy and I went to the restroom with Miguel and Joe. We were in the restroom washing our hands when Miguel told me the news.

"Did you hear that the Police Officers and FBI arrested those guys that broke into Eliza's house. They are going to get ten years in prison, maybe they might get life in prison." Miguel said.

"Really!" I exclaimed.

"I guess you and Eliza got what you wanted. And was that really necessary, Mauricio?" Miguel asked.

"For them to spend time in jail?" I asked.

"No, not that. I meant that you hoped that your long time friend The Dark Cowboy would come out to kill them." Miguel said.

"How do you think Eliza is going to feel if she finds out that you were saying that you wanted The Dark Cowboy to kill them?" Joe asked.

"Not to mention seeing them fry in the chair." Miguel added.

"I love her to death. If anybody else lays a hand on Eliza, I will personally kill them and it will be worse than The Dark Cowboy's killings!" I yelled and tried to calm down and put water on my face. "It was the court that gave them these sentences not me. May God have mercy on them because they are going to needed it."

"You still don't know, Mauricio. Nobody has told you what really happened on that night." Someone else intervened.

"Stay out of it, Primo. This doesn't concern you." Joe said.

"Well, what do you know, it's the son of the crime lord, Primo Mancini that wants to stick his nose where it doesn't belong." Miguel said.

"Haven't you been in trouble your entire life." Joe said.

"Tell me, Primo, you seem to know something." I said and Joe and Miguel wanted to throw him out of the restroom but I stopped them and said, "Guys, allow him to speak his mind. Primo, you were saying?"

"Something else happened on the night when you guys were attacked. It's a cover up. I want you to be careful, old friend and don't trust your loved ones. Be safe at all times."

Primo smiled and left and I decided to forget what he was trying to tell me. Everyone had always hated Primo for a very long time. He was hated by the boys and loved by all the girls in the school but I was his only friend and I thought what he said. So, I wanted to get back to the dance floor and to be with Eliza and I washed my hands and I went back to Eliza and she was happy to see me.

Later on in the evening Eliza and I were talking and we were watching everyone dance. And then they played our song, "It Ain't me Baby," the same song I sang to her in the library over two years ago.

"Surprise!" I exclaimed.

"I remember when you were singing that song in the library. You dedicated to me and that was sweet of you."

"Can you dance?" I asked.

"Of course! I've been waiting for this! Our last dance as seniors." Eliza put her hands on my arms and very gently I pulled her out of the wheelchair. We walked onto the dance floor and started to dance. Everybody started to clap and they pulled back and they watched us dance and they were happy because they felt that Eliza might recover from this. We were dancing and I saw her smile and all of the sudden I heard the alarm of my watch go off and I looked at it and it was twelve o'clock well it was midnight. Eliza and I were alone on the dance floor and I began to realize how much I really loved her. I wished I could spend the rest of my life with her and I hoped to God not to take her away from me and give her at least one more chance in life.

We started to kiss as we were dancing and then all of a sudden Eliza fell against me and slipped out of my arms and collapsed on the dance floor. Eliza was gasping for air and she was grabbing her heart and she was very pale. And one of the Teachers rushed over and started to give her mouth-to-mouth respiration and the FBI Agents were calling the Paramedics but we all felt that they will arrive at the prom way to late. Eliza looked at me and said, "I love you!" And gave me one last smile and just like that she passed away on the dance floor. At exactly midnight she passed away and all of her friends got on their knees and they were crying their eyes out and they were telling her to wake up. I still had Eliza in my arms and I was screaming and crying and I didn't want her to leave me. And the Paramedics arrived way to late and they put her inside the Ambulance and took her away to the Morgue. They asked everyone to go home and the FBI Agents took me back to the house and my parents and my sister, Tania were with me the entire night and they never left my sight.

A week later there was a funeral service for Eliza Caballero and everyone was crying and continued to tell her to wake up, and I went to see her and I felt that she was sleeping and I felt that she could wake up in anytime and give me a huge smile but she didn't wake up at all. And I took three pictures of Eliza and she still she looked so pretty than before. I leaned over to kiss her on her forehead and told her that I love you a lot and I hope to see her very soon but not yet. I gave her a huge smile and I went back to my parents and they hugged me very tight. The very next day Eliza was buried and everyone was throwing her favorite red roses on her casket as they were lowering it on the ground and I was standing in front of the casket and I squeezed the red rose, so hard that my blood came out of my hand and I threw it on the casket. "I wanted revenge!" I exclaimed and I hugged my parents and we all left to the house.

CHAPTER FIFTEEN

THE LEGEND OF THE PACHUCO2K

It was Monday morning where I went to school and I was walking in the hallway when my Counselor and I ran into each other. My counselor told me that I was going to have my final annual meeting at the end of the week. Gee and I wonder what they were going to tell me in my final parole. Well my Counselor told me that I was going to have it by Friday afternoon. And I said thank you and went to the cafeteria and sat down with my friends. And everyone ware still sad because Eliza passed away and they were still crying but I told everyone that we got to move on with our lives because that's what Eliza wanted from us. Then it was Friday afternoon, I was in the classroom when they called me to come over to the conference room. "Bring the Inmate Number 6954324. Miguel smiled and everyone was laughing and so was I. The Campus Police were waiting for me outside the classroom and they escorted me to the conference room and I walked into the conference room and everyone looked at me and bowed down and smiled, "As you were!" I also smiled and they told me to sit down and they were going over the paperwork for almost thirty minutes. And they finally looked at me and they gave me a huge smile. Well as it turns out that everyone in the conference room told me that I was going to graduate from Americas High School and they also wished me a lot of luck in the future and they gave me a huge smile.

I got up to hug everyone in the conference room and they started clapping for me. "Long live Mauricio de la Vega!" They exclaimed and they were happy for me and I was excited and I ran all over the school and hugged everyone. And then the bell rang and I went to my house and told my parents and Tania that I was going to graduate in a couple of weeks. They were happy for me and we celebrated all night long and I know Eliza would be proud of me and she is watching me from Heaven. And I knew that she was smiling from ear to ear and I know that she's not going to like what I planned to do next. Then us seniors took our final picture together at the gym and the Principal was explaining to us what was going to happen at the graduation ceremony. May came around the corner and on the last day of school everyone didn't go home at thirty forty-five. The freshman, juniors, and sophomores stayed outside the school and didn't go home either. But us seniors were taking our final walk inside Americas High School. No one talked at all, we were just walking around the school. We went upstairs to walk around the long hallway and we were happy and sad because we were going to be the third class to graduate. Half of us have been in Americas High School since the year 1997. We have been in Americas for a long time and together we built this school, and we watched this school grow even bigger and bigger. We have known each other since we were little kids, and finally we looked at the clock and it was five o'clock in the afternoon and we went to the front of the school and we looked at each other and we smiled and our tears were coming down our faces. Everyone that was outside started clapping for us and we looked at them and we just passed the torch to the next generation.

We finally went to our homes and waited for the next day. And the next day was June 1st and we went to the Student Complex Center and all of us gathered around and we got into a straight line and we were all cheering and clapping. And I had butterflies in my stomach where all of the sudden they played the graduation song and all of us started walking and the people were cheering us on. We were sitting down for at least five hours and we were listening to the Principal talk and we had other guest speakers that were also talking. And then they started calling out our names. And they called my name, "Mauricio de la Vega!" And I got up and all of my classmates bowed down for the last time and all the people from the bleachers were clapping and I got diploma and they shook my hand. I so was happy and I looked up at the sky and said, "This is for you Eliza!" And in about thirty minutes later we finally stood up and walked at the end of the football field and we threw our caps in the air and celebrated with my friends. We had firecrackers that was lighting up the sky and we all hugged each other and cried. And the ceremony finished and they told us that were are going to be a Country Club, and they told us they had karaoke and we could do whatever the Hell we wanted. But my friends and I had other things in mind and it was nine-thirty when we left to Chris's house.

We arrived at his house and we were still celebrating and we were hugging each other. We went into the house and took off our caps and gowns and put them on the couch. "Congratulations on graduating from Americas High School. And I truly hope that you're ready for the real world." Chris smiled and hugged us.

"Now let's do the senior prank." I said and laughed.

Everyone smiled and Karina and the rest of us sat down and Chris looked at us and said, "First I'm going to give you guys your paychecks. I want everyone to know that I'm paying everybody different because you had different talents." Chris said.

"That's fine." We all smiled and sat down on the couch and we began to noticed that there were twelve briefcases laying on the floor and it had our names written on it.

Chris was standing in front of us and gave us a huge smile. He picked up a briefcase and said, "Christina Bobs! You are a great fighter and for the past couple of years I've been hearing stories that you have beaten up, so many people along the way and you have sent them to the Hospital and I know they've recovered from their wounds. Guess what you're getting sixty-seven thousand dollars." Chris smiled and gave her briefcase.

Christina smiled and said, "Thank you! I want to thank the girls and our great leaders, Mauricio and Primo." She hugged us and sat down.

Chris grabbed another briefcase and said, "Jennifer Callaway! You are a great abductor. And for the past couple of years there has been a lot of people that were getting kidnap in their own homes, and everywhere they went. You've been able to kidnap them without breaking a sweat. You are going to get seventy thousand dollars." Chris smiled and gave her the briefcase.

Jennifer smiled and hugged him. "Thank you!"

Chris grabbed another briefcase and said, "Mauricio de la Vega! For being a great co leader, cofounder of the gang known as the Pachuco2k, and also killing at least twenty-three people. King Mauricio de la Vega, you are going to get eighty-seven million dollars." Chris smiled and gave me the briefcase.

I got up and hugged him so tight. "I did it for you guys!"

Chris grabbed another briefcase and said, "Jessica Hernandez for going around the whole city stealing expensive cars, and trucks and without getting caught by the Police Officers and the FBI. You are going to get thirty-four million dollars." Chris smiled and gave her the briefcase.

She got up and hugged him so tight. "I also did it for the gang!"

Chris grabbed another briefcase and said, "Lorraine Hondo! Jessica was stealing the cars and you were racing every car and truck that she ever stole. And making sure that the Police Officers and the FBI didn't arrest you. And as the matter of fact you were also racing against the Police Officers. You are going to get thirty-five million dollars." Chris smiled and gave her the briefcase.

Lorraine got up and hugged him and said, "I want to thank everyone!"

Chris grabbed another briefcase and said, "Erin Killins! For stealing people's identity and living their lives to the best. Also stealing the reporters identity and giving Mauricio that cool nick name "The Dark Cowboy". You are going to get thirty-three million dollars." Chris smiled and gave her the briefcase.

She got up and hugged him and said, "I would do anything for my friends."

Chris grabbed another briefcase and said. "Primo Mancini! For being the co leader, the cofounder of the Pachuco2k, raping a lot of women, and for helping Mauricio with his mission. Well you are going to get eighty-six million dollars." Chris smiled and gave him the briefcase.

Primo got up and hugged him. "I thank Mauricio and big thanks to my sisters and uncle Chris."

Chris grabbed another briefcase and said. "Cassandra Powell, for exploding the buildings and helping your friends with their missions. You are going to get forty-five million dollars." Chris smiled and gave her the briefcase.

She hugged him and said, "I also want to thank everyone."

Chris grabbed another briefcase and said, "Karina Reyes, the Lieutenant and the voice of the Pachuco2k. For hacking into the system, and blocking the telephone calls, also helping everyone with their missions and making sure that no one got arrested. Well you are going to get eighty-five million dollars." Chris smiled and gave her the briefcase.

Karina got up and smiled. "I thank my friends!"

Chris grabbed another briefcase and said, "Sonia Rodriguez for putting bugs all over the city and taping all the telephone and cell phone calls and we were able to hear everything that they were saying in the whole city. Well you are going to get fifty million dollars." Chris smiled and gave her the briefcase.

Sonia smiled and hugged him and said, "I thank the girls and the two leaders. Mauricio de la Vega and Primo Mancini and I thank you, Chris for motivating me."

Chris grabbed another briefcase and said, "Rosanne Sanderson for stealing everything in the city and for instance stealing money, jewelry, candy, and food. You are going to get, thirty-five million dollars." Chris smiled and her the briefcase.

She smiled and said, "I did it for my friends!"

"Finally this last briefcase is for me. I taught you guys everything I know and I want to tell you is that I love you guys so much." We all got up and hugged him so tight and we started celebrating like one big happy family.

We were still smiling when Jessica got our attention. "Wait a second. We have another surprise!"

"Jessica is right and come with me." Chris smiled and took us to the backyard and we saw eleven storages and there were eleven boxes in front of the storages. And our names were written on top of the storages. "Well this is a surprise and I want it to be like a graduation present from me to you guys." Chris smiled and said, "Christina Bobs please step up to your storage." Christina smiled and went up to her storage. She opened the box and took out a key and opened the storage all the way to the top and she saw her brand new car. She was excited and hugged Chris. "Thanks to Karina and Jessica. Registration it's now under your name Christina, and you even have a drivers license." She smiled and hugged him. So, all of us went to our storages and opened the door and we had our own cars. We also had drivers license and the car was under our names with insurance. We were cheering and hugging each other.

"Okay! Now for the real bonus!" Chris smiled.

We went inside the house and we sat on the couch while Karina and Chris got into the system. "The money that you have on the briefcase well you can spend all of it. But I'm going to put more money on your accounts and give you ATM cards and I'm going to give you the ATM cards in a couple of days. Now let's get started. Give me the names, Karina."

Karina smiled and said, "Armando Guerrero."

Chris put his name in the system and all the information about his parents came out. "It looks to me that Armando had two hundred dollars in his bank account. I'll just transfer the money to the accounts." We waited a couple of seconds for his money to be transferred into our accounts. "His account is close."

"Yes!" We all said.

"We're only going to target his parents and not his other family members." Chris smiled and started searching for more information and took the money away from every insurance they had including the car insurance, life insurance, 401k, and everything else they had. Chris was able to clean their bank accounts and credit card accounts, and all the accounts they have were gone. Everything was cleaned and Chris managed to get them fired from their working place and they are going to take away their precious house. The money was getting transferred into our accounts and we were happy.

"Who's next, Karina." Chris asked.

"Deyna Alberts." Karina responded.

Chris put her name into the system and started cleaning everything they had in their accounts and the left them with nothing and also he managed to get her parents fired from their working place and he had the bank to seal off their homes, the cars, and everything they have inside.

"Next!" Chris said.

"Melissa Owens." Karina said.

Chris started cleaning everything from her accounts and he went after her parents accounts and the money was transferring into our accounts. While we were waiting, Karina ordered Pizza and in about thirty minutes later the Pizza arrived and all of us were eating and in about three hours later the mission was complete. And Chris was able to transfer all the money into our accounts. Plus they were now homeless and fired from their working place. And Chris was going to give our ATM cards in a couple of days.

"That was a lot of work and we were able to ruin their lives. Drinks on me!" Chris smiled and everyone were hugging each other and Chris took out the soft drinks and they were going to celebrate until I ruin the moment.

'Wait a second! I'm glad that were happy that we took their money away and their property away from them." I laughed and said, "Right now I'm in the mood to piss off my parents."

"We should wait for tomorrow and let them find out that the people's money were stolen and their property." Chris said.

"Chris, I'm not going to wait until tomorrow or the next day or in three months from now. Everyone is at the Police Station and it will be fun to hear my father loose his mind because it was a job that they never saw coming." I laughed.

"Mauricio, I know you are still hurting inside because Eliza died a couple of months ago and at least we should wait for tomorrow." Primo said.

"Are you afraid Primo?" I asked.

'Yes, I am, Mauricio. Because I have a girlfriend now and I changed my life for the better." He responded.

"What's your plan, Mauricio?" Karina asked.

"Well you don't have to pay us for this mission, Chris, and think about it as a senior prank. You know free lance." I smiled and looked at Karina, "I'm going to call them and I want you to hack into the system." I said and looked at Primo, "What do you say, Primo. One more time."

"Fine!" He yelled.

Karina was locating the bugs they had inside the Police Station and she turned on the microphones and we were hearing everything. And I started dialing and the phone was ringing. My father answered the prone and said, "Hello!"

I transformed into the monster and started breathing heavily. "Good evening, Agent de la Vega. I hope you are happy that your beloved son, Mauricio de la Vega, graduated from high school and I cannot wait to get him when he's alone in college."

"As the matter of fact, Yes. I am happy that my son graduated from Americas High School and my son is going to become an FBI Agent and also he is going to become the new King of Spain and he is coming after you, for killing and raping his lovely girlfriend, Eliza Caballero. Do you remember our little conversation we had a couple of months ago? That I can come up with any plan I wanted and my men follow it without asking why. Well you said that you can hear everything that goes around this city, well I completed my Plan B. The funny thing is I lied about everything. You were so sure that I was going to pardon you with the crimes that you committed over the years. Well I'm planning to accuse you of everything that happened around here. First you were killing innocent people and now you decided to rape two girls and you nearly killed them. Well one is dead and the other one is still living. And how long does she have to live, Dark Cowboy? And I'm also accusing you of the burning buildings, stealing cars and so on. This city hasn't done anything to you Dark Cowboy. Well since you were my real challenge ever and I know that you like to negotiate with us. I know that you're going to like my two choices that I have planned for you. The first choice is that you can turn yourself in. Nothing bad is going to happen to you, first we're going interrogate you, will get you the best Lawyer this city has to offer, then to trial and spending life in Prison. You will rot there and I can guarantee you that you will suffer from all the torture from the inmates. And the second choice is if you don't turn yourself in, then I'm going to keep accusing you, of all the crimes that you didn't commit just yet. I'll be the hero of the city and you will be rotting in prison where you truly belong. The ball is in your court, Dark Cowboy." My father smiled and laughed.

 Everyone was looking at me and they did looked worried and I smiled and started laughing at him, "And what's stopping you, Agent Pablo de la Vega, from accusing me with all the crimes that I didn't commit just yet. I once respected you Agent de la Vega because you were chasing down criminals and arresting them and keeping the streets safer. But that was in Europe and the Middle East. And now you come home to El Paso, Texas and you couldn't go twelve rounds with Muhammad Dark Cowboy. Maybe your age is catching up with your lack of Police work and your sex life of course. Well I know that it's been a long time since you and your lovely wife haven't had sex because she knows that you have failed to satisfy her in bed in more than twelve occasions, you have failed to arrest me and I've been in front of you so many damn times and you cannot arrest me at all. You have failed as a Police Officer because you couldn't arrest the great Vito Mancini, you've failed as an FBI Agent because you wouldn't catch me The Dark Cowboy, the greatest serial killer that has ever lived. And you have also failed for being the Mayor of this city and you've been a failure your entire life. So, much for the de la Vega tradition. Your motto is making the family proud of your accomplishments. But my motto is that Agent de la Vega failed in everything. Do us a favor, Agent de la Vega, retire from the FBI and disappear into the thin air and stop wasting the air that we breathe. You don't deserve to be in the same place as me."

 My father stayed quiet for a couple of seconds and said. "I'm not going to rest until I chase you down to the ends of the Earth and bury you beneath the ground. I will do anything to arrest you and kill you right on the spot. Like I said, Dark Cowboy, I give orders and my men will follow it."

I laughed even more. "Well Agent de la Vega, I also give orders to my people and unlike you, my people respect me and that's something that you don't have anymore. No one respects you, Pablo de la Vega, let's face it you suck big time and you've dropped the ball." I laughed and my father stayed quiet because I knew have him where I want him. And I asked. "I want to ask you something. Are you sitting in front the computer?"

"No, why?" He also asked.

"Because there is something that I want you to see and there are so many things that I wished to share with you. Now find a computer and sit down."

My father found a computer and we heard everyone asking him what was he doing. We knew everyone gathered around my father and the computer and I wanted them to see the heist that we did tonight. And Karina hacked into the computer that they were on and we heard them talking about the screen looking fuzzy.

"You remember Armando Guerrero?" I asked.

"Yes, he was my son's friend." My father responded and Karina hacked his name and put the information and sent it to them. "What the Hell is this!" My father yelled.

"You remember Deyna Alberts and her family?" I asked them and Karina sent them the information. We kept hearing my father screaming and everyone was also screaming. "You remember Melissa Owens and the rest of the people that I killed, Agent de la Vega!" We kept hearing them and my father was loosing his mind.

"Where are you going with this, Dark Cowboy? We know that you are a cold blooded killer!" He yelled.

"Keep looking at the screen and see what happens, Agent de la Vega." I was laughing so much and looked at Karina and she sent them the information on their houses, their accounts and so on and just like that everything disappeared right in front of their eyes. "Well it looks to me that they no longer have any money in their accounts and everything has been erased and they lost everything, and you never saw this heist coming."

My father and his team couldn't believe what was going on. "Where's their money! What did you do!"

"It's all gone, their money is gone and tomorrow the bank is going to take away their cars, also seized their house and there's going to be a garage sale by the end of the week and they are going to get fired from their jobs and you couldn't do anything to protect them because you were too busy putting more crimes against me and doing other stuff as well. The people of this great city depended on you, Agent de la Vega, and you swore to protect innocent people from likes of us and now innocent people have lost their possessions and there wasn't a damn thing that you can do about it. And like I said, you failed to protect everyone in the city and you never saw this heist coming at all. And remember the conversation we had and I told you that I will let you know when I'll be coming back and wait for a sign. Well I'm sorry to say but this is the sign that you were waiting for and you weren't prepared at all and I thought a great FBI Agent like yourself was prepared for everything. So, much for the great Agent Pablo de la Vega and we are disappointed in you. I will leave you in the presence of the Lord, goodnight and good luck tomorrow with the people. I cannot wait to hear your explanation in front of City Hall." I laughed and hanged up the phone and I was laughing at everyone in the Police Station. We could hear my father moaning like a little bitch that he is and everyone was trying to calm him down.

"This isn't over! Get me someone that can check if they have money in their accounts." My father ordered.

"And this mission is finished! Are you guys in a mood to do another mission?" I asked them.

"Sure! Why not!" Primo smiled.

"So, what's the plan, Mauricio?" Chris asked me.

"Who knows how to tag on the walls?" I asked.

"Me!" Primo responded and said. "What do you want to tag?"

"The Legend of the Pachuco2k" I said.

"I'm ready to tag on the walls!" He said.

"Also we need a couple of buildings to explode." I said.

"It will be done." Cassandra said.

"And now we need to test your cars and we will piss off my beloved daddy and the rest of them. And Chris bring my horse and keep the car for you. What can I say I'm old fashion criminal. Okay, let's have some fun." I smiled..

"We're ready!" Everyone smiled.

"Guys, this is our last mission together. I enjoy working with you, and you guys are my family. But there is going to be a day where once again we come together and have more missions but for now let's enjoy our lives by spending the money and live it up." I smiled and we hugged each other. So, I went to the restroom and changed. Chris brought me my lovely horse. Primo and the girls got into their cars, I hopped onto my horse and we took off to the Police Station. We were monitoring everything that was happening inside the Police Station and we could hear my father and his team still scratching their heads and they couldn't find their money in their accounts. When we got there Chris put three big bright lights next to the wall. Primo started tagging the wall and we saw a couple of people that were walking around the area.

So, we waited until two o'clock in the morning where they finally came out of the Police Station. They were in disbelief and they noticed a couple of people were looking at the wall. So, they went to check it out. They were standing in front of the wall and my mother started reading it. "The Legend of the Pachuco2k!"

"What the Hell is going on tonight?" My father asked.

Then they heard my horse neighing and they turned around and they saw me laughing at them and my ten friends were also there laughing at them. They began to notice that I was on top of my horse and my ten friends were in their ten expensive cars and my father felt that I was the leader of the gang. And I couldn't stop laughing at them and I was turning red and I started talking to them. "Yes, Agent de le Vega we are the legendary, The Pachuco2k. We are the ones that stole the money from all the families and I was charge of doing all the killings and my friends were in charge of the other stuff that was happening around here. Individual we're good but together we are unstoppable and invisible and as the matter of fact we are proud to be legends in the city of El Paso, Texas. The great Agent de la Vega and his team never saw this heist coming at all. And before we go away and spend the money that we stole, I'm going to give you with tonight's forecast. Well it's going to be a hot one tonight and I also hope you have marshmallows." I laughed at them and rode away and my ten friends got inside their cars and drove away into the darkness. We overheard my father over the radio. "What did The Dark Cowboy meant by that?" And my father's question was answered when I gave Cassandra the signal and we heard the buildings exploding along the way and we were laughing at them.

My friends and I were still celebrating our graduation and not to mention the senior prank. I knew my father and his team were scratching their heads and they actually told the people the bad news. That they didn't have any money in their account courtesy of the Pachuco2k and they were going to be homeless and they had a garage sale by the end of the week.

CHAPTER SIXTEEN

THE MASSACRE OF THE MENTAL INSTITUTION

It was Friday afternoon where I was in the living room with Tania and we were watching a movie. On that wonderful day I received a letter and it was from the University of Missouri. It turns out that they accepted me to that University and I was so excited and showed my parents and my sister Tania, they were also excited and they gave me a huge hug. Well at least I wanted to have some pride because I wanted have a good education and I have good morals for once in my life. And on that day I started packing up my things and I have everything that I needed to go to school over there. And on that night my parents and my sister, Tania, took me to eat at *Chico's Tacos* and for the first time in a long we started celebrating like one big happy family. And I knew that I was going to miss that restaurant a lot and including my family and the killings. And more importantly I truly missed Eliza, the love of my life, I made you a promise that I was going to hunt down those bastards that raped you and beat you to death. So, when we got home my parents told me that they wanted to take me to Columbia, Missouri and they wanted to make sure that I will be safe from that psychotic killer. If they only knew that I'm the psychotic killer. The next day my friends and I were hanging out for the last time at Marty Robbins Park. And Chris came to the park and he smiled at us.

"They accepted me to the University of Missouri." I smiled.

"Congratulations! I am proud of you, Mauricio." Chris smiled and gave us our ATM cards and we were hugging him so tight.

"Thank you." I said.

"You have enough to live it up for the rest of your lives." Chris smiled and again he took out another ATM card.

"Another one!" I exclaimed.

"Mauricio, this is just between us and no one will ever know that this last ATM card exists except for us. You don't want to put your friends and family in danger. Well this ATM card contains more than ninety-seven billions dollars and think of it as a thank you bonus for being a great leader and a great friend. You've been like a son to me all these years and I've been saving this ATM card since I was a kid and now I want you to have it." Chris smiled and gave it to me and hugged me so tight.

"Thank you, Chris. I don't know how to thank you for helping us out with our operations. And I'm sorry that I gave you such a hard time during my reign of terror." I smiled and put both ATM cards inside my wallet and said. "One more thing. I want you to bring my horse to Columbia, Missouri, so I can ride it all over town."

"I actually know a man that's going to take good care of your horse. I will make the call and good luck in the future and I hope we see each other very soon and good luck to you guys. I will be leaving tonight." He said and hugged.

"Where are you going?" Karina asked.

"I'm going back to Ireland and spend time with my family and I hope we see each other." Chris smiled and we walked him into his truck and saw him leave and we went back to play softball.

"Now it's time to have fun." I smiled.

"We're not out of the woods just yet, Mauricio." Primo said.

"Why?" I asked.

"Because I found something that's going to bring you more happiness." Karina smiled.

"Tell me!" I exclaimed..

"The other day I hacked into the system and I found out that there's a secret Mental Institution and it's located in the outskirts of Oklahoma City. As it turns out that the secret Mental Institution belongs to the Government and the Federal Bureau Investigation and not to mention the mob as well. That's for the FBI's "prisoners." Who knows what goes on in that place." Karina said.

"My fathers runs that place!" I exclaimed.

"Yes, he does. But your dad lied about Plan B and it wasn't to put more charges against you. It was something else and maybe if one of us gets inside the secret Mental Institution and finds out what's going on in that place. Maybe we may have evidence pointed towards your father!" Karina requested.

"How about I go! I can steal a Nurse's identity and I'll check it out!" Erin said.

"No, Erin! I'll go in!" I said.

"No way, Mauricio! What happens if your dad decides to go there and the plan will be ruin. We can send Primo because half of the patients are rapist and some are killers." Karina said.

"Not Primo, he's already settled down with Madelyn. I'll go and find out but I'm not going to kill anyone. I only need two people for this operation. I'm going to hire Karina and Cassandra for this operation and the rest of you go to school and have fun with the money. And Karina make sure that my father doesn't get reassigned to that place. Pick another FBI Agent and I don't care who it is." I said.

"Just be careful, Mauricio." Sonia said.

"I want to ask you something, Mauricio. How are you going to get into the Psychiatric Ward? Are you planning to enter that place and kill everyone in sight?" Primo asked.

"No I'm not! I'm going to let the FBI captured me and someone has to die for them to capture me. That's where you come in, Karina. I want you to be the voice and tell them to take me to that place." I said.

"Yes!" She said.

"Who is going to die, Mauricio?" Primo asked.

I looked at them and smiled, "My faithful companion, my beloved horse."

"How is she doing to die?" Primo asked.

"I'm going to ride her for one last time in Columbia, Missouri and something has to explode and that's where you come in Cassandra." I said.

"Sounds good." Cassandra said.

"After this we go our separate ways and I hope that we find our happiness somewhere else. It's ashamed that this how it ends for the legend of The Dark

Cowboy and the gang! After this I hung my spurs and guns and move on with life. But I hope that I find those bastards that killed Eliza." I smiled and we all looked at each other and hugged so tight. After that we left Marty Robbins Park and went to our homes. And on Friday afternoon I went to Chris's house and he told me that he sent my horse to Columbia, Missouri and he told me that she is going to be at the fairgrounds and gave me the address as well. I was happy and I grabbed my outfit and put it inside my backpack and we said goodbye to each other and I thank him for everything he has ever done for us. And the next day we were getting ready to leave and I was saying goodbye to my loving sister, Tania, my little munchkin. We hugged for a long time and she was crying. "I hope you find your happiness again. I want to see you smile again." Tania smiled and sobbed.

"Someday, Tania, the old me will come back and I will smile from ear to ear." I smiled and hugged her so tight and kissed her on her cheek. Then my father and I put my luggage in the back of the truck. I turn around and said goodbye to Tania and the city of El Paso, Texas. My father started the engine and we drove off and I looked back and saw Tania saying goodbye to me. That day was nice day for a drive and I knew Texas was a huge state and we were going to pass every city and town Texas has to offer. During the road my parents were talking and laughing and I put on my headphones and I was listening to music the entire time. A couple of hours later we arrived at Forth Worth, Texas. My father went to put gas and my mother and I went inside the Gas Station to buy some snacks. And we got back on the road and my mother was the one that drove this time and we arrived at Tulsa, Oklahoma around midnight. My mother drove for awhile and it was my father's turn to drive and I fell asleep all the way. And the next day we arrived in Topeka, Kansas and I don't know for how long we were driving and I didn't asked and I looked around the city of Topeka, Kansas and it's a nice place to live. We stopped at a restaurant and ate and we were tired from the whole trip. And we got back on the road and hours later we finally arrived in Columbia, Missouri. I loved this small town and we drove around and we were looking for the University of Missouri. So, someone was kind enough to give my father directions and we got there. My father and I got the luggage and went to the dorms and I found my room right of away. I got settled in my room and I was saying goodbye to my parents and they told me that they love me a lot and to call them every single day. I walked them to the truck and I hugged them and watched them go back to El Paso, Texas.

After they left, I went inside and called for a cab and I told the cab driver to take me to the fairgrounds. Twenty minutes later we finally arrived at the fairgrounds and I paid the cab driver. I went inside the fairgrounds and one of the workers told me that there was a horse show and I saw a lot of people enjoying themselves and they were happy to see the horse show. Well three hours later the horse show ended and I was walking around the stables and I saw my lovely black stallion. I went up to her and I started to pet her.

"She seems to like you, Son." The man said.

"I love horses." I smiled.

"Well you can take her out for a ride. I don't mind at all." He smiled. "What's your name, Kid?"

"Mauricio de la Vega." I said.

The man was pleased to have me in his fairgrounds. "Well I heard about your parents. Your father is a very good FBI Agent and he's my grandson's hero and your mother is a great Police Officer. And everyone has heard of you, Mauricio de la Vega, the future King of Spain. And I know the story was bogus but we were so sure that you have royalty blood. And my name George Stevenson. I'm the owner of the fairgrounds and if you are looking for work. I'm hiring everyday to feed the horses and work around the stables."

"I'm looking for a job and when can I start?" I asked.

"Tomorrow morning." George said and smiled. "She wants you to take her out for a ride."

"Thank you!" I had my backpack with me and I got on top of my Black Stallion and we went riding together. And I watched the sun go down and saw the birds fly everywhere and it was a great experience to ride her for the very last time. Well I found a public restroom and I went inside the restroom to see if anybody was inside and I went in to change and put my regular clothes on my backpack. I saw myself in the mirror and I was dressed as The Dark Cowboy. I went back outside and I got on top of my horse again and we started riding like the wind. And as soon my Black Stallion stepped on the ground everything exploded and the whole town heard the major blast. My horse and I fell to the ground and I can say that Cassandra did a good job with her improve. And my faithful companion died right of away and I was on the ground and I was crawling towards my friend. All of the sudden I heard the Police sirens and the Ambulance sirens. And I was excited that our plan worked out like the way we planned but I'm sorry old friend I will see you very soon. And I was laying in front of my horse when the cavalry arrived in time and they got out of their cars. They pointed the guns at me and they told me not move and I was under arrest. They grabbed me and arrested me right of away and they even knocked me out and put me inside the van.

And the next day I woke up in a strange place, my hands and feet were tied up to the bed. I was trying to break free until the Nurse and a couple of security guards came into the room. The guards pointed the guns at me while the Nurse put the tray of food on top of the table and she smiled at me. I asked the Nurse "Where am I?" And she told me that I was locked way in a secret Mental Institution in Oklahoma City. The Nurse also reminded me that I'm a psycho path killer known as The Dark Cowboy and I am too dangerous to be on the streets and that I should be on death row for the murder of twenty-three people. What a bitch and I don't need anybody else to remind me that I'm The Dark Cowboy or how many people I've killed over the years. And I remember every detail that went on in that place and of course I had my sources.

Later on in the morning a helicopter chopper arrived on the rooftop of the Mental Institution and this young hot shot FBI Agent got out of the helicopter chopper and he was smoking a Cuban Cigar and had a glass of Whiskey on his right hand. His name is Stewart Rice, he is second in command of the Federal Bureau Investigation in other words, he is the right handed man of my father, Pablo de la Vega. He is my father's apprentice and Agent Stewart Rice is a very well respected FBI Agent as well. Most people saw him as another Super Cop, and they were comparing him to my father. Agent Stewart Rice also travels all over the world catching criminals, assassins, and terrorist just like my sweet old father. And this hot shot FBI Agent has seen them all but he is about to face his tougher challenge and that is me, The legend of the Dark Cowboy in person and not to mention, the son of the great Agent de la Vega.

After he finished drinking his Whiskey and smoking his Cigar, he finally goes inside the building and the Doctors and his staff welcomed him to the secret Mental Institution. And the hot shot FBI Agent put his Cigar in the trash can and he ask to refill his Whiskey and made a toast.

He gave them a huge smile and raised his glass of Whiskey. "Ladies and gentlemen. We finally captured The Dark Cowboy after all these years on the run! We finally captured him! We should drink to this moment! Cheers!"

But no one wanted to have drink with him because they wanted to show him what they had in the basement. The Doctors took him all the way to the basement where it was heavily guarded by twenty guards and they were armed to the teeth. The Doctor swiped his card and the door opened, and they took him inside and the hot shot FBI Agent couldn't believe what he was staring at.

"Oh, my God. This is The Dark Cowboy in person, man he is so ugly." He said and put his hand on my face and he was shocked. "You're so young and you are going to die young. Give me a gun, so I can kill him because I'm not going to wait when he goes to trial. The great Pablo de la Vega will happy to know that you have captured him and I get to kill him and we are going to get the bounty. Ten thousand dollars for the one that captures him and thirty thousand dollars for the one that kills him. So, cheers once again!"

The Doctor interrupted him while he was drinking his Whiskey and smoking his Cigar. "Well I don't know how to tell you this, Agent Rice, but this is the son of Pablo de la Vega. His name is Mauricio de la Vega, the second and he was captured in Columbia, Missouri and we found out that he is The Dark Cowboy. And yesterday we were doing evaluations on Mauricio and we also ran so many test on him. We found out the problem that he has some kind of mental disorder and is like psychosis. He talks to himself and he yells and his voice changes and curses us all the way to Hell. But did you know that he was going to be the future King of Spain?"

Everyone in that room bowed down before me and I was sitting down on the bed and I was looking down and I was drooling on the floor and I was also shaking and it was a part of the act, so they can think that I'm crazy. And finally the hot shot FBI Agent decided not kill me. "Mauricio! Son, are you alright?"

I looked up at him and said, "Help me! Help me, before he comes after me again. He wants to kill me, I don't want to die!" I sobbed.

"He's been that way since yesterday. He wants us to help him but we don't know how to help him." The Doctor said.

I yelled at them. "He wants to kill me! I want you to help me before he attacks me again!"

"I can see that he attacked you outside Missouri and he put you in his place and I know that The Dark Cowboy is still going to be on the run as always. How can I help you, Son. Tell me everything about The Dark Cowboy, so we can arrest him and throw him in jail for the rest of his natural born life. He has threatened you before. I guess the FBI Agents arrested the wrong person. Boy, Agent de la Vega is going to kill us."

I was going to answer but the Doctor told me to rest and later on in the night they would talk to me once again. Then the Doctors were talking to this hot shot FBI Agent and they couldn't figure this out on their own and they were talking about getting help from another Physiatrist.

"I'm going to stay here and help Pablo's son, so that psychotic killer won't come after him. Did you hear me, Mauricio. I'm going to help you. So, I want you to rest because we are going to guard this building and you will be safer here"

They were about to leave when they heard someone laughing and it sounded like a satanic laughter and I started talking to them and I was growling and my eyes were glowing red. "You cannot protect Mauricio de la Vega from me, you hot shot FBI Agent scum. No one cannot help him, I own his body and I enjoy seen him suffer!"

They turned around and they saw that my eyes were glowing red and I had an evil laugh as well. "This is not happening!" The Doctor yelled.

"At last we meet, you Federal Bureau Investigation scum and allow me to reintroduce myself. My name is the legendary Mauricio Dark Cowboy de la Vega, the greatest serial killer of all time and I know you're a piece crap FBI Agent that was trained by the great Agent de la Vega. And now tell me how are you going to protect, Mauricio, oh, let me guess by planting more mine bombs on the ground and see him getting injured and a little personal note my horse died and I won't forgive you for that. And I'm guessing that there's three hundred-and thirty five people that are working in this secret Mental Institution. And I'm going to kill all off you by midnight and I'm going to send all of you straight to Hell." I started laughing at them. "And I have full control of Mauricio's body and you cannot help him at all. Not even if you pray to your God and hope that I get out of his body. It will not work at all." My laugher continued.

"He is right. No matter what we do is not going to work at all. But we need to bring help from the outside and I know the right person that can help us out with this patient." The Doctor said.

"We're not going to give up. You listening to me, Mauricio! We are not going to give up and I will do everything in my power to help you." The FBI Agent said.

"Bring whoever you please and I will get a kick out of it." I growled and laughed at them.

The Doctors sedated me and I fell asleep and everyone left the room and the guards decided to tied me up once again. Everyone went to the Doctor's office. "There is a possibility that Mauricio might be possessed by the Devil or some Demon that's on the loose. Because his eyes were glowing red and he has that evil voice in him and looked like a monster." The Doctor said.

"How are we going to help him?" Stewart asked.

The Doctor responded. "Well three years ago, I was in Holland, Amsterdam. And I started working with a Psychiatrist and she always gives spiritual advice to the patients that had the same problems as Mauricio and they were able to recover. She is the best there is and she's been doing this for almost twenty years. Her name is Doctor Juanita Van Der AA and she wrote a book about her patients. And right now her book is number five in the New York best selling's list."

"I know who she is, my daughter was friends with her niece, Madelyn Van Der AA. And I can send a chopper to Holland, Amsterdam and bring her over here." Stewart said.

The Doctor agreed and made a couple of phone calls and I'm guessing that Doctor Juanita Van Der AA agreed and he sent a chopper to pick her up and brought her to the Mental Institution. And three hours later the helicopter chopper arrived at the building, the Doctors were there to welcome her and they went straight to the office. "It's nice to see you again, Juanita." He said and smiled.

"It's nice to see you too." She smiled.

They were getting acquainted when the hot shot FBI Agent interrupted them. "I'm sorry for this but we are in the middle of a crisis here. Well Doctor the patient that is here is the son of my boss, his name is Mauricio de la Vega and we may think that he may be The Dark Cowboy too." He said.

The Doctor showed Doctor Juanita Van Der AA all the Medical report they did on me and she agreed to help out. "I've seen patients like him and I've been able to cure them." She smiled.

Then the FBI Agent and the Doctors took Doctor Juanita Van Der AA all the way to the basement. That's where she saw me through the glass window. The Doctor swiped his card and the door open. I was already waking up and the hot shot FBI Agent approached me and said, "Mauricio I'm going to call your parents and I know they are going to be worried for you!" He said and as soon he was going to leave I grabbed him, and I broke his arm in three places and I yelled, "Kiss my ass!" I started laughing even more and the guards came into the room and put me in a straight jacket and took me to the room where she can talk to me. The guards sat me down and Doctor Juanita Van Der AA was looking at my profile and she looked at me and smiled and she also sat down.

"Hi, my name is Doctor Juanita Van Der AA and I'm a new Doctor of this Mental Institution and this is my first day here. I came all the way from Holland, Amsterdam and we are going to work together for now."

"My name is Mauricio de la Vega." I smiled and my eyes were glowing red. "My name is The Dark Cowboy and I'm a legend."

"Well I know everything about you. I've worked with a lot of patients that have psychosis, mental illness, and also possessed. My father was once a Pastor and I have a lot of experience with people that were once possessed. I hope I can cure you." She smiled.

"I can tell you are a great Psychiatrist." I smiled and again my eyes were glowing red and she was scared.

"How about you tell me about yourself and you can tell me anything you want. I want you to think of me as your friend." She smiled.

"That's fair enough. So, you want to know everything about me. This is going to take all day and I've got to warn you Doctor Juanita Van Der AA this is going to be Rated R. Perhaps I should start from the beginning and I will tell you where it all began, Doctor Juanita Van Der AA." I smiled and she took out her pen and paper and wrote while I dictated. Well on that afternoon, I told her everything about me. All the people that I killed, I also told her about Eliza, the love of my life. The secret rivalry I have with my father and along with everybody else. And finally after five hours, I looked at Doctor Juanita Van Der AA and said, "You know the rest of the story! I woke up in this place and I'm talking to the great Doctor Juanita Van Der AA from Holland, Amsterdam."

Doctor Juanita Van Der AA was checking her notes and then looked at me and asked me, "Were you responsible for Eliza's death?"

"No! I loved her a lot. I was willing to die to for her! I wanted to marry her and have kids with her!" I responded.

Doctor Juanita Van Der AA smiled and she was looking her notes and she looked at me and said, "We're done for the day. How about we finish with this tomorrow and there's a lot of test that I want to give you. And I hope that I can help you get that Demon out of your body. From what you told me I can tell that you a great guy. You care about others but it's this monster that's controlling you and made you kill innocent people. And like I said will discuss this tomorrow in the afternoon. I will see you tomorrow!"

"How about later on and I will personally show you the monster that I have inside my body and this Hospital is going to have a river of blood!" I laughed and growled and three guards came into the room and took me back to my room. And I couldn't believe that Doctor Juanita Van Der AA told me that she was going to evaluate me first thing in the morning. Well I wasn't going to wait at all and I made a promise that I was going to kill more people and avenge her death. I wanted to show Doctor Juanita Van Der AA that I wasn't bluffing at all and I broke my promise to the gang and especially Luz Maria Fitzgerald Estrada. The guards took me back to my room and that's where I fell down and told them that my head was hurting so badly and I started throwing up all over the place.

The guards got on the radio and said, "We need a Doctor, this patient is getting sick. Now!" And one of the guards came up to me and picked me up very gently. I looked at him and smiled and I punched him right in the balls and grabbed his gun and shot him and I transformed into the monster and started growling.

"Hold it right there! Put the gun down!" The other guard yelled.

Fine I did the put gun down and ran towards the guard and snapped the guard's neck and he died instantly. I went to the other guard and grabbed his weapons. And five more guards were coming into the room and just like that I killed them and their were blood were splattered on the walls and to the floors. I found my clothes laying around in some table and I put my clothes on and grabbed my backpack. And was once again I was The Dark Cowboy and my eyes were glowing red and I was growling. I finally went upstairs and everyone was screaming and crying. Four guards approached me and I shot them and I also snap their necks and they died instantly. There were twenty-four guards working inside the Mental Institution and I killed all of them and they were laying in a pool of their own blood. And I kept hearing the Doctors screaming, "Call the Police!"

The other Doctor yelled out, "I can't! The damn phones are down and alarms won't go off!" They couldn't call no one and the alarms couldn't work either. Perhaps someone blocked the calls and the alarms. I liked the improve from Karina. And I killed the rest of the guards and I grabbed their guns and bullets.

I could tell that there weren't any guards left. So, I grabbed all the Doctors by their hairs and they were yelling at me. That's where I began to notice five patients that were standing side by side with that hot shot FBI Agent and I was able to recognize them. They were the ones that broke into Eliza's house and raped her and beat her to death. And they were the ones that killed her. And I killed the rest of the Doctors. I grabbed the hot shot FBI Agent by the neck and one of the last guards came up to me and hit me in the head with the nightstick. I was just standing there staring at him and I grabbed the guard's neck and snapped it. And I also snapped the FBI Agent's neck and he also died. And I grabbed the guard's handcuffs and looked at them. "You come with me!" I yelled at the patients and they nearly peed themselves because they were so scared. I grabbed one of them and yelled! "Who hired you to break into Eliza's house? Who paid you to rape her and beat her?" I asked them and they didn't say anything, so I handcuffed them together, and I saw Doctor Juanita Van Der AA that was hiding behind the desk and she was crying her eyes out and I also handcuffed her to the patients. "We have all night long to be together!" I yelled at them and I dragged them to see if there any guards left but they were dead and the Doctors were also dead.

"Don't kill us!" One of them yelled.

"Do you see the dead bodies that are laying around here? And there is going to be more dead bodies laying around if you don't tell me who hired you to break into the Eliza's house!" I yelled at them. "Who hired you?" I yelled at them and they didn't say anything. Well I took them to room to room and killed every patient that was inside the Mental Institution. They were crying their eyes out and again they told me not kill them. And we went back to the front office and I threw them to the ground. I grabbed one of them and yelled at him. "Who hired you?" I asked.

"Please don't kill me!" He sobbed.

"Who hired you?" I asked and punched him in the face.

"I don't know his name but we got our orders from him." He said and pointed at the guy who has curly hair. I looked at the guy who has curly hair and they all said that he was the leader and he gets his orders from someone else. Well these guys were just errand boys. I went up to him and asked. "Who hired you?"

"Just don't kill us." He sobbed.

I grabbed all four of them and snap their necks and they died instantly. "Who hired you?" I asked.

"Please don't kill me!" He yelled and he was pissing his pants and he didn't say anything at all. So, I punched him in the face and I was yelling at him. And he was crying and I grabbed him by his hair and he was screaming. "Please don't kill me!"

I was yelling at the man. "Who hired you to break into the Eliza's house?"

"I cannot tell you who hired us because THEY told me that if I talk that THEY were going to kill my whole family!" The man screamed and cried.

"If you don't tell me who hired you, I will kill you and your family and the one who hired you! Now tell me! Who in the Hell hired you to break into her house!" I yelled at him and pointed the gun at his head and yelled at him again. "Who hired you?"

Then I pointed the gun at his legs and shot him and he screamed and cried and told me something that really shocked me and he yelled out. "De la Vega! De la Vega! FBI Agent Pablo de la Vega is the one that hired us to break into her house! And Vito Mancini. Both of them hired us. That's all I know! I swear!"

I looked at him and yelled, "Liar!" And I shot him in the head and all over his body and killed him. I couldn't believe what happen and I should have asked him more questions but my ego got in the way and I just killed all of them. But why did my father and Vito did this to me and Eliza. I was staring at all the dead bodies and all I could hear, "De la Vega, De la Vega!"

After that incident inside the office, we went outside to find a car. Tonight it's June 17, 2002, the clock struck at twelve fifty-six in the morning. It's my birthday and I'm spending my birthday in this secret Mental Institution. It's a hot night and there's a thunderstorm that's coming into town. I looked up the dark sky and it looked ugly right away. There's a chance that this thunderstorm might turn into a tornado watch and maybe there is a possibly for a tornado warning. The lightning was so bright as the day, the thunder was really loud, the wind was blowing really hard, the rain was pouring down really hard, and the hail was also coming down hard and it was breaking windows and breaking other things in the peaceful town. And I'm staring at the secret Mental Institution that has been own by the FBI and the mob. The patients in this secret Mental Institution are not ordinary patients with mental problems, these are the patients that worked for the mob and they are wanted by the FBI or they might work for them and the other patients are contract killers. Twenty hours ago I was captured and locked away in this secret Mental Institution because they were so sure that I was The Dark Cowboy. I could tell they were celebrating but after their ten minute celebration came to the end when they found out that I'm a de la Vega and they were scared to know that my father is head of the Federal Bureau Investigation. Right away they did a lot of test on me and they failed to find out my problem. So, they decided to bring help from the outside, and they contacted a famous Psychiatrist from Holland, Amsterdam. So, the good Doctor from Amsterdam agreed to help out and we had a couple of hours of conversation and she decided to help me. She said that she wanted to do all kinds of test by tomorrow in the morning. Well there were three hundred and fifty-three people that were inside the secret Mental Institution and they were living their day with no worries until just moments ago where I ended up killing all of them and they were laying a pool of their own blood. Well we were outside and I was staring at the damn building and I was getting hit hard by the rain and the hail. Something bad happen on this night when I killed one of the patients. I still could hear the man yell, "De le Vega. De la Vega. Pablo de la Vega is the one that hired us to break into her house!"

And Doctor Juanita Van Der AA was yelling at me. "Mauricio, we got to get out of here! There's a Tornado coming and it's going to hit us if we don't leave!"

I looked at her and said, "I couldn't protect her on that night we were attacked and it was my father that hired those men to come after us!"

"Eliza is dead! Let her rest in peace! Mauricio, I was Eliza's Doctor and she had all kinds of problems! She wasn't that well and let the authorities arrest your father!"

I looked at her and yelled, "I'm going to find him and then I'm going to kill him!"

"He's your father! You cannot stick to his level. Think about it. And you told me that you received a scholarship to the University of Missouri! You can change your ways, and you also said that you retired for Eliza. You can have a better life. You don't have to do this anymore! There's going to be a day that you will find love once again."

And I heard the loud siren sound and I didn't know what it was. "What's that noise?"

"A Tornado is coming and we need to get out of here!" She responded and grabbed my shoulder. "Come on!"

"You win, Doctor Juanita Van Der AA! No more killing and I do want a better life. And I know my father is going to pay for his action. Send the tape and I'm going to let the government handle him." I smiled and went inside the car. She quickly started the engine and left the area. Doctor Juanita Van Der AA turn on the radio and we heard the weather report. Before the anchor was going to say Tornado, we heard something break. I turn around and saw that the Tornado destroying the secret Mental Institution. She stepped on the gas and we left the area and we arrived in another town and went into a Hotel. We shared a room and on that night. And she started talking about religion and what God wants from us. I knew what I did was wrong but I couldn't help it. I told Doctor Juanita Van Der AA that I got addicted to killing and it was going to be hard not do it again. And finally the next day we went back on the road and we started talking.

She looked at me and asked, "Tell me were you and Primo behind the rapes and the killings?"

I responded with a smile, "Primo and I are co leaders and cofounders of the gang known as the Pachuco2k. Nine girls and two guys and everything that happened over there they were responsible. I was doing all the killings and I hired Primo to rape the girls that I wanted to kill."

"What made you do that?" She asked.

"Because of my ancestor did the same in the late 1700's." I responded.

"Your ancestor, Mauricio?" She asked.

"Yes! He was known as The Aztec Conquistador. I'm known as The Dark Cowboy!"

"I remember when I was a little girl and my grandfather told me about that story. I didn't believe it but I did research on The Aztec Conquistador and it was a legend. But I continued to search for more details. I found out the name. Mauricio de la Vega and you're Mauricio de la Vega the second. The original Mauricio killed his family to rule Spain, there was one survivor. And you are about to do the same thing!"

"I heard that story from this guest speaker we had in elementary school. His name is William Jones. But my father didn't tell me anything about him and his name wasn't on the record books. I thought they named me after a broke down family member and that broke down family member turned out to be a serial killer."

Doctor Juanita Van Der AA looked at me and asked, "You think your father knows who you really are?"

I responded, "I don't know! But I was able to fool the Police and the FBI. And like you said that I should move on with my life. I need to be isolated from the people because I don't know what's going to happen down the road. Doctor Juanita Van Der AA, what if I fall in love or have a best friend then what happens. They might die right in front of my eyes."

"You're a man on the run but no one knows who you really are. And you can live like everyone else. Everything is going to be okay!" Doctor Juanita Van Der AA smiled and we finally entered the city of Topeka, Kansas and we arrived in Columbia, Missouri. Doctor Juanita Van Der AA asked for directions and they told her where the University of Missouri was at. And in twenty minutes later we finally arrived. She parked and we stayed talking for awhile.

"Thank you for taking back here!" I smiled.

Doctor Juanita Van Der AA "You're welcome, Mauricio! And I can tell that you're a nice guy and I hope you find your happiness once again. I just hope you and the Demon that you have inside your body are able to get along."

"We will get along! And are we going to see each other again?" I asked.

Doctor Juanita Van Der AA responded with a huge smile, "Well, Yes! After all my niece, Madelyn, is friends with your baby sister, Tania. Plus she's in a relationship with your friend, Primo and I know they love each other and I hope they get married in the near future. And good luck in the future, Mauricio."

"It was nice to meet you, Doctor Juanita Van Der AA!" I smiled and got out of the car and she started the engine and went away. And I stayed outside the dorms and I started laughing. Maybe she's right. I should enjoy my life and no more killing, so I went inside the dorms. And I hope that I have a good education right here in Columbia, Missouri.

CHAPTER SEVENTEEN

FOUR YEARS LATER COMING BACK TO EL PASO, TEXAS

I was in my dorm room and I started packing up my things and I was getting ready to go home. Well I said goodbye to all my college friends and hit the road. And the next day I arrived in El Paso, Texas., I was driving around the Eastside and the neighborhood where I finally reached my house. My mother and my baby sister, Tania were outside waiting for me. They were sitting down on the bench when I parked into the driveway. I got out of the truck and they came running towards me and I hugged them so tight. Tania was so happy to see me and she started crying and was holding on to me. My mother hugged me too and kissed me on my forehead. After we finished hugging each other, Tania and my mother were helping me with the luggage and we went inside the house and sat down in the living room. Tania and I were sitting down while my mother was in the kitchen and brought three glasses of Juice and she also sat down. We were talking all morning long and my mother and Tania were telling me what they were doing all those years ago. And I told them about my misadventures I was having in Columbia, Missouri. They were not that happy but they liked my other fun stories. After we finished talking in the living room, I grabbed my luggage and went to my room and started unpacking everything and I was putting them in the drawers. After that I was laying in my bed and I was relaxing and I was so happy to be home and I wanted to spend the whole summer with my parents and my sister.

And I decided to call my college roommate, good old Matthew Walsh and I told him that I arrived at my house safe and the weather was great the entire time I was driving. We were talking for about half an hour and we hung up the phone and went to turn on the television. And at the top of the entertainment center, I saw my old high school diploma. And I had the diploma in my hands and I remember when I graduated from Americas High School and it was just four years ago. I put my diploma back at the entertainment center, and I went to open my other drawer and I found the family album and I sat on my bed and I was looking at it.

There were a lot of pictures when I was a little kid and there were a lot of pictures of my family and friends. And there were also a lot of pictures when I was hanging out with my friends. Also there were a couple of pictures where I was hugging Eliza, the love of my life. I was happy to see her again and I know she's happy wherever she's at. I truly wanted to marry her and have kids with her. And to be honest I was planning to retire from all the killings and to spend my life with her but there was another person that got in my way. And that was my father but I made Doctor Juanita Van Der AA a promise that I wasn't going after him anymore. And I should forgive him and there's got to be a reason what he did to us. As I was looking at the picture where I was hugging Eliza, but I couldn't remember her at all and I didn't have any memory of her except the fact that she was my high school sweetheart. After that I put the album back in the drawer and I was laying in bed and I started to remember those summers pretty well. My friends, family and myself had a lot of cookouts in the backyard but it was a lot of fun when we had them at Marty Robbins Park. We usually played volleyball and sometimes we went to the swimming pool and we swam all afternoon long. When I was younger I did the same thing every kid my age did in most summers. I was always looking at the newspapers to see if they were any jobs available. Well there were a lot of jobs available, so I spent most of the summers cutting grass, painting houses, and I was a paperboy for awhile because I was always falling off the bicycle and the damn dogs always chased me down the street. And not to mention that my friends and I were terrorizing the entire city of El Paso, Texas and we did so many awful things to this city and I hope that after four years away the Police Officers, the FBI, and the citizens still remember who we are.

Well on top of all the killings I enjoyed the summer with friends and family. It was great for me but that was so many years ago but somehow I felt that this summer was going to be different than the rest of the summers I had in my life. I turn around and on top of my dresser I found thirty-four letters of little Samantha Jones. And I grabbed the letters and once again I laid in bed and I started reading all of her letters and I was glad that she was doing okay and I know she is having a better education and she was a lot smarter than most of her friends at school. She even sent me a picture and she is so beautiful and she had grown up as well. And later on in the afternoon I went down to the kitchen. My mother and Tania were making lunch.

"Are you hungry, Mauricio?" My mother asked.

"A little bit." I smiled and asked her, "So, where's dad? Did he went back to Europe?"

My mother looked at us and responded, "Well your father was in Washington D.C. And they were planning to close the case against The Dark Cowboy. They were going to send your father to Europe because they finally located Vito Mancini. But on that day the FBI received a horrible video tape from The Dark Cowboy and that psychotic killer threatened to kill everyone inside a Psychiatric Ward and he gave your father one week to go up there and save them. When they got there the building was destroyed and they were looking for the bodies and they spread all over the county and they found the dead bodies laying on the ground. They were so sure that the Tornado killed them and they did an autopsy on them and they found the bullets inside their bodies. The Dark Cowboy killed all of them and he showed no mercy. And since then The Dark Cowboy was never seen ever again and not even the members of The Pachuco2k. So, right now your father is still in Washington D.C. and the FBI planned reopen the case against The Dark Cowboy for all the crimes he committed over the years."

"Gosh mommy! Are you saying that the FBI is going to reopened the case all over again and there's going to be another curfew and another bounty? I wanted to enjoy the summer with my brother and my friends. Curse The Dark Cowboy all the way to Hell!" Tania exclaimed and was disappointed.

My mother smiled and kissed my sister on her forehead and said, "Of course not, Sweetie. There isn't going to be anymore curfews and no more bounties. Your father and the new Mayor of El Paso made it clear that there's not going to be anymore curfews. The people have a lot of faith and now they have the confidence that the Police Officers and FBI Agents can arrest all the criminals and especially The Dark Cowboy and his henchmen." My mother smiled and turned off the stove and told us to sit down. "I have something to tell you guys. I know you guys are all grown up. Tania is anxious to go to college and, Mauricio is on the doorstep of graduation from the University of Missouri. But I've been thinking about it for awhile and I came to the conclusion that I am thinking about retiring from the Police Force and move on with my life and wait for your father to come back home. Your father is also thinking about retiring from the FBI as well."

"What are you going to do now, Mom?" Tania asked.

"If I retired that means I would get to travel all over the world like I always wanted. Your father and I have been thinking about moving to Miami, Florida and that's where old people go to live. Besides you guys are growing up and going to school and I hope you two end up having a good career and we taught you guys everything we know. Tania might be going away to college and Mauricio is going to have a great future ahead. And all I want is for the both of you to be happy with your lives and have a good career ahead of you and start family pretty soon." My mother smiled and hugged us.

"But mom what made you decide to retire from the Police Force? I mean you are a Super Cop and you have arrested so many criminals from all over. You can do anything." Tania encouraged her.

My mother responded with a nice smile. "Well I've reached my fifties, Tania. And I thought I could continue being a Police Officer for as long I wanted but the two of you know that The Dark Cowboy wore me out. As the matter of fact The Dark Cowboy wore out everybody in the Police Department and the FBI. The Dark Cowboy droved us absolutely crazy. And things are different these days. When I was younger I had no problem chasing down criminals and I got to tackle them to the ground. And now you have the new young generations of criminals that looked like athletes. And I couldn't keep up with a twenty year old bank robber and I lost my breathe when I ran for three seconds. The criminals are getting younger, smarter, and more wiser than us veterans and it's up for the new generations of Police Officers and FBI to take them out. And I made the decision to retire."

"Well whatever makes you happy, Mom. Tania and I will be there for you and dad." I smiled

And Tania added, "But mommy you taught us not to give up. We know that you were working for eight hours, so you can take care of us. And now we're grown up and you should continue with your Police work. Whatever happen to the great Beatrice de la Vega that never gave up. I know you still have it in you but don't give up and at least try. You told me that you rather die on the streets than to retire. This is not the mom that I know."

"Tania is right what happen to the great Beatrice de la Vega. The Super Cop! You arrested so many criminals and tackled them to the ground. You are the best there is!" I exclaimed and smiled.

My mother looked at us and smiled and hugged us. "I love you guys so much. And I'm sorry that I got old on you guys and I haven't made my decision to retire but I will think about it. I promise!"

"Please think about it!" Tania hugged her.

"I will think about it!" My mother smile.

So, by the year 2006 my parents were turning fifty-two years old and they have been on the Police Force for thirty-four years. And there is no way in Hell that my parents are going to retire from the Police Force. My parents would rather die on the streets than to retire from an old age and for them that's the easy way out. And it seams that they gave up because my friends and I were way better than them. Well I'm actually responsible that my parents were aging because they couldn't find me and they were chasing an invisible man. They didn't know that the I'm psychotic killer and I've been in front of them several times and they have yet to arrest me. But nobody is perfect and they should keep guessing. And now my parents plan to retire from the Police Force. And I was shock to hear that the good Doctor actually sent out the tape to my father. I'm guessing that it was a threatening video tape and not the evidence tape. So, this was a heads up towards my father and I knew that he was loosing his mind when he saw the video tape and he was going to have more gray hairs. And I have a feeling that things are going to get more interesting around here.

So, half an hour later we sat on the table and my mother served us lunch and for two hours we were eating and laughing. My mother and my sister were glad that I came back home for the summer. After we finished eating lunch Tania and my mother were washing the dishes and after they finished washing the dishes. My mother went to her room while Tania and I were hanging out in her room.

"What do you think of my new room?" She asked.

"I can see that you did a little decorating. What happen to your stuff animals and your dolls?"

"I'm a big girl, Mauricio! I wanted to have changes in my life. I didn't want you to think that I'm still the spoil little Princess that kept stuff animals and dolls in my room. I wanted you to see me like a big girl now!"

"You're will always be my little spoil Princess." I smiled and hugged her so tight. She sat down on her bed and I sat down on her chair.

She looked at me and smiled, "I'm glad you're back, I really did missed you! A lot! I remember when I was a little girl I was used to seen you every single day. And I remember when I had bad dreams and I went into your room and we talked and laugh for hours. I wasn't scared anymore. You took care of me when mom was working all night long. And when you graduated from high school and left. I cried myself to sleep because my big brother had left to college."

"I'm sorry, Tania that I went to a different place. And I'm sorry that I missed the holidays, your birthday, our parents birthday, and your high school graduation. I don't know what I was thinking when I left El Paso and I am too selfish. I'm sorry to let you down but I'm on the doorstep of graduating from the University of Missouri." I smiled and I was too busy killing people in that secret Mental Institution that no one knows that exists and I'm surprised that they didn't put it on the news. I want to tell you that I'm The Dark Cowboy but I don't want you to have nightmares with the things that I want to tell you. But for now I want you to see me as your big brother.

Tania giggled and said, "Don't feel guilty, Mauricio. I will always love you no matter what. You are my big brother and my best friend in the world and I just missed you and I'm so happy that you are back home with us. And we can have fun and I have the summer planned out." Tania smiled and hugged me so tight.

I sat her down in my lap and tickled her and she was laughing. "Well how about this, Munchkin. Let me take you to Ascarate Park and I will make you a promise that on this summer. You and I are going to have fun together. That is my present to you because you graduated from Americas High School."

"Well I have another surprise for you." She smiled.

"Tell me."

"Yesterday, I received a scholarship to Harvard Law and I hope to be there by the spring semester." She smiled and hugged me again.

"Congratulations!" I smiled and hugged her so tight.

"Well we have another reason to be happy and to celebrate."

"You have grown up, Tania." I smiled.

"So have you, Mauricio. And I want to become a District Attorney. And hopefully I will be the one that puts The Dark Cowboy behind bars for the rest of his natural born life. The Dark Cowboy is guilty of what he is done to this city and I will never forgive him what he's done to us. He was about to kill you in our living room. And I promise you and the de la Vega family that are spread all over the world and that are watching us from the Heavens. That I would be the one that throws The Dark Cowboy in jai forever." She looked serious.

I smiled and said, "Come one, Squirt. Let's go to Ascarate Park. How about you get ready and I will go to *Big 8* and get everything that we need to fish. You know the snacks and the drinks." And Tania got up and was getting her clothes and she is still pissed off with my alter ego. Well Tania plans to become a District Attorney and wants to take me out for good. Well good luck baby sis because they all tried to stop me. You're no different from the rest of them. Just take a look at our parents because they have a lot of gray hairs and they lost their pride.

"Okay then! Well I'm going to take a quick shower and I will be ready when you come back from the store." Tania smiled and hugged me so tight.

"I'll be right back!" I smiled and left her room.

CHAPTER EIGHTEEN

LOVE AT FIRST SIGHT

Tania was getting her clothes and went to take a quick shower. While I went to the garage and I got the fishing gear and put them in the living room. Then I got into the truck and went to the store and I arrived at *Big 8* and went into the store. It was a lot fresher inside than outside because it was over one hundred and two degrees. And I saw everyone buying charcoal and food because they were having a cookout somewhere in the city or maybe at Marty Robbins Park. And I went around the whole store and grabbed a couple of snacks and put them on the shopping cart and went to the soft drink section. I was standing in front of the cokes section when all of the sudden I smell something and it was the smell of perfume, and it smelled so good. And I turn around and there was she was. I saw the prettiest girl I have ever seen in my life. She was holding a basket of flowers and ten bags of planting seeds. She just walked past the coke section and I don't think she saw me at all. I grabbed two boxes of Pepsi and I followed her and she walked toward the counter and luckily the cashier was occupied with one of the customers and the cashier didn't have any change at all. And I started walking towards her as quickly as possible and I found myself standing behind this beautiful girl. She looked perfect, she's five feet tall, ninety-six pounds, light skin, long reddish hair, and green eyes. She was wearing a blue blouse with a long white skirt and she had on sandals. She looked like an old fashioned type of girl. Right of away I knew that she wasn't going to be like the other drunk girls I had met in college. I wanted to get her attention and I started sneezing and she finally turned around and she said, "Bless you, Mate!" and gave me a beautiful smile that I will never forget but still I was smelling her perfume and it felt that I smell this kind of perfume before. And I couldn't figure it out where I've smelled this perfume before. And I'm guessing that she must be English or Scottish. We were the only ones there and the rest of the people went to other counter because they were taking a long time to get more money from the vault. Finally the manager brought more money to the register and the cashier started scanning her purchases, the seeds and the flowers. The total was ten dollars but the beautiful girl didn't have enough money to pay for all of her things. So, I took out my wallet but all I had was a fifty dollar bill and gave it to her.

"Here!" I smiled. "So, you can pay for your roses and seeds."

She didn't want to take the fifty dollar bill and said. "No, thank you." She gave me a shy smile.

"I insist. Please take it." I smiled.

"Well thank you!" She said reluctantly and I looked at the cashier and she smiled. The beautiful girl was too embarrassed to take the money but took the money anyway and paid for her purchase. And then she gave me back the change. She smiled and started walking towards the door and then stopped half way there. She turn around and waited for me and I was relieved that she was had decided to wait for me. She looked at me and smiled and I paid for my things and started walking towards her.

"Thank you for lending me the money to pay for my things." She smiled and she was talking to me with a fancy accent.

"You're very welcome. And I wanted to do the right thing and help you out." I smiled.

"Well you seem like a nice guy. And I really appreciate what you did for me today. How can I make it up to you?" She asked.

"Well, how about we go eat *Ciro's* it's just across the street. You are going to like their food."

"Yes, that will be great. And I feel like I can trust you. And I know that you're not that type of guy that don't do this every time you want to meet a girl and pay for her things." She said.

"I don't know how many times I've met a girl at the grocery store and pay for her things." I smiled and said. "I'm kidding well thank your for trusting me. I really appreciate it."

She smiled and I carried her bags of flowers and planting seeds and put them in the back seat of the truck and we also got inside the truck. And I drove across the street and *Ciro's* didn't have that many people inside, so I parked and we went inside the restaurant. Well everyone that worked in the restaurant smiled and said welcome to *Ciros* and they took us to find a table. We found a table that we liked and we sat down and she looked at me and she gave me another smile. And I couldn't keep my eyes off her and I felt that she was the prettiest girl I have ever seen in my life. Then the waitress came to the table and smiled.

"What's going to be your order?" She asked.

"Tacos and a Coke." I said.

"What about you, dear?" She looked at her.

"Flautas and Tea." She smiled.

The waitress wrote down our orders and left and she came back to bring us Tostadas and Chile while we were waiting for our food. And she also brought our drinks and left. We looked at each other and smiled and we started having a good conversation.

"So, what's your name?" I asked and ate a Tostada and I didn't want to eat the Chile.

She responded with a smile. "My name is Luz Maria Fitzgerald Estrada."

"What a pretty name!" I exclaimed. This girl looks so familiar! Where have I seen her before. Wait, I couldn't believe that she's the same girl I rescued a couple of years ago from those drug dealers. She was just twelve years old at the time I saved her life. Well Luz Maria has transformed into a beautiful girl.

Luz smiled and started to blush. "How cute! And, what is your name?"

"My name is Mauricio de la Vega." I also smiled.

She smiled and said, "I like that name. Don't take it the wrong way but your name sounds like a character from a Soap Opera. Like those pretty boys characters that try to act all emotional and all they want is to get the girl into bed and spend time in the beauty salon."

"Well I've heard that before. But I do have a middle name and I don't like it at all."

"What is it? Tell me?" She asked with a huge smile on her face.

"To be honest, it's really embarrassing and I'm sure if we get to know each other a little bit better. I'll tell you."

Then the waitress brought our food to the table and Luz and I finished the Tostadas and the drinks and she wanted more. "Can you bring us more Tostadas and Chile, Please?" She asked the waitress and smiled. "After all Mauricio de la Vega is paying." She giggled and said, "I'm kidding, Mate. And I haven't eaten Tostadas in a long time."

I looked at the waitress and said "Refill. Please and thank you!." And I looked at Luz and said, "Well I don't mind paying just as long I get the chance to get to know you a little bit better." I smiled and I remember her lovely smile and her pretty green eyes.

She winked at me and we started eating our food and I like the way Luz ate, she is very proper with good table manners. She put the napkin on her legs and very gently she ate her Flautas.

"How old are you?" I asked.

"I'm eighteen years old and what about you."

"Twenty-one years old and I'll be twenty-two in two weeks." I said.

"That's cool." She said.

The waitress came back to the table and she brought more Tostadas and Chile and our Cokes and she asked us if everything was okay and we said yes. "Are you from El Paso?" I asked.

"Yes, I was born here and I was raised in Belfast, Ireland. I'm half Cuban on my mommy's side of the family and I'm half Irish from my daddy's side of the family. Well my daddy has been working overseas and sometimes I get to travel with him. And I was attending a boarding school and I usually came back home around the holidays and I get the chance to spend the holidays with my mommy. My parents got separated when I was a little girl but they still get along very well." She smiled and ate.

"How long have you been here?" I asked.

"I arrived two days ago. My mommy and I were happy to see each other. And I'm having so much fun with my mommy. And the other day my mommy even took me out to eat at *Chico's Tacos*. I haven't been there in a long time and Ireland doesn't have *Chico's Tacos*." She smiled and ate.

"Since, I've come back home from college, I've been craving to eat at *Chico's Tacos*."

"When did you came back home?" She asked.

"I arrived in the morning. And I was gone four years and I came back because I really missed my family a lot. My dad isn't here because he is in the

Federal Bureau Investigation and he gets to travel a lot and I'm guessing that he is in Europe right now. My mom is a Police Officer and she's thinking about retiring. And I hope to see my dad before I go back to Missouri."

"I know how you must feel." She smiled and we sat there talking more than eating because we weren't really that hungry at all. Luz saved her Flautas for her mother and I saved the Tacos for my sister. She looked at her watch and said. "It's getting late, my mommy is going to get worried for me. I should be going home right now!"

"If you want I can give you a ride to your house." I said.

"I would like that. Thank you." She smiled.

We got up and I paid for the bill and they said goodbye to us. Luz and I left the restaurant and got into the truck and I took her to her mother's house which turned out to be only five blocks away from my house. I parked in the driveway and we started talking once again.

"Luz, I know this is too soon to ask you but will you like to go out tomorrow or later on in the afternoon?" I asked.

"My mommy wasn't feeling too good this afternoon." She responded.

"Is she sick?" I asked.

"Well this morning my mommy had an asthma attack and thank God I was there to help her out. But my mommy is going to be okay and I will let you know if I can go out later on in the evening or tomorrow night."

"You want my number?" I asked.

"Yes, and I will give you mine." She sad.

I took out my cell phone and gave her my cell number and she gave me her home phone number and I put her home number into the cell phone. And Luz was getting her things together when her mother open the door and came outside. Her mother was wondering who had parked in the driveway. Luz gave me a quick kiss in my cheek and got out of the truck and hugged her mother. Luz and her mother stayed outside talking and both of them waived at me as I left and drove to my house. And I started thinking about the kiss she gave me on my cheek and I also remember the kiss we gave to each other on the mouth. And that was just couple of years ago when I rescued her from those drug dealers. I was so happy to see her again and Luz got so pretty and hot and she has a nice butt as well. She has grown up and turned into a beautiful girl. So, I finally arrived at my house, my mother was outside talking to a neighbor and they were both drinking Lemonade. And I said hi to them and went inside the house to put the food and the snacks inside the refrigerator. And I went to Tania's room and the door was open, and she was talking to someone on the phone and she smiled at me. I sat on her bed and she hanged up the phone. She also smiled.

"Tania, I have to talk to you about something."

"About what?" She asked.

"I met a girl at *Big 8*." I smiled.

"Really! What's her name?" She asked.

"Well her name is Luz Maria Fitzgerald Estrada. She is eighteen years old and she is the most beautiful girl I have ever met in my entire life." I gave her a huge grin and I started describing Luz to my sister. And all she did was stare at me with a huge smile on her face and she wanted to hear more about her. After I finished talking about her, Tania, was still staring at me and she was smiling and I said, "Tania, I know I made a promise that I was going to take you fishing. I don't want you to get mad at me."

"It's okay, I understand. We can go fishing some other time." Tania smiled.

"You really mean that?" I asked.

"I'm glad you met a girl at the grocery store."

"I don't want you to be upset with me." I said.

"Mauricio, you are my big brother and I love you a lot. I want you to be happy." She smiled.

"You are too kind, Tania and I hope that you get the chance to meet her in person." I said.

Tania started giggling and said, "Too late, Mauricio, and I just got off the phone with the bloody leprechaun and Luz told me that she met you at the grocery store and she seems to like you and Luz cannot wait for you guys to go out later on in the evening. No worries!"

"How do you know her?" I asked.

Tania responded with a smile, "Well Luz and I have known each other since we were little kids, Luz is like my little sister. We met in a mother and daughter summer camp and we became best friends."

"Tania, I don't feel comfortable going out with your best friend." I said and I completely forgot that they are best friends. They are closer than sisters.

"Don't say that, Mauricio. Luz said the same thing as you and it will be great to see you two together, and you guys will make a cute couple. She is going to call you in two hours because I convince her to go out with you. You gave her a good impression because you were a gentlemen. And I truly hope that you guys get to know each other better. And I really hope that you tell her more about you, because she hates it when people keep secrets from her." Tania smiled and got up to hug me and I stayed in her room to watch a movie for two hours.

And two hours later Luz called me and said she was ready to go out. I went to the garage and took out my two old bicycles, boy did they had cob webs all over. So I started cleaning them and I put them in back of the truck and I took a quick shower and got out, got dressed and I went to her house. When I arrived at her house, Luz and her mother were outside. Her mother was watering the plants and Luz was drinking Apple Juice and they were laughing about something. Well Luz was wearing a pink shirt and blue shorts and sandals. She had her hair into a ponytail and I parked in the driveway, and got out of the truck. Luz went back inside the house to put the glass on the kitchen and came back outside. Her mother turned off the water and smiled.

"Mauricio, this is my, my, my, mother. My mommy!" She was nervously when she introduce me to her mother. Well her mother and I smiled, we shook hands but she hugged me.

"Hi, Mauricio, I'm Alma Estrada."

"Nice to meet you." I said.

She smiled and asked, "Where are you two going?"

"Oh, we're going to ride the bikes around Marty Robbins Park. Maybe get an ice-cream." I said and smiled.

"So, Luz told me that you paid for her flowers and her planting seeds. And you guys went to eat at *Ciro's*." Alma said.

"Yes, I did. And I did what it was right and I want to get to know her a little bit better." I smiled and while I was talking to her mother, Luz was just standing there smiling. She wasn't much of a talker and all she did was shrugged her shoulders and smiled and was listening to our conversation. And I kept looking at her mother and I felt like that I had seen her mother somewhere before. But I remember the day I saved Luz's life and her mother and my mother came running towards the park and they tried to save her from the likes of me. Well I took her to the Hospital. But where else have I seen her mother before today and the incident at Marty Robbins Park.

"I can tell that you are a great guy, Mauricio, and I'm glad Luz has made a new friend today. She has known Tania all of her life and they are like sisters. And did you know that your mother and I have known each other since we were little kids. We grew up together in Mexico City. I moved here when I turn eighteen years old."

"Have we met before? Because you seem so familiar." I said.

"Well we hardly saw each other because you were always hanging out with your friends and you were too busy with your school work. You and I ran into each other at Clarke Middle School."

"Really! When!" I exclaimed.

"We kind of ran into each other when you made the Honor Roll." She smiled.

"'Oh, Yes. I remember now. I received my honor roll and I started running around the school like a crazy person and I bump into you in the hallway. You congratulated me and I told you that it was my sixth honor roll." I smiled.

"You even hugged me and hugged everyone in the school." She said and smiled.

Luz looked at me and smiled and I was anxious to go to the park and I could tell that she was anxious to go too. "I've go to go now, mommy." Luz said.

"Don't worry about me, Honey. I will be fine. You two have fun in the park. Good luck in your date."

"I will take care of her." I said.

"I know you will. I trust you, Mauricio!" She smiled.

Luz kissed her mother on the cheek and we got into the truck and went to Marty Robbins Park. We took out the bicycles from the back of the truck and rode them around the park. We passed a little league baseball game and continued riding the bikes and then we stopped to rest and sat down in the shade of a big tree.

"Do you have any brothers or sisters?" I asked.

"I'm the only child from my parents first marriage. My mother couldn't have anymore kids. She has been through enough problems in her life." She said.

"What kind of problems?" I asked.

"Well my parents went through a terrible divorce. My daddy moved to Belfast, Ireland and got married. He usually came to work at Washington D.C. I don't know what field my daddy was in the FBI. I think he worked with your dad. And my mommy stayed single and raised me when I came to visit her around the holidays. And I'm proud of my mommy because she is the most respected Teacher in the city of El Paso, Texas but she also wants to retire and move on with her life."

"My mom also wants to retire form the Police Force and I know this was her dream job since she was a little kid."

"I don't blame your mom at all. Well she has been under of a lot of stress for the past couple of years. Because The Dark Cowboy wore everybody out and I never seen your mom this stressed out."

"I cannot imagine what she's going to through." I smiled at her and I wanted to see if Luz remembers me saving her life from those drug dealers but anyway I wanted to get to know her a little bit better. "Do you get along with your step-mom?"

"Yes! She loves me a lot. We're best friends. I love her Irish accent and she taught me the history of Ireland and the language. And I know three languages. English, Spanish, and Gaelic. At the beginning I was nervous when I started talking in Gaelic but now I became fluent in Gaelic. And I have two half sisters from my daddy's second marriage. I'm the oldest but both of my mommy's and my daddy still spoil me. They treat me like a Princess." She smiled.

We smiled and watched the butterflies going around us and there was a ladybug that landed on top of Luz's arm and she giggled and then the ladybug flew away. And I picked up a yellow sunflower and gave it to Luz and she started to smell it. "So, what grade are you in?" I asked.

"I already graduated from high school well I was in a boarding school over there and it was an all girl school. My mommy went to Ireland and saw me graduate. And I plan to go to college here in the states. I'm waiting for a letter from Columbia University and I hope to get their letter anytime this summer. And I'm planning to become a reporter." She smiled.

"That's great and I hope you get accepted." I said.

"What college do you go to?" She asked.

"I'm going to The University of Missouri. And I want to become a Lawyer and I want to make the de la Vega family proud of me and I want to help the people of Spain and this country as well." I smiled and we continued talking for awhile and watched the little league baseball game. Actually we just looked at each other and smiled.

"Have you had a lot of girlfriends?" She asked.

"To be honest with you, I only had one and I had a lot of dates when I was living in Missouri." Yeah, I had dates with college drunk girls and I killed three hundred and fifty three people.

"Are you serious?" She asked.

"Yes, You thought I had more than one." I said.

"Well, you paid for my things so I figured you do this every time you want to meet a girl." She said and smiled.

"You are the first one." I smiled and asked her. "What about you, Luz? Is there someone special in your life?"

"Well I never had a boyfriend at all and it's hard to find the right guy these days. Most guys just wants to have sex and leave the girl pregnant." She looked at me and smiled. "But a few years ago there was someone special in my life but I never saw him again and I hope to see him again."

Well I'm pretty sure that I'm her special someone and I was glad that she remembers the day I rescued her. And all I could say to her is, "You never had a boyfriend at all? Look at you, you are so beautiful and hot."

She blushed. "That is sweet of you."

"So, what was his name?" I asked.

"You're not going to believe me at all and you are going to laugh at me." She smiled.

"I'm not! Try me" I smiled.

"Well his name is The Dark Cowboy and a few years ago he rescued me from a pack of drug dealers! It was right here at Marty Robbins Park. I was attacked and The Dark Cowboy came to my rescue and took me to Thomason Hospital. And on the day I got out of Thomason Hospital, The Dark Cowboy came to visit me well of course he came to my room during the night. The Dark Cowboy was standing by my window and I came into my room and I was happy to see him again. And I thank him for saving my life and I received my first kiss ever. And I hope to see him again." She smiled.

"See I'm not laughing!" I just smiled and I was proud that she remembers the kiss I gave her.

"Yes, you are! You are making of fun me right now!" She smiled and we continue to look at each other and there was a huge smile coming from both of us. Then I decided to impress her, so I got on my bicycle and started doing my infamous bicycles "tricks." Luz was sitting down and she was smiling and paid close attention but I could tell that she wasn't that impressed but she continue to smile. I kept doing my tricks and I was doing great but I didn't see the large rock on the grass and I fell to the ground and landed on my butt for the second time. And Luz came running towards me.

"Are you okay?" She asked.

"I'm so embarrassed and I wanted to show you my bicycles tricks." I said and I was in pain, not.

"You don't have to impress me. I like you for who you are. Just be yourself. I don't want you to act like the other guys." She said.

"I won't do it again! Don't be mad at me." I said.

"I'm not mad, I'm just glad you didn't get hurt." She smiled.

"You are too kind." I said.

"I can't wait to tell Tania what you did today. It will be funny story for so many years." She smiled.

"You are you so bad, Luz Maria Fitzgerald Estrada." I grabbed her by the waist and I started to tickle her and she started laughing out loud. And I was on top of her and I continued to tickle her and she couldn't stop laughing and she was turning red. She said, "I'm sorry!" And then I stopped but she was still smiling and we just looked at each other and she smiled and once again she kissed me on my cheek and we got up and went back under the shade tree. We talked all afternoon long and we continued to watch the little league game. Luz was rooting for the other team and I was rooting in the team in red. So, the team in red won and it was a shutout and I was happy for my team.

"My team won!" I yelled.

She looked at me and said, "You bloody wancer!' She smiled and I looked at her and started to tickle her again. "I'm sorry! I wont say bad things about you!" She continued to laugh and we continued to talk. So, on that day Luz and I were getting to know each other a little bit better. Then we watched the sun set behind the mountains and it was so beautiful. Luz was leaning against me and I put my arm around her and I wanted to hold her tight, and kiss her for a long time. And it was getting dark and we got up to put the bicycles in the back of the truck. I started the engine and went to her house. I parked in the driveway and we talked some more. I could see her eyes sparkle in the darkness and her smile.

"Did you had fun?" I asked.

"I had a great time." She smiled.

"Well me too, Luz." I said and smiled. "Luz, I wanted to ask you something.

Tomorrow my mom celebrates her birthday and I was hoping you and your mom could join us. You know the whole family will be together."

She smiled and responded, "I would like to go. I haven't seen Tania and your mom in a long time. It will be great to see them again and I hope you and I get to hang out and I hope we can also dance." She smiled.

"That will be great!" I smiled and I got out of the truck and opened the door for her. I walked her to the front door and we just looked at each other. She quickly kissed me on my mouth and went inside the house and blew me a kiss and closed the door. I got into the truck and went back to my house, and I went to my room and I fell asleep as soon I landed on my bed.

CHAPTER NINETEEN

OUR PERFECT RELATIONSHIP

I woke up the next day with a big smile on my face and I was hoping to see Luz very soon and I wanted to kiss her all over her body and have her in my arms all day and all night long. But I wanted to take my time and get to know her a little better and I don't want to be in the same situation with the other drunken girls in Columbia, Missouri. And I got up and went to the kitchen, my mother and Tania were in the kitchen making breakfast and they were listening to the radio. My mother was making scrambled eggs and my baby sister, Tania, was making pancakes and I went to hug them, so tight and they looked at me very surprised. Then I walked into the living room and Tania followed me and she was kind of curious about our date.

"I'm happy." I said.

"You kissed her!" She exclaimed.

"Just a quick kiss and that was enough to make me happy. Luz is the most incredible girl I have ever met in my life. She is different from the rest of the girls I dated in college." I smiled and I was grinning from ear to ear.

"Well I'm glad that you guys had fun together and I am glad that you guys are happy with each other and I hope you guys will love each other and get married and have a lot of kids." She said.

"I hope so! But do you think she'll accept my past?" I asked.

"Of course, Luz is going to accept your past. Just be honest with her. She will accept you and she will know that you made a couple of mistakes in your life. Remember what I told you, she gets pissed off when people aren't honest with her! She may be fragile but she has the Irish temperament!" She smiled.

"Well I truly hope that she can accept my past because I really like her a lot." I smiled and hugged her.

"I remember that smiled and it's good to have you back, Mauricio." Tania smiled and her tears started coming down her face. We just hugged each other and we went back to the kitchen to eat scramble eggs and pancakes, and there were so delicious. And on that morning my mother received her early birthday surprise. The three of us were just sitting in the living room, and we were watching television, when a black van pulled into the driveway. We quickly got up and went outside to see who parked in the driveway. The side door opened and it was my father and he came back from Washington D.C and I know he wasn't in a good mood to come back to El Paso because I saw that weird smile he has when he's not in the good mood. But my parents were happy to see each other and my father was glad to see me after all these years and I was glad to see him again. So, later on in the afternoon Tania and my mother started decorating the backyard. My father and I went to *Big 8* and bought paper plates, cups, spoons, forks, and the rest of the food. I told my father that I met Luz and she gave me a quick kiss and he was happy for us. And we went home my parents and Tania were making the food while I was getting ready for the big night.

Then all of us got dressed up and I called Luz around five o'clock in the afternoon and she said that she was ready to go. I got into the truck and went to pick them up, and when I got there her mother was already outside waiting for me. I was outside talking to her mother when Luz came outside to lock the door and she was so beautiful. She looked like a Princess and she looked at me and gave me a shy smile and I was drooling all over her. She had been to the beauty salon for a perm and had her nails done too. She was wearing a black silk dress and I was loss for words. She just looked gorgeous that night. And I helped them get into the truck and went to my house. When I parked in the driveway, Luz and her mother were shock to see a lot of people that showed up for my mother's birthday party.

My parents came outside to greet them and they were happy to see each other. And we went inside the house, and Luz saw Tania hanging out with her girl friends. She went to cover Tania's eyes. "Guess, who you red eye bugger?" She asked.

Tania responded, "I recognize that horrible smell of perfume, your bloody accent and I don't know where your hands have been." Tania turn around and smiled. "You, bloody leprechaun!" They smiled and they hugged each other. They were happy to see each other after all these years and they stayed talking in the living room but Luz wasn't much of talker. Well she was standing there listening to them talk while she laughs and smiles. I went to the kitchen to get something to drink and I was standing there talking with one of my mother's friends and I could hear Tania asking Luz about the date we had yesterday. Well she told them what went on and they were happy for us. Just then my old friends from high school showed up at the party and I haven't seen them since the day we planned to go inside the secret Mental Institution. So, anyway I went upstairs to get my mother's birthday present and meanwhile Tania greeted my friends and they all got to know each other a little bit better. Well everyone went to the backyard and the girls were dancing around but my friend Karina and Luz started talking.

"How long have you known Mauricio?" She asked.

"Since we were kids. He's like my brother" She responded.

"Really!" Luz exclaimed.

"Yes. How did you meet him?"

"We met yesterday at the grocery store, I was buying flowers and bags of seed but I didn't have enough money to pay for them. Well Mauricio paid for my flowers and after that we went to Marty Robbins Park and just hang out. He then started showing me his tricks with the bicycle and fell to the ground." She said and smiled.

"It sounds like you guys had a lot fun." Karina said.

"Karina! How come, Mauricio only had one girlfriend? He is a nice guy and he could make any girl happy." She said.

Karina smiled and said, "It's been a long time since I've seen Mauricio happy." Karina said and was drinking her beer. "He deserves to be happy."

"You have been a good friend to him all these years." Luz smiled.

"Trust me he deserves to be happy! He was once happy but something bad happen and he was miserable. I hope you can make him happy!" Karina smiled.

Then I came back to the backyard and saw Luz and Karina were looking up at the stars. And Luz was trying to connect the stars and she saw me and smiled. Also the girls came back and all of us were together.

"Are you having fun, Luz?" Tania asked.

"Yes." She responded.

"Luz was telling me that you got on the bicycle and started showing her your infamous bicycles tricks and fell to the ground." Karina smiled.

"Yes, I did. And I was so embarrassed."

"Same old Mauricio, always trying to impress the girls with his bicycles tricks and falls off the bicycle." Karina said.

Luz was giving me her look and she was wondering about this. Then everyone was making fun of me. "This is not the first time that Mauricio has fallen off the bicycle when he was trying to impress someone."

"Don't listen to them they are making up stories about me." I said and looked at Luz and smiled.

We were talking for a while and it was around midnight when my Lieutenant, Karina Reyes was getting ready to go to her house, so I decided to walk her to her nice 2006 beautiful brand new car. "Luz is a great girl. And I cannot believe that it's only been two days and she really likes you a lot." She smiled.

"I know and I'm happy that I met her for the second time. And I'm taking it slow you know one day at a time. The Dark Cowboy saved her life at Marty Robbins Park. And I, Mauricio de la Vega met her at the grocery store. And I got to say that I really like her and I haven't stop thinking about her!" I smiled.

Karina looked at me and said, "Well it's really good to see you again. And I am glad to see you happy. And I hope you enjoy your relationship with Luz and I know that you're a good man but it's that thing that you have inside your body that's controlling you!"

"Well let's cut to the chase, Karina. I found something very interesting in the secret blown up Mental Institution." I said.

Karina was afraid to ask, "Well what did you found out?"

"That my father hired those men to come after me and Eliza. He's responsible for her death!" I exclaimed.

"Why would your father do that?" She asked.

"I don't know, Karina. And I let my ego get in the way and I killed him and as the matter of fact everyone died in the secret Mental Institution. And a tornado destroyed the building and the dead bodies went flying all over town!" I smiled.

"You said that you will not kill anyone! This was suppose to be a quick in and out! You promised that you were not going to kill again and you wanted to live in peace!" Karina exclaimed.

"Well I lied and I couldn't help it and remember I'm a psychotic killer! People described me as a border line psycho path. I got addicted to killing, so many people and there is nobody that can't stop me. But I was able to spare Doctor Juanita Van Der AA's life. She was talking to me about the Bible and I should forgive my father for everything he has done to me. Maybe I have changed my life for the better. I'm a good guy after all because I spared little Samantha Jones's life, I spared Luz Maria Estrada's life, and Doctor Juanita Van Der AA's life. But I'm not going to spare my father's life!" I smiled.

Karina looked at me and smiled. "Well don't worry, Mauricio. Your father's secrets is going to come out very soon. Just make the order and I'll check him out. So, I'm going home and have fun with Luz and I will see you later on in the summer."

"I will and take care of yourself." I said.

"That's not all I heard!" We turned around and Sonia went up to us. She looked at me and smiled, "I heard that you were sleeping with a bunch of drunken women! And you had a tough time because you were miserable over there! I know how you are, Mauricio. And let me guess on your first date you slept with them!"

"Yes!" I responded.

Sonia looked at Karina, "Were you behind this?"

"No!" Karina said.

"I didn't think so! So, your father hired those intruders?"

"Yes!" I responded.

"Maybe someone else is behind this!" Karina said.

"Vito Mancini or Pablo de la Vega?" Sonia asked.

"Both, maybe!" Karina said.

"Well we're going to find out! And Luz is waiting for me!" I said.

Karina smiled and kissed me on my cheek and said, "I'm going keep my eyes on the city and Sonia is going to hear their conversations! Well I'm going to go home and I'll see you later!" Karina smiled and got into her brand new 2006 car and went to her house. So, Sonia and I went back to the party in the backyard.

Sonia found a cute guy that she liked and she went up to him. Tania and Luz were sitting down and they were talking and laughing and they were watching everyone danced around. And I sat down with them and Luz put her hand around my arm and she leaned against me. We watched everyone dance and we saw Luz's mother dancing with a young Police Officer and they were dancing to a Kumbia song. Then Luz got up and grabbed my hand and we started dancing too. As we were dancing we were looking at each other and we were about to kiss until we heard Tania cheering us on. Luz started to blush and hid her face on my chest. Our parents didn't mind and they knew that we were having fun.

Luz and I wanted to be alone, so we decided to go somewhere where we won't be bothered at all. We sat behind the tailgate of my truck and Luz leaned against me and I put my arm around her waist and I started to tickle her and she was giggling. And she got up and put her arms around my neck and I had my arms around her waist. I could feel her breathing and she giggled too. We held each other for awhile and we had our first kiss under the moonlight but this was our second kiss. We kissed for about five minutes and there was a little tongue action as well. I was holding her so tight and once again I could hear her breathe. She looked at me and smiled and giggled and we were still holding on to each other and kissing.

We looked at each other and I asked her, "What's on your mind, Luz?"

She smiled and responded, "Well I'm thinking about this being my second real kiss ever and I'm happy that it's you kissing me and protecting me."

"So, this was your second kiss? What was the name of the guy you kissed again" I asked.

She giggled once again and responded, "His name is The Dark Cowboy and then you! And when was the last time you kissed a girl?"

"Well I dated a lot of drunken girls in Missouri and I did a lot of things with them." I responded.

'I'm getting jealous. How can I compete with those girls?" She asked.

"I was just experimenting with them and I wasn't looking for a girlfriend over there. But I may feel something good about you because you are not like them, you are way different from them. They were just college drunk girls. And I didn't like that life at all." I smiled and Luz is the same girl I met a few years back and she even giggled when we were kissing but now she's all grown up.

"I don know how those drunken girls look themselves in the mirror and do the same thing everyday."

"Let's talk about something else." I said.

"You pick!" She said.

"What are the things you see in a guy?" I asked.

"As long he's honest, caring, and I don't go for looks. I don't like pretty boys because they are so dull! And what do you see in a girl?"

"I'm holding her right now and kissing her. I really like you and I don't care about the other women."

"I also like you a lot and I'm glad you're protecting me." She smiled and kissed me.

I smiled and asked her, "What are the things you like to do?"

"Well let's see. I love to dance you know ballet, I like to sing and my mommy taught me how to sing. And I like to go swimming, spending time with my friends and family, and listen to music. And I dream of marrying my Prince Charming." She smiled. "What about you?"

"I like to collect football cards, I also went clubbing with my friends when I was living in Columbia, Missouri. I like to spend time with my family more than my friends. And I like to listen to music." I smiled and there's something else that I might have left out. For instance killing three hundred plus people, and lead the team into action.

"What kind of food do you like?" She asked.

"All kinds and what about you?"

"The same." She smiled.

"You know what I like to do right now. There is something I want to taste again." I said and smiled."

"Tell me!"

"The taste of your lips and I want to hold you all night and kiss you."

"Can you promise something?" She asked.

"Anything you want!" I said.

"I don't want any secrets between us. I want our relationship to be open about everything." She said.

"I promise, now come here to me." I smiled and we started kissing again and held each other for awhile. We stayed outside holding on to each other for a lot of hours. Then it was around two o'clock in the morning and everyone had gone home for the night. My father and Tania were already asleep. My mother, Luz, Alma, and I were in the kitchen talking and drinking coffee. My mother loaned Luz some of her clothes, so she went to the restroom and changed. She came back to the kitchen and was wearing a long white shirt and sweats and she had on sandals but my mother told her to keep them. Well I gave my mother her birthday present and she opened the present and it was an expensive gold necklace that what I got her when I was in Columbia, Missouri. She was happy and she gave me a huge hug. If she only knew where I got the money to buy her present.

"So, Alma are you going to call that young hot Police Officer. You know that one you were dancing with?" My mother asked.

Alma responded with a huge smile on her face. "Well, he's too young for me, Beatrice. I'm a lot older than him and I'm old enough to be with his mother. I'm fifty-two years old and he's thirty-two years old."

"Come on, Alma. Is not going to hurt you to go out with someone younger. Well you can have."

Alma interrupted her! "Beatrice, not in front of my daughter or your son."

"I'm a big girl, Mommy. Besides I want you to be happy and you never know something good might come out in this relationship and is not going you to hurt to have sex with someone younger." Luz smiled.

"She's right, Alma." My mother said.

"I'll think about it. After all my daughter is growing up and maybe she end up marrying her Prince charming somewhere in the future." Alma smiled and hugged her daughter so tight.

Luz looked at me and smiled and kissed me on the cheek. "I hope so."

"So, Beatrice, my daughter tells me that you want to retire from the Police Force." Alma said.

"I'm thinking about it. What about you?" My mother asked.

"I'm also thinking about it." Alma said.

"Our kids are all grown up now and we could move on and try other things." My mother smiled.

"But Luz is still our baby and we can still spoil her. It doesn't matter what we do as long we get to spoil her!" Alma smiled and was kissing her on her cheek and sat her down on her lap. "My little Princess."

Alma and my mother started to tickle her and I was looking at her laughing. "I cannot believe that she's all grown up. The last time I saw you, Luz, you were a cute twelve year old girl. It's ashamed that we didn't get to spend that much time together because of your injury and I hope that this summer we can spend a lot of time together." My mother smiled.

"I hope so." She smiled.

Alma looked at Luz and said, "I hope that Mauricio spoils you and treats you like a Princess."

"Don't worry, Alma. She's in good hands and our relationship is going to be like fairy tale. The Beauty falls in love with a monster like me!" I smiled and Luz blew me a kiss and yeah I'm a monster that kills people.

"You're not a monster, Mauricio. You are a handsome young man. And you two were made for each other." Alma smiled.

"You know I was wondering where my other daughter is at?" My mother asked.

"Madelyn!" Luz responded.

"I didn't see her tonight!" My mother said.

"I guess she couldn't make it. Tania and Jackie haven't seen her in the last couple of weeks. They told me that she's dating Primo Mancini. I hope she's happy!" Luz smiled.

"Tania told me that Primo makes her happy. Well I'm sure that they went to Amsterdam for the summer vacation." Alma smiled.

We continued to talk and by now it was three o'clock in the morning, Alma and Luz were already tired so I took them home. I parked in the driveway and walked them to their house. Alma gave me a kiss on the cheek and said goodnight to me and went into the house. Luz and I stayed by ourselves and we kissed and hugged so tight. I told her that I will call her as soon I got back to my house. And I got into the truck and drove to my house and I parked in the driveway of my house and called Luz and I told her that I got home safe. We said goodnight to each other and I went to my room and fell asleep right of away.

The next day I woke up around eleven o'clock in the morning and it was one hundred degrees and it was so damn hot that I could have boiled an Egg on the sidewalk along with Bacon and Hash Brown. So, I got up and went to the kitchen to get a glass of water and I drank all of it and got some more water. And Luz called me on my cell phone, and she told me to come over, so we can talk and have ice-cream and kiss as well. I took a nice cold shower and got dressed and went to her house. I parked in the driveway and she was sitting down in her mother's rocking chair. She was wearing a white tank top, red shorts, and she had on her flip flops and she was glad to see me. I went up to her and I hugged her so tight and I lift her up but her back was sweating but

I didn't care. While I was lifting her up, her flip flops fell on the grass but she put her feet on top of my mine and we kissed.

"Hey, Sweetie!" She exclaimed.

"Hey, Hunny Bunny." I smiled and kissed her.

"You called me Hunny Bunny! How sweet of you." She smiled.

"I missed you a lot." I said.

"Me too." She smiled.

"But I missed you more." I said.

"No! I missed you more than you missed me." She smiled and put her arms around my neck and we kissed for a couple of seconds."

"How long have you been outside waiting for me?" I asked her.

"Since I called you." She responded with a smile.

"Oh, really. What happens if a pervert comes up to you and grabs you, and takes advantage of you." I smiled and we kissed.

"I'll let him take advantage of me." She smiled and kissed me.

"You're so bad, Luz!" I exclaimed and we kissed for a long time.

While we were holding on to each other, there was a fresh breeze and it blew most of Luz's hair on her face and she put her hair into a pony tail. We were in the shade talking and we were about to go inside the house when she told me to get her flip flops. So, I went to pick them up and gave them to her, she smiled and kissed me. We went to the kitchen and Alma starting making us sandwiches and she sat down and started talking about Luz. She was telling me a lot of funny stories about Luz and I looked at her and she shrugged her shoulders and she blushed and she was eating her sandwich and she also smiled. And the phone rang and Luz went to answer the phone. Alma and I just looked at each other and smiled. And she touched my shoulder and asked me something, "Tell me, Mauricio do you ever think about, Eliza?"

I looked at her and I was really in shock but she smiled. And Luz came back to the kitchen and said, "It was my daddy he wanted to know how you were doing. Well he said everything is fine in Ireland. He wants to talk to you, mommy."

"That's good, Sweetie. I'm also glad that he is doing fine."

It was an awkward moment for me because Alma had mentioned Eliza to me. I haven't really thought about her in a very long time and I didn't know why she would mention her name. Did Alma know her? And why would she mention Eliza's name after Luz left to answer the phone? So, Luz came back and gave her mother the telephone and she started talking to Luz's father. Luz sat down and we were just staring at each other and smiling. I was touching her hand and I kissed her hand and my cell phone rang and it was Tania and we talked for a couple of seconds and I hanged up the phone.

"Who was it?" Luz asked.

"That was my sister, Tania. She wants you to come over." I said.

"Oh, cool! There are a lot of things I want to talk to my big sister." She smiled and she went up to her mother. "I'm going out, Mommy. Tell daddy that I love him so much and a big kiss to my sisters and to my other step-mommy." She smiled and kissed her mother on her cheek and she was talking to her ex husband and we said goodbye to her mother. We went outside holding hands and I open the door for Luz. She smiled and went inside and I went inside the truck and went to my house. I parked in the driveway and we got out of the truck and my sister, Tania came outside to greet us with a huge smile on her face. She quickly grabbed Luz's hand and they were walking in the living room and I could hear them talk on the way to her room. My parents were in the kitchen making lunch and I sat down with them.

"So, what do you think about Luz?" I asked.

"She is a nice girl. And she is like our daughter." My mother said.

"Just don't get your hopes up." My father said.

'Why do you say that?" I asked.

"What your father and I are trying to tell you is that we don't want the two of you to think that your relationship is always going to be perfect. There are going to be some tough times ahead." My mother said.

"What are you two talking about? Luz is perfect and I know there is nothing to fight about." I said.

"Mauricio, there is no such thing as the perfect relationship." My father said.

"You guys are in love and kiss all the time." I said.

"That's fifty percent that we love each other and the other fifty percent is we talk about how much money we're spending and among other things." He said.

"You have to work extra hard in a relationship and don't expect that this relationship to be all perfect. I love you guys so much to see you get hurt." My mother said.

"You know that your mother and I went through Hell when we couldn't capture The Dark Cowboy. We didn't sleep in the same room for a couple of weeks, so you need to work extra hard." He said.

"Just take it slow, Okay. Remember what happened in your previous relationship. I hate to see you two get hurt." My mother said.

"You guys are right!" I smiled and I couldn't believe that my beloved parents slept in different rooms because they couldn't captured me and I knew that I gave them a hard time in their relationship but I know that their love is strong. And my father still blames The Dark Cowboy for his failures.

Then Luz and Tania came down to the kitchen and they were still laughing and Luz kissed me on the cheek. Tania looked at my parents and said, "I cannot believe that you guys slept in different rooms. You see that's why I want to become a District Attorney. I want to be the one that throws The Dark Cowboy in jail for the rest of his life. Maybe the death penalty"

"Honey, don't talk like that." My mother said.

"I know you guys had a hard time capturing The Dark Cowboy and I know that you two got soft on him. And not to mention that my best friend, Luz, is always defending that psychotic killer." Tania was upset and looked at Luz. "And I'm glad that he rescued you from those drug dealers and the fact is that you are alive but The Dark Cowboy needs to pay for all the crimes that he committed over the years." Tania said.

"Well The Dark Cowboy did saved my life from those drug dealers and I think you should be happy about that Tania. And you should thank him that he saved my life." Luz smiled and hugged Tania.

"Well I am happy because you are my baby sister and I worry for you sometimes. But you need to know that The Dark Cowboy attacked my brother, whose now your boyfriend and nearly killed him in our living room and he threatened to kill my daddy and my mommy too. So, The Dark Cowboy needs to pay for his actions for good. End of conversation! And not buts, Luz!" Tania smiled and kissed her little sister on her cheek and they sat down with us and we started talking all afternoon long. And then my parents decided to tell Luz, so many funny stories about me and she told my parents what I did at Marty Robbins Park. All of them were turning red and they couldn't stop laughing at me and they were making fun at me as well. My mother took out the family album and showed her pictures of me when I was a little psychotic killer! "Beatrice, guess what cute name you son has for me." Luz smiled.

"Luz how many times do I have to tell you to call me mom. You're like a daughter to me!" My mother smiled.

"Sorry, I forgot. Mommy, guess what cute name, Mauricio has for me!" Luz smiled.

"Bloody Irish!" Tania smiled.

"Tania, behave." My mother smiled and looked at Luz. "I don't know but I hope it's something

"Your son called me, Hunny Bunny." She smiled.

"How sweet of him!" Tania smiled.

"Your son is so adorable." Luz smiled and kissed me on the cheek.

"Yes, I'm so adorable." I smiled.

My parents continued to tell Luz more stories about me well most of them were the silly things I did when I was a little boy and I'm glad that Luz didn't hear the stories when I was killing people and saw those pictures of all the people that I've killed over the years and it was a good thing. Then it was around eight o'clock that night where the girls were making dinner and they were laughing and talking. My father and I were in the garage talking.

"You know, Son. I'm so glad that you are about to finish college. But did you realize that you had us worried all those years ago."

"I'm sorry, Dad. I was having too much fun with drunken girls and at least I called on the holidays and wrote letters." I smiled and I was wondering if you hired those intruders to come after me and Eliza.

"Well your mother was really worried for you and we understand that you are growing up. So, what are your plans after college?" He asked.

"I'm studying to become a Lawyer and you know I'm planning to make the family proud of me. That's my destiny." I responded with a smile.

"I like that. But have you decided to join me in the FBI liked we talked about because we need new blood to go after Vito Mancini." My father said.

"No thank you, Dad, Because I want to do my own thing. And I know that the de le Vega's have done a lot of things to make them feel good about themselves and I'm about to end the streak. I'm not following in my parents footsteps and I'm planning to do something else in my life." Like becoming a legendary serial killer and yet that bastard of my father couldn't keep up with me and still wants me to follow his silly dream.

"Son, your sister, Tania, wants to become a District Attorney. The de la Vega's have been in the big time for generation and generation. You have the opportunity of becoming somebody important in your life. You need to leave a legacy for your kids. Don't you want to be a legend in your own right and make the family proud?" My father asked.

"You are right about that, Dad. But I want to find my own road of success. And I want to become a legend on my own terms." I smiled.

"Well your mother told me about your little adventures in Columbia, Missouri. I cannot believe that you slept with so many drunken girls. Mauricio what's going on inside that head of yours?" He asked.

"I don't know but I will admit to you that I made some bad decisions in Columbia, Missouri and the best decisions right here in El Paso, Texas." I smiled.

"Have you told Luz about your little adventures in Columbia, Missouri? Because she doesn't like it when people keep secrets from her. She got mad at me for not telling her where I was going to be stationed. She can be a tough girl, Mauricio. After all she has the Irish temperament." He smiled.

"I already told her and I need to tell her the rest of my story!" I exclaimed and asked him something else. "So, mom tells me that you are also thinking about retiring from the FBI. Why are you guys retiring? You guys are Super Cops and you have arrested so many criminals from all over the world. What's the problem, Dad? Did The Dark Cowboy also wore you out!"

"Mauricio, we're getting to old for this job and there's a lot of new young punks that are doing so many crimes. And at our ages well we got too old for this job and it was time for the other young Police Officers and FBI Agents to take over the job. And that's why I want you to become an FBI Agent and I know that you are going to be successful and I know that you will be ten times better than me. I never went to college or finished high school. But you have all the education and with me on your corner you can be successful FBI Agent. And I hope Tania also becomes an FBI Agent as well." He smiled.

Then my mother came outside and said, "Dinner is ready!"

"Dad, you think Luz will understand and accept my past?"

"She will understand just be honest with her."

My father and I went inside to eat dinner and it was so delicious, my mother and the girls cooks really good. And later on in the evening we were still in the kitchen and Luz started yawning and she looked to be tired and sleepy. And I took her home and she went inside the house to turn on the lights from the front porch and we sat down on the bench.

"I had a wonderful time."

"Me too, Baby." I smiled.

"I haven't laughed this much in a long time. You make me so happy and I love spending time with my family." She smiled.

"You look so beautiful when you laugh." I said.

"It's always been great spending time with your parents and my best friend, Tania. They always told me so many great things about you. And you can say that I had a crush you since I was a little girl. And I wish we talked back then and we could have been best friends too. And I already know a couple of things from you and I hope you can tell me the rest of your story." She smiled.

"Well I'm happy that my parents and my baby sister Tania told you everything about me. And I also hope you also tell me more about yourself. And I will tell you everything about me."

"That's fine with me and I feel that we are going to be the perfect couple and we are happy to be together at all times." She smiled and gave me a kiss.

"And I still cannot believe that my baby sister, Tania has a hatred towards The Dark Cowboy."

"Everyone in this city has a hatred towards The Dark Cowboy and I keep on telling them that he's innocent because he saved my life and he's turning good." She looked at me and said, "Rumor has it that you guys have known each other since little kids. What happen between you two?" She asked.

I looked at her and smiled and responded her question. "Well, Luz! The Dark Cowboy and I were once closer than brothers. We think the same, walk the same and it's like staring at a mirror. We were hanging out one evening. When all of the sudden he started talking about killing a lot of people. Because he found out that everyone at school were messing with me, so The Dark Cowboy ended up killing my friends on the Franklin Mountains. That's where I stopped talking to him and he begged me to be his friend all over again and I ignored him. We fought to the death and I left him for death. So, he wanted to hurt me for good and started killing everyone that wanted to help me and befriend me. And one evening The Dark Cowboy came after me and he nearly killed me right in the living room. Until a couple of years ago he came into my room and made a shocking confession. The Dark Cowboy started regretting all of the killings he's done over the years. And he also told me that he saved someone's life." I smiled.

"Did you guys talked about me?" She asked and smiled.

I looked at her and responded, "The Dark Cowboy said, "Mauricio, old friend. I saved a girls life at Marty Robbins Park and I don't know her name and she is so beautiful and I don't think she would give a monster like me a chance. But I was shocked when she gave me a kiss and she even giggled and she was happy that I rescued her."

"Tania told me that he attacked you at your house and he almost killed you. And I couldn't believe that The Dark Cowboy broke his promise. I was so mad at him when I found out what he did. I was planning to confront him and I was going to ask him. Why did he broke his promise, but I should be happy that The Dark Cowboy spared my life and yours too And I should be happy for that!"

"Luz, what happens if The Dark Cowboy comes back to town and you guys see each other?" I asked.

"I will tell The Dark Cowboy. Why did he break his promise and I would tell him to stay away from our relationship. But I told him if he ever needs someone to talk to, I will be there for him but as a friend and I will introduce him to my new boyfriend. Mauricio de la Vega!" She smiled and we held each other for awhile and then we said goodnight to each to other and we kiss and she went inside her home and I went home. And I still felt that Luz still has a thing for The Dark Cowboy. So, that might be a good sign that she might want to know the truth later on in the summer and I hope she can understand the rest of the bloody story. So, I fell asleep and had a peaceful sleep.

And the next day I went to Luz's house around three o'clock in the afternoon. Luz and I were in the living room watching a movie and we started kissing with a little tongue action of course and she looked at me and smiled and continued to kiss. "Let's go to my room and make out so my mommy won't hear us." She smiled and I picked her up and we went to her room. I put her on her bed and I turn the television and I got on top of her and we started kissing with a tongue action. And all of the sudden we heard a strange noise that was coming from her mother's bedroom. We got up and ran all the way into her bedroom and opened the door. Her mother was laying on the floor and she was gasping for air. She was getting pale and I grabbed her and sat her down on her bed.

"Mommy! What's wrong?" Luz was crying.

"Does your mom have any medicine or her inhaler?" I asked.

Alma had the inhaler in her hand but it was empty. Luz opened a drawer and took out the medicine and she was about to give her a shot and she was still crying and I was afraid that she might make a mistake. But Luz succeeded and gave her a shot.

And then we waited for a couple of seconds and I had my cell phone in my hand just in case if we had to call the paramedics. She finally looked at us and smiled. "I'm fine."

"Mommy!" She hugged her mother so tight. "I thought I was going to loose you!"

"I feel better now." She said and hugged Luz.

"Are you sure? Don't you want to see a Doctor?" I asked her.

"I feel better now."

"Thank, God." Luz said.

We took her mother to the kitchen and Luz made her tea. I sat there and started remembering something. I had a flashback and in the flashback I saw Eliza and she was pale just like Alma was a couple of seconds ago. And I could see her laying in a bed somewhere and I guess it was in Thomas Hospital and she was completely pale and was dying, and I also heard the heart monitor beeping so loud. And I didn't now what was going on and why was this happening to me. Then Luz got my attention and asked me if I wanted something to drink. And she stopped sobbing.

"No thank you. But I'm going to leave so you can rest, Alma." I said.

"Don't go, Mauricio. I'm going to my room and get some sleep. Stay with Luz and continue to watch the movie. I'm not going to be in the way." She said.

"I don't want to get in the way either and right now she needs to care of you. And I will come back tomorrow and see how you are feeling." I smiled and gave her a kiss on the cheek and smiled.

"Stay with me, Mauricio." Luz hugged me and kissed me.

Alma got up and smiled, "I'm going to my room so you guys can be together and goodnight to you guys."

Luz walked her mother to her bedroom and she said goodnight to Luz and she came back and hugged me and she was crying. "I thought I was going to loose her."

"Everything is going to be okay." I smiled and we hugged. She grabbed my hand and we sat down on the couch and we were watching the movie.

"Just hold me, Baby." She looked at me and tried to smile. She put her feet up the couch and she laid next to me. And I was holding on to her for a long time. And it was eight o'clock that night where Luz fell asleep and I watching her sleep the whole time. God knows what she was dreaming. And I heard the door open and Alma came to the kitchen for a glass of water and Luz woke up when her mother turned on the water.

"You need anything, Mommy." She said.

"I'm just getting water and goodnight." Alma smiled.

"How long was I asleep?" Luz asked me.

"A couple of hours. I was watching you sleep and you were also smiling." I smiled and kissed her and said, "I should be going home. I'll come back tomorrow so we can be together." I smiled and kissed her.

"I'll walk you to the truck." Luz smiled and we went outside and we were just listening to the crickets. We were holdings hands and she hugged me and started crying again. I was holding her real tight.

"It's okay, Luz, your mom is going to get better." I said.

"I thought I was going to loose her." She said and started wiping her tears. "I'm sorry I don't want you to see me this way."

"I understand, Luz, you are just scared to loose your mom." I smiled and kissed her and hugged her.

She looked at me and kissed me as hard she could. "I'm glad that you are here with me and I wish you can stay the night with me and protect me."

"I'll come back tomorrow and I will have a surprise for you." I said.

"What kind surprise?" She asked.

"You will see and you are going to like it." I kissed her and got into the truck. "I am going to miss you a lot and I want to see you smile again."

"I will miss you more." She said and tried to smile and kissed me.

I started the engine and went home. I parked in the driveway and went into the house, my father was in the living room watching television and my mother was by his side but she fell asleep. I went straight to my room and I was laying in bed and I was thinking about Luz and I was already missing her so much. And Tania came into my room and sat on the bed.

"You are home early. It's eight-forty." She said.

"Yeah."

"Did you guys got into an argument?" She asked.

"No. Of course not." I said.

"Then what happened."

"Her mother had an asthma attack in the afternoon but she is fine. I was about to leave but Luz wanted me to stay with her for the night." I said.

"It's bad enough that she is the only one that takes care of her mother. She is lucky to have you there. I'm going to call her and I'm going to tell her that she is not alone and if she needs someone to help her out with her mother. I will be there for her and I hope you will also be there for her and her mother."

"I care about her, Tania. She wanted me to stay for the night. I mean things are great with us but I just don't have be in the same situation like in Missouri. And I'll admit to you that I slept with a lot of drunken girls. But Luz is different from the rest of them and I want to respect Luz." I said.

"I know you respect her a lot but there might come a day where you guys finally make love. And it's part of your relationship. Every girl dreams of having sex with their Prince Charming." She smiled and asked me, "Are you going to see her tomorrow?"

"Yes, I told her that I will have a surprise for her on that day."

"Mauricio, I don't want to stick my noise in your relationship. And I see how you two look at each other. And I can tell that you guys are in love. You should tell her how you feel about her." She said.

"I do have strong feelings for her." I said.

"That's good and I know you two love each other. And I'll admitted to you that I never seen her this happy since The Dark Cowboy saved her life from those drug dealers. And she even kissed him and besides you make her happy!" Tania smiled and went back to her room and she called Luz to see how her mother was doing. And I honestly thought that I was way too soon for me to tell Luz how I feel about her. At the same time I was thinking about Luz and I was thinking about the kiss I gave her a couple of years ago. Luz still remembers the kiss and I think that we have fallen for each other. Then all evening long I was thinking about the vision I had earlier. This is the first time that I'm thinking about Eliza and why am I thinking about her. I should be happy that she is in Heaven and I know she is happy for me.

CHAPTER TWENTY

SENSING OF PRESENCE'S OF DANGER

It was one o'clock in the morning and I was still wide wake and I didn't felt like sleeping at all. I just closed my eyes for three seconds and I was already asleep and I started dreaming. And I heard the voice of Mr. Caballero that was saying, "Mauricio I want you to meet Eliza."

I heard the sweet voice of Eliza, "Nice to meet you, Mauricio."

"Eliza will you be my girlfriend?" I asked her in my dream.

I heard her sweet voice. "Of course, Mauricio."

I'm guessing that I'm dreaming about her and everything else that went on in the past. It was good to remember her and I hope she's resting in peace. And one of the things that I hate about dreams, is that in most dreams can jump into another dream and to another. Suddenly in my other dream I was sitting down and I felt that I was inside a dark cave. The problem was that I couldn't move at all and I was just looking at everything around me and I noticed that I was paralyzed. And I guess somebody shot me with my own dart gun and I was moving my eyes and I saw everything that happened in that weird dream. And all of the sudden I started seen dead people that were inside the cave and they all had gun shots wounds in their bodies.

They were floating around me and they looked at me and they were pointing their fingers at me. "Mauricio, you kill me! You kill me!" They exclaimed in the dream and they continued. "Mauricio, you kill me! You kill me! You don't deserve to live! You monster!" And I was able to recognize all of them, well these are the people that I killed and they were accusing me of killing them. Well there were at least three hundred plus ghost that were yelling at me.

And then I heard angry voice that was yelling at me, "Mauricio Dark Cowboy de la Vega, you are found guilty for the murder of twenty-three people and you will face death row and may God have mercy on your soul!" And I was able to recognize this Judge pretty well. It was Judge George Fuentes that was yelling at me. And then Judge George Fuentes slammed the gable to the table and it sounded like an echo. He slammed the gable three times and the people were cheering and clapping. And I didn't know what the Hell was going on and I couldn't move or yell at all. I looked around and saw my father laughing at me and he said, "I've finally captured The Dark Cowboy and you will rot in Hell! You son of a bitch!" And I was just sitting there staring at them when all of the sudden the dead people, including my father just disappeared into thin air. It got quiet all over again and there wasn't any noise at all.

And then I woke up because Tania was waking me up. "Wake up, Mauricio!"

I sat up and looked at her and asked, "What's wrong?"

She responded, "Just to let you know that mom and dad are going to fight crime. And I think they are going to be out late."

I smiled, "Okay! Well go to sleep and you know they will bring those criminals to justice."

"I hope so and I'm going to sleep and goodnight!" She smiled and sat next to me and hugged me.

"I'll look out for you!" I smiled and kissed her on the cheek. She went to her room and closed the door. I sitting on my bed when all of the sudden my heart started pumping really fast and I had the sensation of someone being in danger. I got up and opened the closet door and took out my bag. I took out my old outfit and changed. I was dressed as The Dark Cowboy and I couldn't be any more happier than to help my mommy and my daddy out. I also took out my custom made radio and I pressed the second button and all the bugs that were hidden inside the Police Station, the Police Cars and their CB radio sequence were turned on and I could hear what was going on. It's a good thing I can put it inside my pocket and I put on my headphones and I was listening to their calls. And I climbed out on the window and jumped on my rooftop and I was standing there. I closed my eyes and I wanted to make sure where I was sensing of someone being in danger. Well I heard the Police Sirens over the radio and I went to that direction. I was afraid that I might be a little bit rusty, so I started running and I was jumping the rooftops of the houses. And I heard my mother over the radio, "All units I'm pursuing the suspect on foot and I'm requesting for backup." I took out the radio and pressed the map button and she was chasing him on George Dieter. And the other Police Officers were pursuing the other ten suspects and I went to my mother's direction as quickly as possible. I heard my father over the radio, "Beatrice, wait for back up and it can be dangerous!"

She responded, "You will arrive too late and the criminal will get away."

"This is not the time to have pride, Beatrice!"

"Damn! He got away from me!" My mother yelled and the criminal attacked her and they were wrestling on the ground.

"Don't move!" The criminal yelled and he was pointing the gun at her head and that's where I jumped down and landed in front of him. He was scared to see me and he pointed the gun at my face when I broke his arm in three places. He was screaming like a little girl and I took out my guns and I shot him so many times.

I turned around and looked at my mother. "Are you okay, Beatrice?"

She was catching her breathe and she was able to stand up and looked at me, "You saved my life! Why?"

"I thought you needed help, so I came to the rescue. I cannot believe that I saved the great Beatrice de la Vega. No thanks in return and I'm not looking for medals."

She smiled and said, "You spared my life because you want me to tell the story how you kill this criminal and you saved my life."

"You were doing a pretty good job chasing him down. And I killed him, so you can reconsidered by staying as a Police Officer. Remember I was your real competition and you swore to protect everyone from the likes of me. Have I changed your mind into staying as a Police Officer or I need to kill more people. I'll wait for your answer." I was going to walk away from her.

"Thank you for saving my life!" She smiled.

I looked at her and smiled too, "I saved Samantha Jones, Luz Maria Estrada, Doctor Juanita Van Der AA and now you. Well I hope your team are able to arrest them. So, you can tell everyone what just happened here tonight!

Goodbye, Officer de la Vega!" I jumped on the rooftop and went back to my house. Before I went back to my house I decided to break into *Big 8* for the third time and grabbed the roses and went to Luz's house. I took out the radio and turned off the Police Scanner and I decided to press the first button and all the bugs from the people's houses were waiting to turn on. So, I put Luz's address and three bugs from her house were turned on. I wanted to surprise her with the roses but something else was happening.

I heard the voice of Luz over the radio and she started crying for some reason. She wanted to let it go but she couldn't take it anymore and started screaming at the top of her lungs and started crying really loud. She was sobbing and was breathing heavily. She got up and started running in her living room and she opened the front door. And she fell on her knees and she had her hands on her face and started crying a lot. "It's my fault!" She yelled! "It's my fault!"

Her mother came outside to see what was wrong with her. She grabbed her and took her inside before the people went outside. She took her to the kitchen and made her tea and she was trying to calm her down. "What's wrong, Honey?" Her mother asked.

"I cannot take it anymore! I try to forget about the past but it keeps coming back to me." Luz sobbed.

"You're thinking about that day? Is that why you're crying?"

"I saw you today having that horrible asthma attack and I was remembering the day you had that horrible asthma attack. It was my fault." She hugged her mother so tight.

"Luz, it wasn't your fault. You didn't do anything wrong and you know that I had a problem with asthma since the day I was born."

"It's my fault that you and daddy broke up because of me. My baby sister got injured because of me." She was still sobbing.

"Whatever happened between me and your father was a misunderstanding. We didn't get along, so it was best if we got separated." They were still hugging each other.

"I hate my dad. I will never forgive him what he did to you. I hate him!" She yelled.

"Your father loves you! And he wouldn't hurt you. You're his Princess and we just didn't get along. But we still love you and we will do anything to protect you." Her mother said and gave her the tea.

Luz was drinking her tea and was trying to calm down. "Imagine what Mauricio is going to think of me." She continued to drink her tea and said, "He has a perfect life, and he's the perfect boyfriend. He's going to graduate from college and he is going to have a great career ahead of him. And when I tell him about my past and what I did to you and my sisters. He's going to hate me and leave me for someone else."

"You're right! Mauricio is a great guy and he's happy to be with you. And I know he is going to forgive you." Her mother smiled and hugger her.

"I hope he doesn't leave me. I really like him and we get along great." She finally smiled and giggled.

"I love to see you smile!" Her mother said.

Well I threw the roses on the ground and I knew that this wasn't the time to give her the roses so I left home. I hope she can feel a lot better and I looked at the clock and it was four o'clock in the morning and I fell asleep as soon I landed on my bed. I was dreaming once again, and I found myself standing in my own room when all of the sudden The Dark Figure left my body and we were face to face and I saw it's glowing red eyes. And The Dark Figure spoke to me, "You see was just happen a few years ago in the secret Mental Institution on the outskirts of Oklahoma City. Well someone you know sent those men to come after you and Eliza."

I responded, "My father sent those me to come after me and Eliza. And why are you talking to me in the dream?"

The Dark Figure responded and laughed, "Mauricio, this is the place where no one can't hear our conversation. Remember Sonia put a lot of bugs in the city and including your room. So, we can talk about anything in this dream!"

"What's wrong then?" I asked.

The Dark Figure responded, "I can see that you met Luz once again and you plan to stay with her. But there might be a chance that your enemies want to come after you and your loved ones. And I know that you're sensing that someone is in danger at this very moment."

I looked at The Dark Figure and said, "Yes, I feel it. But I don't know who's in danger!"

"I'll go and find out. You stay here and be with Luz and protect her. I'm going to give you half of my power. But there might be a chance that you will also feel my presence from wherever I'm at. You will feel a lot of bad things while you're here and you need to control it."

"You're right if I go to the place where I feel that someone is in danger, they're going to know that I left and they are going to put everything together. Then they will know that I'm The Dark Cowboy. Well I hope you can help that person!"

"Don't worry old friend. You just enjoy the summer with Luz and your family. Now it's time for my spirit to leave your body."

"Can I still help people during the night?" I asked.

The Dark Figure responded, "Like I said I will give you half of my power and you will be just fine. Just be careful with the flashbacks and the sense of someone of in danger." And just like that The Dark Figure left my body and disappeared into thin air. Well I still had half of The Dark Figure's power and that might be enough to sense everything from a long distance. And I could feel my anger going around my body and it felt like electricity. And I saw myself in the mirror and my eyes were glowing red. I was grinning and growling when suddenly I started to hear a lot of worse things than ever before. I heard more explosions and people screaming for their lives. I heard a voice that was screaming, "Help me, Mauricio, Please help me! They are after me and my family!" And that's where I woke up and I was sweating and I looked at the clock and it was six o'clock in the morning. Damn I got two hours of sleep and I couldn't sleep at all and I just laid in bed and I was starting at the ceiling for awhile. And I went to the restroom and washed my face and went back to bed. And I was thinking about the dream I had and the screams. I didn't know who was begging me to help them. And all of the sudden, I started thinking about the bogus order that Karina gave to Sonia a few years back. Well no wonder Primo was there in the first place before I shot Armando and Deyna with the dart gun. And it's a good thing that Primo acted it out the whole time they were arguing. And I started hearing Karina's voice over the radio, "Sonia send Primo over! Sonia send Primo over because Mauricio needs him!" Well Karina was the voice of the gang and who knows what she's capable off. And I hope that it was a misunderstanding order that she gave on that night in the Franklin Mountains. And I finally fell asleep in about twenty minutes later and I didn't have anymore nightmares after that. And three hours later I was sound asleep when my cell phone was ringing and I was having a hard time waking up. Well leave me a message from whoever was calling me but the phone kept on ringing so many times. And I finally woke up and I looked at the clock and it was nine-thirty and I wasn't sleepy anymore. I grabbed my cell phone and it was five missed calls, no voice messages, no text message and it was an unknown number that I didn't recognize at all. Oh, well, I finally got up and went to the kitchen and my mother was making breakfast and she had the radio on and she was also singing while she was cooking. And she saw the look on my face.

"Did you and Luz got into a fight?" She asked.

"No. I had a bad dream and I couldn't fall asleep because it way too hot." I responded and sat down.

"What was it about?" She asked.

I responded, "Well it was a weird dream and it was kind of spooky too. Also I had a dream about Eliza, and Mr. Caballero was introducing us. I saw her smile in my dream."

My mother's eyes got watery. "Well it's good to know that you remember her after all these years. Is that why you didn't want to come back home?"

"Mom, I told you so many times why I didn't come back. But this was the first time that I dreamed about her." I said.

"What made you dream about her?" She asked.

"Luz's mother mentioned her name and just yesterday when she had an asthma attack. I had a vision and I started thinking about Eliza and at the same time I also saw her pale like the way Alma looked yesterday."

"How is Alma?" She asked.

"She is doing good."

"How did she know Eliza?" My mother asked me.

"I have no idea, Mom. Since Alma is a Choir Teacher and I'm pretty sure that she was a student of hers and maybe she was in her class or something like that." I responded and at the same time I was kind freaked out too about the other dream as well.

"Well Mauricio, as long you get to remember her and it makes you happy to think about her." She smiled.

Then I said this, "It's hard to forget the past and just imagine what Luz is going to think when she finds out about my past and when she finds out that I'm still thinking about Eliza."

"She will understand and you need to tell her everything about your past. She is going to accept you for who you are. Who are we to judge one and another?" My mother smiled.

"Luz told me right from the start that we aren't going to keep any secrets from each other. And when I tell her about Eliza and among other things, she might leave me." I said and when I tell my mother and everyone else, that I'm The Dark Cowboy and who knows what's going to happen.

"Do you remember what I told you a long time ago when you got into trouble in the library because you were singing to Eliza?"

"How could I forget it seems like it was yesterday when you told me." I smiled.

"Well you and Luz need to work extra hard in this relationship. It's not easy to be in a relationship. Just be yourself and tell her everything." My mother said.

About that time my father and Tania came to the kitchen and we started eating like one big happy family. My father and Tania saw the look on my face but we continue to eat and tried to have a good meal. After we finished eating our breakfast, my father went outside to get the newspaper and came back to the table we saw the look on his face.

"What's wrong" I asked.

My father responded, "I'm going to read you today's headlines." And he started reading, "Last night was the first time that The Dark Cowboy has been seen in four years. And there was a robbery at the Bank and the Police Officers were chasing the criminals and one of them was Officer Beatrice de la Vega who was chasing a criminal in a empty alley. And they started wrestling on the ground and Officer Beatrice de la Vega was nearly killed when all of the sudden The Dark Cowboy showed up and saved her life. Not to mention that he killed another person." My father was pissed and slammed the newspaper on the table.

"That's good news!" I smiled.

"We have been in front of The Dark Cowboy several times and we have failed to arrest him! And he's killed another person." My father looked worried and he has every reason to be worried because I'm becoming a legend in my own right. And they don't know that I'm The Dark Cowboy.

So, later on in the afternoon I was still thinking about Eliza and yet I was having more flashbacks about her and I usually saw her when she was pale and laughing as well. And I went to my room and started listening to music. I was laying in bed listening to music when I all of the sudden I wasn't feeling too good and I fell off the bed and I got on my knees and I was gasping for air. I felt that someone was in danger but it didn't came from the city. The sense of danger was coming from another place but I couldn't figure out where I was sensing it. This is how I felt when I went to Marty Robbins Park and rescued Luz from those drug dealers. But I cannot go out the window and run like a crazy person because what are my parents and Tania going to think. I cannot disappear and then come back home just like that. Well I was going to leave it to The Dark Figure. And I remember what Doctor Juanita Van Der AA said to me. So, I started praying for an half an hour and I poured my soul into praying. Half an hour later I was feeling a lot better, I was on my feet again but then again I was anxious to kill someone and rescue the person that's in trouble. My head was still hurting and I was getting dizzy but it all went away. And I was afraid that it was going to come back if I don't do something about it. I was sweating and still gasping for air and that's where I decided to tell my mother and father the bad news. I open the door and went to find them but my parents were in the living room watching television and when I got their attention, Tania also walked into the living room.

"Mom and dad can you take me to the Hospital?" I asked.

"What's wrong, Son?" My father asked.

"I have a headache and I feel pretty dizzy. And I was kind of hoping to get a cat scan." I responded.

"A cat scan?" Tania asked.

They saw the look on my face and they knew that this wasn't no normal headache at all. Because I was still loopy from the flashbacks and everything else.

"I'm going to call, Luz. She needs to know about this." Tania said.

"I don't want her to worry." I said.

"With this, Mauricio. You are keeping a secret from her and is not right." My mother said.

"Fine call her and tell her everything that happened today." I said and my parents took me to the Hospital for a cat scan. When we got there they gave me a cat scan and they did a psychical on me. They took blood out and I had another cat scan. After that my parents and I were inside the Doctor's office. We were waiting for the Doctor for at least twenty minutes and then the Doctor came into the room and he was looking at the file. He sat down and smiled.

"So Doctor! What do you think is wrong with me? You think I had a concussion, or amnesia." I said.

"Amnesia?" My mother asked.

"I might have that." I responded.

"This is not a joke, Mauricio!" My father said.

"Have you been on a medication?" The Doctor asked.

"No." I said.

"Drugs, alcohol."

"Not at all." I said.

"What makes you think you have amnesia?" He asked.

I had to lie to them! "It's because I woke up and I saw a bunch of Indians and they were asking me a bunch questions. And I even saw a Doctor, and she was actually there with the Indians and I forgot her name." I responded.

"What kind of Doctor was she?" My father asked.

"I think she was a Psychiatrist. And I don't know what I was doing there or why she was there with me." I said.

"Do you remember the name of the Doctor?" He asked.

I started thinking about it and said, "Doctor Juanita Van Der Aa, I think that's her name."

"That's Madelyn's aunt." My mother said.

"Mauricio, maybe you blocked out the memory of Eliza from your mind and now you are remembering her." My father said.

"That might be that Mauricio. You were pretty shaken up when she past away." My mother said.

"Your mother is right, Mauricio." The Doctor smiled and started writing a prescription for me. "Here go to the pharmacy and get this medicine because you really needed, Mauricio. And it's looks to me that you are having depressive memories and that is why you blocked out everything from your mind. And now you come back home and those memories of Eliza, are coming back to you but very slowly. So, for now I want you to be in bed for a couple of days and take the medicine and you will feel a lot of better. And don't worry everything is going to be fine. You are healthy but you need to take this medicine."

"What if it gets worse?" I asked.

"With the medicine you will be fine." He said.

Just like that the Doctor thought that I was depressed and that's why I was having those weird flashbacks and thinking about Eliza and among other things. So, my parents took me to buy the medicine that I needed and we went back to the house. My mother walked me to my room and she closed the door and we sat on the bed.

"Mom, have you told anyone else. You know about Eliza?"

"I'm not going to say anything to anyone and especially Luz. You are the one that needs to tell her everything." She said.

"Please, I don't want Luz or Tania to know about this. And I don't want to worry them." I said.

"I know but I will not say anything. But for now you need to rest. And it will be a secret from a citizen to a Police Officer."

The door opens and Tania asked me with a smile, "How are you feeling, Mauricio?"

"I feel better, Tania. I'm just need to rest." I said.

"Look who came to visit." She said.

I saw Luz's head and she smiled and walked to my bed and hold my hand and asked, "How are you feeling?"

"I'm feeling much better, now that you're here with me. And I'm sorry for leaving you alone yesterday, I wasn't feeling too good. And I was way too proud to tell you and I didn't want you to be worried for me."

"How could I not worry about you, Mauricio! You are my boyfriend and I care about you." She said and smiled and kissed me.

"What time is it?" I asked.

"Seven o'clock!" My mother responded.

"I wanted to give you a surprise." I said.

"What kind of surprise?" Luz asked.

"How about we go to the movies so we can be alone." I responded with a smile.

"Are you sure you are going to be able to drive to the movies?" Tania asked me.

"I'll drive." Luz smiled.

"Since when do you drive?" Tania asked.

"Since I was fifteen years old! My step-mom taught me how to drive and I have a driver's license." She smiled and showed my sister her drivers license!

"Let me see that!" My mother said and looked at her. "This is a fake Identification Card!"

"No! That's mine mom!" Tania smiled.

"Here's my driver's license!" Luz smiled.

"I also can drive, Luz. I also got my license last week. How about we race tonight?" Tania asked.

Luz looked at me and smiled, "Baby, I've beaten the great Tania de la Vega in everything and she's been a sore looser."

"Is that so." I smiled.

"How about we go outside and race from here all the way to Juarez." Tania smiled.

"How about all the way to Ireland, Mate." Luz smiled.

"To Mars." Tania said.

"Pluto!" Luz smiled.

My mother and I had enough of their argument and my mother smacked them on their heads. "Will you two knock it off. Every time you two are together, your always arguing and compete all the time. And Tania always loses and somehow Luz always wins!"

"She started it!" They both said.

"Enough!" My mother yelled at them.

"Come on, Mother. Luz and I argue because I see this bloody leprechaun as my baby sister and I love her a lot." Tania smiled and they hugged each other and hugged my mother too.

"We love you mommy!" They smiled.

"Okay! You two won!" My mother smiled.

I interrupted all three of them and said, "Well I hate to interrupt this moment. How about I drive and we are going to be late."

"No, Mauricio. I'll drive." She smiled and kissed me.

"We will leave you two love birds alone?" My mother smiled and took Tania with her and they said goodbye to us.

We were by ourselves. "I missed you last night." I smiled.

Luz tried to smile and said, "Me too. And did you know that I hugged my pillow pretending that is you."

"You're too sweet. And I had a dream about you last night."

"What was it about?" She asked.

"All we were doing is kiss and I was protecting you in the dream. We were happy together." I smiled and we kissed.

"You make me happy! And yesterday I was lonely without you, Mate!" She smiled and kissed me. "Let's forget about the Theatre or whatever surprised you have for me there. How about we go to my room and watch the movie. My mommy went out with that hot young Police Officer and she told me that she is coming back in the morning. And I want you to keep me company and protect me all night."

"I would like that." I said.

"I hope you don't think of bad of me." She smiled.

"I'm not. But I don't want your mom to think that I'm taking advantage of you." I said and we kissed.

"Mauricio, I want you to take advantage of me." She smiled and said, "Don't forget your pills!" I got up and I grabbed my precious damn pills. "I'll drive!" She smiled and grabbed my keys and went into the truck. She started the engine and went to her house. She parked in the driveway of her house and asked, "How was my driving?"

"You drive really well!" I smiled.

She smiled and we got out the truck. We were holding hands and she opened the front door. I picked her up and we walked into the dark living room and the dark hallway in the darkness and went into her room, and she turn on the lights. I looked around her room and still she has her collection of horses and has a lot of stuffed animals and she hasn't changed at all. She grabbed her pajamas and she turn on the lights from the hallway and went to the restroom and changed. I was looking at her wall and she still has a lot of pictures of her family and her friends. Also she has a picture of The Dark Cowboy! Luz came out of the restroom and she went to the garage in the darkness and very quickly she put her clothes in the laundry. She came back to the room and she was wearing a black tank top and she was wearing a black underwear. She closed the door and she sat on her bed while I was looking at her movie collections.

"It looks to me that I'm the second man that comes to your room during the night!" I smiled.

"Yes! And with all the respect to The Dark Cowboy. You are going to spend the night with me!" She smiled.

"Which movie do you want to watch?" I asked.

"The Summer of Mauricio de la Vega and Luz Maria Estrada." She responded with a smile.

"I never seen that movie and which part do you like." I asked and went up to her and she put arms around my neck.

"I like the part when the Princess invites her Prince Charming to her room and protects her all night." She smiled and said, "You can touch me anywhere you want."

"I want to respect you." I said.

"I'm a big girl, Mauricio, but we are just going to kiss and you can touch me anywhere." She smiled and we started kissing. I went to turn on the television and the movie started and I turn on off the lights. Well I took off my shoes, socks, and my shirt and hopped into the bed with her. We started kissing and she let me touch her body and I took her clothes too and I started touching her breast and other parts of her body as well. But we didn't have sex at all and that was okay with us. All we were doing was kiss and I was touching her all night long. And I actually thought that I was going to have a peaceful sleep but I didn't. I didn't hear The Dark Figure's voice not yet. So, I found myself walking around in some playground and there were a lot of kids that were playing tag and among other things. I turn around and there was my long lost friend Armando that was in the playground bus and I was playing with him. And I tagged him so gently and he just fell on his own and he started crying like a little girl and everyone was ganging up on me. I turn around and I saw myself on the playground bus and once again there was Armando and Deyna that were playing around and I went inside the playground bus and I was just standing there and I saw him saying something to her. So, she fell down on her own and again everyone was ganging up on me.

And I could hear Eliza saying to everyone. "Mauricio is innocent. He didn't do anything wrong!" I figured that she was trying protecting me from everyone else. And this dream jumped into another horrible dream. I saw a vision that a lot of people were pointing the guns at me and they were laughing at me. Then everyone started shooting at the me but I disappeared into the darkness and I heard more explosions and the screams. Once again I heard the voice, "Help me, Mauricio! Please help me! They are going to kill me!" And I heard more explosions and screaming. And that's where I woke up and looked at the clock and it was ten o'clock in the morning. I sat up and I was breathing heavily and I was sweating as well and Luz looked at me and asked me, "Are you okay, sweetie?" She grabbed my pills and gave me one and she ran to the restroom and brought me some water. I took the pill and drank the water. While I was drinking the water, I kept hearing the voice of someone that wanted my help.

"I just having a bad dream." I said.

"What were you dreaming about?" She asked.

I looked at her and smiled, "It doesn't matter anymore." I kissed her and she smiled.

We heard a noise in the kitchen and something smell good. "My mommy is making breakfast."

"It smells so delicious!" I smiled.

I got up and put my clothes back on. Luz also got up, she put on her rob and put on her flip flops. We went to the kitchen and Alma gave us a huge smile. "I'm sorry that I stayed here. I just going to my house." I said.

"Don't worry, Mauricio. I'm just glad that Luz wasn't alone. Are you hungry?"

"No thank you!" I smiled and Luz walked me to the truck we said goodbye to each other. "I'll call you if you want to do something together."

"Sure. I'll miss you and I'm glad that you stayed with me." Luz smiled and blew me a kiss when I left her house. And I parked in the sidewalk of my house. I stayed in the truck and I was already freaking out about the dream I had and finally I went into the house. I went to the kitchen and my mother was making breakfast for all of us.

"Did you get some sleep last night?" She asked.

"Yes, I did. I spent the night with Luz." I responded.

"Did you guys use protection?" She asked.

"We didn't have sex but we slept together." I said.

"Do you love her?" She asked.

"I don't know but I feel something good about her. Maybe later on I can tell her that I love her." I said.

"Mauricio, I think you should tell her how you feel about her. I never seen Luz this happy." My mother said.

"Well I am going to tell her how I feel about her. And also I'm going to tell her everything. I hope she can understand."

"She will understand."

"What's for breakfast?" I asked.

"Scrambled Eggs." She smiled and served my plate of Scrambled Eggs and Tania and my father also joined us to eat. And we finished eating our breakfast I went to my room and all I was doing was thinking about the weird dreams I was having. And all of the sudden I started feeling the presence of someone being in danger but I don't know where it's coming from. I tried to forget about it and started praying and it went away just like that. And I was laying in bed and I was already missing Luz a lot and I wondered what she was doing right now. I didn't turn on the television at all and all I did that morning and that afternoon is lay in my bed and looked at the ceiling. And Tania came into my room.

"So, how was last night? I want details!" She exclaimed.

"All we were doing is kiss, she let me touched her body and we slept together." I responded.

"I can tell that you guys are in love." She smiled.

"Well I have yet to tell her that I love her. And we get a lot pretty well" I said.

"As long you guys are having fun and getting to know each other." She smiled.

"Yes, that's true." I said.

"Are you going to see her tonight?" She asked.

"Yes"

"Well I'm going to hang out with Jackie and I'm going to sleep at her house. Mom and dad are going to be in a hotel because they wanted to be alone. You guys have the house to yourself." Tania smiled.

"I hope you have fun in the slumber party, Tania." I smiled and called Luz and she wanted to see me so I took a nice hot shower. But first I went to buy Chinese food and I went to pick up Luz. She was sitting down on the bench she was playing around with something and she saw me parked and I got out and we kissed.

"What are you doing?" I asked.

"I found another lady bug. Ah, darn, it flew away." She smiled and kissed me.

"Did your mom got mad?" I asked.

"No! She's happy for us. Why would she be mad?" She smiled.

"Just asking. Listen my parents are going to be away for the night. Tania is also going to be away for the night. We have the house to ourselves. I bought Chinese food so we can have a romantic dinner." I said.

"That will be great." She smiled and we kissed for a long time. So, we went to my house and went inside the house. My parents were just leaving.

"You kids behave and I don't want you to throw a party." My father smiled.

"Let's go, Pablo." My mother smiled and kissed Luz and Tania on the cheek.

"Well I'm also leaving and have fun tonight. Well Jackie and I are going to talk about you two love birds!" Tania smiled and we heard honking. "That's my ride and Luz I want details." Tania smiled and they kissed each other on the cheek.

We took the food, drinks, plates, and glasses to my room. Luz closed the door and we sat on the floor. I was serving her food and I gave her a glass and she saw the carton of Apple Juice.

"Why Apple Juice?" She asked.

"Well that's what you were drinking before we went to Marty Robbins Park." I smiled.

"Ah! You remembered. How sweet of you!" She smiled and I pour the Apple Juice into the her glass and I also had Apple Juice. "Cheers!" We said and we started eating the food and by eight o'clock that night we finished eating. "I'm full." She smiled and she hopped into the bed and laid there.

And I started cleaning everything and she wanted to help me. "I'll do it, you are the Princess, let me clean everything." I smiled and we kissed. And I made her laid there and put her feet up and tickled her feet too and she giggled.

"Hurry back!" She exclaimed and I went to take everything to the trash can. I washed my hands and I came back to the room and she was smiling and she missed me a lot. I turn on the television and I picked her up and had her in my arms and we were kissing. She was taking off my clothes and I took my clothes as well. Well we were in our underwear and we went under the covers and we were kissing and I was touching her body and she was moaning and kissing me hard with a tongue action. Then the next day I woke up and it was nine-thirty in the morning and Luz was in my arms. I was watching her sleep and she was smiling too. And all of the sudden I heard the voice of Primo and he was calling me for help, "Mauricio help me! They are going to kill me!" And I heard gunshots and I heard Madelyn scream and she was crying. I had a vision of my friends that were dying right in front of my eyes. Luz was also there and she was also dying right in front of my eyes. And I started breathing heavily and my heard was hurting pretty bad. I started yelling at the top of my lungs and Luz woke up.

"Are you okay!" Luz exclaimed.

I looked at her and said, "Yes!"

"Another bad dream?" She asked.

"Yeah, but it doesn't matter anymore!" I responded but I was wide awake and it looked so real.

She looked at me and kissed me and said, "I had fun last night!"

"I'm glad you had fun!" I kissed her and I was holding her so tight.

Luz and I laid in bed for awhile and an hour later we finally got up and put our clothes on. Luz and I went down to the kitchen. My mother and my father were making breakfast for us. They looked at us and smiled. "Are you guys hungry?" My mother asked.

"Yes!" We exclaimed.

"How was your night?" Luz asked.

"Good. How was your night?" She asked.

"We had fun together. Your son protected me all night long! I'm never been this happy in my life!" Luz smiled and went to hug my mother and my father. "I'm having so much with your son."

"Well breakfast is ready and we have something to tell you guys." My father smiled.

We sat down and my mother served us scrambled eggs and we were eating. "So, what are you going to tell us?" I asked.

"Yesterday, your father and I had a long talk and we came to the decision. That I'm going to retire at the end of the summer from the Police Force." My mother said and smiled.

"And I'm also going to retire from the Federal Bureau Investigation. Your mom and I feel that we have nothing else to prove and let someone else take over this job. We had a great run on the Police Force." He said.

"My mom and I are going to support your decision." Luz smiled.

"Me too, whatever makes you happy. You guys had good career and good luck in the future." I smiled and deep down inside I was happy that they gave up but who's going to come after me if they're no longer in charge of this case. Maybe this is my father's plan and they know that The Dark Cowboy might be listening to their plan.

We finished eating our breakfast and Tania came back to the house later on the afternoon. And the six of us were spending time together and we went out to celebrate my parent's careers and my sister and Luz knew they made the right decision to retire from the Police Force. And I was surprise that my parents are giving up. Well I guess it was the night I saved my mother's life from that criminal, she was convinced that they will never put the end to my all of my killings. Happy retirement mommy and daddy.

CHAPTER TWENTY-ONE

LUZ'S GUILT

The next day I went to see Luz and I parked in the driveway. I wanted to run at her door and give her a huge hug and kiss her all over her gorgeous face and body. But I decided to take my time but she met me halfway there. We were happy to see each other and we hugged and kissed. And Alma also came outside and she was happy to see me too. Well the three of us were outside talking for awhile and then Luz and I went into the truck and went to Marty Robbins Park but first we went to get an ice cream. And we drove to Marty Robbins Park and we got out and started walking around and we were holding hands and we stopped in our shade tree.

"How are you feeling?" She asked.

"I feel better but I hate taking the pills." I said

"I don't want you to get sick on me and if you do get sick I'll take good care of you. I'll be your Nurse." She smiled.

"I'll stopped taking the pills so you can be my sexy Nurse." I smiled and we finished our ice cream cones and she put her arms around my neck and we were kissing. I saw the look on her face, her eyes were getting watery and she was smiling.

"What's wrong?" I asked her.

"I have to tell you something." She responded.

"You can tell me anything you want." I said.

She looked really sad and hugged me and started crying. "I want to tell you so many things but I am afraid that you will not want to be with me anymore and leave me for someone else." She said and tears started coming out of her face.

"Why am I going to leave you?" I asked.

She looked at me and said, "When I was thirteen years old it was the most difficult time of my life. I was so depressed that I wanted to commit suicide. And this one time I did cut off my veins but I was lucky that my parents rushed me to the Hospital." She started to cry and continued. "I was hanging out with the wrong crowd in Ireland. And I started drinking and doing drugs and I got into lots of fights at school. I was mean to everyone and including my parents and my little sisters and I got in a fight with my one of my sisters and sent one of them to the Hospital. Because I broke her leg and punched her in the face!"

I didn't want to interrupt her and I just wanted her to let go of her pain. "Go on." I said and hugged her.

She looked at me and continued. "I lost my friends because they were ashamed of me, but my family was there for me. They took me to rehab several times, but it didn't do me any good. I ran away from my house several times and I ended up in the juvenile home for a couple of months and I even to boot camp for awhile. After I got out of boot camp, I spent most of my time on the computer talking to a lot of guys." She was wiping her tears with her hands and continued. "Then one day I was on the Internet and I was talking to a couple of guys when all of the sudden a window popped out and I thought it was a guy that wanted to talk to me. Well it turned out to be a girl. This mysterious girl started talking to me about her life and I felt connect towards her. And I started talking to her about my life and it was like she knew everything about my life. Well we became Online buddies and we felt comfortable with each other and she started to comfort me during my tough time, and she was my best friend. And this mysterious girl saved my life and if it wasn't for her I could be dead right now or I could be locked away in the Psychiatric Ward for the rest of my life. And she started talking about religion, God, and if I believe in Him. And I told her that I now believe in Him so much." She smiled and her tears were gone and she looked at me and she was smiling once again. "Then one day I woke up and the sun was shinning on my face. I called everyone and told them how much I love them. My parents took me to Church and it was a Christian

Church. And I let God and Jesus into my life and I was Baptist as well. Tania, my mommy, and your mom also became Christians and they has the same fate as me. That's why your mom is going to retire from the Police Force because she got tired of the violence and she wants to live her in peace. And someday, Mauricio, I will tell you why I did those awful things."

"Well I'm not going to pressure you. I'll just wait for the day you tell me." We kissed and I was holding her tight and we looked at each other, "Luz, I've been meaning to tell you something for awhile." I took a long breather and said, "I wanted to tell you is that I love you a lot, Hunny Bunny."

She looked at me and smiled and once again her tears started coming down her face, "I love you too, Baby!" We kissed for a long time and we looked at each other and smiled and we held each other for a while and I wanted to tell her my other secret which I didn't want to.

"Gilberto." I said.

She looked at me. "What?"

"My middle name is Gilberto!"

"Oh, my God." She started laughing and I was glad to see her smile again.

"I told you I have an ugly middle name."

"But you did warn me from the beginning and still you make me happy. That's why I love you more than you love me." She said.

"Me too, Hunny Bunny."

"I love it when you call me Hunny Bunny." She smiled.

We stayed together at Marty Robbins Park and I took out my pocket knife and I carved our names in the shade tree and I looked around the corner and there was the tree that Eliza and I carved our names a long time ago. And Luz and I kissed and walked around the park holding hands and we stopped in our shade tree and I wanted to tell her the other lame secret. And I hope that she can understand.

"Also there is something I want to tell you." I said.

"Tell me." She smiled.

"Well when I was living in Columbia, Missouri I made a lot of mistakes over there and I did learned from my mistakes. And it turns out that slept with every drunken girl that Columbia, Missouri has to offer. I was so bad back then." I said.

"Do you love them?" She asked.

"I wasn't in love with either of them. I was wild over there and I had no control of myself. I was just wanted to experiment with them. But all I know is that I love you so much. Because you make me a better man."

She smiled and said, "I love you too. And I know you made a couple mistakes in the past but everything is going to workout. I want to spend my rest of my life with you. And I hope we get married."

"And we will have kids of our own." I said.

She looked at away and said, "I hope so."

We kissed for a long time and we stayed together for a couple of more hours at Marty Robbins Park. We left the park around nine o'clock that night and I parked in the driveway of her home. I saw my mother talking to Alma and they were sitting on their rocking chairs, and they were both drinking Beers. We got out of the truck, Luz kissed my mother and her mother on the cheek. And I went to hug Alma.

'What did you love birds do all day?" Her mother asked.

"Just walk around the park and we were talking." She said.

"That's good! Your mom and I were just talking and catching up. And drinking Beers." My mother smiled.

"Well, Mauricio, your mom invited us to the park because we're going to have a cookout." Alma said.

"When?" I asked.

"Tomorrow." My mother said.

"That will be awesome and it has been a while since we had a cookout." Luz said and smiled.

"We are going to celebrate Mauricio's birthday." My mother said.

"Why so early?" I asked.

"It's a long story and I will tell you on the way home." She said.

"So, Alma! How's your relationship going with that young Police Officer?" I asked.

"It's going good!" Alma smiled.

"Are you in love, mommy?" Luz asked.

"I think I am and I'm happy to be with him." Alma said.

"The sex is great isn't?" My mother asked.

"That too!" Alma smiled.

"If that Police Officer hurts you than I'm going to have to kill him!" I smiled and started laughing.

They were looking at me and my mother started laughing. "Oh, Mauricio, is always a joker!"

"For a minute there you sounded like The Dark Cowboy. I was surprised." Alma smiled.

"Well, Mommy! Mauricio and I have a surprise for you as well." Luz smiled.

"What is it?" Her mother asked.

"Mauricio and I are in love!" Luz smiled and hugged her mother and my mother.

"Our kids are in love and they are growing up so fast." My mother smiled and we stayed talking with them for three whole hours and we were saying goodbye to each other and my mother went into the truck. Luz and I hugged and kissed and said goodnight to each other. My mother and I went home and we sat down in the kitchen.

"Mom, what is going on? Why are we celebrating my birthday early!" I asked her.

My mother responded with a smile, "A lot of bad things, Mauricio. Your father is going to be reassigned to go to Mexico City because your friend Primo and Madelyn are on the run. It's because Vito Mancini is after them, well not after them. Vito is after the money that The Pachuco2K stole from the people a few years ago. The money was split in eleven ways and they were given in ATM cards and the eleventh card is somewhere in Mexico City. And it looks like that the ATM card belongs to The Dark Cowboy. Vito Mancini plans to use the money to kill The Dark Cowboy and whoever stands in his way. Your father told me that the card contains more ninety-seven billion dollars."

"Why so much, money?" I asked.

"I don't know. But Perla called me a few hours ago and told me everything that happen to them in the last couple of days. And she also told me that Primo said to her that he was willing to risk his life for his best friend The Dark Cowboy, so Vito won't get the money and now his mother and his girlfriend are in danger."

"What's going to happen to Primo and his family if the Federal Bureau Investigation catches them first before Vito does?" I asked.

"You know your friend, Primo. He has a criminal record since he was a little kid and we figured that somebody framed him because half of the Police Officers and the FBI Agents are also after the ATM card. And I think that's where everyone is going to show their true colors. And Vito doesn't care about anyone than himself and he is going to kill his only son in order to get the money. Vito Mancini is using the Police Officers and the FBI Agents to get that card! And Primo plans to intercept the ATM card before they do." She said.

"I just hope that my dad is able to save them and get rid of the money for good." I said.

"Well I'm glad that your father saw you and he is happy that you're going to graduate from college and he's proud of you!" My mother said and smiled. "Well it's time to go to sleep because tomorrow we are having a cookout but Tania doesn't know about this and I don't know how to tell her because Madelyn is also like her baby sister."

I just smiled and I went to my room and I was worried for my friend Primo Mancini and his family. And I will like to know is why are those knuckleheads in Mexico City. They know that I have that ATM card that's worth ninety-seven billion dollars and I have it in my wallet. So, I'm guessing that's the real reason why I felt someone was in danger. And I guess Primo called me the other day and there was five missed calls. After all Karina is able to hack into the phones too and she is able to hear things. Karina is the voice of the gang and I bet that she's misguiding Vito and his men, so they can fall intro the trap. I guess Primo and his family are safe from them. Well they come back here Primo and the girls have some explaining to do. And I started thinking if this was their plan right from the beginning. And I started to remember that Karina's father is in the CIA, also known as the Central Intelligence Agency. There might be a chance that they might go to Mexico City. After all Anthony Reyes was the one that trained my father to become an FBI Agent. And I figured that Karina has all of the evidence when I was killing people and Primo raping girls. And she can send the evidence to her father and they would come in and try to arrest us. So, I have a feeling that Karina and the girls might be in Mexico too. Those were my speculations on that evening. And at the same time I wouldn't want to put my mother, Tania, and Luz in danger. But maybe Primo and his family needed my help and that's why he called me and I was sensing him in danger all along. Well old friend, The Dark Figure is also there to help you out. Well I stop thinking about it and went to sleep.

So, the very next day I woke up around ten-thirty in the morning, my mother and Tania were putting the food together and I helped my father put the grill in the back of his truck. They were on their way to the park and I went to pick up Luz and her mother. And we arrived at the park, my father and I were putting the steaks and the burgers on the grill. Luz and Tania grabbed their towels and went running to the swimming pool and it was outdoors. They didn't bring their swimsuits but they went swimming in their long t-shirts. And I could see them from where I was standing at and I was glad to see Luz and Tania were enjoying themselves in the swimming pool. And then Tania and Luz waved me to come over. So, I walked my way to the swimming pool.

"What's up?" I asked.

"Luz wanted to know if you could swim with her because the Irish leprechaun wants to see you without a shirt." She smiled.

"Is this true, Luz?" I asked.

"Tania, I already saw Mauricio without a shirt and we slept together twice. Do you remember, Tania!" She smiled and looked at me. "You should join us in the pool."

"I would love that but I don't have a change of clothes and I don't want to get wet." I smiled at Luz and I was about to go back to the grill and she grabbed my shoulder and I felt she wanted to tell me something and I got a towel and gave it to her and she looked at me and smiled and gave me a kiss on the cheek. I put the towel around her and I wanted to hold her tight. She was drying her hair and her shirt was still wet and I could see the color of her bra and something else.

"Hey, Tania. I'm going to talk to Mauricio." Luz said.

"You are going to tell him that you want to marry him and have a lot of babies." Tania smiled.

"That will be nice." She smiled and I grabbed Luz's hand and we sat down on the chairs and we watched Tania swim around the swimming pool and I could tell that she was having a good time in the swimming pool. "Sweetie, I want to tell you something.' She said.

"What are you going to tell me?" I asked.

She looked at me and her tears coming down her face before she was going to tell me what she wanted to say to me. "A couple of years ago, my mommy came to visit me in Ireland because my daddy called her and told her that I was doing drugs and she was worried for me. My mommy kept on telling me to stop doing drugs. On my good days she pleaded with me and she even got on her knees and begged me to stop doing drugs. And one day my mommy wanted to take me to see a Psychiatrist and I didn't want to go and she grabbed me, she started crying and she was telling me to get some help. I was so mad at her and I cursed her to Hell and I pushed her so hard and she fell to the ground. She started having problems breathing, my step-mommy gave her the inhaler and it didn't work, then my daddy gave her a shot and didn't work at all. So, they rushed her to the Hospital. And I ran all the to my room and cried all night because I thought she was going to die. But three hours later my step-mommy and my daddy came back to the house and said that my mommy is going to be okay. I was still devastated and I was crying all night long and I made the mistake to I cut my veins. My sisters were screaming and they rushed me to the Hospital and on that night my mommy came into my Hospital room. I cried in her arms and told how sorry I was. She told me that she still loves a lot and from there I went to get the help that I needed. Even now when I close my eyes, I still see my mommy having that horrible asthma attack. I would never forget the look on her face when she was having problems breathing. I feel responsible for my mommy having that asthma attack, and I was hurting everyone and it was my fault that my parents slit up and my sisters were also hurt."

I hugged her so tight and said, "It wasn't your fault. Your parents are fine and they get along pretty well, they love you a lot, just as I love you. You don't need to feel guilty anymore. That's in the past."

Luz looked at me and was sobbing, "I know but it just hurts so much to let it go. Sometimes I worry about the past coming back haunt me!"

"Don't worry about it. I'm here for you. Sometimes you get to let go of that awful past! My little Princess!" I hugged her and kissed her.

She looked at me and smiled. "How much you love me?"

"I love you a lot." I smiled and I sat her down in my lap and hugged her. "Have you told, Tania?"

"Not yet. I still need to tell her that Madelyn is on the run in Mexico City with her boyfriend, Primo Mancini. When I tell her that I was on drugs and our friend, Madelyn is on the run with the son of the crime lord, that is going to crush her even more. And last night I only got four hours of sleep." She finally smiled and wiped the tears off her face.

"You should tell her because you guys are best friends." I said.

"She's my big sister, and I don't want to bring her down." She smiled and looked at Tania. "It was hard for me to tell you about my past and it's going to be even more harder to tell her."

My cell phone rang and it was my father and he told me that the Burgers are ready and we should come to eat. Luz waived at Tania and they went to the restroom and put their clothes on. And I was waiting for them and I saw everyone having fun in the swimming pool. Then for some reason I was having another flashback and it was the memory of Eliza.

I saw myself saying to her. "I want you to make me a promise."

"What kind of promise?" She asked.

"Promise me that we're going to be together forever." I said.

I remembered Eliza saying, "I promise."

"I love you a lot. " I smiled in the flashback. And I was still standing there and I was thinking about Eliza and I was still wondering why in the Hell am I still thinking about her. Luz is my girlfriend and Eliza is in Heaven and I know she's happy for me. And then I heard Luz and Tania giggling when they came out of the restroom and they came running towards me and we went to eat.

While we were eating, I kept thinking about the flashback I had earlier. And I also remembered that Alma had mentioned Eliza and I still wondered how did she knew Eliza. And I looked at her mother and she was smiling at me. We stayed at Marty Robbins Park until eight o'clock that night. The girls started cleaning the table and my father and I picked up the grill and put in the back of his truck. We put the extra food and everything in plastic bags and put them in the back of the truck. My father said goodbye to Luz and they took Alma home. They three of us stayed at Marty Robbins Park and it's a good thing that the lights of the parked were still turn on. Luz and Tania went walking around the park. Luz had her hand around Tania's arm and I knew she was telling her everything because they were wiping their tears with napkins. They were half way to the baseball field and they stopped and just stood there looking at each other. And they hugged each other and they started crying. And Tania wiped Luz's tears with a napkin and they talked for a long time and two hours later they finally began walking back where I was standing. They were holding hands and Luz and Tania were trying to connect the stars and they were laughing again. And I was sorry that my sister, Tania had been upset but it was the right thing to do. Tania and Luz hugged me and we left the park and we dropped off Tania at our house.

Luz and Tania looked at each other. "Bloody Tania." Luz smiled.

"Bloody Irish, and bugger." Tania smiled.

"Are you going to be okay?" Luz asked.

"Yes, I am. Are you going to be okay?" She asked.

"Yes, I am. And we should pray to God and hope that nothing bad happens to Primo, his mom, and our friend, Madelyn." Luz smiled.

"You are right. I love you, you rascal." Tania smiled and they kissed each other on the cheek and Tania got off the truck and went inside the house and I took Luz home. We sat in the darkness and we just held each other.

"What are you thinking?" She asked.

"You, Luz. I saw the color of your bra." I said.

"You were drooling all over me." She smiled.

"That's the second time I drooled all over you. I love you a lot." I said.

"I love you more."

"So, did you told her everything?" I asked.

"Yes. I had to tell her everything. We grew up together and I love her."

"I love my sister so much and I don't want her to be in the that kind of position." I said and kissed her. "Are you still worried for your friend, Madelyn?"

"Yes. I don't want anything to happen to her." She said.

"Don't worry. Madelyn is in good hands. I know Primo for a long time and he is not going to let anyone lay a finger on her. He will do everything he can to protect the girl he loves. Just like me, I would not let anyone lay a finger on your gorgeous body except me."

"So, you would protect me from the bad people." She smiled.

"Of course." I said and I did it before and I can do it again.

"My body is your body. And I told you from the start that you can touch me anytime you want too and I don't mind and you don't need my permission." She said.

"Are you sure?" I asked.

"Yes. Well not public but when were alone. I feel comfortable around you and I'm offering my body to you." She smiled and said. "I am glad you are here with me and I love you a lot."

"Me too, Hunny Bunny." I said.

"I love it when call me Hunny Bunny." She smiled and giggled.

We held each other for awhile and two hours later, Luz started yawning, so we kissed and we said goodnight to each other, and she went inside and I went back home. And the next day my father was getting ready to leave to Mexico City and he said to goodbye to us and he promised Tania and I that he was going to bring our friends back in one peace and they were going to get

Jesus Morales

rid of the money for good and they were going to try to captured Vito and his henchmen. So, my father left and I was in charge of my mother and my baby sister Tania.

And on that night I spent the night at Luz's house. She was in my arms and I was watching her sleep. I put my hand on her forehead and I was seen what she was dreaming about. In the dream, I saw my mother driving around Marty Robbins Park when she saw Alma and a young Luz Maria at Marty Robbins Park. My mother smiled and parked her car and went to say hi to them. And I could tell that Luz was around twelve years or thirteen years old because she looked so young and had braces on her teeth and she looked so cute.

"Hey, Beatrice!" She said.

"Hey, Alma. What are you two doing here?"

"I hope you're not going to arrest us because we're having a picnic?" Alma asked and smiled.

"Of course not." My mother said and smiled. "Who's this pretty little girl?"

"You know my daughter, Luz. She just got here from Ireland, she was living with her father for awhile." Alma said.

"You remember me, Luz?" My mother asked.

"Yes, how you been, Mommy?" She said and smiled.

"I've been good. Tania would happy to know that you're back in El Paso." My mother said and hugged her so tight.

"I'll call her when I get home. Right now I want to spend this day with my mommy." Luz smiled.

"That's good. And I know how much Luz and Tania missed each other." Alma said and smiled. "So, are you still going around to see if people are been safe?"

"Well I'm going to go home and get some rest because we're going to have a long night. But first I'm going to *Peter Piper Pizza* and bring my family food. You guys want to come?" My mother asked.

"That will be great." Alma smiled and started to pick up everything and put it in the car. "Let's go walking we need the exercise."

"Mommy! Can I stay here and wait for you guys to come back. I want to run around the park. I promise to be safe." Luz said.

"Of course. You just be careful." Alma smiled and kissed her on the cheek. My mother also kissed her on the cheek and left walking to *Peter Piper Pizza*.

Luz saw them walk away and she took out her water bottle. She started running around the park for about fifteen minutes. And she stopped in front of a tree and rested, she was trying to catch her breathe. And she began to noticed that a black van was parked near the parking lot and she thought that it might a couple of kids that were going to play soccer in the park. She drank some water and rested for a couple of minutes. Then she started running around the park and on the way back to the shade tree, she still noticed that the black van was still there and no one got out of the van and then a man got out of the van and he was wearing a nice suit. He was calling to her.

"Young lady!" He exclaimed in the dream and Luz heard someone say. "Young lady."

She turned around and said. "Are you talking to me?"

"Yes. I'm lost and I'm hoping you can give me directions." He said.

Luz noticed that the license plates was from California. "Sorry, but I'm not suppose to talk to strangers."

"I know but I need directions. My mom is in the Hospital and I don't know where the Hospital is at." The man said.

"What's wrong with your, Mom?" She asked.

"She has heart problems and I don't know for how long she's going to last. Please I just need directions." The man said.

Luz felt that the man was telling the truth and went up to him. "Okay, which Hospital are you looking for?" She asked.

"Thomason Hospital." He responded and Luz went up to him and smiled and gave him directions. The man smiled and took out his gun. "Get inside the van."

"Please don't kill me!" Luz yelled.

"I said get inside the van. I'm going to kill you if you don't obey me. I just want to talk to you." He said and pointed the gun at her head. "Get inside the van!"

Luz started crying and the man grabbed her by the hair and put her inside the van where four other men were inside waiting for her. They were drinking and doing drugs and they had a twelve year old girl inside the van that was crying her eyes out. The man that was wearing a suit was still grabbing her hair and was laughing and also was drinking. Then they tied her arms and put her on the floor and they started to rape her. She was screaming and calling for help. The man in suit was raping her and punching her in the face and slapping her and telling her to shut up. But she continued to sob and cried for help and he taped her mouth and she continued to yell. They took turns raping her and they were punching her and slapping her all over her body. They even put several objects into her vagina and that might have caused her some more pain along the way. They started to drug her as well and continued to rape her. They even took off the tape and forced her to do a lot more activities with her mouth. When all of the sudden they heard a strange noise that was coming from outside. And it almost sounded like a knock from inside the van and they put the tape back at Luz's mouth and she thought that it was my mother and her mother that came to the rescue. She tried to make a lot of noise and there was another loud bang. They put their clothes back on and one of them went to check it out. He opened the side door and went outside. While they were inside waiting for him for at least thirty seconds and all they could hear was Luz breathing from the pain and crying. Then they heard the man scream. "What the!" And they heard gunshots and that might have scared the men completely. They got startled because they thought it was the Police or the FBI that shot their partner in crime. Then the back door opened and the men were frightened because they were staring at me and my red evil eyes and I was laughing at them. Luz barely lifted her head just for a couple of seconds and saw me staring at them. The men were terrified and the man in the suit was brave enough that he was about to turn on the engine when I shot him in the head and the blood was spilled all over the window and including their faces. Three men were left and they nearly peed on themselves. I took out my other Magnum and shot the remaining two in the head. Luz noticed that the side doors were still open so she crawled her way out of the van and landed hard on the sidewalk.

 Meanwhile back in *Peter Piper Pizza* where someone came running inside the restaurant. "Officer de la Vega, there's been gunshots and it came from Marty Robbins Park."

 "Are you sure?" She asked.

 Another person came in running. "The Dark Cowboy just killed four men at Marty Robbins Park!"

 My mother and Alma looked at each other. "My daughter is at the park." Alma said and sobbed.

 My mother got on the radio and ordered. "All units. The Dark Cowboy has been spotted at Marty Robbins Park. I'm requesting for back up. I'm going to go to the park and arrest him." She said and looked at everyone. "I want everyone to stay here and do not move at all! You too, Alma."

"I'm going with you. My daughter is out there." Alma said.

"Fine let's go." She said and they ran all way to the park.

Meanwhile the man was still breathing heavily and was crying his eyes out. "Please, don't kill me! I will give you anything you want."

"Anything!" I reloaded my Magnum and shot him in the head and killed him and it was a bloody mess inside the van. I was laughing and I turned around and saw Luz laying in the middle of the sidewalk and she was face down. And I could hear her breathing and sobbing because she was in so much pain. My mother and Alma finally arrived at the crime scene and they saw Luz laying in the middle of the sidewalk. My mother also saw five dead people next to the van and she could see the blood all over the van.

"What did you do to my daughter!" Alma yelled.

"Freeze do not move. You are under arrest!" My mother yelled.

I was holing something in my hand and I threw it at my mother and she caught it and she looked at it. "It's drugs these men were raping her and drugging her." I said and went up to Luz and got on my knees.

"I said don't move! They may be drug dealers but you are still under arrest for the murders of eighteen people! And now twenty-three people!" She said and continued to yell. "Step away from the girl!"

I actually ignored my loving mother and took off the tape and she started crying in so much in pain. My mother told Alma not to move at all and both of them saw Luz in so much in pain and she was crying and was calling for her mother and for her father. Just then the cavalry arrived and so many Police Officers and FBI Agents got out of the cars and pointed the guns at me and I didn't put my hands in the sky. My mother went to the van and found bags of weed and cocaine and many other weapons they had inside the van and she felt that these guys were drug dealers and maybe they were henchmen from the mob. I picked up Luz and she was in so much pain and said. "Help me."

"Put the girl down!" One of the Agents yelled.

"Hold your fire." My mother ordered everyone. "He saved her life from these drug dealers. So, hold your fire!"

Everyone began to notice that there was a horse in the middle of Marty Robbins Park. I called my Black Stallion over and she came up to me and I was petting her. Well my horse wasn't even there at the time I saved Luz's life but you know how dreams are. Very I gently put Luz on top of the horse and I also got on top and was holding on to her. "We need to get her to a Hospital. I'm going to need your help, Beatrice."

"Fine." She said and looked at her team. "Half of you come with me and the rest of you take the drugs and everything else back to the Police Station. Call the ambulance so they can take them to the morgue. Is that clear?"

Everyone nodded and half of them stayed behind and they were collecting all the evidence from inside the van and they called the tow truck to take the van back to the Police Station. The other half planned to escort me all the way to Thomason Hospital. Alma rode along with my mother and they turned on their police sirens and most the cars got out of the way and they thought they were after me. We rode off all the way to the Hospital.

My mother and Alma got out of the car and went running inside the Emergency Room. I jumped out of the horse and picked up Luz and put her in my arms and went inside. My mother was talking to the Security Guard when he saw me enter the room. He took out his gun and my mother also took out her gun and pointed at the Security Guard.

"Put the gun down! We need a Doctor for this girl. She was beaten and rape." My mother said.

"My daughter needs help." Alma said.

I began to notice that the fat Security Guard was still standing there and was scared to see me, and I gave Alma her daughter. "Hold her for a second." I said and took out my two Magnums and the people took cover and ran away from the door. I was shooting at the door and kicked it open. I went inside to find a Doctor, Alma took Luz inside and my mother also went inside and ordered for a Doctor. I took out my Magnum and yelled for a Doctor and then all the Doctors were finally cooperating and decided to treat Luz. They put her in a bed and she was still in pain. And I grabbed Luz's hand and said. "You're going to recover."

She squeezed my hand so tight and said. "Thank you for helping me!" She said and tried to smile.

I also gave her a smile but she was in so much pain to notice and I left the Emergency Room and my mother followed me all the way outside. When the team saw my mother that was walking behind me and they also took out their guns. "Put your guns down! That's an order." She yelled at them and looked at me. "So what now?"

"Just because I saved a girl doesn't mean that it's over." I said.

"You don't have to kill people."

"You left me with no choice, Beatrice. You should have brought me your son when you had the chance. This would not be over until Mauricio is finally dead. You already know that and someday your son and I will face each other and settle the score. Like I said this will not be over until your son is dead and I will burn his corpse!" I exclaimed.

"So, this will never end between you and my son?" She asked.

"No! Whenever you are ready to give up your son and we can finally face each other. The fight to the death!" I exclaimed and jumped on my lovely horse and said. "Just tell your son that I will see him very soon." I said and rode off away. And then the dream took me to another place and I found myself in Luz's room and I saw myself in the mirror and I was dressed as The Dark Cowboy and she came into the room and smiled and closed the door.

She whispered to me. "Hi. It's nice to see you again."

"How are you feeling" I asked quietly.

"Better but the Doctor told me that I have internal injury and I cannot have any babies and I'm sad."

"Don't worry I already took care of them. They are buried fifty feet below and there are now going to be worm food." I said

"Why did you save my life?" She asked.

"You were calling for help and I was in the area. But I was happy that I killed five more people. And that you were safe from them." He responded.

"Thank you again for saving me." She smiled and sat on top of the bed. "But why do you kill people?"

"I want revenge. That's all you need to know. I'm glad that you're doing okay but there was a problem." I said.

"What kind of problem?" She asked.

"I counted six drug dealers that were inside the van and I shot only five. I'm guessing he got away when I turn my attention to you and right now I'm looking for him." I said.

"There was five of them and they drugged me." She said.

"Yes, they were drug dealers And I'm going to hunt the other one down." I said and was going out the window.

"Wait." She said and grabbed my hand. "I know there's good in you because you saved my life. Let the Police handle those drug dealers. Don't kill anymore

Jesus Morales

people you must forgive this person that hate you so much. Will you do it for me."

"I'll be thinking about it."

"Okay. If you need somebody to talk to. I will always be here for you. I'm here as a friend." She said and smiled.

"Okay. I like that idea." I said and shook her hand and she was so pretty and said, "I'll try not to kill anymore people and I might forgive this person." I said and went out the window.

Luz watched me from the window and saw me ride away in my horse. She smiled and felt that she made a new friend. She will pray for me and hope that I will never kill again. As I was watching Luz sleep, I heard more explosions and people were screaming for help. I wanted to see if my mother and sister were doing okay. I wrote Luz a note and I jumped out the window and started the engine and went to my house. I parked in the driveway and went into the house. I went to my mother's room and my sister's room and they were sleeping. So, I went to my room and I laid in bed and I was happy that Luz was dreaming that I saved her life from those drug dealers. And I got sad because there was another life that I couldn't save and it was killing me as well.

CHAPTER TWENTY-TWO

THE POWER OF LOVE

I remained in bed until twelve o'clock in the afternoon and I went to do a few things that I needed to do, for instance gathering my thoughts and I was worried for my friends, so I went to buy a double quarter pound from *McDonalds* and I felt so much better. And I finally went to Luz's house around four o'clock in the afternoon. I parked in the driveway and Alma waved at me and she was in backyard and I went inside the house and went to the backyard. Luz and her mother was pulling weeds off the ground and Luz was a complete mess, she was sweating, her hair was all over the place, she had mud on her knees and arms. But I didn't care I still love her no matter what. Alma and I were talking while Luz continued to pull weeds off the ground and she fell down and landed on her butt. She quickly got up and giggled. And the phone rang and Alma went inside the house to answer the phone. Luz and I stared at each other and smiled.
"Hey, Hunny Buns, you look great." I said.
"I'm a mess, sweetie." She smiled.
"It's okay, I still love you like that. You even looked sexy." I smiled.
"I want to kiss you but I will get you muddy and sweaty." She said.
"I don't care if you get mud of my clothes and I get put them on the washer

and take a shower and it's no big deal no worries." I smiled and I grabbed her by the waist and we kissed for a long time.

And Luz took off her gloves and hat and we grabbed two chairs and sat in the shade and there was a fresh breeze and it blew most of Luz's hair and she put her hair into a pony tail. "I talked to my daddy in the morning." She said.

"What did you guys talk about?" I asked.

"I told them that I found someone I love." She smiled and winked at me. "My daddy didn't believe me but my mommy told him that I'm in love. I guess my mommy convinced my daddy that his little girl is in love."

"Are you in love with me?" I asked.

"Of course silly." She smiled.

"We deserve to be happy." I said.

"Yes, we do." Luz smiled and got up and grabbed the hose, she turned on the water and was washing her legs, feet, her arms, and hands and got a towel and she was all dried up. She sat next to me and she put her legs on top of my legs."

"You have mosquito bites." I said.

"My mommy told me not to scratch them but it's hard to scratch."

"I have a spray for mosquitoes bites and its in my truck. I'll be back. Don't you move, Luz." I smiled and I went to my truck and found the spray right of away. I was only gone for a couple of seconds but Luz acted that I was gone for five years .

"I missed you a lot." She said.

"Me too." I smiled and sat down and she put her legs on top of mine and we looked at each other for a couple of seconds. I started touching her legs and sprayed on her legs. Luz looked at me and smiled and then she leaned over for me to kiss her.

"Am I interrupting?" Alma asked.

We looked at her mother and started laughing. "I'm sorry, Alma."

"That's okay, you guys are in love. And I've never seen my daughter this happy and that's all it matters."

"I really love Luz." I smiled and looked at Luz. "You are the most incredible girl I've met in my life."

Luz smiled and hugged me so tight and we kissed. "You guys can go out, Luz and I can finish this tomorrow." She said.

"Are you sure?" I asked.

"Yes, of course." She said.

Luz went inside to take a shower while Alma and I put the shovel and the rest of the stuff into the garage. And we went to the living room and we talked for awhile. We also were drinking lemonade and continued to talk. Then Luz went to the living room and we said goodbye to her mother. Her mother went to her bedroom to take her nap and I wasn't so sure what Luz wanted to do other than to be kissing and be in my arms all afternoon long. She put on her sandals and grabbed an envelope from the coffee table and we went to my house. Luz didn't open the envelope and I was wondering about it. We parked on the sidewalk and went inside the house. We sat down in the living room.

"What's in the envelope?" I asked her.

She smiled and responded, "I received the letter from Columbia University and I haven't opened the letter. I'm so nervous!"

"Open it!" I smiled.

"You open it!" She smiled and gave me the envelope.

I grabbed the envelope and open it. I started reading the letter and I looked at her and said, "You got in!"

Luz looked at me and was happy. "I got in! Oh, my God! I cannot believe that I got in!"

"I'm happy for you!" We hugged each other.

"Wait! That means I get to leave to New York but what about us, Mauricio?"

"Well I'm going to graduate from The University of Missouri and I can move there. And it's going to work out!"

"I don't want to loose you! I love you a lot and we're going to work hard on our relationship if we're far away from each other." She smiled and hugged me.

And Tania came to the living room. "What's up?"

Luz looked at her and smiled, "I got accepted to Columbia University!"

Tania smiled and they hugged each other. "I'm happy for you but what about my brother. You guys are starting your relationship?"

"It's going to work out! I faith in our relationship!" Luz smiled.

"I also have faith in our relationship!" I smiled and we hugged each other.

"Well do you guys have any plans today?" She asked.

"Other than the big news. Not really!" Luz responded.

"We have plans to be kissing and that's about it." I said and smiled.

"Well how about we to go to *Cielo Vista Mall* and it will great if the three of us did something together." Tania said.

"Sure." I said and looked at her.

"I'm in the mood to go out shopping and I hope that my Prince charming spoils me today." Luz smiled.

"Anything you want, Luz. My job description is to make you happy and to spoil you for the rest of my life and to love you a lot. And also going to spoil my baby sister too." I smiled and we went to *Cielo Vista Mall*, which is the biggest mall we have here in good old El Paso, Texas. So, the girls went to looked at the clothes and I stayed outside the stores and looked around the Mall. I hadn't been there for a long time and I had forgotten how crowded the Mall gets during the summer. And we went upstairs to look at the rest of the stories, since I was paying for both of them, Tania and Luz grabbed half of the clothes in the stores. They also went to get shoes and more make up. And I was already tired from walking around and I didn't know why Luz and Tania were not that tired. In spite of being tired and I still had a great time with the love of my life Luz and my baby sister, Tania.

And three hours later Luz and Tania finally finished shopping and we went to the Food Court and we ate at *Subway*. While we were eating I saw my old high school Teacher, his name is Mr. Caballero and he was there with his girlfriend. They were walking by the Food Court and they were headed down to the escalators. I was glad to see that he was doing fine and I saw Luz and Tania laughing and they were turning red. Then at eight o'clock that night we went home and I walked Luz to the front door and she gave me a hug and kiss, and she also blew a kiss for Tania and Tania also blew her a kiss and she went inside the house and we went home. My mother was in the living room and Tania showed her what I bought her at the Mall and she went to he room.

"Aren't you suppose to be working?" I asked her.

"I'm taking time off. I want to recharge my batteries." She responded with a smile.

"I hope you are able to recharge your batteries in time to captured more criminals. I know that you still have it in you." I smiled.

"How about we have dinner? Just you and me." My mother smiled.

"I like that!" I smiled and we went to have dinner together. We decided to go to *Denny's* The waitress came and we ordered breakfast for dinner and the waitress brought our drinks and my mother and I started having a conversation.

"How are things with Luz?" She asked.

"Things are going well. But!"

"But what, Mauricio?"

"Luz received a letter from Columbia University. She was happy and like you said we need to work hard in this relationship."

"I'm glad that Luz is going to Columbia University. I know you two are going to work hard in this relationship. You're about to graduate from The University of Missouri and she might need some company over there." My mother smiled.

The waitress brought our food and we started eating. "Mom did The Dark Cowboy saved your life a couple of nights ago?" I asked.

"I hate to admit it but The Dark Cowboy did saved my life. But he's still a criminal and we need to arrest him." She said and ate.

"I remember when The Dark Cowboy told me that he was going to kill people. I don't how he felt when he took someone's life away." I said and ate.

"It doesn't feel good when you take someone's life away. The first time I killed someone I was just nineteen years old. I was arrogant at that time after all I was hanging out with the likes of your father. And I thought it would be a great idea to kill the criminals, I was too lazy to catch them, so I shot them to death. Well I ended up killing twenty criminals and they all had families. When I shot them and they were just trying to feed their families. I couldn't live with myself. I just hope that you don't take someone's life." My mother smiled and ate.

"I promise that I'm not!" I smiled.

"I just hope that you guys end up getting married. Because I can tell that Luz really loves you a lot." She smiled and three hours later we went home and I was glad to have a peaceful sleep this time. The next day I woke up around nine o'clock in the morning. I got up and went to the restroom and I started feeling uneasy once again. I was breathing heavily and was praying and it went away but not all the way. I got dressed up and I was on my way to Luz's house and I saw the Ambulance coming behind me and I stopped for them to go by me and I love the sound of the sirens and those were the good old days. Then I drove again and I saw the Paramedics at Luz's house and they were running to her house. And I parked in the driveway and I also ran inside her house. I went to the living room and Alma was on the ground and she was having problems breathing and she was very pale. One of the Paramedics was trying to calm Luz down because she was getting hysterical. The Paramedics put Alma inside the Ambulance and said they were taking her to Thomason Hospital. And I went to hug Luz and she was crying on my arms. And I told her that everything will be okay and her mother is also going to be okay. Then Luz went to change her clothes and brushed her teeth and went to Thomason Hospital. And it took us at least half an hour to get to the Hospital. And we finally got there and we went inside the Emergency Room and they told us that her mother was Intensive Care Unit. We took the elevator and I was holding onto Luz and the elevator door opened and she almost ran toward the receptionist to ask for her mother. And I grabbed her by the shoulder and we went walking to ask for her mother.

Luz was not allowed to see her mother, so we had to sit and wait for so many hours. And Luz cried most of the time and I tried to comfort her and she was leaning next to me. And thirty minutes later Luz and I were in the hallway of the waiting room and I called my mother and told her that I was here at the Hospital and Luz gave me her father's phone number and I told my mother if she can call him. And Luz saw the Doctor and he was looking for her, so she went to talk to him and I was still on the phone with my mother and I hanged up the phone.

"Mauricio!"

I turned around and there was my old high school Teacher, Mike Caballero, and he's Eliza's brother and I was glad to see him after all these years. Well I haven't seen him since my high school graduation. "Mike what are you doing here?"

"Monica and I were having lunch at the cafeteria. She now works in the Annex. I was going to leave until I saw you and your girlfriend waiting for the elevator. I saw the look on her face and I thought something was wrong." He responded.

"You're right. Her mother had an asthma attack. I hope she gets better." I smiled. We talked for awhile and Luz went to see who I was talking to. She smiled and I introduce them and they shook hands. Luz was getting ready to leave and we said goodbye to Mike. We left the Hospital and left to her house and Luz had stopped crying. During the way home, Luz was telling me what the Doctor had told her and it was good news, her mother was going to be alright but she needed to rest for a couple of nights.

Then she asked me. "Who were talking to?"

"That was my old high school Teacher, he helped me with Geometry." I answered nervously.

"Why are you nervous?" She asked.

"I'm just worried for my mother-in-law." I looked at her and smiled.

She leaned next to me and I put my arm around her and she was upset. We were getting to her house and I parked in the driveway. "Since we've been together, you have never told me anything about your past, except that you went to school in Missouri and dated a lot of drunk girls. And I told you personal things about me. And I've never told Tania or anybody else but you haven't told me anything."

"To be honest I don't remember that much about my past." I said and smiled.

"Stop playing around, and I told you right from the start that I don't want any secrets between us." She said.

I didn't want to tell her that I was The Dark Cowboy but it's a good thing that I had another flashback and I had a vision of *Concordia Cemetery* and there was a gravestone. "Okay, no more secrets." Saved by the flashback and I started the engine and took her to Concordia Cemetery. I had no idea where I was going but some reason I was so sure that I was going to find answers there. We parked and we got out and walked around the cemetery and she saw a tombstone.

The tombstone read, "Eliza Caballero, born in 1983 died in 2002." Luz read very slowly. And Luz looked at me and cried. The flashbacks came back. And I remember saying to Eliza. "Eliza will you be my girlfriend."

And she said, "Of course, Mauricio."

I also heard a voice. "You two make a cute couple and I hope you guys get married and have a lot of kids together." And everything about my relationship with Eliza kept coming back to me and I want to thank my memory for that. And it's good to remember her and now I wanted to move on with Luz.

We left the graveyard and we leaned against the truck and I had my arm around Luz. "Eliza was my girlfriend and the guy that I was talking to at the Hospital was her brother. I met her while he was tutoring me." I said and from my vision I started to describe Eliza but I realized I couldn't remember her at all and the only thing I remembered was her laughter and her beauty. And I continued, "Eliza and I have known each other since we were little kids and we were together for over two years and she passed away from a heart disease." I said.

"I'm so sorry, Mauricio." She smiled.

"I couldn't do anything to help her. She was dying right in front of my eyes and there was nothing I could do just watch her die." I said.

Luz looked at me and had tears coming down her face. "You did everything you could to make her happy, and you gave her your love. She was lucky to have you just as I'm lucky to have you in my life. So, you don't need to feel guilty."

I looked at Luz and smiled and we kissed. Then we headed back to her house and I called my mother and told her that I was going to spend the night at Luz's house just in case she needed me. I didn't want her to stay alone and I wanted to sleep on the couch but Luz wanted me to sleep with her on the bed. But first she went to take a shower while I was laying in bed. And I remembered what happen to me in the restroom . I started sensing the presence of danger. And it was Alma that needed my help and if I could arrived in time she wouldn't be at the Hospital right now. What will be the excuse, I cannot say that I'm hanging out with my friends because they are not here. There went to college and I cannot say that I was eating in a restaurant or still sleeping on the couch. Well I'm sorry Alma that I wasn't there to help you.

Luz turned off the water and she put her tank top and her underwear. She was drying her hair and we laid there in bed just holding on to each other.

"Are you okay?" I asked.

"Yes, with you here I feel safe." She said.

"Don't worry everything is going to be okay. You mom is going to recover and your friend Madelyn is going to come back home and you guys will have a slumber party and it will be like old times."

"I hope so." She said.

"So, how come you didn't have a boyfriend?" I asked and I wanted to change the subject so Luz wouldn't be sad.

"Because most guys are into drugs and others just want to get girls into bed and leave the girl pregnant. And also sleep with drunken girls just for the Hell of it!" She said and looked at me and smiled. "No offense, Sweetie."

"It's the same thing everywhere." I agreed with her

"When you were in college, did you slept with every girl you saw?" She asked me.

"Kind off but I was bored because I wasn't in love with them. But I know that I made a couple of mistakes in my life and I was able to learn from them. And I'm in love with you." I said.

"Me too. I will love to marry you someday and we are in love and we care for each other." Luz smiled and she looked at me and we started kissing for a long time. "Make love to me."

"Are you sure?" I asked.

"Yes." She said and smiled.

We started kissing and we took off our clothes and we made love all night long. And it was a magical night for us. Then later on in the night I started having another weird dream and it was about my senior prom that Eliza and I went to a few years back. Eliza and I were sitting down with our friends until they played our song and it was called "It Ain't me Baby." She saw so happy and we got up and started dancing in the dream. And I could see my friends and everyone else were moving away from the dance floor. I saw them clap for us but I couldn't see Eliza's face it was only a blur in the dream. And I only saw her smile and then she put her head on my shoulder. We started kissing and as I was looking at her, Eliza turned into a skeleton and I started screaming at the top of my lungs. I continue to scream and I woke up and I heard Luz crying in her sleep.

"Please! Stop! Let me go! Don't rape me!" She continued to yell and she finally woke up, sat up and looked around the room. She finally looked at me and started crying her eyes out and I hugged her so tight. "I was dreaming about something so horrible!" She cried.

"Everything is going fine, Eliza." I said.

"You called me, Eliza." Luz sobbed.

"I meant, Luz and I'm sorry, Luz. I was dreaming about Eliza."

"Just hold me, Mauricio." Luz cried for awhile and said, "What were you dreaming about?"

"I don't want to remember, just as long I'm here with you."

"I love you." She said and she was crying for her mother and her depression of the past. And I was holding on to her so tight and we finally fell asleep. And I was worried for her and everything else that's happening this summer.

Then the next day when I woke up and Luz wasn't there in bed. I went to the restroom and she was in the kitchen making me breakfast. I went to the kitchen and hugged her and she turned around kissed me.

"I'm happy because we made love last night and I wish we could enjoy it but if it wasn't for our horrible dreams." She looked at me and said, "Look at us, Mauricio, a couple of weeks ago were just two strangers that met. Remember when we were happy, we were having fun and now we're having bad dreams and we're sad."

"Everything is going to be fine." I said and hugged her.

"What's wrong with us?" She asked.

"Every couple goes through with this, I went through this with Eliza. But something else brought us together and all I know that this is the best summer I had in years and all I now is that I love you a lot." I smiled and I had a feeling that it had something to do when I saved her life a few years back.

"Me too." She said.

We sat down and ate scrambled eggs. "These are good scrambled eggs." I smiled.

"I'm glad you like them and I hope I get to make you breakfast when we get married." She smiled, "And can we go see my mommy later on." She said.

"Of course." I said and looked at her and smiled.

We finished eating our scrambled eggs and Luz went to take another shower and I went home to take a shower as well and we got dressed and I came back to pick her up and went to Thomason Hospital. When we arrived at Thomason Hospital Luz and I went to the gift shop and bought a lot of balloons and we headed towards the elevator and we arrived at Intensive Care Unit. The Doctor was standing there and he was talking to the Nurse. The Doctor saw us and he came up to us.

"How's my mom?" Luz asked.

"Your mother is resting now but we did all kinds of test on her and she's fine now." He said and smiled.

Luz started crying and I was holding on to her. "Thank God that my mommy is going to be okay!"

"Of course she is." I said and hugged her tight.

"We're going to keep her here for a couple of nights." He said.

"That's fine!" I smiled and Luz was able to calm down when the Doctor took us to see her. We looked through the window and she smiled and waved at us. We went into the room and Luz hugged her mother so tight. "How are you feeling?" Luz asked and her tears started coming out.

"I feel better and I'm ready to run a marathon." She responded with a smile.

"When are you getting out?" I asked.

"In a couple of days." She smiled and looked at us and saw the look on our faces. "Did you guys get into a fight?"

"Now, we just had a rough night." I responded.

"Mauricio, kept me company and he heard me scream in my sleep and he protected me all night long." Luz said and smiled.

"You two make a terrific couple and I hope you two end up getting married and have a lot of children." Alma said.

"Oh, Mommy! We just met! Plus we haven't talked about getting married." Luz smiled and she was grinning from ear to ear.

"But you guys made love last night!" She said.

"No, we didn't." She couldn't stopped smiling.

"I know you guys made love because Luz never smiles when she has a conversation, she waits to smile at the end of the conversation and right now she cannot stop smiling. She looks like the *Joker* from *Batman*." She looked at her and smiled and touched her hand. "You lost your virginity, Luz."

"I'm sorry to disappoint you, Mommy. And for the second time in my life. I don't know what to do without you." She said and wanted to cry.

"Stop blaming yourself, Luz. I'm not angry with you two having sex, it's part of your relationship. I'm glad to see you happy and in love." She smiled and hugged her.

"I thought you were going to die." Luz said.

"I'm alive that's all it matters." She said.

And my cell was vibrating and I went outside to see who it was. It was a text message from Luz's father. I came back inside the room and said, "Your dad called, Luz."

"Go and talk to your father and be strong for me." She smiled.

"I will be strong for you and for Mauricio. And I'm going to go downstairs and talk to daddy." Luz smiled and went downstairs to talk to her father. Well I was still standing in front of Alma and she just smiled and I decided to sit next to her. I didn't want to make things worse than already is but I had to ask her.

"Alma, on that day when you mentioned Eliza to me. How did you know Eliza?" I asked her.

Alma smiled and responded, "Eliza was my student at Clarke Middle School. I was her choir teacher and we were close friends. We talked about everything and one day Eliza came running into my classroom and said that she met a great guy and that you guys were in love. The way Eliza talked about you, Mauricio, and it seemed that she really loved you a lot and wanted to marry you and have a lot of kids. She told me so many great things about you and I was glad to see her happy. Eliza was different from the girls at school and what made her special is that she was caring, thoughtful, friendly, and loved to help people. She changed people's life."

I responded, "I don't remember Eliza at all, and I started having flashbacks when you mentioned her name. And I don't remember that much about her just her smile and her laughter." I said and I wanted to cry. "And I feel the emptiness inside my body like there is something missing and I don't know what to do because I'm going crazy here. The depression pills are not helping at all."

Alma touched my hand and smiled. "I know who you really are. I don't know what happen to you that you no longer have any memory of Eliza or your dark side."

"My dark side?" I asked.

"Yes, Mauricio. You are The Dark Cowboy." She said.

I was shocked and how did she know that? And all I can say is this, "Who is The Dark Cowboy?" I asked and I wanted to know where she would go with this.

"The Dark Cowboy was inside you the entire time, ever since you were born. The Dark Cowboy is part of you, like your long lost brother. You know like Cain and Able, one is good and the other is bad."

"You are saying that I have a curse." I said.

"It was a gift but you didn't know how to control it. This monster was controlling you and made you kill so many people along the way. And you need to find the answers that you are looking for." She said.

"How do you know that?" I asked.

She responded with a smile. "A close friend of mine told me that you were out of control and you had a hard time controlling the evil spirit that was inside your body."

"So, did I just transformed into The Dark Cowboy and killed my friends and everyone else?" I asked.

"Well as the matter of fact you did control it but you were able to disguise yourself and used the costume, so no one would know that a monster was killing people. During the day you were Mauricio de la Vega, and during the night you were The Dark Cowboy and you were some kind of monster underneath the costume. But you saved my daughter's life when she was attacked at Marty Robbins Park and I thank you for saving her life. And you saved your mother's life as well. And I know there's a lot of people that you want dead but there might be good in you after all." She smiled.

Well my future mother-in-law has me in a corner that I cannot get out. "To be honest, Alma. I don't remember that much about Eliza but I do know that I'm The Dark Cowboy and I've been anxious to kill someone but I'm controlling myself. And not to mention that I have the ability to sense when someone is in danger. I'm guessing that Primo needs my help and I sensed when you were in danger. And I couldn't save you two because I don't have an excuse. And I know everyone thinks that I killed Eliza but I loved her a lot. And what's hurting me inside is that I was able to rescue Luz from those drug dealers and I couldn't rescue Eliza from those intruders and that's the part of me that still haunts me to this day." I said and looked at her, "How am I going to tell Luz that I am The Dark Cowboy and I was the one that was doing all the killings. Luz defends me because I saved her life. She is in love with The Dark Cowboy and I don't know if she truly loves me." I said.

"Don't be upset with yourself, Mauricio. Luz will understand because she changed a lot over the years. And you two are in love and why don't you let her decide because you're the same person. Maybe you guys were meant to be together." She smiled.

"That's what I'm thinking too." I smiled and Luz came back to the room and smiled at me. And I calmed down when she came in and I was trying to act cool around her.

And the Doctor came into the room and told us that Alma needed to rest. Luz kissed her mother her forehead and I also kissed her and she smiled. "I'm going to see you tomorrow." Luz said and smiled.

Alma tears started coming down her face and said, "Yes, Luz. You are going to see me tomorrow. And I love you, my Princess and I'll be fine." They hugged each other and we left the Hospital. We went inside the truck and went to her house and I parked in the driveway.

"Do you want spend the night with us?" I asked.

Luz hugged me and responded, "Yes, that will be great. And knowing Tania she will be happy and your mother will also be happy. And I forgot that tomorrow is your birthday and I hope we can come back here to my room, so we can make love that will be my present to you." She smiled.

"I really love you, Luz and I really want to marry you and have a lot of children." I smiled.

"I want to have a big family with you." She said and smiled and I started the engine and went to my home and Luz told my mother and Tania what the Doctor told her and they were happy that her mother was going to be okay and they were planning to give her a huge surprise when she gets out of the Hospital. And I was still wondering who told Alma that I was The Dark Cowboy and she thanks me for saving her daughter's life. Well I'm guessing someone broke the rule of my identity. So, I tried to enjoy dinner with everyone and I wanted to continue my relationship with Luz and without any distractions at all. And after dinner my mother washed the dishes and I was helping her out. Luz and Tania were kind of quiet and my mother wanted them to cheer up. "How about you guys have a slumber party? I want to see you two smile and have fun!"

"That will be great!" Luz smiled.

Tania smiled and said, "Okay, I'm going to send a text message to Jackie ,so the three of us can have a slumber party and we can pray and hope to see Madelyn before the summer ends and she comes back home safe. And come on Luz I'll lend you some of my pajamas." Tania smiled and was getting ready to have a slumber party, so she called her other close friend. Jackie Lewis, well she is deaf. And she actually send her a text message and told her to come over to the house. Tania loaned Luz some of her pajamas and Luz went to take a quick shower. I was still in the kitchen with my mother and we were talking. My mother was sitting down drinking her coffee, and someone knocked on the door and Tania went to open it well it was her friend Jackie and they hugged each other. She said hi to me and hugged me. Tania and Jackie decided to bring snacks from the grocery store. So, my mother took them to the grocery store, I was in the kitchen when Luz came out of the restroom and she smiled. Luz and I stayed by ourselves and I picked her up and went to my room. We started kissing until we heard something fall down and we got startled. The noise came from inside the closet And we went to open the closet door. We found a box that was laying on the floor and I grabbed it and I wanted to know what was inside the box. I put the box on top of the bed and opened it.

"Let's see what's inside the box." Luz smiled.

I took out some letters, "These are love letters that Eliza wrote to me." I smiled and gave them to Luz and she was reading all the letters and was happy and was wiping her tears.

"She really loved you a lot." Luz wiped her tears.

I also took out a notebook and we were looking at it and it had pictures of us. That was our own yearbook and we nominated ourselves as the best couple at Elementary School and the best couple on the planet Earth but we did became the best couple in Americas High School and everyone loved us so much. And finally I took out a perfume and I sprayed it at Luz's arm and we both smelled it. "This was Eliza's perfume and it smells like the day I met you at the grocery store."

"Are you serious?" She asked.

"Yes! That's weird!" I responded with a smile and finally I took out Eliza's diary and it was red. "It's her diary and don't you have one?"

"Yes, I do! Oh, my God. It's been a long time since I've written in my diary. I was just a little girl when my parents gave me my diary for my fourth birthday. And I think I have it in my room." She said and smiled.

"If it's okay with you that we should save Eliza memories!"

"You should and it's great to have memories of her." She said and smiled and then the front door open and Tania and Jackie came inside the room and took Luz with them to have a slumber party. I went to the kitchen ask my mother if we have another box. And she told me that there's a box in the garage. So, I went to the garage and grabbed the box and went to my room. I was putting Eliza's memories inside the new box and put it back in the closet. And I started watching a movie and I was happy that they were having fun. But I was more excited that I had a peaceful sleep

The next day I woke up and looked at my calendar, today is June 17, 2006 well this was the anniversary at the secret blown up Mental Institution and it's also my birthday. I was happy and went to the restroom and I heard someone singing. And I went to the kitchen and saw the backdoor open and Luz was outside sitting on the bench. I joined her outside.

"Good morning!" I said.

"Hey, baby."

"Did you sleep well?" I asked.

"Yes, and I had a dream about you." She smiled.

"What was it about?" I asked her.

She looked at me and smiled, "That we got married and had a lot of children and for our honeymoon we went to the Virgin Island and we were happy together." She smiled and kissed me. That's weird I had the same dream as her. But that was a long time ago and she leaned against me and she was humming. And once again a lady bug landed on Luz's arm and the lady bug was walking around on her arm. "I think this is the same lady bug I was playing with on more than three occasions." She smiled and there were a couple of butterflies that were going around us and one landed on her nose. "How cute! The butterflies' legs are tickling my nose." Luz giggled and a couple of birds landed on her legs and she was giggling too. Then the butterflies, and the birds flew away and also the lady bug also flew away. "Take care!" She smiled.

"I love it when you are in a good mood." I said and we kissed.

"Happy Birthday!" She looked at me and we kissed for a long time.

"How sweet! You two are in love!" Tania smiled.

"Breakfast is ready!" My mother yelled.

"Will be right there." I said.

We went inside the house and everyone hugged me, my mother told me that I should wait for Saturday because she wanted to have a big party so all the relatives could come and celebrated with me. Then later on in the afternoon Luz and I were outside sitting on the bench.

"I want to give you your present." Luz said and kissed me.

"What is it?" I asked.

"Me! We should go back to my room and we can make love all night long." She smiled and we kissed.

And in about three hours later Luz and I went to her house. She locked the door and I carried her to her room and we were also kissing. I gently put her on top of her bed and it was a magical night for two of us. But I had a lot of surprises coming up for Saturday, one of my surprises was that on, Thursday morning Luz and I went to pick Alma up from the Hospital.

We brought her to my house and we stayed in the kitchen and my mother made lunch for everyone. "You are wonderful cook, Beatrice." Alma said.

"Thank you!" My mother said.

"Rumor has it that you are going to recover and you are going to be the old you all over again." Tania smiled.

"Bless you Tania. You have been a good friend to my daughter all these years. But I want you to be a favor, Beatrice."

"What kind of favor?" She asked.

"I don't want you to retire from the Police Force because I know that you still have it in you and I'm not retiring either. I want to be a Teacher for as long I want to!" Alma smiled.

"My job is a lot harder than yours. Your job description, is to teach students to sing. And my job description is to keep criminals off the street and sometimes you need to learn when to walk away. Because I don't want to be a washed up Police Officer!" My mother said.

Luz's tears started coming down her face. "Beatrice! I mean mommy, I remember you taught me not to give up and with all the things that were happening to me. You still told me not to quit just keep moving forward. And someday I was going to recover from my drug problems! And I was able to recover!"

"My daughter is right, Beatrice. You might want to think about that." Alma said.

"Mom, you don't have to go to Miami." Tania said.

"I think you should reconsidered by staying here and continue with your Police work. I know you're anxious to arrest The Dark Cowboy! I have a prediction that you're going to take out the greatest serial killer of all time without breaking a sweat and before the summer ends!" I smiled.

"I'll think about it." My mother said and smiled and we hugged her so tight.

We finished eating and after that Alma and Luz spend the night at our house. And the other surprise was that the next day at exactly four o'clock in the afternoon, a black van pulled into the driveway and we went outside to see who it was. My father and Anthony Reyes, Karina's father came out of the van with a huge surprise and opened the side door, and Primo Mancini, Madelyn Van Der AA, and Perla Mancini got out of the van and gave us a huge hug and we were happy to see them again. Well my father being the arrogant man that he is, he showed us today's newspaper and he even read it to everyone. "The FBI and the CIA have finally captured mob leader Vito Mancini. And finally after twenty years on the run, the CIA and the FBI have finally captured him." My father had a huge smile on his face and said, "One down and one to go" and my father was mentioning The Dark Cowboy, yeah good luck with that one. I doubt that my father arrested Vito Mancini, well it was the CIA that captured Vito Mancini and his henchman. And I know my father was happy for no reason at all and I think he should be more professional like Anthony Reyes. My mother and Tania hugged my father so tight and I don't know if I should congratulate my father for not arresting Vito or I should kill him in front of everyone. And maybe Karina and the rest of the crew has some explaining to do to me.

And later on in the evening we had a cookout in the backyard and we were laughing and celebrating like one big happy family. Well my father was celebrating because he thinks that he made the family proud and he could care less about the rest of us. Karina and the girls also joined us in the backyard and Primo and the girls were also there celebrating and they saw the look on my face but this wasn't the place to talk. Then on Saturday afternoon my mother made me a big a huge party, so everyone went to my birthday party and we were having fun. And I introduce Luz to all of my family and they liked her immediately. The de la Vega family were encouraging me to marry her and we smiled and hugged each other. And I told them I am just as soon I'm finished with college. And it was close to midnight when everyone went home. Luz and I were in my room and she was combing her hair. She saw the look on my face

"What's wrong, Sweetie? Did you enjoy your birthday?" She asked.

"Just thinking." I responded.

"You're still thinking about Eliza?" She asked.

"Sometimes, I miss her a lot, and I guess because she was my first love." I responded.

"I know she was your first love." Luz answered and said. "And I wish I could have met her in person."

"You two would have been inseparable but Eliza is in the past and I want to spend my rest of life with you. I love you so much."

Luz put her arms around my neck and we kissed for awhile and I was holding her tight and she pulled away. "What's wrong, Hunny Bunny?" I asked.

We sat on the bed and she responded with a smile, "I'm pregnant!"

"Really?" I asked.

"Yes. I just found out this morning." She smiled and kissed me.

"We should have another celebration." I said.

"It's a miracle and I thought I could not have any babies because of my internal injury! Plus I was praying to God and hoped that I could get pregnant and have a healthy baby." Luz sobbed and hugged me and we kissed.

"We are going to be parents. We're going to live a great in Spain and we're going to rule that magnificent country."

Luz looked at me very seriously. "I don't want our kids to live the way I used to live, you know with the drugs, suicide and I was always getting into trouble at school and at home." She started crying and said,. "I already know where I'm might going to end up when I die."

"In Heaven, of course." I said.

"We both know that I'm going to end up in Hell with all the bad people. Even though I became a Christian. And I accepted Jesus and God into my life and who knows if they are going accept me in Heaven." She said.

"Come on, Luz! That was in the past. Besides you changed your life for the better." I said.

"Yes, but even though I got over the drugs, suicidal, and among other things. And what hurts me the most is the fact that I was raped and it's something I've got to live with the rest of my life. It still hurts, Mauricio, and even though it was a long time ago, I can't forget it at all." And Luz told me everything about the day she was raped but I already know the story she's going to tell me. So, I had her in my arms and she started telling me, "Well my mommy picked me up from the airport and we hugged each other and I wanted to have a picnic at Marty Robbins Park. So, we went to the grocery store to get some food and we were in line to pay and I saw the newspaper and it was the first time I read about the murders."

"Murders?" I interrupted her.

"I asked my mommy about the murders, well my mommy just smiled. And the cashier told me that there was a serial killer on the loose and the Police Officers and FBI Agents had not caught him yet. They were calling him "The Dark Cowboy!" They said that he came out at night and killed everyone that stood in his way. My daddy told me everything about Vito Mancini and he was crime drug lord but they said that this killer was worse dangerous than the mob. Even the Mayor of El Paso, Texas had decided to put on a six o'clock curfew, so no one was allowed to go outside in the night." She said.

"Go on." I said.

"The manager told my mommy to take care of me and before we left, the cashier said to me, "Beware of The Dark Cowboy. You can't run and hide from him, so all you can do is pray and hope that he doesn't come after you and kills you. And eats your soul!" I looked at the cashier and wondered what she meant by that. I looked at my mommy and she smiled, and she told me not to worry at all. So, my mommy and I were having our picnic at Marty Robbins Park, just then your mom came and I was glad to see her. So, we talked for awhile and we were going to go get some Pizza but I wanted to stay and run all over the park. Well they left walking and I started running all over the park and I saw a black van that was parked on the street but I kept running and when I got close to the street, and the van was still there. And all of the sudden this guy came out and wanted directions, so been the nice and naïve girl that I am. I went to give him directions. And all of the sudden the man points the gun at me and grabs me and pulled me inside the van. They tied me up and started raping me and drugging me and punching me." Luz started sobbing.

"It's okay, baby." I said.

"No, it's not okay. I want to tell you everything." She grabbed a Kleenex and wiped her tears and continued. "They were doing all kinds of weird stuff to me. They put weird things into my vagina and that caused me to have internal injury. And then there was a loud bang that was coming from outside. One of them went outside to check it out. Well they waited for him to come back and then we heard him scream and we heard gunshots and the back doors opened and when I looked up at the back door, I couldn't believe what I was staring at, even though I was drugged and delirious from the pain."

"What did you see?" I asked.

"I thought I was seen things but I know I was conscience and I was staring at The Dark Cowboy! His eyes were glowing red like there was something evil in him and he had an evil laughter in him. And one of the gangsters was about to turn on the engine, and The Dark Cowboy shoots him in the head and the blood was spilled in my face and all over the van. So, with all my strength I had left in my body, I crawled my way out to safety and I landed hard on the sidewalk. The Dark Cowboy killed everyone in sight and that's where your mom and my mommy came and the Police and the FBI also came. The Dark Cowboy picked me up and I guess he flew all the way to the Hospital. I was in so much pain and he took me to the Emergency Room at Thomason Hospital. After that I got involved with the wrong crowd and started doing drugs."

"Whatever happened to The Dark Cowboy?" I asked.

"I don't now but he came to visit me in my room and I was happy to see him. And I never knew why he spared my life but I thank him for that. Also my daddy is so religious and took me to Church every Sunday and that also helped me lot."

"Well I know you had an awful experience and you changed your life completely, and look at you now. You are going to be a mother, and we're in love. And you are devoted to God and you're going to college and you're going to have a great career ahead of you. You don't need to worry anymore. Because I'm here for you and I love you a lot."

She looked at me and smiled and she wiped her tears away, "Thank you, Mauricio for helping me handle my past and I love you a lot." Luz continued to sob and I hugged her so tight that I could feel her breathing. "The power of love! I hope we stay together forever."

CHAPTER TWENTY-THREE

UNEXPECTED SURPRISES

Luz and I kept talking and laughing until we saw a bright lightning and we heard a loud thunder that was knocking it's way into the city and it started to rain really hard and the wind was blowing really hard as well. Once again the thunder struck really loud and the lights in the entire city went out and my parents and Alma went to light up the whole house with the candles and they also turn on the stove. Tania came running into my room and hugged Luz and they were already freaking out and they wanted to cry too. I was standing in front of the window and for some reason I started having the same flashbacks and they were like migraines. I grabbed my head and I couldn't see anything but I could hear what was going on. And I heard a voice of the man that was screaming at the top of his lungs. "De la Vega! De la Vega! Pablo de la Vega hired us!" My heart started beeping so fast and everything was slow motion. And I heard my father telling me, "Mauricio step away from the windows! You are going to get hurt!" I was still standing there when the windows broke and the glasses hit me on my and it knocked me to the ground and I only saw a glimpse of the red evil eyes. And I heard Luz asking me, "Honey, are you alright?"

I was covering my face but I kept hearing the same voices and I got on my knees and I wanted the voices to leave. They were all screaming and begging for their lives. I also heard explosions and the gunshots. Then I heard the same voice that was talking to me. "Remember who you really are, Mauricio de la Vega. Don't be afraid, Mauricio de la Vega." And it got worse from there and I was still on my knees and I had my hands on my head and I was trying to block out the voices. And again I heard the same voice, "Soon we will have our revenge Mauricio de la Vega. Now it's time for us to be united once again!" And I started feeling all my anger and it felt like the electricity was rising up my whole body and I was breathing heavily and I had the sensation that I wanted to kill someone. The wind was blowing really hard and the candles fell to the ground and all of the sudden the house was completely dark and there was a fire in the living room. My parents, Alma and Tania were throwing water on the floor while Luz kept on yelling at me, "Mauricio, what was wrong?" And my parents, Alma and Tania came back into the my room and they were telling me if I was okay.

The wind continued to blow even more harder and there was another loud thunder and it started to rain even more harder and hail started to come down and they were hitting everything and the front door opened. And everyone took cover when the other windows broke and just like that it was over. It got quiet and I finally got up and continued to breathe heavily and started laughing out loud. My parents and Alma went to close the front door and went to pick everything up from all over the house. Meanwhile I continued to laugh and I was saying, "I'm back! I'm back!"

And then Luz got my attention. "What are you talking about?"

I open my eyes and the whole room was glowing red. "Why is the room glowing red, Mauricio? What kind of tricks do you have up your sleeves?" Tania asked and laughed.

Then the lights from the whole city came back and I was back to normal once again and I turn around to hug Luz and Tania. They were wondering what was going on. And just like that the storm also went away without an explanation. I'm guessing that The Dark Figure wanted to make a dramatic entrance to enter my body once again. So, Tania and Luz stayed with me and I sat on my bed and at the same time my head was hurting because of the window smacked me in my head. My mother came back to my room and brought me water and some aspirins. The girls stayed with me while I drank my water and my depressive pills. I was sitting down and they were trying to figure out what was wrong earlier but I was smiling at them. After Tania went to help my parents and Alma with the broken glasses.

"Hunny Bunny, I need you to calm down and think about our baby." I said and kissed her and hugged her.

Luz sobbed and smiled. "I love you a lot and I thought you were going to die tonight and I'm glad that you are okay. And have you taken the pills?"

"Yes, I have, Luz!" I said and smiled and I picked her up and I had her in my arms. She stopped crying and was smiling once again. And I started to tickle her and she was laughing and I sat down on the bed, and she was sitting down on top of my legs. And again I started to tickle her to make her feel happy again. She was laughing and I kissed her. "All I want is to make you happy, Luz Maria Estrada." I smiled and we just held each other for awhile.

She looked at me and smiled and said, "Well I want to be known as Luz Maria Fitzgerald Estrada de la Vega. Well I guess I'm going to have to shortened my name! Luz Maria de la Vega!" She smiled and kissed me and we held each other. She looked at me and giggled, "But I also remember when I was in your arms and you took me to Thomason Hospital. And you came to my room and you gave me my first kiss ever and a couple of years later here we are again."

I looked at her and I was in shock and I asked her. "What makes you think that I'm The Dark Cowboy?"

"Well we have a strong connection toward one and another. And I knew that you are The Dark Cowboy all along. We had our first kiss in my room and our second kiss under the moonlight at your house and right there I knew that you are the famous legendary Dark Cowboy."

"You love him don't you? Because he saved your life?" I asked her.

"It was you that saved my life silly." She said and smiled, "A Princess gets attacked by a pack of drug dealers and her Prince Charming rescues her. And I'm glad that you are my rescuer and I love you more than ever. But I'm jealous! How many girls have you saved?" She asked with a smile.

I responded with a smile, "Samantha Jones, Doctor Juanita Van Der AA, you, and my mother."

"I heard about Samantha Jones. The news was spread all over the world. They have been looking for her. So, where is she? Did your friend, Primo raped her?" She asked.

"No. And Samantha Jones is in a boarding school! And I made her mother a promise before I killed her, that her daughter was going to have a good education. Her daughter was there at the wrong place, at the wrong time!" I smiled.

"You're a good man after all! And I'm glad you saved Madelyn's aunt and my mother-in-law." She smiled.

"How come you didn't say anything!" I smiled.

She looked at me and smiled, "I wanted you tell me! How come you didn't tell me?"

"Because I didn't want to loose you! I know over the years you've heard so many awful stories about me. I was afraid that you're going to leave me." I said.

"I was just a little girl when I heard those awful stories about you. And when you saved me at the park. I didn't believe in those stories. I thought I would see you again and I was hoping that you will tell me how everything began. After all I love you a lot and I'm not going to leave your side. I support the decisions that you make." She smiled and kissed her.

"How does the fairy tale end, Hunny Bunny?" I asked her.

She smiled and said. "They live happily ever after."

"Now you know about my secret. You got to understand why I chose to kill them. They were working for the mob!" Yeah, right I killed them because they didn't want me to be around Eliza and I felt that they were going to stick their nose in our business. Maybe I should keep that secret to myself and I'm sorry Luz. "Well I have a crazy idea, Hunny Bunny! How about we run away together. Let's have an adventure together and see the world. Eliza's grandfather once told me that you got to risk everything in order to be with the one you love. Well I love you a lot, Luz and I'm willing to risk everything to be with you." I smiled.

She looked at me and smiled, "Well I'm also willing to throw away my scholarship to Columbia University just to be with you. And I want to see the world and be together forever and love each other."

"Tomorrow in the afternoon, we will leave together and go to Spain and you can have anything you ever wanted in your life. And we can raise our new born child over there. But I don't want you to throw away your scholarship to Columbia University. And I was thinking of dropping out of college and continue the rampage." I smiled.

"Well Mauricio, I think we should wait when I have the baby. At least we should be here with our family and I want them to see the baby and then will go away together to Spain." She smiled and kissed me.

"You are right, Luz, my beautiful Princess!" I smiled and I was holding her so tight and I started to tickle her and she was laughing again and I put her on the bed and we were kissing for a long time.

And she looked at me and she wanted to tell me something and she said, "Mauricio, there is something else that I wanted to tell you for a long time. But I want my family to hear this too." Luz and I went to the living room, my parents, Alma, and Tania they started watching a movie. "I want to tell you guys something!"

My father turned off the television and asked, "What's wrong?"

Luz looked at us and we sat down, "You remember when I told you that I was talking to a lot of guys on the Internet and to a girl?"

"Yes, I remember!" I smiled.

"Well we were talking for a couple of years."

"Really?" Tania asked with a smile.

"She started to help me like the way she helped her boyfriend with all of his problems."

"Her boyfriend had problems? What else is new?" Tania said.

"She told me that her boyfriend had different problems. He had problems at school and he was in Special Education. The way she talked about him, she really loved him a lot. She was telling me everything about him and I was so happy to hear her talk about her boyfriend. And I wanted to have the same boyfriend as hers." Luz looked at all of us and continued, "She was born in El Paso, Texas."

"That's good that she's from here? And are you going to visit her because she saved your life?" I asked.

Luz smiled and continued, "She told me that they were together for two years until one day we were talking and she told me that hadn't felt so good. She was telling me about her heart problems. She also told me that the Doctor diagnosed her with a heart disease. And she had been see a Psychiatrist since she was a little girl because she was traumatized when her friends were murdered right in front of her. She didn't tell her boyfriend that she saw a Psychiatrist! And she died four years ago."

"Where are you going with this, Luz?" I asked.

She started crying and responded, "Her name was Eliza Caballero!"

I was shocked to hear this and I was loss for words. "Did you say Eliza. You talked to Eliza?"

"Oh my God!" My mother exclaimed.

I started yelling at her, "You knew Eliza and you never told me anything!"

"It's true, Mauricio!" Luz sobbed.

"I don't believe you!" I yelled.

"You got to believe me. We were meant to be together. Maybe Eliza was trying to get us together."

I was shocked and my parents were hugging me and I looked at Luz. "What would happen if she hadn't died. Would be a possibility that I would cheat on her and leave her for you."

"That doesn't matter anymore, Mauricio!" Alma said.

"We love each other, Mauricio. And Eliza even sent me a letter and she wanted us to read it when the right time comes." She got up and hugged me, "I love you a lot!"

As I was hugging her and I had a flashback and all I could hear was someone typing on the computer. And I saw the words and I could see Eliza typing away. I saw what she wrote, she wanted us to meet because her time was running out. And it makes sense now. Eliza and I were starting out our relationship when I saved Luz at the park. I couldn't stop thinking about Luz ,so I acted like a jerk around Eliza. Things happen for a reason and I guess I have to move on with Luz. I looked at Alma and my parents. "You guys knew about this?"

"We knew that she was rape but we didn't know that she knew Eliza." Tania responded.

Alma said, "I mentioned my daughter to Eliza and I told her about her drug problems and Eliza was glad to help her out. You know that Eliza loved to help other people. She was fine after she went to see Doctor Juanita Van Der AA and she cured Eliza. And I gave Eliza, Luz's email address and they started talking but Luz never told me about Eliza. But Eliza did told me that she was helping her out. Eliza tried to help Mauricio and two people that had problems were cured and now they meet each other four years after her death."

"I didn't meet her, Mommy. I just talked to her Online." She looked at me and said, "Eliza told me so many wonderful things about you. But she never told me your name and I had to figure it out on my own. I fell in love with you from the moment Eliza told me about you and your parents said the same thing as Eliza."

"I don't know what to say!" I exclaimed.

"Mauricio it all makes sense now. Your past and Luz's past it involved with the same person. Eliza showed you guys the way. Maybe she's the reason you guys are together." Alma said.

"I love you!" Luz said and kissed me as hard she could.

I looked at her and said, "I love you too." And we hugged for a long time and our parents and Tania were also hugging us. And I started thinking as Mauricio de la Vega, I had my encounter with two girls that loved me a lot. As The Dark Cowboy I nearly killed Eliza back in the Franklin Mountains and I saved Luz's life at Marty Robbins Park. Well I am responsible for Eliza's death. I scared Eliza completely when I killed Armando and Deyna right on front her eyes and I couldn't protect Eliza on the night we were attacked in her own room. This is what Eliza wanted from us and damn we're going to stay together for the rest of our lives.

And it was eleven o'clock that night where we were still wide awake. I was in my room listening to music while Luz and Tania were outside sitting down on the bench and they decided to call Madelyn and Jackie. So, in about an hour later Jackie came to the house, and Primo and Madelyn also came over to the house and they stayed outside talking. And I went outside to join them and I was just standing there talking to Primo.

"I cannot believe that you never told me that you knew Eliza." Tania said.

"I didn't met her, I just talked to her Online." Luz smiled.

"Well you have told us that we don't keep secrets from each other. That's something that you requested from the beginning, Luz!" Madelyn smiled.

The front door open and my mother brought us glasses of Orange Juice. "What an ugly evening. First the storm and my shocking confession." Luz said.

My mother responded with a smile, "Don't worry about it. It took a lot of courage."

"Mommy! Did you liked Eliza?" Luz asked.

"My mother responded with a smile, "Well Eliza was a wonderful girl. May she rest in peace. You should have seen them together. Eliza was Mauricio's first love and Mauricio had problems asking her out. Well he wanted to impress her with the bicycle skills and he sang to her in the library. Until I had a long talk with him and they were boyfriend and girlfriend."

Luz smiled, "I really love Mauricio and I really want to spend my life with him."

I know you do. I'm glad to see you two happy. I was suffering because Mauricio lost his first love. And my little Princess was having problems. And I'm glad that you guys changed."

"We deserve to be happy." I smiled and hugged Luz.

"I guess we're going to plan two weddings." Tania smiled.

"Two weddings?" My mother asked.

Madelyn showed her ring, "I'm getting married!" And she hugged my mother.

"Well I have yet to propose but I'm going to buy her the ring. I have ninety-seven billions reasons to buy her ring and have a wedding of the century." I smiled.

"I'm happy for you guys!" My mother smiled.

We stayed talking until two more hours and they went to their house and we had a peaceful sleep. The next day my mother made a delicious meal and all of us ate at the table. My father looked at us and smiled. "Today, I'm going to speak in front of the people and we are going to take away all the murder charges against The Dark Cowboy. And Beatrice and I thought about it for the last couple of days. And I came to the conclusion that I'm not retiring from the Federal Bureau Investigation. I want to continue with this dream." He said.

"And I'm going to stay on the Police Force." My mother smiled.

"That's great." I said.

"I know, Tania, is going to be living in Boston for awhile and she can stay with us during the summer." My father said.

"That's good because we have a surprise as well." I said.

Luz smiled and said, "I'm pregnant!" And everyone started clapping and we were hugging each other and we sat down and continued with a lot of surprises.

"What are your plans, Alma?" My father asked.

"I'm going to continue teaching at Clarke Middle School and I'm going to teach Luz how to raise a baby." She responded with a smile and Luz hugged her mother so tight and everyone was happy for us and we finished eating and later on in the afternoon Primo, Madelyn, Jackie, and Primo's mother Perla came to visit us and we made a cookout in the backyard, the girls went to the room to talk. Our parents were in the kitchen talking and Primo and I stayed outside and we were cooking the food.

"You didn't tell her about me?" He asked.

"Who?" I asked.

"Doctor Juanita Van Der Aa." He responded.
"I told her everything that went on" I said.
"You don't remember anything do you?" He asked.
"Yes! I hope I see her again."
"You are in luck because she is town." Primo said.
"Well I don't want to bother her but I just want to be happy with Luz. I think we should be happy because we are in love." I said.
"You are right! I already settled down with Madelyn. No more raping women and no more missions. Also I want out of the gang and I hope that's okay." He said.
"We didn't sign a contract and we're not going to have anybody hostages. Everyone is free to do whatever they want. And I know you settled down and I settled down. But the world might need me." I said.
"Whatever makes you happy?" He said and smiled.

Then the food was ready and we started eating together like one big happy family. And later on in the afternoon my father spoke in front of City Hall and he said that The Dark Cowboy is innocent and all the charges are going to be dropped. My father was explaining to everyone that the people that were killed worked for Vito Mancini and now that he is jail they were going to kill him. And he also announced that he wasn't going to retire from the FBI and he also announced that my mother is not going to retire from the Police Force. Well everyone started clapping and they made The Dark Cowboy into a hero and I was kind of happy about that. Then the whole city was excited to hear the news that Vito Mancini was finally captured and The Dark Cowboy was declared innocent. And later on in the night I was alone in my room and I was taking a nice cold shower and I got dressed and stayed in my room and I was thinking about everything that happened on this crazy summer. I looked at the calendar and summer was about to finish. I had to make a tough decision to make and if I wanted to stay here with Luz until our baby is born and throw everything away or go back to Columbia, Missouri and finish school. But I took out a quarter, heads I stay and tails I go back to Columbia, Missouri and be miserable all over again. I flipped the coin and it landed tails and that sucks I have to go back to Columbia, Missouri. But I started laughing about it and said, "Screw it I'm staying here for sure" And I went to bed and I had a nice peaceful sleep.

The next day I woke up and I heard someone laughing in the kitchen. I went to the kitchen and the girls sitting down and they were talking and laughing. I saw Alma, Luz, Tania, Jackie, Madelyn, my mother, and Primo's mother and they were eating breakfast. My father and Primo came back inside and all of us were eating together. Then Luz and her mother went back to the house to take a quick shower and they were going to do a few things at the house. Then in the afternoon they came back and we were sitting on the living room. Luz and I were outside kissing and we were holding on to each other.

"Guess what?" She asked.

"What?" I also asked.

"I have a surprised." She said.

"You're going to have twins?" I asked.

"No, but that will be nice." She smiled and said, "Actually, my daddy is coming to town and he wants to meet you. He's also a close friend of your parents and they also grew up together."

"I cannot wait to meet him." I said and continued to kiss.

We went back inside and everyone was getting ready to throw a party because Luz's father was coming to meet me and see his baby girl, Luz. We were outside having another cookout. My parents, Luz and her mother went to the airport to pick him up while Primo and I put the steak and the burgers on the grill. Jackie, Perla, and Tania brought everything to the table and they set the table pretty nice. And in about half an hour later we finished cooking and we covered the food with aluminum. And Primo and I were in the kitchen making Kool-Aid while the girls in the room listening to music. And we heard the front door open and we heard my parents talking and everyone was laughing. We heard Tania, Perla and Jackie saying hi to everyone.

I heard my father talking Luz's father. "Chris, do you want a beer?"

Primo and I looked at each other and said. "Nah! It cannot be him."

"Hey, you knuckles heads come to the living room. You never guess who came to visit." My father said.

We put the drinks on the tray and went to the living room. Then Primo and I stalled for a second and we couldn't believe who we were looking at. I dropped the tray and the glasses broke and the Juice was spilled all over the floor. My mother and Alma and Tania got up to clean the spill and picked up the glasses and put them on the trashcan.

"Are you okay, Son? Because you have that look that you seen a ghost?" My father asked me and my mother, Tania, and Alma went back to the living room and sat down. Alma looked at me and smiled.

"Mauricio, this is my daddy. His name is Chris Farrell Fitzgerald. He's been friends with your parents since they were little kids." Luz said and smiled.

"We have met before, Honey. It's nice to see you again, Mauricio. I haven't seen you since you were in Americas High School. And I know his friend Primo Mancini, the son of the crime lord and they were childhood friends. Primo is like Mauricio's bodyguard." He said and smiled.

"It's nice to see you again, Chris." Primo said.

"What about you, Mauricio. Are you happy to see me again after all these years?" He asked.

"Of course. I'm sure Luz told you that we're in love." I said.

"I'm aware of it." He smiled and looked at Luz. "I understand that my baby is pregnant. And are you planning to ask her to marry you or are you going to leave her for someone else?"

"We will as soon I have the money to buy the ring." I said.

"I don't think that's going to be the problem. I think you have ninety-seven billion reasons to have the wedding of the century. Isn't that right!" Chris smiled and everyone started laughing.

"Daddy, I don't want you to be upset with me." Luz said.

"I'm happy because you are in love."

"What's matters the most is that they are in love and they are going to have a baby and they are going to get married in the near future." Alma smiled.

"I agree." My mother said.

"How about we continue with this conversation in the backyard because I'm starving." My father said.

We went outside eating and everyone was laughing and talking except Primo and I because we were uncomfortable with Luz's father. And around eight o'clock that night we were still in the backyard talking and laughing. Chris's cell phone rang and he went inside the house to answer it. It was Luz's step mother and Luz went inside to talk to her too. I went inside the house to go to the restroom. And I overheard Luz and her father talking in the living room and he was happy that she was in love with me. Also Madelyn was getting ready to leave, so Primo decided to walk her to the car and they went into the house. Madelyn was saying goodbye to us and Primo walked her to her car. The three of us stayed in the living room. Luz hugged her father so tight.

"Sweetie, why don't you go outside, I want to have a conversation with your boyfriend, Mauricio." Chris smiled and Primo came back to the living room. "I also want to talk to his bodyguard, Primo."

"Go easy on, Mauricio, I really love him a lot." Luz said.

"I am, Sweetie. Don't worry about it." Chris smiled and Luz hugged her father and kissed me and went outside and he said, "You guys looked surprise but shocking to see here.

"Yes! How come you didn't tell us that you had a daughter?" I asked him.

"We were doing a job together and I wasn't planning to get emotional and tell you about my private life." He said.

"We did so many jobs together, Chris. We were one big happy family and we didn't keep secrets from each other. And I want to know is why Mauricio's ATM card had so much money in it. You know the ninety-seven billion dollars. And do you realize what I went through in Mexico City for that ATM card. I put Madelyn and my mother in danger" Primo said.

"They are still breathing, Primo." He said.

"So, that card was really mine?" I asked Chris and looked at Primo and asked him. "How much did you get in the rapes?"

"Close to eighty-six million dollars. All I did was rape women and helped you out with the killings." He said.

"You know why I gave you two so much money. Because you guys are the best, you two are the co founders and the co leaders of the Pachuco2K. The members of the group didn't get hurt and they are out there spending their money and you guys haven't spend the money."

"I did get hurt, Chris, I didn't have the memory of Eliza, and everything else I did in my life. But I do have the memory once again. Why did you allow the girls to do those jobs behind my back?" I asked.

"What are you talking about, Mauricio" Chris asked.

"Karina sent out a tape and an audio and it had my greatest hits." I responded.

"You know that Karina is the voice of the gang." Chris smiled.

"So, everything I went through in Mexico City. It was Karina that was responsible for this mess!"

"Yes! And that's all I know!" Chris said.

"Why would she do that?" Primo asked.

"Karina and the girls disobeyed our orders. Karina and the girls have some explaining to do!" I said.

"Look Mauricio I really appreciated that you saved my daughter's life from those drug dealers." Chris smiled. "So, what's the problem here? You guys are mad that I didn't tell you about my personal life. Well I have a life and I wanted to be a private one. You guys should respect my privacy!"

"You are right, Chris. We should respect your decision." Primo said.

"Chris, you didn't give me the ninety-seven billion dollars for no reason. You gave it to me for something else."

"You never know you might need it when you plan a wedding with my daughter." Chris smiled.

"Well I heard Vito wanted the money." I smiled.

"Vito Mancini doesn't like you Mauricio. You killed his men and he wants to buy the Police and the FBI Agents." Chris said.

"Are you worried, Chris?" I asked.

"Yes, I'm worried for my daughter and for my wife and kids back in Ireland." Chris said.

"Well I might have a challenge and I hope Vito Mancini is the right one that give me some real competition." I said and smiled.

"You never worry do you, Mauricio?" Primo asked.

"Sometimes but I have ninety-seven billion reasons to motivate your father, Primo." I smiled and took out my ATM card from wallet.

Chris and Primo smiled, "You son of a bitch!" And we finished talking and then the backdoor open and everyone came inside and we heard them laugh. They brought everything to the table. Jackie was getting ready to leave and she said goodbye to everyone. Chris and Alma stayed the night with us and they slept on the couch. Luz and I were alone in my room.

CHAPTER TWENTY-FOUR

HAPPILY EVER AFTER

Luz was sitting down on my bed and I went to the restroom to put on the outfit and I was looking myself in the mirror and my eyes were glowing red. I was started laughing and growling.

"You look great and now I can't wait for us to get married. I know there is going to be day that The Dark Cowboy is going to come back to save a lot of people!" She kissed me and hugged me. "Mrs. Mauricio Dark Cowboy de la Vega."

"But!" I said.

"But what?" She asked.

"I can walk on the walls, stand in the ceiling, I can float on the air, I can run very fast, I can sense when someone is in danger, I have incredible strength, and not to mention that I'm a wanted man. Just to let you know that The Dark Cowboy is going to have a lot of enemies that want to kill me in a bad way. Like Tania is going to become a District Attorney and who knows what she's capable off. I don't want to put you at risk." I said and hugged her.

"I love you a lot and I want to be with you. I have a choice too and I'm willing to risk my life for you and for our love and our baby. You accepted my past and I'm accepting your life too. But you are a different serial killer. You care about your friends, family, our relationship and we are going to have a baby very soon. You don't need to worry anymore because I love you no matter what." She smiled and she took my bandana from my face and my hat and she started to kiss me.

"I hope you don't regret it." I smiled.

"I'm not going to regret it. This can be your hide out and I will keep this secret safe and take it to my grave. And I will promise you that." She smiled.

I smiled and said, "A Princess gets attack by a couple of drug dealers and gets rescued by her Prince charming." I hugged her so tight and kissed her. And I went to the restroom to change into my normal clothes and put my old outfit back into the backpack. "Your parents know the secret about me."

"How do they know?" She asked.

"I'm guessing that your father told your mother about my secret. Well your father was the one that recruited me and my ten friends when we were little kids. He paid me a lot of money to kill people but I didn't do it for the money or the fame. I did out of pride and honor, well you know about the de la Vega tradition. And I didn't know Chris had a family and I wish he could have told me about you. And just to let you know that I didn't have any regrets when I was killing them. But the only thing I regret is that I couldn't protect Eliza on that night we were attack in her room. I don't know what was I thinking. Eliza was beaten and rape and I couldn't stop them from killing her and she died right in front of my eyes. And it looks to me that I took care of them and I found out who was the one that hired them." I said.

"Mauricio, at least you tried to protect her from those intruders and that's all it matters. You don't need to feel guilty anymore. And maybe you didn't want her to know that you're The Dark Cowboy! So, her boyfriend who loved her a lot and did everything he could to protect her because you really loved her a lot. And I don't believe that you wanted to get her into bed and leave her for someone. Because you really loved her." She smiled and hugged me.

"You're right, Baby. I did loved her. As Mauricio de la Vega I failed to protect her from those intruders and I wanted revenge. As The Dark Cowboy I killed those intruders and I showed them no mercy. And like I said, Eliza is in the past and you're going to be my future wife and we are going to be parents." We kissed for a long time and hugged each other.

"That's right, Honey. As long you guys have each other. That's all it matters!" We turn around and it her was father that walked in and closed the door. And he asked. "So, what now, Mauricio and Luz?"

"Well I marry Luz, the love of my life and we're going to have a family pretty soon. And I'm still going to be The Dark Cowboy and I will continue to do the things I do best." I said and smiled.

"I'm glad to hear that. And I remember on the day you went crazy on me and it turns out that saved my daughter's life from those drug dealers. There is a possibility that there's good in you, and not bad for being a dangerous psychotic serial killer. But I want you to know that there are still a lot of evil people out there. Mobsters that are killing innocent people and Vito is still giving orders while he's at prison. Rumor has it that he's coming after you and he is going to send a whole Army to kill you and he's also after the money." Chris looked at Luz and said, "Baby, you know that I love you a lot and are you willing to take a risk for this? I lost your mother because I was a terrible husband to her and I lost her and I don't want to loose you too."

Luz smiled and said, "Daddy, I want to spend my rest of my life with Mauricio de la Vega. And we really love each other and we are going to have a baby together. I'm willing to take that chance!"

"Well I can get you an alibi because you're really going to need it from the other people. And I'm starting an *Agency of Spies* right here in El Paso, Texas and you already know about the job description. Also I'm going to pay you for every evil person you want kill. But we're going to make it look like a business that creates buildings from all over the world. You know that kind of stuff so the people won't know about our secret business. And Karina is going to be the voice and the original gang is going to be there too. And I hope that you don't have a grudge for what they have done."

"Thank you, Chris! Well you can pay me for every time I get to travel but paying me to kill people it's priceless and it's going to be messy too. And why not pay for our honeymoon! And no hard feelings between Karina and the girls! They were doing their jobs!" I exclaimed and smiled.

"Fair enough! And I thought serial killers aren't suppose to fall in love!" Chris smiled.

"Well things are going to change!" I smiled.

"That's going to be a great a story. A Princess falls in love with Mauricio de la Vega also known The Dark Cowboy!" Luz hugged me and giggled.

"Yeah, that will be great!" I smiled.

Chris and I shook hands and he went back to sleep in the living room. Luz and I slept together and we had a good night sleep. And three weeks later the crazy summer finally ended and things were going to change for the better for me personally and I don't know about my father and everyone else. And on that afternoon all of us were together in the living room and we were making a toast to our happiness in life. "To one big happy family!" My father exclaimed and he looked at Jackie and asked her, "What are your plans for the future, Jackie?" He asked her and Tania did the sign language for her.

Jackie responded while Tania said, "Cool! Jackie says, that she's going to become a Medical Examiner. That means she's going to open up dead bodies and I'm happy for you, Jackie."

"That's great!" My father smiled and looked at Primo and Madelyn. "What about you guys?" He asked.

Primo responded with a smile. "Well I've already settled down. After all of the bad things I've done over the years. No more raping women and I'm glad that I'm no longer in the spell of The Dark Cowboy. And I'm finally happy to spend my rest of my life with Madelyn and have a lot of kids together." Primo smiled and Madelyn said, "Don't forget that we're planning for our wedding and we're going to get married in a year. But I'm also going to go to college and become a Psychiatrist like my aunt Doctor Juanita Van Der AA. My aunt took me under her wing for the last couple of years and I feel that I can help others." She smiled.

"Wow! I'm happy for you guys." My father smiled and looked at Tania, "What about you, Honey?"

"I'm going to Harvard Law and hope to become a District Attorney. I know my daddy pardon The Dark Cowboy's actions but I will make sure that psychotic killer is behind bars, and along with the rest of the criminals in the world. And who knows I hope Doctor Madelyn Van Der AA ends up curing them and Jackie can open them up and check if they have bullet holes inside their bodies. And maybe if the District Attorney doesn't work out. I'll join the FBI." She smiled.

"That's good to know that you have dreams and you care carrying the family tradition. And you Chris?" My father asked.

"Mauricio and I are going to be business partners. We're going to become Architects and were going to be spread our company World Wide. You will see unique houses from all over the world. People will die to see our houses that we built!" Chris smiled.

"That's good! And you Luz?"

Luz responded, "I received a scholarship from Columbia University. I'm hoping to be there by the spring semester. And I want to spend the rest of my life with Mauricio and I hope to have a lot of children in the near future." She smiled and looked at her friends and her parents and Luz did sign language for her friend Jackie. "We are growing up!" She smiled and her tears started coming her face and her friends hugged her so tight.

"What are your plans, Perla?" He asked.

"Well I'm going to divorce Vito Mancini and I'm still going to be on the Police Force." She smiled.

"What about you, Alma?" He asked.

She smiled and said, "Well, I've been dating this young Police Officer for the past couple of weeks and we got serious. I never thought that I was going to fall in love again not after what happen between Chris and I." She smiled and showed everyone her huge diamond ring and everyone was happy for her.

"You're getting married, Mommy!" Luz smiled.

"Yes!" She smiled.

"You deserve it Alma. And I know we have been divorced for a very long time. At the same time we raised our beautiful little girl. I'm glad that you found someone else and I was a lousy husband to you right from the start. I'm sorry for everything I did to you." Chris said and Alma hugged him.

"It's all forgotten!" Alma smiled.

"And as for Beatrice and me. We found out that we were getting too old for this job. And I was a great FBI Agent and I arrested so many criminals in the world. But The Dark Cowboy wore us out and I know it was the right decision to remain with the Federal Bureau Investigation and continue with my career and helping out the young FBI Agents. And I got to say that The Dark Cowboy was way better than me and if I had the chance to see him again. I will love to shake his hand and get out of his way because he is the best serial killer of all time and a hero to this city. And also The Dark Cowboy has every right to be a legend in his own right. The Dark Cowboy's story is going to be legendary for so many years. The Dark Cowboy is going to be known as the one that was able to fool the Police Officers and the FBI Agents. But I also want my story to be legendary for so many years and over than that I'm going to chase him down." My father smiled.

My mother looked at us and smiled. "I was eighteen years old when I came a Police Officer in Mexico City. I was single at that time and during the night

I was usually out there on the streets fighting crime and keeping the streets safer. Until I met the man of my dreams and together we took criminals off the street and we had two great kids and I busted my butt for you two. And to be honest I didn't care about my life after I failed to captured The Dark Cowboy and people died on my watch. I hated everyone and I was unhappy with my life. Even though I had you guys, that wasn't enough to keep me happy until three more girls showed up into my life. Jackie Lewis, Madelyn Van Der AA, and Luz Maria Estrada and I am proud that you girls were also a part of my life. You four were always there for me when I was dealing with my depression and when I was ready to quit my job and thank you girls for not letting me quit." My mother's tears started coming out of her face and the girls hugged her so tight. "So, I wanted to be a Police Officer for as long I wanted too."

"We're happy for you, Mommy!" Tania smiled and they hugged her.

We stayed talking in the living room for a couple of more hours. Then at the end of the week my father was about to go back to Washington D.C but he decided to stay a couple of weeks with us. My mother went back to work and she was tackling criminals to the ground. Jackie Lewis went off to college and we said goodbye to her. Primo started working in a rehab center as a consulted for kids that are delinquents and rapists and they hope they get rehabilitated. Madelyn Van Der AA went to the University of Texas at El Paso and she also hoped to become a Psychiatrist just like her aunt, Doctor Juanita Van Der AA. My baby sister, Tania started working in a grocery store and hopes to go to Harvard by the spring semester. Also Alma left us her house and she was moving in with her young fiancée and she will be married very soon. And I moved in with Luz and we turned her old room into a nursery and we stayed in her mother's bedroom. And Chris hired contractors to build his "business." We planned to bring criminals to justice because we didn't have the confidence in the new generation of Police Officers. Also his wife and two daughters moved out here. And Luz made the wise decision to stay here and raised the baby at the house. She also hopes to go to Columbia University in the spring but for now, she joined Tania at the grocery store.

And another surprised the nine members of the Pachuco2k decided to help Chris and I with our "business." Luz and I went to his house and we saw the girls sitting down in the living room.

"No, hard feelings, Mauricio!" Karina smiled.

"Not at all!" I smiled and we hugged each other.

"Well there's ten of us and it's not the same without Primo! I think we should convince him to come back!" Karina said.

"How about we call him!" Chris smiled and he called Primo and twenty minutes later he came into the house. We were sitting down in the living room.

"What's this about?" Primo asked.

"Well we're going to convince you to come back to the gang!" I smiled.

"I told you I've already settled down with Madelyn!"

"Me too! But I'm still going to continue." I said.

"All of us are going to continue and we're not going to walk away from the gang." Karina said.

"Come on! What happened to the Virgin Killer?" I asked.

"What's the matter, Primo? To chicken to continue!" Karina smiled.

He looked at us and said, "Okay! You guys won but I'm not going to rape anyone. I'm just going to torture and find out what they know!"

"We're back! The return of the Pachuco2k!" Karina smiled and we hugged each other.

"When do we start?" Primo asked.

"Tomorrow at midnight! And we should be prepare because we might be a little but rusty!" I smiled and after that Luz and I went back home. And the next day I finished moving into Luz's house and we started to paint her old room and we started to decorate the whole house as well.

On that day the gang came into the house and we were in the living room. "How are we going to do our comeback?" Karina asked.

"Well I'm planning to do it first. Remember The Dark Cowboy hasn't showed up in a while and my parents and Tania are happy. Why not give them a shocking surprise and at midnight we're going to help the city once again." I smiled and I decided to give my sweet old gray hair daddy more gray hairs and wonderful present from us. And I know he's going to like it more than Tania and my mother. I went to the room and opened the backpack and took out my old outfit. I went to the restroom and changed and I was The Dark Cowboy once again. I called Chris and told him that I have a great idea and he came over right of away. I told him about my plan and I guess he liked it too. He brought me a huge box and put it in the back of his truck and I got into the box and Chris and the girls started wrapping it like a Christmas present. And later on in the evening where Chris went to my parents house. My parents and Tania were in the backyard and Chris put the present on the floor and rang the doorbell. My father open the front door and saw the present on the ground.

"What's this?" My father asked.

Chris responded, "Well I don't know, Pablo, it was here when I pulled into the driveway."

"Well bring it in and see who sent it." My father and Chris picked up the box and put in the living room. "It doesn't say who sent it or who is it from."

"Open it!" Chris smiled.

My mother and Tania came into the living room and Tania asked, "What's with the box?"

"I don't know but I'm going to open it." My father responded and he started to open it and when he finished taking the Christmas wrapping. I jumped out of the box, Chris, my parents, and Tania fell to the ground.

I was floating in the air and I was laughing and growling. "I'm back!"

My father yelled. "Dark Cowboy you are dead to me!"

"That's funny I don't remember a funeral service. I was having a vacation at the Virgin Island. I was spending the money that we stole a couple of years ago. The war is not over, Pablo de la Vega! We will see each other very soon. We're preparing a plan to have our comeback! Just wait for a sign and keep your eyes and ears open!" I growled and grabbed the couch and threw it on the window and jumped into the darkness. And I overheard my father having a breakdown.

"He's back! What are we going to do?"

"I guess we're going to have to arrest him!" My mother responded with a smile and laughed.

"Curse you to Hell Dark Cowboy!" Tania yelled.

And I arrived at my house and went inside. Luz was in the kitchen making dinner! "How did it go?" Luz asked.

"Great. My parents and Tania were shocked to see me." I smiled.

Luz smiled and asked. "Do you feel better?"

"Yeah!" I smiled.

"I'm hungry! I'm craving for Chinese Food!" She smiled.

"I'm going to buy something to eat and I'll come back." I smiled and went to get Chinese Food and bought some drinks. Then I heard a loud thunder that was knocking it's way into the city and it started to rain and I rushed back home. I took the food and the drinks upstairs to the room and I went back to get the plates and napkins and forks and I went back to the room. Luz was already in her nightgown and smiled. We sat down and we started eating and we were having a good conversation. And we kept hearing the rain and the thunder. We were getting ready to eat when my radio started beeping.

"What is it, Karina?" I asked.

"Someone is robbing the Bank. And there's five of them." She responded.

"I'll be right there!"

"And I'll guide you, Mauricio!" Karina said.

I looked at Luz and she said, "Good luck." She gave me my outfit and I went to the restroom and changed. I started loading the guns.

"The food is going to be cold!" I said.

"I'll wait for you. When you come back will eat. And be careful!" Luz smiled and kissed me.

"I love you!" I said.

"I love you more. Now go and save the city."

We went downstairs and she open the front door. I hugged her and jumped to the darkness. Karina told me where they were robbing the bank and I was jumping in all the rooftops of the houses. And I arrived where the bank is been robbed by those criminals. How does the story end? It ends with me killing these bank robbers and the streets will be covered with blood. I'm the serial killer known as The Dark Cowboy.

NEW STORY

THE CHOSEN ONE

INTRODUCTION

Tania de la Vega, Jackie Lewis, Madelyn Van Der AA, and Luz Maria de la Vega meet for the first time at Camp Jesus. And it turns out that their parents have also known each other since their little kids. Their daughters meet and right away they became friends. And during the summer they share their dreams on what they wanted to do when they grow up but all they were talking about is how much they love fairy tails and they would love to marry their Prince Charming. When summer camp ended they went back home and they started going to school together and went to each other's house. Their mom's always told bedtime stories and they told them how a Prince would rescue a Princess and they live happily ever after. And every weekend they will hear those stories and it brought joy to their lives. But unfortunately the killings began, people that got beat up on the streets, explosions and women been rape everyday and that changed their plans for the future. Well things changed for them, Jackie getting a scholarship to another college. Madelyn falling in love with Primo and Luz falling in love with Mauricio. And Tania stands alone and in she vows to put The Dark Cowboy to justice and now at eighteen years old. She throws away her scholarship and becomes an FBI Agent. Tania decides to investigate the killings all over again and her parents warn her that it's too dangerous and they are afraid that something bad might happen to her. Tania ignores all the warnings and continues her investigation. Until she realized that The Pachuco2k are right on her trail and they make it impossible for her to solve the case.

ABOUT THE AUTHOR

All my life I wanted to become an author, so when I was ten years old I started writing a lot of book reports and at the age of thirteen years old I wrote ten stories. When I was in high school I started reading "To Kill a Mocking Bird," "The Giver, "The Diary of Anne Frank," Those authors inspired to become an author. And I imagined myself talking to the people and telling them about my life and the books that I wrote. Churo Town is my first book. I currently reside in El Paso Texas.

Made in the USA
Coppell, TX
27 February 2022